THE
KING'S
BEAST

THE
KING'S
BEAST

A MYSTERY *of the* AMERICAN REVOLUTION

ELIOT
PATTISON

COUNTERPOINT
Berkeley, California

The King's Beast

Library of Congress Cataloging-in-Publication Data
Names: Pattison, Eliot, author.
Title: The king's beast : a mystery of the American Revolution / Eliot Pattison.
Description: First paperback edition. | Berkeley, California : Counterpoint, 2020. |
    Series: Bone rattler
Identifiers: LCCN 2019047032 | ISBN 9781640093188 (paperback) |
    ISBN 9781640093195 (ebook)
Subjects: LCSH: Franklin, Benjamin, 1706-1790—Fiction. | United States—History—
    Revolution, 1775–1783—Fiction. | GSAFD: Historical fiction. | Suspense fiction.
Classification: LCC PS3566.A82497 K56 2020 | DDC 813/.54—dc23
LC record available at https://lccn.loc.gov/2019047032

Hardcover ISBN: 978-1-64009-435-2

Cover design by Lisa Pompilio
Book design by Jordan Koluch

COUNTERPOINT
2560 Ninth Street, Suite 318
Berkeley, CA 94710
www.counterpointpress.com

Printed in the United States of America
Distributed by Publishers Group West

10 9 8 7 6 5 4 3 2 1

PREFACE

THE REVOLUTION THAT TRANSFORMED THE thirteen colonies into the United States was in many ways one of the great mysteries of human history. This wasn't only because no one knew what the outcome would be—there was no precedent for a successful democratic uprising against a powerful government—but also due to the extraordinary new threads being woven into the American tapestry. The period leading up to the American Revolution was a time of extraordinary intellectual exuberance. The edge of the vast American wilderness was being probed and mapped, and the boundaries of natural philosophy—which wouldn't be called "science" until the next century—were rapidly expanding. The proliferation of printing presses, schools, and economic opportunities were empowering individuals in unprecedented ways. As important as this unleashing of knowledge was to the process of revolution, so too was the self-discovery occurring among the two million men and women of the colonies.

Years later, looking back on the struggles that led to the birth of the United States, John Adams observed that "the Revolution was effected before the war commenced. The Revolution was in the hearts and minds of the people." From the perspective of 1769, when this book opens, the American colonists are already engaged in subtle forms of rebellion, as they begin to realize that their traditional British identity is less and less important to their hearts and minds. That transformation is being accelerated by an out-of-touch king who pursues policies designed to inhibit the economic and intellectual freedom of the colonies and permanently weaken the native tribes.

As a vital bridge between the tribes and the colonists and as a secret operative of the Sons of Liberty, Duncan McCallum finds his life growing increasingly complex. The British troops occupying Boston have grown to staggering numbers, equal to nearly a fifth of the city's population. The Townshend Parliament has imposed punishing duties on key imports, prompting the Sons of Liberty to organize pacts for the boycott of British goods and develop secret plans for the expansion of American industry. As liberty poles—rallying points for patriots—proliferate, Parliament has invoked a law from the reign of Henry VIII to order colonial dissenters transported to England for trial. The economic and intellectual pursuits of America are poised to explosively conflict with the policies embraced by the distant king, and despite being in the Ohio wilderness, Duncan unexpectedly discovers himself at their treacherous point of collision.

As with all my books in this series, my story lines are built around actual events of the period. As the story opens in 1769, tales of the mysterious *incognitum* fossil creatures found in the Ohio country are stirring excitement not just in East Coast settlements but in Europe as well. Daniel Boone has just arrived in those frontier lands, foreshadowing new tensions with the tribes, which London is keen to exploit. British repression has precipitated the Virginia Resolves and the Massachusetts Circular Letter, both statements of colonial outrage at Parliament that become unifying cries throughout America. Benjamin Franklin's role as London agent for several colonies has been jeopardized by his rift with the aristocracy. At least the transit of Venus, the greatly anticipated astronomical event of the year, is devoid of the volatile politics that contaminate everything else—until Duncan painfully learns otherwise.

THE
KING'S
BEAST

Chapter 1

Spring 1769
The Kentucky Wilderness

T HE CHAIN OF MEN WORKED feverishly, passing bucket after bucket of muddy water from the pit that Duncan McCallum stood in. The youngest members of their keelboat crew ran the buckets back to the pit as they were emptied, excitedly handing them down to the broad-shouldered man who stood beside Duncan, thigh-deep in the muck of the pit. Ezra's good-natured calls to the crew above them were becoming forced, Duncan realized, for he saw an unexpected cloud on his friend's countenance and had begun to hear whispered prayers in the tongue of his African tribe.

"Praise God! 'Tis a miracle!" came a cry in an Irish brogue from above as Duncan once again pulled at the slippery object of their attention and it began to rise into view, raising a chorus of enthusiastic cheers. Duncan looked up at the strange gallery of keelboat crewmen and Indians standing by the hole of muddy water, then reached under the surface and with a heave lifted four more inches of the huge knobby bone into the air.

"*Magnifique!*" exclaimed Pierre Dumont, the French scholar who had accompanied Duncan from Philadelphia. "A leg as stout as an oak!"

"God protect us! Lucifer rises!" hissed the diminutive man in black homespun who hovered above Duncan. The captain of their keelboat, true to his devout Cornish roots, had agreed to accept the Reverend Podrake as a passenger exploring sites for new missions because he had hoped the man would act as chaplain for their remarkable expedition. However, the thin, sour man was proving more of a burden than a blessing.

Duncan and Ezra found a grip on the mud-covered bone, which Duncan took to be a giant femur, and pulled together, raising it another few inches. Nearly two feet of the bone extended from the pit, and much of it was still buried in the slime. The tall, loose-limbed man in buckskin at the end of the pit gave a low whistle. "Could have fed a settlement all winter," he observed in his languid manner. He seemed to be conversing with the long rifle in his hands, which he held pointed in the direction of the forest. The frontiersman had met them at the Ohio River landing, confiding that he had been sent to aid the Sons of Liberty, but seemed more interested in the tree line around the large, sulfur-smelling clearing than in their extraordinary excavation. Duncan was not sure if the gruff man named Boone was watching for his two tribal companions who had disappeared when they had exposed the bone, or for something more menacing. Three days earlier they had steered their keelboat toward a burning farmhouse but had arrived too late to do anything but dig graves. The region had become a refuge for many displaced tribes and wandering warriors, some of whom had not accepted the terms that had ended the tribal rebellion a few years earlier.

"Get a harness 'round the treasure!" shouted one of the excited crewmen gathered around the pit, drawing a frown from Ishmael, Duncan's companion. The men of their keelboat spoke often of the rumors that aristocrats in London and Paris were paying fortunes for ancient relics such as Duncan was uncovering. "Worth its weight in silver, I wager!" the man crowed.

Ishmael, nephew of Duncan's closest friend Conawago, shouldered the man back from the edge of the pit. "This bone is for Dr. Franklin," the young Nipmuc tribesman growled.

"I don't see why this particular—" The riverman's protest was interrupted by a clap of thunder. He jerked about at the sound and his eyes widened as a bolt of lightning sliced off the limb of an oak at the far end of the clearing.

"You must be familiar with Dr. Franklin's work," Ishmael said with a satisfied grin, nodding toward the smoldering limb.

The riverman glanced with sudden worry at the smoking tree, then turned wide-eyed toward Ishmael, as if realizing the young Nipmuc was suggesting the distant Franklin had dispatched the lightning. He backed away then, as rain was beginning to fall, beat a hasty retreat toward their camp, while the others gathered around the pit laughed.

The downpour quickly reversed the progress they had made in emptying the pit and gave poor prospects for advancing their task further that day. The crew from the keelboat soon abandoned their work, and Dumont ran off to a smaller bone that was being exposed by the torrent with the exuberant and now familiar cry, "*Incognitum!*" Journals in London and Paris had taken to calling the mysterious creature, its remains discovered by travelers on the Ohio, the American *incognitum*, the American unknown.

Soon only Duncan, Ezra, Ishmael, and Boone remained at the pit. As the frontiersman tied a leather cover over the firing pan of his rifle, Ezra climbed out of the muck, then extended one of his huge mahogany hands to help Duncan up. Ishmael extended Duncan's tricorn hat, grinning at the muddy water that sluiced out of his britches and down his bare calves. Duncan cuffed Ishmael with the hat and was about to make a jest about the long arm of Dr. Franklin when he noticed the surprisingly somber expressions of his other two companions. Boone was looking at the immense bone with an uneasy, almost frightened gaze. What Duncan saw on Ezra's face was not fear, but something that hinted of shame.

Duncan was about to speak to the African, who had been such a jovial companion on their voyage down the Ohio, when Ishmael touched his arm. He saw now that Ezra's lips were moving, his soft words drowned by the torrent. One of his hands had slipped inside his tunic and was grasping the necklace he wore underneath.

Ezra's action seemed to disturb the lanky woodsman, and Boone took a step toward him, raising an arm as if to pull him away. Then Ishmael stepped between the two men. "Not your concern, Mr. Boone," he warned.

The woodsman cast an irate glance at the young Nipmuc, then retreated several steps and once again silently contemplated the knobby end of bone that still protruded from the rapidly filling pit. "T'ain't worth the blood," he declared, then turned and disappeared into the sheeting rain.

Duncan stared after the taciturn Boone, not certain he had heard correctly, not wanting to read alarm into the strange words. He became aware of Ishmael tugging at his elbow. The Nipmuc raised an open palm toward Duncan, as if to say they must leave Ezra alone, and pulled Duncan toward their camp.

"What did he mean about the blood?" Duncan asked as they made their way across the soft, boggy ground.

"I don't know. Last night when most had gone to sleep Boone freshened his powder and sharpened his knife, as if expecting trouble. I sat beside him and began sharpening my own knife. Boone nodded his approval. I thought he was worried about some of those rough characters in the village just down the river, but then he said, 'The Shawnee know there's ghosts in the old Lick. Ancient ghosts. First man ghosts, monster ghosts, giant buffalo ghosts. And the ghosts,' he said, 'ain't altogether happy about outsiders stealing their mortal remains.' He said the Shawnee don't call this the Bone Lick. They call it the Gods' Gate."

The chill that ran down Duncan's spine was not from the dampness. He knew enough from his years of living among the tribes to recognize the importance they attached to relics of the dead. He never intended to be a bone stealer. He had come for the cause of freedom at the request of the Sons of Liberty.

The cook, Ezra's cousin Gideon, had prudently rigged a large piece of canvas over their fire and the long flat rocks they used as eating tables. The crew of the *Arabella*, the keelboat they had taken from Pittsburgh, were now gathered around the crackling fire with mugs of tea while Gideon prepared an early supper.

"To hell with this," one of the older rivermen groused. Duncan followed his gaze to the rivulet that had begun flowing under one of the tents where the crew's bedrolls lay. "Beg pardon, parson," the man added with a glance at Reverend Podrake, who sat reading his Bible with a smoldering expression. "But there's dry bunks on the *Arabella* less than an hour's walk from here," he declared, then retrieved one of the bedrolls and gestured to the rest of the crewmen. "Unless ye want to spend the night like a mudpuppy, ye should head for the boat with me," he said. He laid a soggy hat on his head, then set off at a rapid pace down the wide buffalo track that led toward the cove where the *Arabella* was moored.

The remaining men laughed as the youngest of their company darted off after the man, stumbling in a calf-deep mud puddle, then they laid a blanket over one of the flat boulders and began tossing dice. The reverend cast a disapproving glance, then stared out toward the rain-veiled Lick. As Duncan poured Ishmael and himself mugs of tea, he realized Podrake wasn't gazing at the clearing as such; he was staring toward the dim ghostlike figure who was praying over the huge bone. Ezra had now raised his outstretched hands toward the sky. As Duncan watched, he turned to address the arches of ancient ribs rising out of the boggy ground. For weeks Ezra had shared his excitement about their mission, but his joy had inexplicably disappeared after arriving at the Lick.

Duncan retreated to the small tent he shared with Ishmael, grateful that the young tribesman had not only erected it on a ledge above the camp but had also lined the floor with dry pine boughs and moss. He sat in the entrance, nursing his tea as he watched Ezra with new foreboding. The miasma over the Lick seemed to be worming into Duncan's brain. It was as if the appearance of the first ancient bone had jarred open a dusty chamber in his mind he had never known existed. He had been taught by one of his Highland uncles, and later by the Iroquois, that the earth had places of great spiritual power, secret sites where men encountered mysteries of the planet that were greater than themselves, where powers from under the earth could work miracles or strike terror. Duncan and Ishmael had sensed it immediately when they had arrived at the Lick at sunset the day before. In the center, casting shadows of eerie black arches down the wide clearing, had been the massive rib cage Ezra now spoke to. The creature would have been as large as a cabin. The Lick was more than just some mineral-rich clearing that attracted animals. Its deposit of massive bones could be explained by neither European nor tribal knowledge. The tribes were inclined to call such places mysteries sent by the gods, and tended to treat them more as a miracle than a problem to be solved. Among the scholars of Europe, the Lick had begun to cast a shadow, for some suspected they were glimpsing creatures that were mightier than man, and others warned that they were witnessing the ongoing work of God, a divine workshop that no man should tamper with.

Duncan had been struck dumb when arriving at the Lick, for he had not anticipated the strange majesty of the place, but he had also felt an icy knot in his gut. Ishmael too had halted, wordless on arrival, and had begun whispering a Nipmuc prayer. Duncan had struggled to put words around his own unexpected reaction until Ishmael had spoken. "It's like stepping into the church of someone else's god," the young Nipmuc had said.

They had assuaged their odd sense of guilt by walking reverently among the bones in the twilight of that first day and paying homage to each exposed skeleton by burning a small mound of fragrant leaves before it. A solitary buffalo had looked up from a patch of snow-white soil and stared at them with an oddly expectant expression. It was a place where the earth was reaching out, his old friend Conawago, Ishmael's uncle, would say of the Lick. Not for the first time Duncan wished Conawago were with him, but the gentle old Nipmuc had declined to join the expedition and Duncan had not pressed him, for he had suspected his closest friend was about to leave on one of his periodic spirit quests in the deep forest.

He desperately wished now he could ask Conawago if it was proper to remove the ancient bones, for he increasingly wondered if by pulling up the enormous bone that day they had opened an entrance to some world they did not belong in. The Lick spoke to something deep inside him, something from his clan's primeval past, a world populated by fairies and banshees. Why had these mysterious creatures, these outliers of nature, congregated here? Was this a place of ancient butchery or ancient reverence? And why, asked the voice that had been nagging him for weeks, were the bones of the *incognitum* so vital to Benjamin Franklin and the Sons of Liberty that they had urgently sent him on this mission?

Duncan watched Ezra performing his ritual for several more minutes, trying to make sense of what the former slave was doing. He had come to greatly admire the quiet, stalwart man whom he had first met in the house of Benjamin Franklin in Philadelphia during a late-night meeting hosted by Franklin's wife, who was often her husband's surrogate while he was in London. Duncan had raised no question when the sponsors of the expedition had told him Ezra would join Duncan and Ishmael, for they had explained that he had been on the Ohio before. He had simply assumed Ezra had been selected for the combination of that knowledge and his great physical strength. But now Duncan reflected on how Ezra had been on surprisingly familiar terms with the leaders of the Sons and wondered if there had been more behind the choice of this freedman, who had been a cheerful companion on their voyage but always guarded when Duncan asked about his past. At the landing the day before, Duncan had thought he had seen a flash of recognition between Ezra and the Shawnee warrior traveling with Boone. But that seemed impossible—and if it were true, why keep it secret?

He extracted a tattered letter from inside his waistcoat and read it for what might have been the hundredth time since leaving Philadelphia.

*The threat to the colonies grows more acute each day. If they could bend the prime minister into silence I swear they would make membership in the Sons of Liberty a capital offense. Only one path, both secret and treacherous, remains if we are to avoid the bloodletting. You must bring me the relics from the Great Lick in the Kentucky lands. Time, and secrecy, is of the essence. American in-*cognitum *and its* mortis antiquae *may save us yet. God speed and God preserve our liberty.*

B. Franklin
Craven Street, London

Franklin's wife had thrust her husband's letter to the leaders of the Sons, al-ready tattered from circulation within their circle, inside Duncan's waistcoat as he left her house that night, bound for Pittsburgh. Duncan was not sure why he had been selected for the strange mission, but the leaders of the Sons in that Philadel-phia meeting had spoken with desperation in their voices and pleaded with Dun-can to carry out the mission so urgently requested by Franklin. Sarah, Duncan's betrothed, had bitten her lip and tearfully nodded when he had told her they had to delay their wedding once more. Now, arduous weeks later, he was at the myste-rious Lick, facing the American mystery creature. *The* incognitum *and its ancient death may save us yet,* Franklin had written.

The sun was rising into a clear azure sky as they set out across the Lick the next morning. Deer browsing on the salt at the edge of the sulfurous bog looked up, then bounded into the shadows. A raven flew low and dismissed them with a raucous caw. The ground underneath was boggy and the sulfur smell more in-tense after the rain, but the men were not to be discouraged. They walked in a line, swinging buckets and leaning shovels on their shoulders, singing one of the French ditties Pierre Dumont had taught them during their long days of poling the *Arabella* downriver. The ebullient Frenchman led three men carrying a scaffold of lashed logs with a mounted pulley he had devised to erect over the pit.

"Ivory!" one of the rivermen shouted, and half the line broke away to inves-tigate a small horn-shaped object that protruded from the ground. Pierre pushed through the men and dropped to his knees, then, with sudden, intense effort, began scooping away the wet earth with the small gardener's shovel he carried. By the time Duncan arrived, he had exposed several inches of the curving ivory.

"*Mon Dieu*, Duncan! Can it be a tusk?" Dumont exclaimed. He happily agreed to Duncan's suggestion that he stay with four men to excavate the new discovery while Duncan and the others recovered the large bone they had discovered the day before.

It took nearly an hour to raise the scaffold and lower the water to the level of the day before, and Dumont and his men were already prying their tusk, nearly seven feet long, out of the mud by the time Duncan had rigged a rope to the pulley and lowered himself into the muddy pit. He attempted to reach under the huge femur to fasten the rope, but something new was blocking it, probably a root. He paused to scan the flat once more for Ezra, who had left the Lick but had not appeared at breakfast, then pushed with his back against the bone's exposed end, bracing his feet against the wall of the pit. The bone shuddered, then began to rise. Duncan watched the pulley, calling for the men to pull in unison, but a moment later the rope went slack and the man closest to the pit staggered backward, crossing himself. Another dropped to his knees with a terrified groan and vomited.

"The demon is among us!" Reverend Podrake gasped and clutched his hands together in prayer.

Duncan followed their gaze to where the bone crept out of the water. Clutching the femur was a huge muddy hand.

In his horror, Duncan flattened himself against the wall of the pit. He did not even realize that he was struggling to push himself up over the edge until Ishmael jumped in beside him and grabbed his arm to calm him. The young Nipmuc took the gourd of fresh water that hung from his belt and emptied it over the hand, washing away the grime. The flesh was newly dead, the skin a mahogany color.

"Not ancient," Ishmael declared in a grim tone. "And not a demon."

"Ezra!" Duncan cried and struggled forward, dropping down to futilely grope for his friend's body.

"Stay," he heard Ishmael say. The word was directed at the rest of the crew, who were backing away. "He was our friend," Ishmael said. "We must do the right thing. Pull the rope as we planned." He took the rope that Duncan had left dangling and fastened it lower down, around the breadth of the bone, submerging half his head in the process.

Minutes later they had pulled the great artifact out of the pit, releasing the body that had been pinned under it. The mask of mud on Ezra's face made him appear more like some horrid gothic statue than the joyful traveling companion whose deep bass voice had often echoed in song down the river at night.

Duncan could not recall a task more painful, or more hideous, than transporting the body of his friend out of the pit and across the fetid bog. He first tried with three others, one man to each limb, but as they sank to their shins in the mud, the riverman holding one of Ezra's legs pitched forward and fell sprawling across the dead man. He spat frantic curses as he struggled to his feet, then retreated, wanting no more of the task. Finally they cut pieces of rope to cradle the body, but Ezra's head kept lolling down, dragging his face in the mud. At last Gideon, tears streaming down his face, brought a section of canvas for a litter. Several more men came to carry the corpse to camp.

An hour later Ezra's body lay on one of the slablike table stones. After bringing buckets of fresh water, the rivermen retreated to the Lick, where Dumont, having expressed his deep regret over Ezra's fate, had reminded Duncan of the urgency of their mission and resumed the retrieval of artifacts. Gideon, murmuring prayers in his native language, refused all help in cleaning the body, except from Ishmael, who had been whispering his own prayers in a different tribal tongue. As they finished their task, Ishmael inserted fragrant cedar stems between the lifeless hands Gideon had crossed over Ezra's heart.

Duncan struggled to push down the agony of the death as he looked over the Lick, trying to understand the tragic accident. He had not seen Ezra since sunset the evening before, when the freedman had continued his vigil in the fading light. Worried about the former slave, Duncan had risen in the night, when a dense fog had settled over the Lick, but when he had started toward the flat, Gideon had appeared out of the shadows to stop him. "Not yet," Ezra's cousin had cautioned. "He be back when it's done; can't interfere when a man speaks with the gods."

There was clearly a secret between the two Africans, something that touched on the sacred, and even now Duncan was loath to pry into it. Weakened by his hours in the rain without rest or nourishment, Ezra must have tried to remove the bone by himself, slipped, and been pinned by it. It was the only possible explanation. He had mired himself in the mud with no firm surface to push against, but in his struggle had slipped farther under the heavy bone and been trapped by its weight. Duncan himself had once nearly died in a Virginia bog, being sucked into a pocket of quicksand, so he well knew the dangers of a mud pit. But why would Ezra think he had to retrieve the bone alone in the gloom of night? It made no sense. A crew was coming after sunrise to perform that very task.

Ever since agreeing to travel to the Lick, Duncan had known there were secrets surrounding their mission. But those were secrets of Philadelphia and London, secrets of the Sons of Liberty leaders and Benjamin Franklin, secrets that surely did not reach hundreds of miles down the Ohio. He and Dumont had been trusted with a straightforward task that simply called for Duncan's frontier skills and Dumont's scholarly knowledge. Indeed, now that the sun was drying the ground, Dumont was using that knowledge to assemble an impressive collection of giant ribs, huge vertebrae, and more long curving tusks. The giant femur had already departed with a party of four men carrying it in a sling, with instructions to wrap it with blankets and a cushion of pine needles and moss when they reached the keelboat.

Duncan turned at the sound of whispers from the shadows beyond their camp. The woodsman Boone had returned, and now he stood under an oak with his two tribal companions. The three seemed to be arguing about something, and one of them was now pointing at Duncan. Boone grew silent, gazing uncertainly at Duncan, then hesitantly approached Gideon and whispered in his ear. Gideon too stared at Duncan, and Ishmael took a step in Duncan's direction as if he might need protection.

"This Seneca," Boone said as he approached, jerking a thumb to the taller of the two natives, "says we must let the body speak to you. He says he has seen you at council fires and that the wise women of the League consult with you about these things."

Duncan cast a new, appraising gaze at the tall warrior. If the man was of the western Iroquois, he might indeed have seen Duncan at one of his frequent visits to Iroquois council fires. "These things?" he asked Boone.

"Death."

"Dying," the Seneca said, as if correcting the woodsman.

Ishmael relaxed and cast an apologetic glance at Duncan.

Boone scratched the stubble of his jaw and studied Duncan with new interest. "For some reason the Iroquois call you the Deathspeaker," he said and shook his head. "Makes me shudder just to say it," he added, tightening his grip on his long rifle.

Duncan looked at Gideon, who nodded, then carefully washed his hands, rolled up his sleeves, and stepped to the body of his friend. "I was trained as a physician in Edinburgh," he explained. "I will have to touch him, to closely examine his body."

"But it was an accident," Ishmael interjected. "Surely that is obvious. A terrible accident." His voice trailed off as the Seneca moved closer to the slab on which Ezra lay. The tribesmen were always uneasy when Duncan conducted what they considered his communication with corpses. They wouldn't lightly ask the Deathspeaker to do so.

Gideon and Ishmael had already removed Ezra's filthy shirt, and with clenched jaws they braced the dead man into a sitting position as Duncan examined his back. He paused over the web of old scars along the former slave's spine, the work of an overseer's whip, and felt the skin crawl along his own spine, which bore similar, more recent scars from months Duncan had spent enslaved on a Virginia plantation.

Probing the flesh along Ezra's shoulders and neck, he discovered a soft, spongy spot at the base of his skull. Making no comment, he helped lower the body onto the slab and studied the rest of the dead man's skull, pausing over another spongy spot along his left temple. He braced himself and opened Ezra's eyes, now cleaned of mud and clearly showing the red stain of burst capillaries. Next he studied the lifeless arms and hands, which revealed several small cuts in the palms, and only quickly scanned the tattoos on his torso, knowing that since they were done by a tribe across the ocean, they would be meaningless to him.

"He had always worn a necklace underneath his tunic," Duncan said to Gideon. "Did he still have it?"

"I removed it," Gideon replied with an edge of warning in his voice.

Duncan returned Gideon's defiant stare a moment, then reached inside his own shirt and pulled out the totem he had worn since his early years with the tribes. "I am well aware of how to treat things touched by the gods," he assured Gideon.

The cook gave a reluctant nod, then stepped to one of the wooden boxes he kept spices in and extracted a braided lanyard with a leather-bound bundle hanging from it. The worn leather, pocked and with a greenish tint, was unfamiliar to Duncan. It bulged from an irregular shape inside, just as Duncan's own quillwork totem pouch did. Gideon held it out as if he wanted Duncan to take it. Duncan leaned forward but did not touch the bundle that Ezra had grasped while praying. "Sometimes a totem is taken as a trophy," he said. "I wanted to know if he still had it, and if so, what people it was from." He quickly saw, however, that the last inquiry had no simple answer. Several objects were tied around the bundle. He recognized the feathers of an owl, a solemn protector of the woodland tribes, fastened with a strip of black-and-white skunk fur along one side of the bundle, but the other side held objects unfamiliar to him. A three-inch claw was fastened tightly against the bundle, and a large white bead of what must have been ivory carved with intricate patterns was sewn into its end.

Gideon recognized Duncan's confusion. He pointed to the pocked leather. "Crocodile," he explained, then "*Ingwe*" as he indicated the long claw. "Leopard." Lastly, he pointed to the beautiful bead. "Protector," he stated.

"Protector?" Duncan asked.

"Protector spirit," Gideon said in an insistent tone. He was clearly not inclined to explain further.

Duncan did not voice the question that leapt to his lips. Why would Ezra wear a talisman that combined symbols of his African tribe and those of the American woodland tribes? He examined the dead man's legs and feet, then stepped back so he could address not only Gideon but also Boone and his native companions.

"Ezra suffered two blows before he died," he declared. "A slight one here"—he indicated the patch of slight discoloration on the left temple—"then on the back of his skull, more severely. Perhaps he slipped," Duncan admitted, "hitting the side of his head on the bone, then fell backward onto an unseen rock. If he fell unconscious into the pit, he would have quickly drowned."

"You don't sound convinced," Boone observed.

"Both of the blows are well defined, rectangular in shape. They would have been rounder if his head had glanced off the bone and a rock."

His companions chewed on Duncan's words. It was Ishmael who broke the silence. "You mean he could have been hit with a club or war hammer."

Duncan nodded. "The blow on the back could have been enough to kill him. There are many fresh abrasions on his hands and wrists. Perhaps they were all from his labors yesterday, but I tend not to think so."

"And if not?" Boone asked.

"He was defending himself with his bare hands. He was attacked."

"But the truth of it can never be known," Gideon said forlornly.

Duncan leaned over the body. "Ezra can tell us the truth," he stated. "I am going to push on his chest. If it was an accident and he drowned, water will be discharged. If he died out of the pit and his body was placed there to look like an accident, only air will emerge." When no one objected, he pressed the dead man's ribs. Nothing emerged, neither water nor air. Confused, he bent and tried again. The chest was tight, with none of the movement he expected from emptying lungs. He opened the dead man's jaw, holding it open with one hand as he extended the fingers of the other down Ezra's throat.

The rumble of protest from Gideon died away as Duncan drew out a rolled and crumpled piece of paper. It was stained with blood, saliva, and at the topmost portion, muddy water. The natives with Boone gasped and backed away.

Gideon groaned and a tear rolled down his cheek. "I don't understand," he said in a hoarse voice.

"He didn't fall and hit his head," Duncan replied. "He was knocked unconscious and this paper was forced into his throat. His windpipe was bloody, which means the paper was pounded down with a stick or a handle of some kind to be certain it blocked his breathing."

"A handle?" Gideon asked.

"The handle of a tomahawk or maybe a pistol barrel," Ishmael suggested, then looked back to Boone. The woodsman's companions were gone.

The torn and bloody paper had been a letter, though most of its writing had been dissolved or rendered illegible. Duncan lay it flat at the edge of the rock. He made out the words *Philadelphia* and *Covenant*. Only the last line and signature, protected by being folded repeatedly, was fully intact. *God grant you the protection of a worthy partner for your noble mission*, it said in an elegant hand. Duncan stared at the signature, disbelieving.

Ezra had been choked to death with a letter from Benjamin Franklin.

Chapter 2

THE DISCOVERY THAT EZRA HAD been murdered made the weight of his death almost unbearable. No one spoke, and they paused in their work only to look up when a wood buffalo emerged at the far side of the Lick and gave a long, lonely bellow. Duncan, Ishmael, and Gideon had finally finished wrapping Ezra in soft deerskins brought by the taciturn Boone when Gideon broke the mournful silence. "This place of sulfur and fog is no place for his grave," Ezra's cousin said.

Boone seemed to have been considering the same point. "There's a little meadow above the river landing, a place of spring flowers and birdsong," he suggested.

Gideon agreed, and Duncan spoke to Pierre Dumont and the crewmen preparing to carry the next load to the boat. They laid out a length of canvas and carefully placed the body on it. As four of them lifted the litter, Gideon rushed forward, knelt, and touched his forehead to the shrouded head, murmuring in his African tongue as tears streamed down his cheeks.

"We must have the burial at dawn, with Reverend Podrake reading from his Bible," the French scholar announced, "for the captain is eager to set out for Pittsburgh. He says that storm came early, the first of many spring storms, and if we tarry they will strengthen the current and surely slow our passage." Dumont sighed as the litter disappeared down the track, then pulled out his list of discoveries to review with Duncan. "All our weeks of travel and so little time to explore now that we're here. Only a day's work, really."

"But such an impressive day's work," Duncan replied in genuine admiration. In addition to the giant femur, Dumont's collection included the tusks, several huge rib bones, a dozen great vertebrae, a score of small unidentified bones, a dozen relics in the shape of thick bricks, and a skull that appeared to be from a vastly oversize bison.

"Over forty artifacts," Dumont proudly declared, "though in Philadelphia we will sort only the very best to send on to London. But Franklin certainly must have this!" He pulled a cloth covering from an object he had lifted from his bedroll. It was the skull of what seemed to be a great cat, except that it had two long spikelike teeth extending five inches from its upper jaw. "We will stun them in London with our fanged wonder! They will see that the colonies have teeth!" Duncan had almost forgotten that the Frenchman was planning to escort the bones to Franklin.

Dumont's gaze drifted toward the wide buffalo trail that led to the boat landing. "The tusks are the finest ivory I have ever seen. I should have sent a warning to the captain."

"I am sure he will take great care in packing them," Duncan replied as he watched Boone disappear into the forest. The woodsman seemed strangely restless, and Duncan could not help but wonder why he would have troubled himself to bring deerskins for Ezra's shroud, which was a custom of the tribes, not the colonists.

"No, no, about the second boat. This country abounds with fortune hunters."

Duncan hesitated, then raised an eyebrow at his friend. "There was no second boat, Pierre."

"It appeared the day we arrived, just before dusk. You and I had already come here but those who stayed on the *Arabella* saw it pass in the waning light, which was bright enough to reveal a black-and-white checkerboard pattern along the top of its hull. It veered into the bank downriver, toward that little settlement we heard about. Our business may no longer be a secret. One of those tusks would be worth far more than an entire cargo of furs in New Orleans, and vastly more in London or Paris."

"The *Muskrat*," put in one of the Irish crewmen, spitting the name like a curse. "She's known for slick practice. Takes on cargo that's kept under black canvas, if ye get my drift."

"Surely the captain put out a guard," Ishmael said.

"No need," said the Irishman. "The boys who just returned said she departed before noon today, back up the river."

"You mean downriver," Duncan said. "Keelboats go downriver to sell their goods in the Louisiana lands."

"Not us. Not them. They went back up, poling against the current like we'll be doing soon."

"She came for a day, then turned around?" Duncan asked, new worry entering his voice. "As if her business was finished." *Not us. Not them.* As if her business was the same as Duncan's.

The riverman shrugged. "Maybe they had business in the settlement, a rough place of drunks and sharps, I hear. Maybe they picked up some cargo or a passenger. Maybe they needed to make a better camp 'cause they needed repairs or someone took bad sick. There's good sandy landings a few miles up."

Duncan frowned, wondering if it was time to reveal to the others that Ezra had been murdered. He turned to confer with Dumont, but as he did so the Frenchman cried out in alarm. Some of the crew had nearly dropped one of his giant ribs, and he darted away to lecture them about the fragile, irreplaceable nature of their cargo, then decided to follow as they left. "I will speak to the reverend about the burial," he called over his shoulder, and was gone.

As Ishmael and Gideon readied the camp for a meal, Duncan wandered out into the Lick, gagging as he passed a crack from which particularly potent fumes leaked out. He settled onto a broken vertebra that someone had cleaned off for use as a stool. This was not the visit he had anticipated. He had looked forward to studying the legendary Lick with an explorer's glee, intending to make detailed notes and sketches to share not only with those who had sent him on his mission but with Conawago and Sarah as well. He had thought they would have a week or more to explore the extraordinary place. Nothing had gone as anticipated. More than anywhere he had ever known, the Lick seemed a place unconnected with the rest of the planet. There was something threatening about the sulfurous clearing, but also something reverent, and he bemoaned that it was so close to the river, making access too easy for those who would exploit it. Men would come to mine it not for its knowledge, but for the silver that collectors would pay for its relics.

Once more he recalled Ezra's expression when they had first glimpsed the Lick.

The freedman had shared Duncan's excitement, but on reaching their destination that excitement had quickly faded to confusion, then pain. What had he sensed about the place? Duncan had too hastily treated their work at the Lick as just a task for the Sons of Liberty. Ezra had recognized a deeper significance in the Lick, and if Duncan had bothered to try to understand Ezra's reaction, he would have taken more precautions. The closing words of the letter he had pulled from Ezra's throat haunted him. Franklin had prayed that Ezra would find a worthy partner to protect him. But Ezra had only found Duncan, and Duncan had failed him.

His inability to explain the death gnawed at him as he rose to wander through the eerie forest of bones, trying to make sense of Ezra's fate. Had he been killed while trying to stop others from taking the bone, or had he been killed in an attempt to force a secret from him? The pounding of the letter down his throat hinted not so much of vengeance as of angry frustration.

Duncan returned to find Gideon alone, mixing molasses into a pot of simmering beans. "You and Ezra were close," he suggested.

"From the same plantation, even the same tribe, though we lived in different villages and he was several years older. His mother and my mother were sisters. He and I were taken by the slavers together and finally won our freedom together. After we came out on the Ohio the first time, he knew I loved the river and helped me get this job on the keelboat."

Bitter memories of Duncan's own time spent working beside Virginia slaves flashed through his mind, and he recalled a moonlit night on the water when he had confessed to Ezra that he too was a freedman, having served a seven-year bond and captivity on a plantation. "I seldom meet men who have had the chance to buy their freedom," he said.

A melancholy grin rose on Gideon's face. "He and I made healing potions and such, things we learned from the old women of our tribe when we were young. Folks began buying them and found they worked better than the doses they got from their own doctors. We saved our money and bought our freedom. Before we left, we taught others how to make them, so they could earn enough to buy out their own bonds."

"I had almost forgotten this was not the first Ohio trip for either of you." Duncan recalled how reticent Ezra had been when asked about his past, but knew how painful his memories must have been.

"Our old master had shares in one of those land companies. He offered good wages for us to join his survey expedition."

An unexpected question occurred to Duncan. "What happened on that expedition?"

Gideon considered Duncan's question, then shrugged. "It changed both our lives." As he spoke, another group of rivermen appeared from the track to the river.

"Gideon," Duncan said, keeping his voice low, "I need to know if he gave you anything. Something for safekeeping? Something someone else might desire?" The cook's only response was to tighten his jaw. "I can't understand why he was killed. If he had a secret I need to know it, for it may help me find the killers. And it may tell us if more lives are in danger."

Ezra's younger tribesman straightened, frowning at Duncan, then reluctantly stepped to the piled cooking supplies and from its center withdrew an object wrapped in an old shirt. He laid it on their makeshift table. When he looked up, there was warning in his eyes.

"Nothing to do with those Philadelphia people," Gideon said. "Yesterday he asked me to get it to an old man we know in Carolina."

Duncan had expected a message, or some kind of secret token. "You mean something he found in the Lick?" he asked in confusion. When Gideon did not reply, he pushed back the cloth to reveal one of the brick-shaped objects they had not yet identified. It was nearly eight inches long and over four wide, with a shimmering chestnut patina on the sides and tapered at the bottom. Its top surface was packed with long, rough, curving ridges. "Carolina," he said as he studied the relic. "Where you and Ezra won your freedom. You mean an old man on your plantation? A tobacco slave?"

Gideon slowly nodded. "A wise man from across the ocean. I don't know the word for what he is. The tribes here, they would call such a man a shaman. But men from Europe might call him a witch."

Duncan lifted the relic, surprised at its weight. He had not yet had the chance to examine any of the artifacts in detail. Something from his old days in medical school clawed at his memory. "Will we ever solve the mystery of such things?" he wondered out loud.

"But I know what it is, Mr. Duncan," Gideon said. As if to explain, he gestured for Duncan to follow him down the hill to the edge of the Lick. They walked to a pile of rotting logs that appeared to have been thrown there in a storm. Gideon pointed, and Duncan saw that the bottom log was no log at all but a long slightly curving bone that had a row of identical oblong holes along its top. "I was only a boy when the neighboring tribe captured us and carried us to those black ships on the coast," Gideon explained. "But I remember how when I was very young the ground trembled in the night and I ran to my mother in fear. Do not be frightened, my mother said, for they are our protectors. Then she carried me outside to see. I never knew living creatures could be so big. She said they were mountains that had been granted life by the gods so they could protect our tribe. They were very wise, wiser than men, my mother would say, so wise they always knew when they were dying, and then would all go to the same place, so the old gods could greet them as they entered the next world. When you became a man in our tribe, you were taken to that sacred place to spend the night alone among the bones. I was looking for firewood after making camp when I found this. Ezra said he had seen many of these that night he had been left alone in that place."

Gideon took Ezra's relic, which Duncan had tucked under his arm, and gestured him to kneel so he could look at the end of the long bone that was obscured by the logs.

"Blessed Michael!" Duncan exclaimed as he saw more of the brick-like objects, still in their sockets. "A jaw!" He finally recalled his old lessons about the fauna of Africa. "You speak of elephants!" A professor in Edinburgh had kept a similar tooth in his office and would sometimes bring it to class to debate whether it derived from an herbivore or carnivore.

Gideon solemnly nodded. "Sacred to our people. If the creatures here weren't elephants, Ezra said, then they were American cousins of elephants. And elephants were the protectors of our people. The old man in Carolina, the shaman, he would know the right prayers to say over their remains, and Ezra said maybe then they will come back to help our people. All those years on the plantation he had a recurring dream. In it, elephants were pulling down the manor house."

"Ezra was saying prayers," Duncan said, "because this too was a dying place of old, wise creatures."

Gideon ran a tentative finger over the ridges of the ancient tooth. "He was worried 'cause he didn't know the right words. He wanted to calm the gods' anger, so they would still listen to our people. Ezra told me he hadn't known these were the creatures we would find here, that this was what Mr. Franklin was seeking. He said that our tribe would have considered it a grave sin to take the remains away from their sacred dying place, that white folks don't understand that there were places where gods visited, 'cause they don't have the same gods." Ezra's cousin led Duncan back up the hill as he continued his explanation.

"If strangers came to take away such things in the land of our birth, our tribe would have driven them away with spears and arrows. He said maybe this was his destiny, to be here to explain to the gods that Mr. Franklin had a sacred use for them, that Mr. Franklin was something of a shaman himself and so must have known. He said the great storm yesterday meant the gods were taking notice but that so far they were not convinced. He said if only we could get this tooth back to Carolina, the old man would find a way to speak to the gods and the spirits of those dead ones. Or maybe, he said, the tribes who live here know the right prayers.

"I took him some food in the night, though I was frightened because of those awful brimstone fumes and the mists swirling about. It was like the Lick was of the earth, and not of the earth. I said that to Ezra and he said it was true, but that none of the Europeans understood that, maybe not even you, which scared me even more. Now I wonder if maybe it was a sign, maybe it was an angry god who killed him. Or maybe the gods needed him on the other side to explain why men came to disturb this place." Gideon shrugged. "Ezra said maybe the others would help too, the chosen ones."

"The chosen ones?"

They had reached the camp. Gideon took back the huge tooth and began to wrap it again. "I asked him what he meant and he tapped his pocket where he had kept that letter from Mr. Franklin during most of the voyage. He said maybe in America there are different kinds of shamans, and maybe men like you and Franklin could find a way, those who work in the shadows to plant seeds of truth."

"Us? We were the chosen ones?"

"He trusted you. He said maybe you and Mr. Franklin knew different prayers that might still reach these gods. He said everyone knows lightning is a path to the gods."

The words stabbed at Duncan. Ezra had trusted him and now he was dead, murdered by an unseen hand because Duncan had missed something, had not understood the lethal path that Benjamin Franklin had sent them on. He looked back over the Lick, where fingers of fog now reached out of the lower ground. The gods were beckoning.

He turned to the young freedman. "You said where he had kept the letter. Do you mean he no longer had it when he arrived here?"

Gideon screwed up his face and touched his own totem, under his shirt, then lowered his voice. "I don't know. There's some kind of magic at this place. He had that letter signed by Franklin, yes. But one night last week we were sitting at the stern watching the stars and he took it out. He said he had decided it was too dangerous to keep. As I watched he tore the letter up and threw the pieces into the river. It was gone, I am sure of it." Gideon looked to Duncan as if for an explanation, but Duncan had none. The cook shrugged, whispered "magic" again, then returned the tooth to its hiding place and brought a mug of tea for Duncan. "Captain will want you to inspect the cargo before we set out." He shrugged again. "I wish we could stay longer. Ezra's spirit is not settled."

Duncan sipped the hot brew and nodded. "For Ezra's sake, it's best that we go."

"Best for Ezra?" Gideon asked.

"We owe him justice," Duncan said. "It was no angry spirit that knew about the letter from Franklin, and killed him because of it. His killer is on either our own boat or the one racing ahead of us for Pittsburgh." As he spoke another group of the rivermen arrived, instantly drawn to Gideon's fragrant pot over the fire. Dumont unexpectedly stepped from the shadows of the track, looking winded and pale. He ran over to Duncan.

"I thought you were going to the boat," Duncan said, then noticed that his friend's clothing was soiled and torn.

"*Mon Dieu, mon ami!*" the Frenchman said. He was breathing heavily, and his face was streaked with dirt. "It is a blessing we can stay no longer. *Sauvages!*" he muttered, shaking his head as he looked toward the cook. "How can I tell Gideon?"

Duncan glanced toward the woods, then at his rifle that leaned against a nearby oak. "What savages?"

"Our party carrying Ezra back to the river was beset by a dozen warriors. No one was badly hurt. But they stole Ezra's body!"

The company was reduced in number, and spirit, when they gathered for their meal at sunset. The treasures from the Lick had been hauled to the boat and half the tents struck and carried back to the river by those who would sleep on the *Arabella* that night. Gideon's biscuits and beans seemed to lift the men, however, and by the time Boone and his two native companions reappeared, quickly consuming what was left in the pot, some of the rivermen—former blue water sailors—were singing about the enticing ladies of Spain.

The tight-lipped Boone offered a meager smile as Gideon poured out cups of hot cider, and soon even the tribesmen were tapping their feet to the songs.

Gideon and the remaining crew, exhausted from a stressful day, had dropped into their blankets by the time the flames died in the fire ring. Ishmael left Duncan with Boone and his companions to wander out into the now moonlit Lick, the remaining rib bones glowing like the arches of some ruined cathedral. Boone pushed the kettle back into the coals and chipped pieces from a block of compressed tea into it.

Duncan gave voice to the suspicion that had been shadowing him all evening. "You know where his body is."

Boone gazed out over the Lick, where Ishmael moved ghostlike among the tendrils of ground fog. "This land is not your plaything, McCallum," the woodsman declared.

"I'm sorry?" It occurred to him that Boone had never explained how he had known of the Sons' secret expedition. He recalled that the woodsman had been absent the night before, when Ezra was murdered.

"Years ago, men from those land companies back east would just draw lines on maps and call them claims. Then some came to put up markers proclaiming this valley or that mountain range to be theirs. Now they come in secret, taking sight lines and measurements, then racing back to have some tame magistrate sanctify their greed with a damned wax seal."

"I am no land agent," Duncan protested.

Boone ignored him. "Those bones are part of this Kentucky land. They are here because the gods of Kentucky put them here. I can't decide which is worse, stealing the land or stealing from those land gods for glory back home."

"You're here to chastise me on behalf of the gods?" Duncan spat. "Or perhaps you are so land-hungry yourself that you want to frighten anyone who might be a competitor?"

Boone's eyes flashed as hot as the embers. "You earn land by soaking it with your blood and sweat, not with hot wax and a guinea to a foul judge!"

"That is between you and the Shawnee, I suspect," Duncan shot back.

The tribesmen laughed. Boone grunted, as if conceding the point, then poured the simmering tea into mugs and handed one to Duncan. He accepted it as a gesture of conciliation and drank. The tea had an unusual hint of anise and spice, but he relished the brew and drained his mug.

"You should have studied his tattoos better," Boone said.

Duncan shook his head to clear a sudden cloud in his brain. He seemed to be sinking, and held onto his log seat to stay upright. "Tattoos?" he mumbled, then pitched headlong toward the fire.

Shadows moved. Owls called. A wolf howled. Duncan's eyes fluttered open and he fought to collect his senses. He was moving but not on his own legs. His head was flopping and the world was upside down. He struggled to lift his head and saw that he was slung over someone's back. A man spoke in a tribal tongue he did not recognize. He faded back into unconsciousness.

Visions came, nightmares of skeletal monsters and man-shaped demons with horns coming out of their skulls. Through a smoky miasma, he thought he saw the long face of the woodsman Boone, holding a bundle of smoldering twigs. Small pots spread before him gave off an eerie glow.

Suddenly cold water sluiced over his head and he shot up with a Gaelic curse on his lips. Before he could stand, someone shoved him down. He shook his head and his eyes cleared. One of Boone's tribal friends stood over him, one hand pressing on his shoulder, an upturned gourd in the other.

It was no nightmare of his imagination. This nightmare was real. He was sitting in a cavern, or perhaps a chamber carved out of the living earth, that was lined with bones. Curving ribs were spaced along the walls, rising along the ceiling like gothic arches. Pillars made of giant stacked vertebrae stood between the bone arches, each capped by a huge skull inside which pots of burning fat flickered. Some of the skulls appeared to be of large bison and giant bears; others were of creatures Duncan could not identify. Smaller skulls were arranged before him in a broad oval that contained something covered by a buffalo robe.

Boone and Ishmael sat on either side of Duncan, both looking deeply worried. Across the oval of smaller skulls, three fierce-looking figures sat before a pile of embers on which bundles of fragrant twigs smoldered. The two flanking the central figure wore the tops of bison skulls on their heads, from which sharp, stubby horns extended. The man between them sat on a throne made of tusks and wore a breastplate of bones over his bare torso. Fitted over his head so that only the center of his face showed was a skull with an intact jaw from which two long, slightly curving fangs jutted downward, similar to but bigger than the skull Dumont had shown Duncan. The effect was terrifying at first glance, for the skull was fitted so perfectly to the man's head that the fangs appeared to extend out of his own mouth. His bright eyes glowed in the shadow of the skull.

Duncan realized he was in a holy place of some kind, and that the man with the fangs had to be the chief of the holy men, a high priest or shaman of the tribes. The shaman did not acknowledge Duncan but gazed reverently into the skull oval. In the flickering light Duncan made out strands of silver hair over the haunting eyes.

One of the two men with the bison skull caps lifted a bundle of the smoking twigs toward Duncan, gesturing with them to his chin and forehead, then handed them around the circle. Duncan understood. At Iroquois council fires the ceremonial pipe was passed around, its fragrant smoke at once calling in the spirits and purifying those present. Duncan held the smoldering bundle close to his mouth when it reached him, letting the smoke wash over his face, then nodded at the fanged priest.

"*Jiyathontek! Jiyathontek!*" the shaman abruptly called, his voice dry as ash, then looked up toward the heavens. He was, to Duncan's great surprise, speaking in the tongue of the Mohawk, offering greeting to the gods.

One of the horned men, responding to Duncan's reaction, spoke in perfect English. "You have no Shawnee. So Chief Catchoka will use the tongue of our Mohawk brothers," the tribesman explained.

"You the Ancient Ones came before," the old man intoned, raising his hands high. It had the sound of an invocation. "You the Ancient Ones knew the first ways of the earth. You the Ancient Ones tamed the earth for the people and took your blessed giants with you to the next world. You the Ancient Ones then ended your own time to allow the people to inhabit the endless forests."

As Duncan had learned from sitting at Iroquois council fires, tribal elders spoke with powerful eloquence. Those few words were a story of origins, and would have been passed down through the mists of time. He studied the bone chamber with new reverence. Tribesmen long ago, perhaps even centuries before, had built this secret shrine and passed down its ceremonies in a sacred chain from generation to generation. The mysterious leviathans who had left their bones at the Lick had died taming the earth for humans. It was as good an explanation as any Duncan had heard.

"Praise for those who have gone before," the old shaman Catchoka said, then offered a chant in the Shawnee tongue. The two priests beside him repeated the words, which were then taken up by Boone and his companions. The old chief gazed expectantly at Duncan and Ishmael, who did their best to repeat the words. He kept staring at them, and in the eyes between the fangs Duncan saw an unexpected mix of sadness, confusion, and anger. With a chill he realized that he might have been brought here to be punished for disturbing the bones.

"You took the bones without asking the gods," Catchoka declared, confirming Duncan's fear. "For all the life of our tribe the bones have rested in this place, where the gods intended to put them. Now they will go with you," the shaman said.

"Some of the bones are packed in my boat, yes," Duncan agreed in a nervous whisper.

"You misunderstand. The gods will follow the bones. No one can stop them now. They have great power. Lives will change." Duncan sensed no anger in his voice now, but rather something like pity. "They are old earth. You are new earth. You will suffer the consequences. You will die, again and again."

Duncan was struck dumb by the horror of the words, and by his own deep shame. In his haste, in his zeal to honor Franklin's request, he had failed to recognize that the bones would hold deep meaning for the tribes.

Catchoka sighed, then swept his arms to indicate the chamber they sat in.

"Even among the tribes most do not know this place exists," the shaman said. "It is between worlds. If you sit here alone you can feel the gods breathing. It can be ter-rifying. I was not the first choice to take up the fanged helmet. To wear it one must stay here alone five nights and five days. My older brother was chosen but when our people came after his vigil, the gods had taken him. I had spent much time sitting in the Gods' Gate as a boy and had spoken of my visions of huge creatures no man alive today has ever seen, so the elders chose me to replace him. The bones changed the course of my life." Catchoka stared at Duncan over the fangs. "Now they will try to trust you. If you stray from the truth in this chamber, you will die," the old man stated. "If you survive, they will change your life as well."

Duncan gazed around the circle of men, then solemnly nodded at Catchoka. He slowly reached into a belt pouch and extracted a narrow band of white wam-pum beads, then touched it to his heart and lips before draping it over his wrist.

Catchoka instantly recognized the gesture. The fanged head nodded. "You are a truthsayer among the Iroquois," he acknowledged. "I do not recall ever seeing a European with such beads. If those Iroquois gods have not killed you yet there may be hope," he said, then made a small gesture to his attendants. They rose from his side and stepped to the oval of skulls.

"You will suffer the consequences," the shaman said again. "But first you will share your secrets, Deathspeaker." The two men carefully pulled back half the buffalo robe, revealing Ezra's body.

Duncan shut his eyes, fighting a new wave of emotion at the sight of the dead man. Why would the Shawnee bring Ezra to their secret shrine? "He was my friend," he said.

"He was my friend," Catchoka repeated. "When I first met him he was with one of those survey parties that came from the east. I could see he had a big heart, and a bigger spirit. His party took sick and stayed a month in our village upriver. He became like one of us, running in the forest on our hunts. The night he joined with us he told me his other name. *Ajoka* was his true name, given by his tribe. You need to know that secret, given us by Ezra. *Ajoka*. Now you know the first truth of him."

The shaman fell silent and aimed his challenging gaze at Duncan again. "So far all the secrets have been mine, Duncan Deathspeaker."

Duncan felt his heart racing. This place was indeed not of the world he knew.

He felt shamed that he'd never seen the complexity in the African named Ajoka or gotten close enough to share the secret of his real name while he lived. Now he had so little to honor the dead man with. He began anyway. "My friend Ezra, known on the other side of the great water as Ajoka, did not die of an accident as the men of his boat believe." The shaman extended a hand and beckoned Duncan toward the body. Duncan rose and paced around the oval of skulls as he studied the dead man once more. "Ajoka was attacked from behind, struck unconscious, then his killers stole his breath by stuffing a paper down his throat. His killers went to great trouble to make it look like the old bone had killed him."

"The paper had your writing on it," the shaman stated.

Duncan stiffened, then realized he meant European writing, not his own writing. "It was a letter from a great American peacemaker."

One of Catchoka's attendants extended a soiled piece of paper to the shaman. Duncan saw that it had been wadded up and then straightened, and he suddenly recognized it as the letter that had choked Ezra. "Was this a letter to Ezra?" the shaman asked as he held it out for Duncan to see.

"I don't know. I think so. Most of it was destroyed in the act of murder." Duncan knelt by Ezra's bare chest.

"So he was killed by this American peacemaker."

"No, no," Duncan protested.

"A trap set by the peacemaker."

"No," Duncan said again. "It wouldn't be . . ." His voice trailed off. He realized that if Ezra had been on his own secret mission for Benjamin Franklin, there might have been others secretly trying to stop that mission.

Catchoka's gaze grew more insistent, and he made an impatient gesture toward the body, which was bare to the waist.

Duncan felt a pang of guilt for having ended his first examination of Ezra after finding the cause of his death. He had noticed the markings on his friend's body, but he had not studied them. Duncan had read stories of tribesmen's lives in scar images and tattoos inked on their torsos, but the images he saw now, done by a tribe on a different continent, he could not decipher. Along the top of Ezra's torso, from one shoulder to the other, were patterns of raised flesh. The skin had been pierced to create a circle of pinpoint scars, then two rows of small rectangles, some of which had been stained with something crimson, making a sharp contrast with the mahogany skin. There were two small star-shaped scars, three small shapes that seemed to be representations of animals, and two larger, jagged scars, positioned over the right and left pectoral muscles, that had been made many years earlier. Something sharp had been inserted into Ezra's flesh. Duncan shuddered as an image of a defiant captive being tamed by being hooked in his flesh and dragged flashed through his mind. Gideon had said a neighboring tribe had captured them to be sold as slaves.

Although the rows of bar-shaped scars reminded Duncan of the wampum bead patterns used to distinguish tribes of the Iroquois Confederation, he could find no message in them. The tattoos below the scars were different. His eyes widened as he saw two stick men, one leading the other by a neck rope, and a three-masted ship.

"It wouldn't be?" Catchoka asked, reminding him he had not finished his sentence.

"It would not be the way of the man who wrote that letter to intend a death."

"It is not for you and me to know the ways of such a man."

Duncan looked into the eyes that glowed inside the fanged skull. "I don't understand," he confessed.

"Lightning carries messages between the gods."

Duncan stared in confusion at the shaman, then glanced at Boone to see if he was following Catchoka's meaning. The woodsman grinned back.

"The one who sent the letter, Deathspeaker," Catchoka stated, "is the man who tamed the lightning."

Duncan's jaw dropped open. The old shaman in the ancient fanged skull was speaking of Benjamin Franklin. Catchoka gestured toward the last rows of tattoos on Ezra's body in explanation. Three small images were over his left rib cage: a broad-limbed tree opposite a fish, a sign of home or domestic life. Between them was a lightning bolt.

Duncan found himself shaking his head. "It isn't what—" he began, his voice gone hoarse. "Ezra couldn't have—"

Catchoka waved the paper at Duncan. "The spirits will decide what Ajoka and the lightning wizard intended," he stated. Before Duncan could react, he dropped it onto the glowing embers. Duncan forlornly watched as the letter burst into flame, sending its message toward the spirits.

Catchoka thrust a fist into the air, as if striking a blow at some unseen enemy. "The truth is before you, Deathspeaker! Are you a child that you are too frightened to speak of it?"

Duncan looked back at the smaller images along Ezra's rib cage. First came a flying bird, then a keelboat and a bundle of arrows. "After he won his freedom, he came down the Ohio the first time, with surveyors." He pointed to the boat, then the arrows. "That is when he befriended the Shawnee." He hesitated over the next two images, a deer and a bear, then leaned over Ezra's bicep to discover another tattoo, also that of a bear. Duncan rolled up his own sleeve to reveal the tattoo of a turtle above his elbow, in the same position as Ezra's bear. "He had a relationship with a deer person perhaps, and was adopted into your tribe," he said, surprise evident in his voice. "Bear clan."

A slight nod of the shaman's head told Duncan he was right. Catchoka pointed to the turtle image. "You understand then. Your blood too was mixed with that of the tribes." The old chieftain rose, helped to his feet by the men beside him. He stepped into the circle and gently lifted up the entire robe. There was a second body lying beside Ezra. It was a young woman in her prime, wearing a doeskin dress decorated with elaborate quillwork. Catchoka bent and lifted her lifeless hand and laid it on Ezra's. "My granddaughter, Singing Deer," he said in a choked voice. "We found her in the forest edge near the Lick. She had been waiting for Ezra to finish speaking with his gods."

Catchoka had spoken of the night Ezra had joined them, the night Ezra had shared his secret tribal name. He had meant the night Ezra had married the chieftain's granddaughter.

The old man did not bother to wipe away the tear that rolled down his leathery cheek and fell out of the fanged jaw. "The ones who did this are from your world, McCallum. We will not be able to find them. You came here because of the lightning tamer. Ezra came here because of the lightning tamer. You are linked. He told our friend Daniel Boone that he trusted you. You have to become a hunter for the Shawnee now, our stealthy wolf. You must be our eyes, our claws, our hope. These men who snuffed out three good lives cannot go unpunished. You are the only one of that world we can trust to make them pay."

Duncan took a moment to find his voice. "Three?"

Catchoka pointed to Ezra. "My adopted grandson." He pointed to the young woman. "My granddaughter, his wife." He pointed to a slight bulge in the woman's belly. "My great grandson."

A great weight pressed down on Duncan's shoulders. "They all died because of a letter from Franklin," he said in a sorrowful whisper, "and because we were at the Lick."

"Truths from your world, not ours," Catchoka said, as if agreeing.

"Men come and go," Daniel Boone observed. He too was staring mournfully at the dead couple. "Some with proper London accents."

"Meaning what?" Duncan asked, turning to the woodsman.

"In the river settlement there were strangers asking questions. Just like the tribes, the British have scouts and hunters, some looking for signs along a trail."

"Signs of what?"

Boone rose and aimed a bony finger at the tattoo to the left of the lightning bolt. "Of whoever drops out of that tree, ye might say."

With a chill Duncan finally recognized the image of the tree. It wasn't just a tree—it was the big oak he had seen near the Boston Common. It was the Liberty Tree, the sign of the Sons of Liberty. Ezra had been bonded not just to a Shawnee beauty but to the Sons as well.

Duncan gestured to the woman. Catchoka nodded, and Duncan bent over her, looking into a face that had been vibrant and beautiful, now grown gray and stiff. She had unhealed abrasions along the side of her face. He lifted the quillwork band that been laid, but not tied, over her neck, thinking to examine the bones of her neck. But there was no need. Her throat had been sliced open with a single deep cut made by a strong arm and a razor-sharp blade. When he found his voice again it was hoarse. "I think there were two men. At least two men. She was fighting one man and he hit her, causing the wounds on her face. But unlike Ezra, she did not suffer blows that would have made her unconscious. While she was fighting one man, I think another came at her from behind and sliced her throat."

A choked cry came from the fanged skull. "Coward!"

They sat in silence, letting the fragrant smoke wash over the bodies. One of the men by the shaman began a low, mournful chant. After several minutes Boone and his companions rose and disappeared down the tunnel that opened into the chamber. Soon the crackle of a fire echoed down the tunnel.

When Boone and his friends returned, they were carrying steaming mugs.

When the Seneca had distributed the mugs with a solemn nod to each man, the shaman removed his fanged helmet, revealing a stern countenance wrinkled with age. His forehead was covered with an intricate pattern of tattoos. His eyes still glowed.

"Europeans are blinded by their ignorance," Catchoka declared as he extended his mug. "We see that you are a good man, a friend to the tribes. But you don't understand, McCallum, that Ajoka died in a war, a war of hunters fighting in the shadows, shadows that will soon overtake you." No, Duncan wanted to protest. Ezra's killers only wanted Ezra, had killed him and fled. They had stopped his secret mission, not Duncan's. He held his tongue.

"If you don't become one of those hunters," Catchoka continued, "you will die too. The gods go with you now, into the world that killed Ezra. They will have to decide about that world, decide if they are with you or against you. There will be blood in the night. If you are weak, they will give up on you, and you will die forever." The foreboding in his voice hung over the chamber like a dark cloud. The chieftain drained his cup. Duncan drained his own and tried to decide whether it tasted bitter because of the brew or because of the shaman's words.

Beside him Boone gave a low cackling laugh as Duncan found himself leaning back against the rock wall, his head swimming again. "Better pray we got it right, Highlander," Boone said as Duncan's vision blurred. "That nightshade be powerful stuff. It'll put ye under for hours, but if we got it wrong ye'll never wake again."

Chapter 3

DUNCAN HOVERED IN A THICK fog. He struggled to recall where he was or how he had gotten there. He willed his limbs into motion and more than once he thought he had risen to his feet only to discover that he was still on his back, blind and unable to move. His world was dark and stifling. The only things that reached him from beyond the miasma were a musty stench, rhythmic sounds of men marching, and, between their short marches, dull thuds as from a club striking something. Prison. He was in prison again. In Scotland, in his first prison years earlier, the guards had marched, then stopped frequently to open and shut heavy cell doors.

Nightmarish visions seized him. He was running, chased by furious, fantastical beasts with huge tusks and fangs. He stumbled into a bog, sinking in the mud as the monsters swarmed ever closer. With his final breath he realized these must be the old, vengeful gods. A giant bone pinned him in a pool of water and he was drowning, drowning for what seemed hours, but never dying. He watched from above as Conawago and Sarah stood mourning at his grave. His grandfather's ketch sailed toward him on a black sea and the old man, flesh hanging off his dead bones, welcomed him to purgatory. An aged tribesman wearing a fanged helmet ate dinner with a jovial, bespectacled gentleman as little lightning bolts flashed over their heads. The tribesman pointed at Duncan and spoke in an apologetic voice. "There will be blood in the night."

Sometimes he heard his name called from down a long tunnel. He tried to answer but could not move his jaw. Then Sarah came. He was in the schoolhouse where he had first taught her to renew her English after being raised by the Mohawk, and where she had first taught him about the Iroquois ways. He was walking hand in hand with her amid blooming apple trees and she played the impish Iroquois maiden by running and hiding. She would pounce on him from a tree and they rolled in the grass, laughing, until fangs grew out of her mouth and she bent to rip his flesh.

More vivid images came. He recognized them as memories. His mother and sisters danced around a Beltane fire. A beautiful woman lay dead in a chamber of bones. He slipped deeper into his fog, all sense of reality gone. A lanky woodsman in buckskin grinned at him, then looked up at a severed head impaled on his rifle barrel. The jovial man who had dined with the shaman shot lightning out of his palms. An urgent but garbled message about murder, liberty, and King George gnawed at the back of his mind.

Something struck his cheek, then again, harder. "Duncan!" came a pleading voice. Someone was violently shaking his shoulders.

Suddenly his eyes opened. "Ishmael!" he gasped.

The young Nipmuc took Duncan's hand between both his own and pressed it. "Thank the spirits, at last!"

Duncan slowly took stock of his surroundings. He was lying on the stern deck of the *Arabella*. The captain and half his crew were staring at him, some with obvious disappointment. A long rope was bound around Duncan's body.

"The captain was going to drag you behind the boat," Ishmael explained in a sour tone as he untied the rope.

"Praise the Lord!" the Reverend Podrake declared as he bent to help Ishmael, "Our worshipful vigil has been rewarded!" Ishmael grimaced.

"Drag me?" Duncan asked as Ishmael helped him to his feet.

"With the best of intentions, McCallum," the captain said in his own defense as he extended a dipper of water to Duncan. "The waters of the Ohio are known to have restorative powers." He nodded toward Pierre Dumont, standing by the cabin hatch with a relieved smile on his narrow face. "Either that or the *monsieur* said we must hang ye up by yer heels."

Duncan looked over the stern of the boat, then into the sky as he drank from the dipper. It was nearly noon. "We left at daybreak?" he asked.

Ishmael and the captain exchanged an uneasy glance. "Boone and his friends carried you to the boat. We left at daybreak. Yesterday," the captain said.

Duncan stared in disbelief. "I have been asleep for a day and a half?"

"Not sure it was sleep," the captain, an austere, hard-driving man of Cornwall, replied. "More like dangling a foot in your grave," he added, then turned to his crew. "No one gave you leave to gawk! Poles in the water, boys! Ain't getting to Fort Pitt by wishing it so!"

The captain, wary of encountering drifting logs and snags in the night, ordered camp to be made under one of the river's massive sycamores. After pitching their tents, the rivermen encircled the huge tree, joining outstretched arms to measure its circumference. It took six of them to span the trunk and one of them quipped to Duncan that it was old enough to have seen his great monsters when they still had flesh on their bones. The other men hooted with laughter but Ishmael fixed the man with a withering gaze. "It is a grandfather tree," the Nipmuc declared. "All the wisdom of the forest flows from such trees. At night, if you know how to listen, you can hear their whispers."

The men stared uneasily at Ishmael, then backed away from the tree. One of them hesitated, then patted the tree and muttered an apologetic "no offense intended, old man." Another, who had been gathering dead branches from under the tree, carefully lowered the branches to the ground, crossed himself, and retreated.

The captain had not left the boat while his crew made camp. As the sun was setting, he summoned Duncan up the plank that had been laid between the *Arabella* and the riverbank. He pulled a piece of charred wood from the little brazier they sometimes used for midday meals, then knelt and drew on the deck. First he inscribed an arc indicating the big bend in the river they had rounded before mooring the boat, then a large island ahead of them that defined a channel along the southern bank. "That's our route," he said. "Without that southern channel, we have to go out into midstream and fight the stronger current. Means we lose at least half a day."

"So we will take the channel," Duncan said, not understanding the captain's anxious expression.

The captain handed Duncan his telescope and pointed to the mouth of the channel. In the sun's setting rays he could see a tree that had fallen, blocking the channel.

"Damn them to hell," the captain growled. "No going around that."

Duncan focused on the bank and made out the jagged stump. "You suggest it was felled to keep us from the shortcut?"

"Aye, this very afternoon, I wager. Look at it. The foliage is still fresh. It's no coincidence. 'Twas the *Muskrat*, God rot them!"

Duncan realized he meant that the obstacle was the work of the keelboat ahead of them. He had been trying to convince himself that Ezra's killers had no interest in their precious cargo, but the tree could be evidence otherwise. "I wager, Captain, that the same boat bears away Ezra's killers."

"Maybe yay, maybe nay," the gruff Cornishman replied. "But blocking that passage be a grave enough sin. When we find them Muskrats at Fort Pitt they will get a thrashing they'll not soon forget."

Duncan's half-hearted effort to convince the captain they could move the tree was interrupted by a sharp whistle from Ishmael. He turned to see the young Nipmuc on the bank pointing downriver, where in the dying light a canoe with three men was rapidly approaching their camp. The buckskin-clad man in the bow raised a hand and pointed to a small sandy beach fifty yards from their camp.

Daniel Boone hesitated as Duncan emerged from the forest behind the bank. Duncan offered no greeting, just silently approached the woodsman and slammed a fist into his belly. Boone collapsed onto the sand, gasping, but held up a hand to restrain his two native companions from leaping onto Duncan.

"Your damned brew almost killed me!" Duncan snapped.

"Can't see as yer suffering," Boone said as he braced himself with his long rifle to regain his feet. "Damned tricky proposition," he said, rubbing his abdomen, "trying to translate the measures given by that old Shawnee grandmother. My Shawnee ain't good enough yet so they had to go from the Shawnee tongue to Seneca to English." He shrugged. "Came out to me as a dram of the nightshade juice. Afterward I found out she meant enough to fill the cap of an acorn." Boone rubbed his belly. "Hell, the long sleep left ye no weaker, McCallum."

"It was no sleep. It was nothing but nightmares for a day and a half! I should—" Duncan paused as Boone reached inside his tunic and produced a piece of paper.

"Ezra's killer was trying to intercept this." the woodsman announced.

Duncan's anger evaporated. He reached for the paper but Boone gestured him to sit on a nearby log. The woodsman muttered to his native companions and they began gathering firewood. As they worked, Ishmael appeared out of the brush. Producing his flint and striker, he soon coaxed flames out of the kindling.

"The tribesmen are right quiet about their private affairs," Boone declared. "And Catchoka weren't there in his bone chamber to speak of family. He was there to speak for the Ancient Ones. But yesterday, after the bodies were readied for burial, he said I must find you. What he didn't tell you was that his granddaughter was going back with Ezra. After he finished his job for the Sons," Boone said, nodding to the paper, "he was going to his old plantation to introduce her to his African clan before returning to the Shawnee lands to live. They were going to build a cabin at one of the river landings." Duncan eyed the paper, which Boone still gripped tightly. "She had this wrapped in doeskin and tied around her waist."

"You mean she was carrying it for Ezra. Hiding it for him."

"Maybe if they had found it they wouldn't have had to kill," Boone suggested. "When they didn't find the message, they had to kill the messenger. But they never searched her," he said and extended the paper to Duncan. "Those who don't know the tribes always underestimate the women. It was Ezra's task, so it was her task too."

Duncan chewed on the words. Ezra's task. The paper no doubt reflected his separate mission for Benjamin Franklin, a mission kept secret from Duncan.

The fire had become bright enough to read by. It was a heavy, expensive paper, rare to see on the frontier, and it was not a letter but a map, an intricate map of the great river system from Fort Pitt to New Orleans. Four circled *X*s were scattered along the map, each with a mark or a signature, the northern two of which were labeled St. Louis and Kentucky. The Kentucky signature, in a stiff but legible hand, was that of Catchoka. At the bottom right the paper was marked AGREED, with the signature of someone named A. O'REILLY. It had nothing to do with the Lick or the bones.

Duncan pointed to the marks. "A series of confirmations along a map of the passage to New Orleans. Why would Ezra die for this?"

"Ain't for you and me to cipher out," Boone said, raising an inquiring glance from Duncan. "It'll mean something to the one it's meant for. He was to take it to Fort Pitt."

"It meant something to those who killed him," Duncan pointed out. "And surely Catchoka must know something about it if he signed it."

"He said it was something very important Ezra had asked him to do, about assuring the safety of certain riverboats."

"Who brought it to Ezra?" Ishmael asked.

"Two men in a fast canoe brought it to Catchoka, to sign and give to Ezra. The chief gave it to his granddaughter, for she would be the first to see her husband. The couriers came from the west, from downriver."

"They left this paper and returned downriver?" Duncan asked. He did not miss the quick glance Boone aimed at his Seneca companion.

"People come and go on this river," Boone said. "Hard to say."

The Seneca gave a grunt as if in disapproval. "He speaks with the dead, Daniel," the tribesman said, then nodded to Duncan. "I spoke with them, then followed them," the Seneca said. "I offered them help but they declined, said they had survived the great Mississippi and had to report back to their leader. They just crossed the river and landed on the north bank. They abandoned their canoe there and took the old warrior trail to the northeast. They carried very little, just weapons and small pouches that probably held food, as if they expected to be running the forest for a great distance."

"That trail goes how far?" Duncan asked.

"All the way back to the people," Ishmael said.

Duncan raised an eyebrow. The young Nipmuc meant the Iroquois. The man before them was an Iroquois, though of the oft-defiant Seneca clans. "They were from the League? Oneida? Onondaga?" he asked, referring to the two tribes most closely connected to the heartland of the Iroquois League.

"A Mohawk can't open his mouth without his tongue giving him away," the Seneca said. "One Mohawk, the other Oneida."

"Why ask about Oneida?" Boone asked.

"They are great wanderers. I have many friends among the tribe," Duncan said, sharing a glance with Ishmael. Duncan's particular friend Captain Patrick Woolford ran special, stealthy missions out of his office as deputy superintendent of Indians. Could he be the leader the couriers spoke of? His agents were nearly all Oneida, and those who weren't were from the tribe of Woolford's wife, the Mohawks. But Duncan had never heard of Woolford deploying his secret hunters such a great distance, and Patrick was on extended leave in England.

"They each had a long rifle and a war ax," the Seneca offered. "Probably good enough."

"Good enough?" Duncan asked.

"On the southern bank a black-and-white boat was tied to a big willow. Not long after the two started up the Iroquois trail, a dugout pulled out from the shadows of that willow, in a great hurry. The three men in it beached their boat on the far bank and started up the trail, following the Iroquois. I asked about them in the river settlement and was told they were just some out-of-work trappers desperate for coin, that the night before two Englishmen came and spoke with them, and afterward those three bought a jug of rum and flashed a purse of coins. The Englishmen dressed like rangers from the old war, but they weren't real rangers because they treated all the tribesmen like servants."

Duncan gazed out over the darkening land on the far bank. Days earlier there had been Iroquois there, perhaps some warriors he knew. If they had evaded capture by their pursuers, they would be approaching the Iroquois lands by now. If not, they had probably died hideous deaths. He might have thought he had stumbled into some bloody frontier feud, and that the recent passage of the Iroquois was just a coincidence, but for two letters signed by Benjamin Franklin. He had come down the river thinking he was on some scholarly adventure. Now, going back up the Ohio, he knew he was caught in a web of violent intrigue that stretched into Iroquois country and across the Atlantic to Franklin in London.

"When you met us at the river landing you said you came to help the Sons," Duncan said to Boone.

"Didn't say which sons," Boone replied with a grin. "Didn't know if I was going to dig graves or make friends at first. The Shawnee held a war council, considering whether every man of ye should be put down if ye made a move toward the bones. Catchoka said no, because Ezra was one of the tribe and he would never choose to help evil men. And his granddaughter said Ezra was helping the Sons of Liberty, whose tree was on his chest. So I was dispatched to take a look-see and report back."

Duncan silently weighed the words. "I thought you were an ambassador for the English to the Shawnee. But it was the opposite."

Boone shrugged. "If I am going to make a new home in this land I have to get along with the Shawnee. And I keep thinking of something Catchoka said to me the day you arrived. 'If the bones are moved, there will be a bloodletting.' But neither of us thought the first blood would be that of Shawnee. That changed everything. The old chief took it as a message, and a rebuke."

"Rebuke?" Duncan asked.

Boone stirred the fire with a stick, sending up a shower of sparks. "You didn't listen well enough, McCallum. The gods will follow the bones, Catchoka said. But then he said no one can stop them."

Duncan stared into the flames, struggling to understand. "The shaman didn't want the gods to leave," he suggested, "but the Shawnee were powerless to stop them."

Boone answered with a solemn nod. "When changes come to their world, they start at the Gods' Gate, for that is their connection to the other side. They know their world is shifting." The woodsman fixed Duncan with a hard stare. "He didn't only tell you that you must be their claws."

Duncan thought back on his hour in the bone chamber. "He said I must be their eyes and their claws."

"I had to drug you," Boone said, a hint of apology in his voice, "but before you drank that tea, Catchoka talked about the gods going. They have to go with you now, he said, into the world that killed Ezra. But do you recall what he said next?"

"He said the gods will have to decide about the shifts in the world." Duncan considered the words for a few heartbeats. "He was worried, not just about whether I could find the killers. He was worried about the Shawnee."

"He fears what the gods will find, Highlander. He fears they may get lost in a world they do not understand. He fears the European god will crush them. He fears they may never come back." For some reason Boone cast a cool, challenging gaze at Ishmael. "Even if those bones find a fate that satisfies the gods, he is convinced they will not return if Ezra and his granddaughter are not avenged. He didn't just say you were their eyes and their claws. He also said you were their hope."

Duncan could find no response. He had wanted so badly to believe that Ezra's death had nothing to do with him. But the *incognitum* and its gods had made it otherwise.

They sat for long silent minutes, listening to the frogs and crickets. The moon-silvered river stretched out before them, the path to a destiny none of them wanted.

"Come sup with us," Duncan finally suggested to Boone and his friends.

Boone cast a skeptical eye toward the camp of the rowdy rivermen. "The captain still got that jug of rye?"

"I thought someone said you were a Quaker."

"My blessed mama was a good Quaker to be sure. But that don't make her son a monk," the woodsman replied, and lifted a burning brand to light their way along the bank.

"You're a long way from anywhere, Daniel," Duncan observed. The two men had warmed to each other as they ate Gideon's bountiful meal of fried fish and corn bread, and now sat against the roots of the huge sycamore.

Boone gave a grunt that might have been a laugh as he finished lighting his clay pipe. "I was born in Pennsylvania province, in the Oley Valley near Reading town. One day when I was sixteen my father came in from the hay field all glum. My mother said, 'Squire, I declare you look like you lost your best friend.' 'Sweetheart,' says he, 'I realized today that anywhere I stand in my field I can see the smoke of another man's chimney.' So we packed up and moved to North Carolina. I never quite understood until after I was married and standing on my own porch one day and spied folks building a cabin down in the valley, not even a mile away. From that day on I felt penned in. I had to be free of all that civilizing. Don't need another man looking over my shoulder all day. Running with the stags in the Kentucky mountains, now that's freedom. Some days I just watch the buffalo, for hours, just for the joy of it. The only men are the tribesmen who are part of the forest themselves. The wild land has a way about it. The tribes understand that and connect with the land in ways most Europeans don't, or can't."

"An elder of the tribes once told me that the forest soil is in their blood," Duncan said.

"The tribes talk about the spirits in the trees and the gods in the forest." Boone looked upward as he spoke, into the limbs of the aged tree. "I heard a preacher once tell a warrior friend of mine that such talk is sacrilege, that there's no room in the Bible for such things. My friend said that's because the men who wrote his Bible lived in the desert."

Boone puffed on his pipe before turning back to Duncan. "They say the leaders of the Sons of Liberty are mostly merchants and tradesmen. So tell me this, Highlander: Do they think they have to buy their liberty? Or does the king have to buy it from them?"

Duncan cocked his head at the unexpected words.

"What I've been trying to cipher out," Boone continued, "is whether freedom means something different to those Sons of Liberty living in their big homes in Boston and Philadelphia than it does to those living in cabins and lean-tos in the wilderness."

"Does it matter?" Duncan asked. "Is freedom really different for a blacksmith in a Hudson village and a warrior in the Kentucky wilderness?"

"That's like asking if freedom is different for an eagle and a workhorse." Boone drew on his pipe and blew smoke toward the stars. "I'm thinking it *is* different, very different, and maybe it's that difference that got Ezra and his wife killed."

"But how could—" Duncan's question was cut off by the discharge of a musket. The sentry in the camp was firing at something in the night.

Boone was a step behind Duncan as they ran to the sound of the shot. The woodsman cursed as they reached the camp, then cocked his rifle and aimed at a shadow moving on the river. He fired, then shrugged, uncertain of the outcome, and reloaded.

As he did so, cries of abject terror split the night. A riverman scrambled past Duncan, stumbling as he fled the river. Not from the river, Duncan saw as he was nearly knocked down by another desperate poleman, but from a monster approaching on the river. "He wants the bones back!" the riverman cried. An angry god was coming for them.

Even the intrepid Boone was shaken. He instinctively raised his rifle, then lowered it again. "Christ on the cross!" he gasped. "What is that thing?"

"God's retribution! Our punishment for sacrilege!" Reverend Podrake had arrived, looking bedraggled from slipping in the mud, and extended his Bible like a shield in the direction of the dragon-like beast.

Even from a distance they could see that the huge creature walking on the water had curving tusks on which a man was impaled. Its boxy head was bobbling up and down as if it were chewing. Four legs extended out of the hulking body. They made no movement, but still the creature eerily progressed toward them. The entire creature, including its tusks, was on fire.

"The devil's hound!" one of the Irishmen called, crossing himself as he took refuge behind a tree. As he spoke, the beast turned in their direction.

"Shut yer teeth, ye fool!" another man snapped from the shadows. "He heard ye!"

Podrake spread his arms and beckoned the crew. "Pray with me! Pray to save your immortal souls!"

Several men hesitantly rose out of hiding, as if to comply, but then the wind shifted and the beast turned again. Duncan realized he could see the moonlit bank on the far side through its body and he began to make out its crude, scaffold-like framework. "Not a beast from hell," he called out as he ran to the bank for a closer look. "It's from the men who killed Ezra! Get the poles to fend it off!" he shouted, but then the creature turned sideways to them, driven by the river current. "It's only timbers!" Ishmael shouted. "Just timbers and reeds lashed together on a raft of logs. And that's no man on its tusk, it's an effigy of reeds!"

Boone raised his rifle once more and fired. One of the flaming tusks shattered, dumping the body into the river.

The captain was the first to join Duncan on the bank. "I declare," he muttered as they watched the burning monster drift downstream. "Had us well scared, I don't mind saying."

"Just wood soaked with grease or lamp oil," Duncan explained, trying to ignore his own racing pulse.

"A lot of trouble for a prank," the captain observed.

"Not a prank. It was meant to stop us, or slow us."

"If it's to slow us, why do this in the night when we're not even underway?" the captain asked.

It was a good question. "Are all your men accounted for?" Duncan asked.

With a few angry shouts the captain gathered his men. "The two tribesmen we hired as extra polemen ran off into the woods. Probably won't see them again.

But why?" he asked. "How does this obstruct us? That damned tree in our channel is the obstruction!"

"I don't know," Duncan said. "Unless it was to drive the crew away from the boat."

The captain yelled for his mate to check the tethered keelboat. He paced impatiently, watching the burning creature disappear down the river, then cursed again and marched to his boat, Duncan a step behind.

Duncan could see from the mate's grim expression that the news was bad. "Every pole is gone," the squat, muscular man reported.

"God's breath!" the captain barked and pushed past the stunned man to leap onto the *Arabella*, darting to the racks on the cabin walls where the poles were stored at night. They were empty. "Look for them!" he roared.

"They're floating toward the Mississippi," Duncan said. It would have been the work of a few moments to throw the poles into the river. Without the long poles used for pushing against the bottom, the keelboat could never progress up-river. "I've seen spares below," he recalled.

"Four spares, yes. But ye may have noticed we use ten," the captain muttered. "Four will get us nowhere against this current. It'll take a day or more to find the hickory we need and then cut 'em down, peel 'em, and shave 'em to shape." The Cornish man spat tobacco into the dark waters. "I declare, McCallum, this expedition of yers is cursed."

Duncan looked over the captain's shoulder at Boone, who fixed him with a meaningful gaze as he held out the mooring line. "Not cursed, Captain," Duncan said as he studied the rope in Boone's hand. "Not tonight. Tonight we were lucky."

"In a pig's eye!" the captain snorted.

"They didn't come to steal the poles," Duncan said, then took the rope and held it up for the captain's inspection. It was half severed. "They came to steal your boat and the shots discouraged them. They must have just tossed the poles as they fled."

"I know a grove of hickories less than a mile from here," Boone said. "And if they be the ones who killed Ezra and the chief's granddaughter, I'll soon have a score of warriors cutting wood so you can take up the pursuit." He directed a warbling whistle to summon his native companions, then spoke rapidly to them before turning back to the captain. "They'll have a couple trees down already when I arrive with your men in the dawn."

"Not all the men," Duncan said as he eyed the frame posts of the cabin. "I want two with me, and tell them to lay out all the *Arabella*'s canvas."

Duncan felt as if a great burden was lifted from his shoulders as the Pittsburgh docks at last came into view. They had pressed relentlessly, even keeping underway at night when the moon was bright. It had been hours after leaving the grandfather sycamore before the captain finally ended his nervous muttering about saltwater sailors poaching his boat. He had seen the approving grins on his crew's faces, but didn't acknowledge the success of Duncan's plans, with a reluctant nod, until a strong gust stretched the canvas overhead, the stays went taut, and the boat began making headway against the current.

The captain had been loath to surrender three of his precious spare poles and had fumed as Duncan and Ishmael had cut two of them shorter to act as booms. By the time the remainder of the crew returned with new poles, Duncan and Ishmael had raised their makeshift mast, tied the canvas onto the booms, and hung their sail.

Soon the following wind had strengthened enough that his sturdy boat was making twice her normal speed, and the captain was sufficiently satisfied to release his men to work on shaving and shaping the new poles. Now, as they finally glided into the small port, Duncan saw his quarry. The black-and-white checkered keelboat was readily visible, tied to the farthest wharf.

"Easy, McCallum," the captain said as he watched Duncan stuff a hand ax into his belt. "This is a military post. Best we let the provosts of Fort Pitt think this is just another spat between watermen, which they be well accustomed to. When boats return home the crews tend to get energetic, if ye catch my drift. My boys ain't forgotten they had the bejesus scared out of them by that flaming monster. And it weren't right for them to block the channel and try to steal my *Arabella*. But tossing our poles, that be as grave a sin as can be imagined on the river. No better than river pirates." As he spoke several of his men gathered behind him, each holding an ax handle or barrel stave. "Let us soften 'em up for ye."

"My feud is with their passengers," Duncan said.

"And ye think their passengers have been just tarrying on the boat until ye arrive? That boat's been here a day or more."

Duncan gazed in disappointment at the moored boat as the truth of the captain's words sank in. For days he had been so ravenous for revenge that he had not thought beyond their arrival at Pittsburgh. He handed his hatchet to Ishmael. "Find teamsters and two wagons, then you and Pierre get our cargo loaded with proper cushioning," he instructed the young Nipmuc and leapt onto the rough planks of the wharf. "We leave at dawn," he called over his shoulder, then slipped into the throng of traders, trappers, and tribesmen who crowded the street below the walls of the great fortress.

Duncan paused by a smithy where an ox was being fitted with shoes to gaze back at Ishmael. Earlier in the week he had found the young Nipmuc in the small hours before dawn sitting on top of the cabin, gazing westward with an uncharacteristically troubled expression. Duncan had wordlessly joined him, folding his legs under him in the tribal fashion.

"That Catchoka," Ishmael had said after several minutes, "he acted like I understood about the bones. Boone was going to drug me too but the Shawnee wouldn't let him, saying I was one of them." Duncan did not understand the anguish in the youth's voice. "Before we carried you back to the boat Catchoka gave me this." Ishmael opened his palm to reveal a lanyard with a curving object. A bear claw, Duncan thought at first; then he saw how it glowed in the moonlight and recognized its longer, more subtle shape. It was a fang from one of the ancient cat skulls.

"He said the old gods are fierce. He said he was glad one of the people was going to be their companion, that the gods were going with me into a new kind of battlefield and I would know when they needed my warrior's hand." Ishmael glanced at Duncan, then fixed his gaze on the moon. "He seemed to think I should be honored by his words, but I didn't feel anything but fear, Duncan. We didn't know what we were doing when we took those bones. We just gathered them up like they were some old sticks on the ground. They have great meaning for the tribes, we know now, but they also have great meaning for those Englishmen who killed Ezra, and we don't know what that is."

Duncan struggled to find a reply.

"Ever since that night of the burning monster I haven't slept well," Ishmael confessed. "Not because of the monster, but because of what Boone said. It's as if the Shawnee expect their gods to become lost and we have to be their guide. Us! We are more lost than anyone!

"When I left that shrine cave Catchoka came out and pressed this tooth against my heart. 'These are the bones of our soul,' he said, then just went back inside. Our soul. He thinks we are the same, but his tribe is nothing like my tribe. We were born a thousand miles apart, in different worlds. I was raised with European ways. I wish I could say I was of the same people as Catchoka, but I can't."

"You are the same blood as Conawago," Duncan said, reminding Ishmael of his uncle. "Conawago and Catchoka are not so different. You are not foolish enough to think you have the wisdom of their years. But one day you will have their years, and their wisdom, as only one of the first blood could have. Wear it close to your heart," he added, nodding to the fang. "Your fear is the opening. Without that fear I think the door to the old gods will stay closed to you."

Ishmael stretched the lanyard out, holding the ancient fang toward the moon. "The bones of our soul," he said, uncertainty still in his voice. He looped the lanyard around his neck, nestling it beside his tribal totem.

Since that night he had spoken no more of the fang, or of the old gods. But now he showed a new confidence, and an almost angry determination, as he directed the unloading of their cargo.

Duncan sat in the shadows at the back of the settlement's largest tavern, watching as the workers from the new coal mine entered for their end-of-day pot of ale. The miners and rivermen had taken up a ribald song, then broken into a cheer at the arrival of a man in a dark green waistcoat, who climbed halfway up the stairs and then paused and pitched a shilling to the tavern keeper to buy a round for the entire company, raising more cheers from the weary customers. As he hurried up the stairs, he met Duncan's eyes with a quick, nearly imperceptible nod.

Five minutes later Duncan tapped on a door in the upstairs corridor and opened it without waiting for a response. Jonathan Reynolds was the most prosperous trader in Pittsburgh and occupied a spacious set of rooms that took up the entire front of the two-story building. He sat now at a small worktable by a window that looked out over the wharf. "The provost marshal had to send soldiers down to break up a brawl involving the *Arabella*'s crew," he said without a greeting. "Not a propitious start for your journey to Philadelphia, McCallum," he continued, sounding peeved. "You were to transfer your cargo with as little attention as possible."

Before replying, Duncan stepped to the window. One of the *Arabella*'s crew sat slumped against a tree as if only half-conscious. Another, now loading cargo onto a waiting wagon as Dumont supervised, had a long bloodstain down his shirt front. "They had some unfinished business with the *Muskrat*," he said to Reynolds, who had sold his commission in the army two years earlier to start his trading post.

"But judging by the great bundles being loaded into the wagons, it seems your mission was a success." Reynolds had warmly greeted Ezra when they had arrived in Pittsburgh at the outset of their journey, and had been of great help in provisioning the *Arabella*. Duncan had later learned that the two had met when Reynolds had been downriver trading with the tribes during Ezra's stay with the Shawnee.

"We have a remarkable collection of zoological antiquities," Duncan confirmed.

Reynolds seemed not to sense the stiffness in Duncan's voice. "Excellent!" he exclaimed, then shot an expectant glance toward his door. "Almost forgot!" He sprang to his feet and darted into the next room. He returned a moment later with a contented air, carrying a muslin sack with a bulky object inside. Duncan did not know Reynolds well, but the energetic, affable man was a friend of Duncan's particular friend Patrick Woolford, deputy superintendent of Indian Affairs. Although Reynolds never spoke of it, Woolford had told Duncan that he had left the army in a fury after his commander, General Amherst, had allegedly tried to distribute disease-ridden blankets to the tribes living near Fort Pitt. Reynolds now aided not only the Sons of Liberty but also Woolford's sometimes secret, sometimes unofficial missions on the frontier and had built his own network of sutlers and trappers in the Ohio territory.

The merchant's face glowed as he set the bag on the table. "Ordered it special from Philadelphia," he declared. "Not one of the cheap ones used for trade goods, but the best in the city, the kind the wealthy Quakers set on their tables," he added, then with a flourish folded back the sack to reveal a shining copper teakettle. "He said it was what she wanted most in all the world," Reynolds explained. "He told me he would gladly pay with furs next spring but I will decline. I mean to tell him I am honored to make it my wedding gift to them."

An immense sadness swept over Duncan as he gazed at the finely worked kettle. "You best sit down, Reynolds."

The news of the murders of Ezra and his bride struck Reynolds like a physical blow. He sank his head into his hands and listened as Duncan recounted the events at the Bone Lick. "Not his wife too? Singing Deer? God, no!" For a moment Reynolds's anger flared and he hammered the table with his fist. "She was so young, so lively, quick as an otter." He put a hand on the kettle. "For weeks I've been anticipating Ezra's joy on seeing this." His gaze drifted out the window, toward the ancient bones being transferred into a wagon. "He was the son of a great chieftain of his African tribe, and she the granddaughter of the great Shawnee shaman." He pounded the table again. "Why, Duncan?"

"Because he was working for the Sons of Liberty."

For a long moment Reynolds seemed to stop breathing. "But no one knew," he whispered, slowly shaking his head.

"The letter that choked him to death was mostly ruined but I made out the word 'Covenant,' and the signature of Benjamin Franklin."

Reynolds grimaced, then rose to fetch a stoneware bottle and two glasses from a corner cupboard. "Only local corn whiskey," he said as he poured, "but the farmer mixes in maple syrup to help it go down." He poured and pushed a glass to Duncan. "Drink. Then talk."

Duncan left out no detail, including both Ezra's strange vigil in the boneyard and his own blind passage to the bone chamber of the Shawnee prophet, followed by Boone's report of two Iroquois being pursued by bountymen.

When Reynolds finally spoke, his voice was hollow with pain. "Those two are safe," he said, "but not those damned hounds who pursued them." He answered the question on Duncan's face. "When my—when those two reached Venango to the north, they sent me a message saying they had delivered the paper to the Shawnee as ordered and Ezra would bring it to me after getting Catchoka's signature. They added that some bountymen tried to interfere with their return. Our couriers were Mohawk and Oneida, not likely to retreat. Their hunters won't hunt again. Were they the ones who killed Ezra and his young bride?"

"I don't think so. Your men coming upriver had delivered the message, you said, and I take it their pursuers were hell-bent on learning its contents. They didn't know it had been delivered to the Shawnee, who gave it to Ezra."

"But the message is lost nonetheless," Reynolds said in a forlorn voice.

"Not exactly," Duncan said, then extracted the map delivered to him by Boone and laid it before Reynolds. It had meant nothing to him, but the former officer gave a surprised grunt, then studied it with obvious satisfaction. "Thank you, McCallum. At least Ezra's mission was completed. You performed double duty, as it were."

"You can cipher out its meaning?" Duncan asked, then indicated the signature at the corner. "You recognize this Irishman?"

Reynolds's lips curled slightly and he poured them each another two fingers of the whiskey and drained his glass before replying. "You are trusted by Hancock, Adams, and Charles Thomson," he said, referring to the leaders of the Sons of Liberty in Boston and Philadelphia. "But what do you know of the Covenant?"

"Used to be what the tribes called the bond with the British that kept the peace for decades."

Reynolds shook his head. "That's been gone for too many years. You must know about the Non-importation Pact."

Duncan shrugged. "The Sons and others are trying to organize a boycott of English goods to protest against the Townshend duties." The punitive duties were causing hardship throughout the colonies and protests against them were reaching the ferocity of those against the Stamp Tax years earlier.

Reynolds nodded. "The colonies are the biggest market for British manufacturers. Choke off those purchases and the tradesmen of Britain will run screaming to Parliament. But to make it work we need new imports, and to advance manufacture of goods on this side of the Atlantic, something London abhors. It means shifting patterns of trade, which is why we've been trying to open channels for import of French and Spanish goods, through the back door, as it were."

"Benjamin Franklin suggested smuggling up the Mississippi and Ohio?"

"The leader of the Covenant has the code name Hephaestus, after the Greek god of industry. Hephaestus says we should think of it more as opening the colonies to the commerce they deserve. Ezra was going to be our western eyes and ears, and help the boats coming upriver."

Duncan glanced down at the signature of the Irish O'Reilly. "The old Louisiana lands are now held by the Spanish," he pointed out. "The Spanish and the river tribes."

Reynolds indicated the signatures on the secret message, starting with the one in the corner. "Alejandro O'Reilly was born in Dublin, but he became a mercenary for the Spanish king and today he is Generalísimo O'Reilly, the new Spanish governor of Louisiana. And the other marks are all from chieftains along the rivers. We will have to pay tribute for each passage, but this paper means they all gave their consent." He grew more enthusiastic as he spoke. "This is momentous news!"

Duncan weighed his words, and his enthusiasm, grateful that Reynolds had found something that banished his despair over Ezra and his wife, however briefly.

But Reynolds quickly sobered. "I had written a report after meeting Ezra on his first voyage, suggesting that he could play a role. I wasn't aware that Franklin knew him already, and he quickly endorsed the idea. I asked for a letter from Franklin, and set forth the points to be included." He paused as if to weigh his own words. "Jesus bloody wept!" Reynolds said with a despairing groan. "I said the letter might be used to further the arrangements to the tribes and boat captains, so it needed to explain the route, the role of Ezra at one of the Shawnee landings, even a confirmation that a small percentage of cargos would be paid as tribute." Reynolds's voice seemed to shrink. "It would have been like a map, a chart for defeating the plan and killing Ezra."

"You did not kill Ezra or his wife, Reynolds."

When Reynolds offered no reply, Duncan tried a different approach. "The Iroquois speak of the gate to the western lands, and of the Senecas as the gatekeeper of the west," he observed. "You are the Sons' gatekeeper." He gestured to the paper before them. "The plan survives. With your help it will assure harmony in the Ohio lands. The Sons can build trust with the tribes this way. You can lay the foundations for peace in these lands."

Reynolds stared into his glass. "This land has settled into my heart," he said. "I went back to England for a few weeks last year, to buy inventory. It was stifling. After being in the American wilderness for three years I felt I was being suffocated. No matter where I went it seemed like I was under the thumb of the king. New taxes, new rules on trade, new rules on voting." He gave a sardonic grin. "America ruined England for me. I want this land to be more American and less English. And I believe the Sons have another gatekeeper for the New York frontier, a Highlander in Edentown."

Duncan raised his glass in salute. "To our dangerous sentiments," he declared, and they drained their glasses. He stared out toward the river, the pathway of commerce, and murder. "Who else knew? Did you correspond directly with Franklin?"

"Never. My contacts are in Philadelphia. They have ways to correspond secretly with Franklin."

"Not too secretly," Duncan observed. "The killers would not have known enough to stalk us if all they had was your note. They acted based on the letter from Franklin to Ezra, sent to him from London."

"Meaning?" Reynolds asked.

"Meaning they learned what they needed in London, months ago. They came from London to Pittsburgh, where they hired new conspirators on a black-and-white checkered keelboat."

"The crew of the *Muskrat* were just watermen earning some extra silver," Reynolds observed. "They are fools but not criminals. Their lips loosened quickly when they started spending it on ale. They had two well-paying passengers who left on fast horses an hour after the *Muskrat* docked."

Duncan wrapped his fingers tightly around his glass. "The two men who killed Ezra."

"It seems likely." Reynolds made a rumbling sound in his throat. "London," he spat. "Meaning someone powerful in government who is set against the colonies and who has a spy in our network," he concluded, then poured a last round of whiskey. "There is no other possibility. You and I might be prepared for such battles, McCallum. But it wasn't you and I who suffered, and what spilled the blood at the Lick is something new to the tribes, new to most everyone. Our friend the former slave and his Shawnee wife died in the cause of American liberty."

Chapter 4

DUNCAN PAUSED ON HIS WAY to the wharves to examine the wounded crewman slumped against the tree, who had suffered a bad gash on his forearm. "Ishmael saw to it," the man said, and Duncan nodded with approval at the dressing of moss and cobwebs, the native remedy for hemorrhaging wounds.

"Nae trouble yerself," the man said as Duncan studied another wound on his head. "A snippet of rum and I'll be right as rain. 'Tis the captain who needs ye, in the far storehouse. He's got the bastard with 'im," he said, pointing to a row of crude structures that ran along the waterfront.

A crewman of the *Arabella* was standing guard at the door of the shed and waved Duncan inside. The captain sat at one end of a table of rough-hewn timbers on which two candles burned. At the other end a battered man was tied to a chair.

"This gentleman be the mate of the *Muskrat*," the *Arabella*'s captain declared. "Another Cornishman, imagine that. He took his beating like a man since he knew he deserved it."

"Where's your captain?" Duncan demanded of the mate.

The man frowned and looked down at the table, speaking through a swollen lip. "We had no cargo to trouble us, just them passengers flush with silver. The captain ran north up the Allegheny an hour after landing, said I should pay a month's berthing fees and he'd be back by then for a proper trip. He has a woman up Venango way."

"Then where are the two murderers?" Duncan asked in a low, harsh whisper.

The man's eyes flashed with fear. "Christ on the cross! We didn't know about that dark business, I told yer captain already, I swear it! They showed up with fat purses, saying they needed to get to the Lick as quick as ever we could. When the captain said he had to wait for a cargo, they produced a pile of silver and paid the value of a full boat and even hired more men for extra poles. It was like they was in some desperate race. We didn't understand what we was racing against until they saw the *Arabella* pulled up at the landing by the Lick. Then they took out a telescope, studied the shore, and clapped each other on the back, saying we'd all have a keg of ale to share that night."

"How did they know it was the *Arabella*?" Duncan asked.

"I knew her well enough, though they didn't ask. They knew 'cause there was something tied to a tree by the landing. A yellow cloth. As soon as they saw that yellow cloth, that's when they acted as if they had won a prize.

"We was that surprised then when they said keep going. We found a little cove a mile downriver and tied up there near that rundown settlement. They went inside their cabin and came out in hunting clothes with right fine weapons. Each had a dagger, a pistol, and a tomahawk. Put me in mind of the English soldiers I saw when I fought on Champlain. Ye know, the ones who trained alongside the rangers in the French War. Off they went into the forest, even though a hard rain had started. We didn't see them 'til the next morning. They were angry as hell when they returned but said we had to leave for Fort Pitt right away, to put miles between us and the *Arabella*."

"Not before your passengers met with three men in a dugout."

The mate looked up at Duncan in surprise. "Yea, well, them were just some hard cases from that settlement looking for quick coin. Shifty eyes. Shifty hands. Glad they never came on board, for we was hard pressed to race back up the river."

"So you could chop that tree to block the channel!" the captain spat.

"And build a monster for burning," Duncan added. "Then try to steal the *Arabella*."

Their prisoner shook his head emphatically. "Didn't know anything about stealing another keelboat. We ain't pirates. The tree and the raft creature, sure, but our passengers said that was to be a big joke on the *Arabella*. Then we was told to stand ready to take over the *Arabella* for them when she drifted free. I think they meant to sink her, 'cause we didn't have the crew to handle two keelboats. But some marksman ended that. A damned good shot given the dim light—got old Tom right in the shoulder before we could reach the *Arabella*. We had enough of that business. We don't mind fending off savages from time to time but we ain't gonna raise arms against other rivermen."

Duncan exchanged a long glance with the captain. Did he understand the significance of the man's words? "And your two passengers, who were they?"

"Haughty gents who kept to themselves. Told us their names were Alexander Pope and Samuel Johnson. I recollect that the former schoolteacher we had on the crew laughed at that, though he kept the joke to himself."

"He thought perhaps they were names of convenience?" Duncan suggested. Apparently only the onetime schoolteacher had been familiar with famous English writers.

"P'raps so. None of my concern, now, was it? The river is awash with secrets, and it don't do to poke yer nose into those of other folks. Mind yer own biscuits, my dear ma used to say." The Cornishman gazed down at the table and spoke with remorse. "They paid a lot of silver. The bigger the purse, the bigger the secret. And they brought extra kegs of ale and rum. They could have declared themselves to be Merlin and Moses, for all we cared."

The prisoner shuddered when Duncan extracted the knife from his belt and drew back in fear as Duncan leaned over him. "Tell me more about them," Duncan said, and cut the man's bindings. "I'll brew you some willow bark tea when you're done to ease your pain. Start with everything you remember about how they dressed that night they went on shore by the Lick."

The mate of the *Muskrat*, once he realized that Duncan intended him no further harm, was more than happy to salve his conscience by cooperating. The men had gone into the night with high leggings of hunter green tied around their thighs and tight brown waistcoats. The older one was the taller of the two, of Duncan's own six-foot height, his companion a few inches shorter. The one called "Samuel Johnson" had black hair and was near to forty years and his companion, "Pope," had brown hair and was three or four years younger. "They never wore wigs," the mate recounted, "but still put on the airs of refined gentlemen and both carried snuffboxes with enameled images of naked Roman ladies in a bath. They made us build a wall inside the main cabin so they had their own compartment where they slept and played cards and studied papers and such."

He glanced at Duncan and hesitated, then nodded as if deciding something. "Ye done me fair. I owe ye. So I'll tell ye they spent more money on a couple rough characters here, told them to keep the *Arabella*'s passengers from traveling to Philadelphia for a week or two. One of 'em started carrying a heavy hammer in his belt, like maybe to break some bones. Excepting they ain't expecting ye so soon. A couple hours ago they was besotted with rum in the tavern by the cooper's shop."

The captain answered with a perverse gleam. "Then ye shall point them out to us so we can truss 'em up and throw them in our hold for a couple days," he said with a nod to Duncan. "While ye can be well on your way to the Quaker city."

The mate shook his head and asked the *Arabella*'s captain, "How the devil did ye get here so fast? Our skipper said we had four or five days to relax here but then to make ourselves scarce."

The captain pointed to Duncan. "This crazy Highlander spent too much time sailing as a boy," he explained with a grin.

"I don't understand something," Duncan said. "You say you were rowing to the *Arabella* that night of the burning monster but turned around after your companion was shot. But someone still reached the *Arabella* and dumped the poles."

The mate shrugged. "And didn't I say someone tied a yellow cloth to a tree at that landing so we knew it was the *Arabella*? He waved to us, a little man dressed in black."

The captain insisted on joining Duncan and Ishmael as they searched the taverns of Pittsburgh. They found their quarry in the fourth one, slumped over a table in a shadowed corner with a tankard of ale and a half-eaten sausage beside a leather purse, his drowsy head supported with one bent arm. The captain dropped several silver coins on the table beside him.

Reverend Podrake looked up with a startled expression, which instantly turned to worry as he recognized the three men. "What's this?" His words were slurred, but he was alert enough to lean back to avoid the reach of their arms.

"Yer passage money," the captain said. "We've decided to take it out of yer hide instead."

Podrake's face drained of blood. A croaking sound rose from his throat, and he attempted to rise, only to be shoved back into his chair by Ishmael.

"You joined us just to spy on us and sabotage our boat," Duncan accused, then turned to Ishmael. "What do we do with spies and saboteurs?"

"In my tribe," the young Nipmuc said, "we would put such men in a kettle and slowly boil them, slicing off the meat as it cooked." It was a lie, but it had the desired effect. Podrake was so stricken his hands began to shake. "Though I think in old England it was just beheading. A lot cleaner. I'll go find an ax. There's a pigsty over by the hill. The hogs will know what to do with the body, though I hear the flesh of a liar is always sour."

Podrake's hand shot to his neck. "Dear God, no! You misunderstand!" His drunkenness had burned away.

"What do we misunderstand?" Duncan demanded. "Your pretending to discourage our expedition on religious grounds? Trying to steal the *Arabella*? Throwing our poles into the river? Were your prayers just as false?"

Podrake frantically looked about as if seeking a way to flee, then sagged. He clutched his tankard and stared into it. "It wasn't like that," he said. "I am a servant of the Great Jehovah. My prayers are true."

"Yer soul to the devil!" the captain spat, and turned to Duncan. "Let me take him, McCallum. My crew will pry his limbs off one by one. He'll be feeding river eels by morning. If we had known earlier, he would have been thrown in the Ohio with a rock bound to his foot."

Podrake let out a terrible wail, so loud it silenced the rest of the tavern.

Ishmael turned to the other customers. "Sore tooth," he loudly explained, "poor wretch just learned it has to be pulled." Several customers laughed, and others raised their tankards to Ishmael and turned back to their business.

Podrake clasped his hands and raised them to Duncan as if in prayer. "I beg Christian mercy, sir! I was lost and they gave me shelter. I knew nothing of their wretched business when they hired me. I never imagined bloodshed!"

Duncan pushed the reverend's leather pouch and heard the clink of coins. "They paid you well," he countered. "Judas silver."

Podrake covered the pouch with his hands. "The money is for my church," he protested.

"You have no church," Ishmael growled.

Podrake's face twisted with torment. "I was pastor with a respectable church in Lancaster town. But there was a misunderstanding over the miller's daughter. It seemed a propitious time for me to take the word of the Lord to the frontier."

"In other words, ye hightailed it out of Lancaster ahead of a tar and feather mob," the captain said.

"They say the frontier is a place for new beginnings, do they not?" Podrake replied, steadier now. "It seemed the hand of Providence at work when they approached me in this very tavern." He clutched his purse more tightly. "Jehovah was interceding in my tragedy. They paid enough for me to build a new chapel in the wilderness. God will forgive all if only—"

The captain's hand hit Podrake's jaw like a slab of wood, knocking the pastor against the wall. "Enough! Ye shared bread with us for weeks and then tried to steal my boat! Mr. Boone frightened away yer conspirators but ye still cast off my poles!" He leaned over Podrake with a menacing whisper. "There's military justice in this town. We could give evidence that would have ye hanged in a week!"

Podrake pressed his hand against his jaw, already discoloring from the blow. A strangled noise came from his throat. "Hanged? I committed no mortal sin."

"The blood of Ezra is on your hands," Duncan said. He recalled how Podrake had been almost invisible during their return voyage, growing more pale, and more nervous, as he spent hours every day reading his Bible in the hold.

"Never! How was I to know?"

"I recall you favor brightly colored handkerchiefs. You signaled the killers with your yellow one tied to a tree!" Duncan shot back. "Do you deny it? I recall seeing it on the passage down the river. Where is that handkerchief now?"

Podrake looked down, avoiding Duncan's eyes. "The wind," he said, his voice cracking. "You know how the wind on the river snatches things."

The captain slapped him again. Blood swelled up from his nose. "Just a signal!" Podrake cried. "How was I to know what purpose it would serve?"

"How did they know Ezra was on that boat?" Duncan demanded.

"I don't know. They knew everything already, knew you would be going down the Ohio, knew about Ezra, knew about your intentions for the old bones."

Duncan chewed on the words. Nothing in the plan Reynolds had described, the plan betrayed in London, would have mentioned the *incognitum*.

"You prayed with Ezra sometimes," Ishmael recalled. "I remember when he asked you to pray for his wife, because he worried about her." The heat had left his eyes, leaving only sadness.

"How could I have known a murder was intended?" Podrake groaned.

"Three murders," Ishmael corrected.

"No, no. Not possible."

"Ezra, his wife, and their son, soon to be born," Ishmael spat. "He was killed in the womb, before he could even taste the breath of this world."

Podrake seemed to shrink. His mouth moved but nothing came out except strangled murmurs. "Not possible," he finally repeated.

"They were murdered by your employers," Duncan stated in a flat voice. "You were part of their conspiracy. You made the murders possible."

Podrake spoke into his tankard. "I had a church in Lancaster," he repeated in an anguished whisper, then reached into a pocket and produced his tattered Bible.

"The only chance you have to avoid the rope, Reverend," Duncan growled, "is to tell us everything you know about the two men who employed you."

Podrake, his hand shaking, lifted his tankard and drained it. "I was only with them a few hours, here in Pittsburgh. They said their names were Johnson and Pope. Pope had the air of a strong, vigorous man, with a roundish face. Johnson had a long face with dark, penetrating eyes. He had a more polished air about him, like he had finished one of those colleges in England. They had come from New York, they said, and were with a land company, though they didn't strike me as men of commerce.

"I was down on my luck, you might say, needing a fresh start. They bought me a pitcher of ale and told me the *Arabella* was going downstream to retrieve the bones of the famous *incognitum* that the London journals speak of. The bones were very valuable, they said, though I couldn't imagine why. They needed an educated gentleman like me to compose an eyewitness report for one of those journals, and they said the value of such a report was in surprising the public, and they couldn't allow the chance of the secret leaking. They said the report would drive up the prices of land they had purchased, allowing them a quick profit. First they suggested I sign on as crew, but I protested that I did not have the physical resources to push a pole all day. Then they suggested that I offer to go as a missionary scouting out a site for a new school in the Ohio lands. That's how I got the idea for my new church, and I saw then that Jehovah was playing a hand."

Podrake clutched his Bible in both hands. "What I said at the Lick wasn't a pretense," he continued in a bitter tone. "I meant my words about the monstrosity. It is an act against God to glorify those bones or speak of the creatures as extinct. It is not possible that Jehovah would create entire species only to cruelly destroy them." It was an argument that had already surfaced in articles about the *incognitum*, written by men who had never seen the bones.

"No one knows if the creatures were extinguished. All we know is that no one in these lands has ever seen them alive," Duncan pointed out. "The continent is vast, and one day men may yet find them in America."

"It has to be so," Podrake said in a desolate voice.

Duncan studied the shattered man, then called for the barmaid to bring a bowl of stew and a mug of strong tea.

The captain pushed the pouch of coins toward Duncan. "Yer going to need to rent the best horses at every coach stop from here to Philadelphia," he stated. "Ye can't stay with the bones, McCallum, or ye'll never catch up with the bastards."

Podrake lifted his head. "It's mine!" he whined.

Duncan glanced at Ishmael, who nodded agreement. "Dumont and I will stay with the wagons," the Nipmuc said. "But you must go."

Duncan opened the pouch and extracted five of the heavy coins and dropped them in front of Podrake. "A friend of mine named Frederick Post, a Moravian, has started a mission for the tribes on the Muskingum River north of the Ohio. You will go to him and say I sent you. You will tell him you played an inadvertent role in the deaths of two Shawnee and must serve penance. One of these will pay your expenses. You will give Post the rest to help the mission and you will work for him for one year."

A murmur of protest rose from the captain. "The devil should hang! One word to the provosts and he'll be in chains before dark."

Podrake looked up at the Cornishman with a terrified expression, then leaned toward Duncan.

"Do you understand?" Duncan demanded. "One of the sutlers, Mr. Reynolds, will be traveling there soon. I will speak with him this very night. You will go with him, and I will get reports from him and Post. If you leave in less than a year, I will let the Shawnee know you aided the murderers. They will find you, and they will make sure you suffer a most unpleasant death."

The reverend nodded stiffly. "Post. Muskingum. One year," he murmured.

"Ye can't trust 'im," the captain warned.

A long, dry sob wracked Podrake's body and he bent, arms crossed over his belly. He seemed to have shrunk.

"We can trust him," Duncan said, studying the miserable man, "because he knows it is the only way he can wash his blackened soul clean."

"Prithee, sir," came a soft, consoling voice. "Take a sip of my good black tea."

Duncan opened his heavy eyelids to see a woman in a gray apron bending over him with a steaming mug. He shook his head to clear his senses.

"Is my stew so bad that you had to mix the dust of the road into it?" the woman said as she sat the tea beside him.

With a mumbled apology Duncan moved his hand from the edge of the bowl in front of him, where his sleeve had been soaking in its contents.

"When did you last sleep, lad?" the woman asked with matronly concern.

Duncan tried to push the fog from his mind. "Nearly four days ago, in Pittsburgh, not counting a few naps along the road," he mumbled. "The moon was bright enough to ride through the nights."

"Blessing to good General Forbes," she said, "God rest his soul." The Scottish general had broken his health in building the western road to Pittsburgh during the French War, and died not long after its completion. Troop commanders may have boasted of their victories, but it had been the Forbes road that had defeated the French in the west.

Duncan had gulped half his tea before he realized the woman had spoken Gaelic, and with a familiar accent. He lowered his mug and saw now her ruddy cheeks and the red curls that strayed from under her linen cap. "The west of the Highlands?" he asked in the same language.

"Isle of Skye, my dear, clan of McCrae. My father was forester for the great laird." The woman glanced about the tavern, confirming that the other patrons were well tended, then pulled out a chair and sat. "It's been too long since I was able to speak the tongue of the isles."

Duncan recognized the inquiry in her eyes. "Clan McCallum. Nigh Lochalsh, so we were neighbors. My people built boats and raised hairy cows. I am named Duncan."

Mrs. McCrae's face broke into a faraway smile. "Oh, the bonny coos. I dearly miss the sight of their shaggy ginger coats scattered over the high braes."

Duncan, fully awake now, began eating the stew with great relish. The Scottish woman's smile grew as she watched him. "Ah, look at ye," she said. "Ye put me in mind of the braw lads competing at the gatherings whilst we kept great kettles of cock-a-leekie soup warming on the fires." She turned and called for a barmaid to bring Duncan a second bowl and a pot of ale. "It's a poorly kept secret that I mix ale in my stew," she confided, "but I save the best for washing it down."

Duncan only had a vague recollection of stumbling into the Lancaster tavern, barely able to keep his eyes open, but now took a moment to admire the tidy, spacious, open-beamed chamber with a large fireplace at one end and a bar cage at the other. "I take it you belong to this fine establishment," he said between mouthfuls.

"Oh, aye. My husband and I opened it years ago but he went to Abraham's bosum these two years since. And my son is at sea so I manage the tavern myself." She saw the way Duncan kept glancing at the other patrons. "Who is it ye seek, Mr. McCallum?"

"Two men riding hard from Pittsburgh."

"I've not had any others falling asleep in their stew this week, if that's what ye mean." She shrugged and surveyed the room. "The secrets of my travelers are theirs to keep," she said in a stiffer tone, then rose, as if wanting to avoid trouble.

"*Redeat*," Duncan said as she turned away.

The word stopped her.

"You have a white rosette in your apron," Duncan observed.

She self-consciously lifted a hand to the silk rosette pinned to an apron strap. "A worn-out memento. I keep forgetting to remove it."

"I was imprisoned and transported to America for giving aid to the Jacobite cause, years after Culloden," Duncan confessed. "Kings come and go, but the truth endures."

Mrs. McCrae sat again, glancing about as if for eavesdroppers. "At every Sunday meal Mr. McCrae would set a bowl of water on the table and hold a glass of wine over it."

Duncan was well acquainted with the simple ceremony. "To toast the king over the water," he said. The cherished Young Pretender who had led the last Scottish rebellion, Bonnie Prince Charlie, was across the ocean living in Rome, but was still revered by many Highlanders. Duncan chose not to mention that friends who had been to the Holy City reported that the true king had become an inveterate drunkard.

Mrs. McCrae's face brightened. "There's more of us in America than ye might suspect," she said.

He paused at the hint of invitation in her words. "I was only a boy at school in Holland at the time of Culloden. I wasn't there, but I still have nightmares of the massacres that followed. My father and his brothers were hanged. I see the troops abusing and killing my mother and sisters. Sometimes I see them bayoneting my six-year-old brother."

The tavern keeper studied him with a gaze that was at once stern and sympathetic, one that he had often received from the aunts of his youth. "Finish yer stew, *Ghaidhealach*," she said, using the Gaelic for Highlander, then abruptly rose. She soon returned with a dusty bottle and two dram glasses. She silently filled the glasses, pushed his empty bowl away, and set one in front of him. "*Slainte*," the Highland matron offered as she put her glass to her lips.

He downed the whisky with a grateful smile. "I recall that it was Clan McCrae who defended Eilean Donan castle for the McKenzies when the McDonalds attacked it."

She beamed and filled their glasses again, then quickly drained hers. "And were made hereditary constables of the castle for the service. We had many fierce warriors. But my favorite was Duncan of the Silver Cups because he put down his sword and became a poet. They say he was a braw, handsome man with wheat-colored hair like yer own." She filled her dram and lifted it once more. "To Duncan of the Silver Cups and Duncan of the four-day gallop." She emptied her glass again, then leaned forward. "Now tell me of these two men ye seek, *Ghaidhealach*."

Mrs. McCrae listened attentively as he related what he knew of the men, just saying they had murdered friends of his. She turned to study the dining chamber. An adolescent boy appeared carrying an armful of firewood, and she had a barmaid summon the youth. "Mathias tends the stable," she explained. "And to other special tasks," she added as she bid the boy sit.

Mathias immediately knew the two men Duncan sought. "Coldhearted bullies they were," he said. "They had nigh killed their mounts but showed no mercy, and one cuffed me when I suggested the poor creatures had earned extra oats. Seeing how the horses were shaking so, I said I hoped they survived the night. The other says if not, no doubt the tavern stewpot would be full on the morrow. 'Tweren't right. What did they care, their friend was waiting with fresh mounts."

"Friend?" Duncan asked.

"Aye, they asked me did I know of a man wearing a red feather in his blue hat who was waiting for them. I said sure, a man with a blue hat and a big S-shaped scar on his cheek. He said he had come up from Virginia, and had been waiting three days at the tavern down the street. Except the groom there said he hadn't been idle, he was keeping busy in town," the boy confided.

"Speak clear, lad," Mrs. McCrae said. "How do ye mean busy?"

"Us grooms stick together," the boy explained to Duncan, "'cause we share rental horses and stalls when one tavern fills, and such like that. He was asking questions, pressing coins in palms, and said he was interested in a big Conestoga wagon that had came up from Virginia filled with barrels of flour."

"Flour?" the proprietress asked. "Not likely, lad, when more than enough is available from the Pennsylvania mills."

The boy shrugged. "Maybe that's what made him so curious. Once he found 'em in the warehouse he studied the barrels and made a note of the address in Philadelphia written on top, where they're to be delivered. My friend watched him from the hayloft, on account of the man's sharp eyes, always searching where they had no business."

"Where's this man now?" Duncan asked.

"I told you. He had horses ready for his friends. They ate dinner in a private room, then he took them to see those barrels. The next morning off they went, the two on the Philadelphia pike and him off to the west, toward the Harris ferry. I remember seeing him through the crowd at the ruins of the tinsmith's shop, which had burned down in the night."

"Are those barrels still here in Lancaster?"

Mathias nodded. "Being shipped in a day or two. I can take you to see 'em right now." He brightened as he stood. "And ye can see our planetary device, it's not far from the warehouse!"

"Not tonight, lad," Mrs. McCrae said. "In the morning. Now see that Mr. McCallum gets set up in the back bedroom over the kitchen, by himself. Tighten the bed and see that he has the good down quilt from the chest in my own room. It's not every day we host a Highland warrior."

Duncan was barely conscious by the time he lay down in the spacious bed. Even when the roosters started crowing he only rolled over, though he started having unsettling dreams of being chased by monstrous animals ridden by men with devil's horns, and then, worse, of watching from a battlement as Sarah was being chased by the same demons. At last a ray of sunlight touched his face and he opened his eyes to see the groom Mathias standing by his bed.

"It's two hours since the cow was milked," the boy said as he extended a pewter mug, "but Mrs. McCrae said I was to save some for you." He backed away as Duncan sat up and accepted the mug. "I can show you the barrels and our amazing device," he reminded Duncan before he turned. He paused at the door, patting the pockets of his waistcoat. "Oh, and most every traveler on the Pittsburgh road stays at one of the taverns here on High Street."

Duncan took a big swallow, then swung his legs off the bed. "I don't follow, Mathias."

"Mother McCrae has me check with the other taverns and the post office when those she calls long travelers come in, because people usually expect them to stop in Lancaster. Ain't the postal office grand? Sometimes I think about posting a letter to some made-up name in Boston or Charleston just so I can imagine its journey. But Mother McCrae scolded me when I told her, said it would be an abuse of the postal trust, whatever that means. I collect letters for travelers, which is almost as good."

"A kind sentiment," Duncan said. "But I won't be receiving any letters here."

With a perverse grin the boy proved him wrong, producing a crumpled envelope. "'D. McCallum,' it says, 'traveler from the west, Lancaster Post Office.' Traveler from the west. Sounds like a knight on one of those quests. I want to be one someday. Oh, and there was a ha'penny owed."

Duncan tossed the boy a penny as he pulled on his britches, then grabbed the letter out of his hand and latched the door as Mathias ran down the hall, clutching his reward.

Duncan's heart leapt as he recognized the handwriting, and his hand trembled as he broke the seal. *Beloved D.*, it began:

Lest you drop your precious cargo and rush to take the first boat north, please know that I am not in Edentown. For important reasons of shared interest I have journeyed to Philadelphia and you will find me at the Preston House, 419 Mulberry Street, though some are taking to calling it Arch Street. If I am not there I will be with Mrs. Franklin or with those who sent you on your journey. I will not begin to express my affectionate longing for you here since I am sending copies of this missive to unknown postmasters in Carlisle, York, Harris Landing, and Lancaster but I assure you I will express it well enough when we meet and at last we shall make our final plans.

The letter was signed *SR* and beside it was a drawing of a deer and the Mohawk word for the shy forest creature *Ohskennonton*. His heart quickened. Sarah was invoking the tender moments when their relationship had blossomed, when they began sharing English and Mohawk words in the Edentown schoolhouse.

Duncan sat as if in another dream, reading the unexpected letter over and over. He had been separated for months from his betrothed and had assumed it would be another three or four weeks before they were reunited at Edentown in the Catskills. Now he would see Sarah much sooner, perhaps even the next day. *Our final plans.* Sarah was speaking of the plans for their long-awaited wedding.

He was so lighthearted as he entered the kitchen that he embraced Mrs. McCrae, then laughed as, clucking like a hen, she brushed away the flour that had rubbed onto his waistcoat. She pointed to a linen napkin covering a plate at the end of the long table. "Fresh biscuits and bacon," she announced, "though ye slept so long we should be serving ye lunch." Duncan chatted with her between bites, mentioning that he had friends coming from the west with two wagons who might enjoy her stew. He was on his last biscuit when through the window he saw Mathias waiting outside.

Minutes later the young groom was leading him down an alley toward a substantial brick building when the boy paused, then guided Duncan down a second alley to a shed with stone walls. A youth in his teens sat against the door, apparently asleep. When Mathias kicked him, he gasped and leapt to his feet.

"Jonathan Wentzel, you slaggard!" Mathias cried and kicked again. "You took a solemn oath!"

The sentinel straightened but did not look Mathias in the eyes. "No one entered," he mumbled.

"What if those scoundrels came back?" Mathias barked. "The vandals! The Huns! You have a duty to civilization and you doze like a common drunkard!"

Despite his chastising, the older boy blocked the way when Mathias reached for the door latch. "Password," he demanded.

Mathias gave an approving nod. "Beyond Mercury to Earth."

"Across the wide heavens," the guard answered, and stepped aside.

The room was dimly lit, but the sunlight filtering through the small, high loophole window lit the brass tube of Mathias's planetary device. "Ain't it grand!" the boy boasted. "Those scrubs thought they had us beat but our Society outfoxed them!"

Duncan was growing more confused. "It's a telescope," he ventured, for the purpose of the long two-inch-wide tube mounted on a tripod seemed obvious, although he was not familiar with the brass rectangle mounted perpendicularly to the tube.

"More!" Mathias beamed. "We are ready for the glorious third of June! America shall know the shape of her universe!"

"We? The third?" Duncan asked, silently chiding himself for giving in to the boy's strange game when he knew he should be searching for a fresh mount.

"The Philosophical Society of Lancaster and Environs. We correspond with the esteemed society of scholars in Philadelphia, the American Philosophical Society!" Mathias declared, pointing to a long chart, pinned to a board on the wall, that showed three precise fold marks and a ragged edge on one side, as if it had been extracted from a journal. "It's never been properly done in America but it will now, if God shines on us. My momma says we are lucky to be alive in this year since we will be in heaven long before the next one."

Duncan yielded to his curiosity, bending to the paper to study its intricate diagrams and equations. *Preparation for the June 3 Transit of Venus and Calculation of the Distance to the Sun,* it read in large type along the top, then *American Philosophical Society.* Duncan had friends in the Society, some of whom were waiting for his crates from the Lick. Smaller type along the bottom declared *In Gratitude to Charles Mason.* He looked up from a drawing of a telescopic device on the paper and saw that it matched that of the device before him.

"Your bullies from Pittsburgh thought they could stop us, but they didn't know the skill of our jeweler in town. We made him an honorary member for the fine repair work he did."

Duncan still struggled to fit all of the groom's words together. "Surely you don't mean the two men I was asking about?"

The sullen sentinel answered. "We are so proud of it that we like to tell visitors. We have a brotherhood of scholars, we like to say."

Mathias sighed. "I told ye, ye can't say that because the schoolmarm and her daughter are in it," he chided, then turned to Duncan. "We like to show all visitors, so they can tell the world how important Lancaster is becoming. They seemed quite surprised, and complimented our work, but then before dawn we found them running out of here, laughing as they leapt on their horses and rode off. We found the tube on the floor, dented, and the old tripod smashed to splinters."

"The paper," the older boy muttered.

"Oh yes," Mathias recalled, and retrieved a slip of paper tucked in a crack in the wall mortar. "They dropped this when they were doing their mischief." He handed the paper to Duncan.

It was a list, written in a precise, well-educated hand. *Buttons, spoons, combs, lamp plates, dippers, betty lamps, plug burners.*

Duncan could make no sense of the tale or the paper, other than that it resembled a shopping list, and silently concluded that Mathias and his friends had somehow offended the men and the vandalism had been their reprisal. Mathias declined to take the list back, as if he wanted it gone from his snug scholars' sanctuary, and Duncan pushed it into a pocket. "We were going to see those barrels," he reminded Mathias, and saw the disappointment on the boy's face. "I must hurry to Philadelphia," he added, "but I shall tell Mrs. Franklin of your great device. I shall name you to her."

Mathias's eyes went round. "The wife of the great Franklin?" he gasped.

"I count Deborah Franklin as a friend, yes."

"And assure her that we do have a chronograph," the youth at the door added. "We need a chronograph to record the points of the transit, but the parson said he would loan his to us on the great day."

"A chronograph," Duncan repeated distractedly. "The barrels?" he asked Mathias. "Then we must find a horse."

Mathias was slowly recovering from the surprise of Duncan's news. "Oh, aye," he said, breaking from his trance. "Mrs. McCrae had me out at dawn, securing the best remount in all the town."

The barrels were in the large brick warehouse Duncan had seen earlier. Mathias waved at the teamsters loading wagons, then led Duncan down a stone-flagged aisle lined with stacks of casks, crates, hogsheads, and bundles of tanned skins. In a corner under a row of windows were a score of barrels marked FLOUR in black painted letters, all bound for a Philadelphia address marked on top, shipped from the same mill in Virginia, and all bearing shipping numerals chalked on the top, from one to twenty. Duncan walked among the barrels, trying to understand why the murderers' accomplice from the south would have thought it important that Ezra's killers see them. It was a mystery, but not one that he could allow to distract him from his urgent business in Philadelphia.

"They were only interested in certain barrels," the groom explained, pointing to a small black X on the side of one, inscribed near the top. Each of the bars of the X ended in small black balls. "This sign is on half of them."

"Why put a sign on only half the barrels?" Duncan asked. "If it was a miller's mark, he would put them on all the barrels."

"Not a miller's mark. I told ye. My friend was watching from nearby. The signs were not on the barrels before they entered, he is certain." Mathias shrugged. "Maybe ye can ask them in Philadelphia."

"Ask whom?"

"Whoever's at that place. All the barrels have the same destination marked on the top. Preston House, on Mulberry Street."

Duncan hesitated, then extracted Sarah's letter and reread the last lines with a chill. The barrels marked by the accomplice of Ezra's killers were all going to the address where Sarah awaited him.

Chapter 5

H E RODE HARD ALONG THE Conestoga Road for three hours, then, not knowing when he would find another mount, climbed down and led his big bay for nearly a mile. By the time he had repeated the pattern twice, occasionally nibbling on the bread and cheese Mrs. McCrae had stuffed in the saddle pouch, he had reached a cluster of buildings marked by a crude sign stating MORGANTOWN. For the sake of his horse, he took a meal in the solitary tavern and then rented a room for a few hours' rest. He rose in the small hours and was back on the road long before dawn, his mount falling into a long, easy gait that ate up the miles.

He did his best to keep the horse from straining, but he could not keep his own mind from racing. Why was Sarah in Philadelphia? She was firmly anchored to Edentown, which had become a thriving community almost by her willpower alone. Sarah was a fixture there, the arbiter of disputes, the patron of the school, the sponsor of resettlement by craftsmen, and most of all the vital, calming link between the Iroquois and the settlers. Just weeks before, she had warned Duncan that because of the increasing tension between the tribes and the settlers who kept pushing west, she felt she could not stray far from her town. In her letter she said she had gone to Philadelphia for "important reasons of shared interest," but the reasons must have been urgent indeed. What was the sudden crisis that had dragged her away from her beloved settlement? He passed the miles weighing their shared interests. Harmony with the tribes. Strengthening Edentown. Educating the children of settlers. Marriage. Avoiding her demonic father, who wanted Duncan dead. But surely none of these would have caused her to abandon Edentown for the Quaker city.

Duncan had become sufficiently familiar with the grid pattern of Philadelphia's streets that he had no trouble finding the livery stable to return his rented mount, leaving another shilling to assure the horse would have both added grain and an extra day of rest. Feeling unsteady himself after so many hours of hard riding, he found a table at a quiet tavern and drank several cups of strong black tea, keeping one hand on the leather knapsack he had brought from Pittsburgh. He couldn't shake the sense that despite the violent mysteries that stalked his journey, the greatest mystery was that represented in the bag, the mystery of ancient earth. *You took the bones without asking the gods*, the aged Catchoka had declared. *The gods will follow.* Once again Duncan tried to parse the words, wondering if the gods would follow to punish him, or to protect him. There had been more words. *There will be blood in the night. You will die again and again.* In the fables of his Highland youth there had been reluctant mortals given missions by the gods that lived under the earth. Those who tried to outsmart the gods never survived, suffering hideous deaths. The tribes considered that the bones had been entrusted to them by their gods. Duncan had broken the trust. Had Ezra sensed that? Duncan wondered. He had not spoken with Duncan after they had exposed the big bone in the pit. Had he died believing Duncan had betrayed the gods?

Not for the first time on his journey, Duncan extracted a little bone, roughly cylindrical, no larger than the top joint of his thumb, with a central hole running down its length. It was an *incognitum* bone, taken from the bone pit. Although he could not tell if it was from a toe, a tail, or some other mysterious appendage, it surely belonged to the ancient beast. He rolled it in his palm with a sense of foreboding. It had become a reminder of his duty, his shame, and the treacherous, unknown path before him.

Preston House was a half hour's walk away, just below the fields of the Northern Liberties. It was a spacious clapboard house that, like many in the district, appeared to have housed a shop or business in its ground floor. The windows at street level had been whitewashed, perhaps to obliterate the slogan that was now a dim shadow on the glass. WILKES AND LIBERTY, it said, a defiant call, invoking the British defender of freedom, that was seen and heard much more often on the streets of Boston and New York than in conservative Philadelphia. Above the ground floor, however, Duncan saw a prosperous-looking residence with elegant brass candlesticks visible on the windowsills and brightly colored quilts draped out the windows of the third floor. He rapped with the large brass doorknocker, to no avail, then stepped back to look for signs of movement in the windows above, without success.

Hoisting his knapsack to one shoulder, he moved down Fifth Street to Market Street, turning into the bricked walkway in the middle of the block that led to a handsome house in the middle of a walled courtyard. The front door was opened on his third knock by a tired-looking woman in a white apron and cap. "Deliveries in the rear," she instructed, then hesitated.

He smiled, brushing his hair back, and nodded to the woman. "I am pleased to see you in good health, Mrs. Hanks."

"Mr. McCallum?" she asked, then pushed the door wide open. "Lord, we didn't expect you for another fortnight or more!"

"Urgent business hastened my return," Duncan replied, looking past the housekeeper. "I was hoping to find Sarah Ramsey with Mrs. Franklin."

"Oh dear, and didn't they have luncheon here not two hours ago! But Mistress Franklin went off to the government house to hear the debates and Miss Sarah—" She paused and turned toward the kitchen. "Priscilla!" she called. When there was no answer, she gestured for Duncan to follow her down the hall to the rear of the house. They found the young scullery maid picking peas in the kitchen garden, singing to herself so loudly she could not hear Mrs. Hanks call from the back step. Duncan slipped past the housekeeper and, stopping at the end of the garden, tossed a pebble into the girl's basket. The sudden irritation on her face vanished as she recognized him.

"Duncan!" she cried, dropping her basket as she leapt forward to throw her arms around his waist. "Thank God the wilds did not kill you!" The girl had helped Duncan on more than one of his visits to Philadelphia. Laughing, he pushed her to arm's length, then fished a glistening black stone from a pocket and handed it to the girl, who pushed back her curly mop of hair to see it better. "Obsidian," he explained. "From a cliff on the Ohio. A token of my appreciation." On his last visit, Priscilla had diverted a patrol searching for a secret Sons meeting by screaming "Thief!" and chasing an imaginary culprit down a nearby alley.

They sat on the back step as he responded to the girl's barrage of questions about his journey before inquiring about Sarah.

"Oh, Miss Ramsey!" the teenage girl swooned. "I should have been broken-hearted to learn you had a woman other than me in your life," she teased, "excepting it's *her*. She has the most amazing manner about her. T'other night at the table she spoke in the Mohawk tongue, just imagine! She named the vegetables and the meat and such. Mrs. Franklin says it reflects a fine Christian heart for her to take the time to learn the language of her heathen neighbors."

Duncan grinned. Sarah took every opportunity to spread learning about the tribes, but few, and certainly no one in Philadelphia, knew that she had been raised as one of the wild heathens herself. Her fine heart, moreover, had much more to do with the Iroquois chieftain and matrons who had been her adopted family than any Christian learning.

"Do I have to follow her trail like a frontier hunter," Duncan asked at last, "or will you tell me where she has gone?"

Priscilla furrowed her brow. "Not at the artisan house, not until evening."

"Artisan house?"

"The big house on Mulberry where she stays."

"You mean the Preston House?"

"That's the one. There used to be a silversmith there, and before that a candle-maker. Sometimes she walks around the shops. She takes notes about new goods from England. Sometimes she buys them and takes them to Mr. Thomson."

"Mr. Thomson the Latin tutor?" Duncan asked.

Priscilla nodded. "The one you met with last time," she said with a knowing grin. "And sometimes she goes to listen to her birds."

"Birds?" Duncan asked.

"Oh yes, I think she misses her forest. There's even a robin she's named. Sometimes she says 'I am off to see my robin,' or sometimes 'off to hear my Siko sing.'

But not today, 'cause today she went toward the waterfront. She likes to watch the ships."

Duncan spent a fruitless hour searching the waterfront, then headed to a small brick town house two blocks from the State House. He went straight to the rear door and rapped three times in rapid succession, followed by two evenly spaced slower knocks. A voice rose from inside and chairs scraped on the floor. Charles Thomson had a front door life, dedicated to students from affluent families, and a back door life, dedicated to the Sons of Liberty.

Duncan watched as an adolescent boy, clutching a book and released early from his lesson, appeared around the corner and skipped down the walk to the street. Moments later the rear door opened.

The tall, round-faced man gave a start as he recognized Duncan. "McCallum!" he exclaimed. "Praise God!" He glanced over Duncan's shoulder, then gestured him inside. "We did not expect you so soon!" The scholar leaned into a darkened doorway off the kitchen and spoke a quick command. A boy of perhaps ten, rubbing sleep from his eyes, stumbled out of the room and darted to the back door. "Tell him our voyageur has returned!" Thomson called after the boy, then turned and offered Duncan some tea.

Less than ten minutes later, another of the coded knocks sounded at the door and Thomson admitted a well-dressed man with a prominent aquiline nose.

"Mr. Mulligan," Duncan said in surprise. "I didn't expect to find you in Philadelphia." Hercules Mulligan was a New York tailor whose daytime employment was as a haberdasher to British army officers and whose nights were often dedicated to New York's much more active contingent of the Sons of Liberty.

Mulligan acknowledged him with a cursory nod. "I have customers who were transferred to Philadelphia." He shot a pointed glance at Thomson. "Delivering their new uniforms was a convenient excuse for me to travel here."

"Mr. Mulligan has helped with shipping arrangements for your treasure," Thomson explained, urging them into his front parlor. "And shipping expenses," he added with a grateful nod to the tailor.

Thomson leaned into a front window and looked up and down the street. "I don't see your wagons. You do have the treasures?"

In reply, Duncan reached into the knapsack he had so carefully guarded and dropped a large object onto the table. Thomson gasped. A pleased rumble rose from Mulligan's throat. Thomson reached out with a tentative finger to touch it. "The *incognitum* is before us!" he exclaimed. "A miracle! From the lands of the savages to our fair city! Is it—" His brow furrowed. "A toe?"

"We found several of these along a long, curving jawbone."

"A tooth! Dear Lord, the creature's head must have been as large as this room!" Thomson's eyes grew even wider as he ran his fingertips over the ridges of the tooth. "Oh, the ages! Ages and ages!"

Mulligan stayed silent, studying the tooth with a satisfied smile. Thomson went to the window. "We must find a quiet place for your wagons," he said, hesitated, then came back to stroke the relic again.

"The wagons," Duncan reported, "have not yet arrived. They are still traveling from Pittsburgh."

"But Duncan!" Thomson protested. "Mr. Franklin trusted you and Ezra to—" He halted as he saw Duncan's grim expression.

"Mr. Franklin is just a stranger across the sea," Duncan said. "I went down the Ohio for my brothers in the Sons. And I didn't gallop back all the way from Fort Pitt because of the bones. I came in pursuit of murderers."

Thomson jerked his hand back as if the ancient tooth had bitten him. The two men stared at Duncan as he lowered himself onto one of the chairs by the table. He held his head in his hands a moment, then looked up. "Ezra is dead."

The next two hours were torture for Duncan, but he felt he owed these leaders of the Sons every detail of what happened at the Lick and on their return to Pittsburgh.

"Are there not blood feuds among the tribes?" Thomson asked. "You said Ezra had taken a native wife. No doubt there were members of the tribe who resented having an . . . an outsider marry into their blood."

Resentment flared on Duncan's face, but he pushed down his emotion. "I know of no people more tolerant than those of the tribes," he replied in a cool voice. "And the tribes have no spies seeking out letters from Benjamin Franklin. I told you, it was a letter from Dr. Franklin that choked away Ezra's life breath. That was not done by a tribesman. The letter was about your Covenant."

Thomson's brows lifted. "That was not your mission, Duncan."

"It was Ezra's mission and he died for it, died for the Covenant's plans for Mississippi trade."

A disapproving rumble came from Mulligan's throat. "Not your mission, Duncan," he echoed.

Duncan ignored their ire. "The killers were two men from England, whom I have pursued from Pittsburgh. They must be found!"

"The city is awash with Englishmen," Thomson observed. "Do you have their names? Do you know their faces? Their destination in the city?"

"I know little about them. One is tall, about forty with black hair, the other a few years younger, of more compact build, and brown hair. They are soldiers, I am convinced, but do not wear uniforms."

"Or once they were soldiers," Thomson suggested.

"There are scores of men who could answer that description," Mulligan pointed out. "I could think of a dozen just among my customers. Need I remind you that Ezra had a different mission from yours, and they must think they ended that by killing him, so their business is concluded?"

"I told you, they tried to steal the boat with the bones on board," Duncan said with thin patience. "They gave their names as Samuel Johnson and Alexander Pope."

Thomson rolled his eyes. "That tells us nothing other than they have a modicum of education and a twisted sense of humor. And no doubt they were just trying to slow your pursuit, nothing more."

"They came down the Conestoga Road, just a day or two ago."

"With more than a hundred others each day. This is Philadelphia. They won't dare lift a hand here."

"They are impetuous in their violence," Duncan pressed. "Before they left Lancaster, they tried to destroy an astronomical device that belonged to some local society of scholars."

Thomson stared in disbelief. "A telescope?" He slammed a fist onto the table with uncharacteristic vehemence. "The Philistines! Can it be true? Will it be usable?"

Duncan and Mulligan exchanged confused glances.

"Charles," the New York tailor said, "you have lost us."

"The transit!" Thomson cried. "Don't you understand? This changes things!" Without an explanation he sprang to his feet and summoned the boy from the kitchen. Bending at his desk, he hastily scribbled a note and handed it the boy. "To Mr. Rittenhouse and then to Mr. Biddle! Posthaste!"

When he turned back to Duncan there was an odd desperation in his eyes. "You must remember more. We must find these hoodlums!"

Duncan was still trying to grasp the sudden alarm in the normally taciturn Thomson when Mulligan spoke. "Charles, collect yourself. You seem more moved by vandalism against some telescope than the murder of one of our agents."

Thomson lowered himself into a chair, gripping its arms tightly as Mulligan refreshed his tea. "The Royal Philosophical Society in London scoffed at our efforts in 1761 to measure the last transit of Venus. They publicly spoke then about how Americans could never offer anything of scholarly value. Now they have ridiculed our preparation for June 3, even mocking our own Philosophical Society. Such arrogance for fools in Pennsylvania to pretend they can match the natural philosophers of Europe, they say. But what they really fear is that we will exceed their own efforts. Many of them have still not forgiven Franklin for leading the way in electricity."

Thomson saw the uncertain expressions on his companions' faces, so he described the efforts the scholars of Philadelphia were taking to assure multiple observations, including regular prayers for fair weather on June 3. "We will have three different teams from our Philosophical Society," he explained. "One at the State House, one on the farm of Mr. Rittenhouse, and another down on Cape Henlopen at the mouth of the Delaware." He seemed frustrated at their lack of reaction to his announcement. "We must rally! We must ship the bones and focus on defending our instruments! Don't you see, the size of the universe is at stake!"

"I'm sure it is," Mulligan offered uncertainly.

Thomson rolled his eyes. "If Philadelphia can correctly chart the times and angles when the planet enters and leaves the disc of the sun, then we, the natural philosophers of Philadelphia, can be the first to tell the world how far it is to the sun! Not London or Paris or Berlin, but Philadelphia! The king himself has built an observatory in London for his own observations, but we all know how awful the weather can be there. Captain Cook was dispatched to the South Pacific months ago for the transit, though no one can know if he will reach Tahiti in time. We have a reasonable chance of making the best observations on the planet, of making history. No representation in Parliament? By God, they will have to take notice of us then!"

Thomson produced a journal from his desk that set forth the complex equation first established by Edmond Halley in the prior century, then turned the page and unfolded the same chart Duncan had seen pinned to the wall of the shed in Lancaster. For a few moments he forgot about the murders and let himself be drawn into Thomson's explanation of the equation, then related how he himself had spent many enjoyable nights in Edinburgh with a professor and a telescope up on Castle Hill. But his attention soon lagged and he kept glancing outside at the dimming daylight.

Mulligan did his best to guide the discussion back to preparations for the shipment of the *incognitum* and away from what he characterized as the childish act of vengeance on a telescope. He finally noticed Duncan's wandering gaze and an inquisitive grin rose on his face. "Surely you have reunited with your coconspirator from the Catskills?" he asked.

"I know not where to find her," Duncan confessed. "Not at Preston House, not at Mrs. Franklin's."

Thomson glanced at his tall case clock. "In her short time here, your enchanting friend has been the recipient of many invitations, trust me. But she declines most and has been raising eyebrows by visiting dining establishments with distaff companions and no gentleman in escort."

Duncan grinned, knowing Sarah would take delight in bucking Philadelphia convention. "I can remedy that if I but knew what establishment she was visiting."

Thomson shrugged and thought a moment. "There's no more than four or five candidates. The inn on Elfreth's Alley, the London Coffeehouse, the Blue Anchor, the Three Doves . . ."

"And the Wild Boar," Mulligan added.

Reciting the list of taverns in his mind, Duncan hurried through the streets, dodging vendors hauling away their street carts and nearly colliding with a lamplighter as he was climbing down his short ladder. He grew more despondent as he exhausted his list and was no longer hopeful when he finally entered the Wild Boar

Inn, between the State House and the port. He had worked up a thirst in his quest and after ordering an ale found a stool at a long high counter that offered a view into the more formal, and much larger, dining chamber.

Duncan was tired and forlorn and his exhaustion began to grip him as he realized he did not even have a bed for the night. A bewigged British officer speaking in self-important tones to two other officers jabbed him with his elbow and Duncan was about to complain when a soft, throaty laugh rose from the dining room, instantly banishing his sour mood.

Sarah Ramsey sat at a table on the far side of the chamber with two other women of her own age, one with blond hair and the other brunette. Sarah was turned sideways to him as she spoke with amusement to her companions. He eased off his stool, then paused, resisting the temptation to rush to her, to let her enjoy more of the evening with her friends. It was rare for her to be away from her responsibilities at Edentown, rarer still for her to be out socializing in a public establishment. Duncan settled back, filled with a warmth he had not felt for weeks.

The soldiers beside him were also enjoying themselves, engaged in lively banter that touched on the poor quality of tea in America, rumors of another regiment being deployed by General Gage to Boston, and whether oysters were better from the Delaware or the Chesapeake Bays.

"Sweet Jesus, what a filly!" the officer closest to Duncan gasped. "Just look at her!"

With a chill Duncan saw that the man was gazing at Sarah.

The bewigged officer unexpectedly turned to Duncan. "Do you happen to know her name, sir?" he asked. "The auburn-haired beauty at the far table, in the dark green dress."

Duncan collected himself, knowing the slightly inebriated officer posed no threat to Sarah. He shrugged. "I am newly arrived in the city," he replied.

"Their escort has apparently abandoned the ladies. Perhaps a king's officer should offer his service."

Duncan gave a whimsical smile. "That might pose a challenge. I trust you have battlefield experience?"

"You suggest such forwardness would not be well received in this most Quaker of cities? I confess I am not well acquainted with its conservative ways," the officer said with a sigh, then he turned to fill Duncan's tankard from the pitcher of ale he had been sharing with his companions. "You seem a man of the world, sir. How do I go about navigating your colonial mazes?"

The shorter officer beside him gave a grunting laugh. "Navigating colonial women, I believe you mean, Major."

The major raised his tankard and touched it to his companion's as if to concede the point. "I am bred for conquest, Lieutenant Nettles," he said with an oily smile. "It is my essence, and my burden."

"And may God show mercy to your enemies," the lieutenant said, lifting his own tankard.

"Because blessed King George does not," the major rejoined.

Duncan inconspicuously studied the uniforms of the soldiers, recognizing the one farthest from him as belonging to an infantry unit stationed at Albany, but he was not familiar with the ornate, brocaded uniforms of the other two. "You make it sound as if you are at war," he suggested.

The major gave an amused laugh. "The fantasies of idle soldiers." As he spoke, his eyes shifted back toward Sarah. "The fantasies of idle soldiers," he repeated in a lower voice, much more pointedly.

"Stick to the barmaids and recent immigrants from England," Duncan said as he sipped his ale. "Those provincial women tend to have skills that may be unfamiliar to you."

"Provincial?"

"The ones bred in the colonies, outside the cities."

"You know this damsel to be such a creature?"

"Look at her. The healthy glow that comes from country air. The brooch she wears may look like yellow metal, but it is only carved wood," Duncan pointed out with some confidence, since he had carved the burnished maple-leaf brooch himself. He leaned closer and whispered. "And proper Philadelphia Quaker women would never venture out without a male escort." As he spoke, Sarah laughed again. The blond woman with her turned to speak with the serving maid and Duncan realized he knew her. She was Olivia Dumont, Pierre's younger sister, whose intellect and curiosity matched those of her brother.

"Then certainly she needs a proper companion."

"You miscomprehend, sir. I am not saying she is need of protection. I am saying you are the one to be protected. They can be wild, the frontier women."

The major refilled his own tankard, and Duncan's. "You miscomprehend *me*, sir. The wilder the prey, the more satisfying the hunt." The major tilted his head back so far to drink that his wig went slightly awry.

"She may scalp you," Duncan warned lightheartedly as he dropped a coin in the small pail held out by a boy soliciting ha'pennies for the orphan fund.

The major turned to the officer at his side. "James, surely there must be a game room here. Perhaps we could invite the ladies to a few hands of whist. The tavern keeper no doubt has a deck of cards we can borrow."

"It sounds too much like a defensive campaign, Major," Duncan chided. He was surprising himself, but he knew Sarah was more than capable of dealing with the tipsy soldier.

The major considered Duncan's words and nodded. "A flank attack it shall be. James, bring that waif back."

Moments later the major had hoisted the boy up to sit on the high counter that divided the public drinking room from the dining chamber. "Good ladies and gentlemen of the City of Brotherly Love," the major announced in a rich baritone. "If you can but spare a moment for a noble cause, we shall have some entertainment while filling this fine lad's pail. 'Tis a game we use to help the king's charities in London." The diners quieted as the major explained that the lieutenant would compete with all comers in acts of great prowess, the first being to construct a house of ten playing cards standing on edge. The major withdrew a coin from a pocket and laid it on the table. "I put my shilling on Lieutenant Nettles here as the man who can complete the structure faster than anyone in the room. Come challenge him by putting up your own shilling. If you lose, your shilling goes in the pail. If you win, you get my shilling."

The major quickly had half a dozen contestants in line and the amused barmaids cleared a space on the long counter as the tavern keeper produced the playing cards. As Duncan stood in the shadows, mostly watching Sarah with weary contentment, the lieutenant prevailed over all the competitors and the pail had six new shillings in it. The nimble lieutenant next beat all comers in balancing a fork, prongs up, on his fingertip, then the major wandered through the diners, encouraging more competitors. He paused at Sarah's table, repeating his invitation.

Sarah did not acknowledge the major, even when he suggested the ladies might best the lieutenant, who now was clearly impaired after drinking several tankards during his exploits. When he put his hand on her shoulder, Duncan's cheer evaporated. He was about to dart to her when with exaggerated effort Sarah lifted the major's hand away, raising laughter by stating that surely a great warrior for the king should know better than to risk the loss of his hand.

At last, with a meaningful glance at Duncan, the major extracted the knife he carried on his belt. It was a slim, elegant weapon, not of military issue. He handed the knife to the lieutenant, who tossed it from hand to hand as a serving girl, following his instructions, spaced half a dozen apples on the mantel over the fireplace. As onlookers gasped, the lieutenant suddenly threw the knife over their heads, pinning an apple to the wall behind it. Three gentlemen among the crowd of diners quickly took up the challenge, and their shillings were soon in the waif's pail. The major retrieved the knife from the last throw, then placed the remaining two apples closer to Sarah's table and with a deft toss sent the blade through the air so that it landed point first, embedded in her table.

As the major advanced with a gloating expression, Duncan stepped into the dining chamber, behind the officer. Sarah's eyes lit and she flushed with excitement as she saw him, then recognized his quick hand signal. She was well acquainted with the silent signals used by Mohawk warriors, for she had taught them to Duncan. She quickly shifted her gaze away, and Duncan realized the major had mistakenly taken her sudden animation as a reaction to himself.

"I have heard much about the prowess of colonial damsels," he exclaimed with new vigor, stretching his arms to indicate all three women at the table.

The woman with the long brunette hair gingerly extracted the knife and held it out. "See how it shines so!" she said in a girlish voice. "And, oh my, there are even jewels in the hilt!"

"The dagger was made for me in Italy," the major boasted, then held up another coin, a guinea, and spoke to Sarah. "If you pin an apple, the coin goes in the boy's pail. If you lose, you pay no penalty other than joining the lieutenant and myself in a game of whist." He fixed Sarah with an eager smile. "Or perhaps piquet, a game for two?"

Sarah acknowledged Duncan's second set of hand signals with a fleeting grin, then touched the gleaming dagger. "But it looks so sharp, General," she cooed.

The major gave a sigh. "A mere major, mademoiselle, though I appreciate the sentiment. If you prefer to forgo the embarrassment, we can just retreat to the parlor now. Shall I order some port?"

Sarah had the blade in her hand now, balancing it. "Does the pointy end go first?" she asked as she stood, then gave a pouting frown toward the mantel. "But the target is just miles away, Major."

The major gave a silky laugh and stepped to the mantel to move the apple closer. As he began to turn back toward Sarah, the knife flashed over the tables. With a resounding thud it embedded itself in the back of the mantel, pinning not the apple but the tail of his wig to the wall.

"Bloody hell!" the major gasped. His face drained of blood. As he pulled away, the wig slid off his head.

Sarah curtsied to him. "Out in the rustic lands we call that a grandee haircut," she explained, drawing hoots of laughter from the crowd. "If you ever make it to the wilds, Major, tie your hair down."

The two women with her gave their own mocking curtsies to the officers and followed Sarah out of the tavern.

An instant later Duncan was on the cobbled street, sweeping Sarah off her feet with a hearty laugh as she clamped her hands onto either side of his head and kissed him. After a long silent embrace she pushed him away, keeping hold of one hand.

"This is my betrothed," she announced to her amused companions.

"I certainly hope so," said the dark-haired woman with a laugh. Sarah introduced her as Madeline Faulkner, visiting from London.

"We have met, Monsieur McCallum," declared the blond woman, who extended her hand good-naturedly. "When I consigned my awkward brother to your care."

"And not a day went by on the Ohio when Pierre did not speak fondly of you, Mademoiselle Dumont," Duncan acknowledged. "A renowned natural philosopher in her own right, he would often say."

The blond woman laughed again. "Not as renowned as my excitable brother." She surveyed the street. "Where are you hiding him? I am so anxious to inspect your treasures."

"Alas, I rode ahead of the wagons," Duncan said. "But with fair weather they should arrive in two or three days. And if you wish to whet your appetite, I left an ancient tooth with Mr. Thomson."

"The thrill of it!" Miss Dumont exclaimed. "We must go immediately!"

Madeline Faulkner feigned a yawn. "We must get you to London, Olivia dear, so I can show you a proper evening's entertainment."

As they walked through the dimly lit streets, Duncan arm in arm with Sarah, all three women fired questions at Duncan about his western expedition. He kept his answers lighthearted, steering clear of the tragedies of the journey, and soon they were knocking at Thomson's door. The tutor greeted them cordially. "Mr. McCallum has brought a piece of the *incognitum* puzzle!" he exclaimed before Duncan could explain their visit. As her two friends stepped inside, Sarah gently tugged his arm.

"I believe we will take the air," Duncan announced, and Thomson excused them with a genteel nod.

Once more Duncan refrained from speaking of the darker aspects of his journey as Sarah questioned him. "The bones will be here soon and you will have all their mystery before you," he said when she pressed him to explain the objects the Sons of Liberty had sent him to retrieve from the Lick. He turned their conversation to an explanation of her unexpected journey from Edentown, but she echoed his own words.

"The mystery will soon be before you," was all she said, then pulled him into the shadow of an elm and kissed him again.

Their route was pleasantly rambling, taking in much of the northern tier of the city, but eventually they approached the compound of Preston House. From the crook of a small tree she produced a key, then opened the door and led him up a dark stairway into a spacious residence. Some of the furnishings were threadbare and all were dusty, but the sitting room was comfortable and afforded an elevated view over the street below.

"Mr. Preston was a wealthy merchant who died a dozen years ago," Sarah explained. "His widow has grown too frail to maintain such a large house, so she lets others use it. She is more assertive in her beliefs than most Quakers I have met."

Duncan considered her words. "Meaning she supports the Sons of Liberty."

Sarah answered with a smile. They stood by the front window and held each other, watching a plodding horse draw a cart of hay to the livery stable down the block. Duncan turned toward a tapping noise coming from the rear of the house. He passed through the double door that led into a musty dining room, then to an open window overlooking the enclosed courtyard. In the center of the stone-flagged yard, a man with a white beard was tending a fire under a steaming kettle. A breeze wafted the vapor toward the window, and Duncan recognized the acrid, slightly metallic odor. The man was boiling horns cut from cattle, to soften them for cutting and stretching flat so they could be used for shaping combs, spoons, and other useful implements. But why, he wondered, was the man doing this at night, and why in the Sons' secret compound?

"It was good of them to let you stay here," Duncan said to Sarah, returning to the sitting room. "They couldn't know how long you would be waiting for me."

Sarah wrinkled her face in an expression that was at once peevish and amused.

He cocked his head. "I don't understand."

She shot him an impatient frown.

It took him another confused moment to understand as he recalled the letter she had sent to him in Lancaster. "You are here because of the Sons?" he asked. "But why Philadelphia?" It wasn't as though Sarah had never helped in his secret work for the Sons, but that had always been on the New York frontier. As he spoke, he heard the tapping sound again and realized it was coming from the floor below them.

In reply, she took his hand and led him down a back staircase. The heavy oak door at the bottom opened into a shop lit by bright oil lamps, where two men, two boys, and three women were bent over workbenches. They all looked up and offered cheerful greetings to Sarah.

"Isn't it exciting?" Sarah exclaimed.

Duncan was not sure how to reply. Instead he walked along the workbenches. The workers were leaning over wooden rods and sheets of horn with drills, saws, and punches. At the end of each bench was a small crate they were filling with the fruits of their labor. He bent and scooped his hand into a crate.

"Buttons?" he asked in surprise.

"We shall do this in Edentown, Duncan! Mrs. Pratt"—she indicated a plump woman wearing a white apron and kerchief on her graying hair—"says she will come and teach our people."

Duncan tried not to show his confusion. Why was Sarah using a secret Sons house to make buttons? "I was not aware we suffered a shortage of buttons," he said, regretting his words instantly as resentment flashed on Sarah's face.

"Not for us! For the colonies! For the Pact! Mr. Thomson, Mr. Mulligan, and I gathered information by visiting merchants in Philadelphia and New York. Nearly all import their buttons from Cardiff and Bristol. This is how the people of Edentown will help the cause of liberty."

A smile slowly rose on Duncan's face. The Sons were quietly working not just to establish new trade routes but also to set up manufacturing shops to replace those of Britain. He recalled reading Sarah a letter from Samuel Adams, months earlier, urging him to make inquiries during his travels to identify craftsmen who might expand their operations, especially with the help of some capital from John Hancock and other wealthy Sons. "The Covenant," he whispered.

Surprise appeared on Sarah's face, but she did not respond.

"We can sell for half the price of what those English factories charge and still make a going concern of it," said a rough feminine voice from behind him. Mrs. Pratt had paused in her work and now stepped forward to examine Duncan. Without warning, she reached out and grabbed his tunic, pulling him closer. He was about to object when he realized she was studying his clothing. "Look at ye. Two buttons missing and Lord knows what shape yer small clothes be in." She turned to the young girl. "Becky, dear, make Mr. McCallum a pouch of the new horn buttons, the walnut-dyed ones, I think." She punctuated her request with a spit of tobacco juice into a heavily used spittoon. "Ye can be like one of those promoting cads. When someone admires yer buttons ye can tell them they come from the soon-to-be-famous Edentown Buttonworks," she said, then slapped Sarah on the shoulder and offered her appraisal of Duncan. "He's a passable specimen," she said. "After ye two are hitched ye'll need to get familiar with each other's fastenings," she added with a guffaw and another slap. "Mr. Pratt knew all of mine well enough, may the rascal rest in peace."

Sarah showed Duncan her store of materials, including sheets of horn and lathe-turned rounds of walnut and cherrywood. "Back home we can pay the Iroquois for the antlers of stags and slice them into discs. Oh, and tin. We have good forge-made stamps for cutting through sheets of tin. And the smith at home made some bullet molds last year. I will ask him to make some button molds so we can use pewter."

Duncan warmed to see her excitement. She had long been frustrated at seeing Duncan off on missions for the Sons while she stayed to manage Edentown and had bitterly complained when friends had died in the Sons' cause while she stood by safely at home. The Iroquois had bred a warrior's spirit in their adopted daughter.

Sarah led Duncan back out into the courtyard. "Soon we shall have enough supplies to keep Mrs. Pratt busy for months, and then we shall make our own materials. Friends from the south are helping."

Duncan paused, remembering the barrels in Lancaster. "Supplies hidden in barrels of flour, perhaps?"

Sarah's eyes flashed. "How could you know that? Yes, from our secret allies in Williamsburg, where the governor is most irate over the Pact. Nothing that might support manufacturing in the colonies is allowed to openly leave Williamsburg. Once those barrels arrive, we can extract their secret cargo and all will be packed up for Edentown. I think they will like Mrs. Pratt there. She's a bit unvarnished but very droll. She tells me coarse jokes about men and women, and the more I blush the more she laughs, saying if I am betrothed I must learn about such things. Yesterday she urged me to put tobacco in my cheek! She said it would put fizz in my mouth for when my man nips me."

They laughed, and Duncan pulled her close and kissed her again. "Your mouth is perfect the way it is, *mo nighean*," he said, then held her tightly and whispered in her ear. "*Mo chridhe.*" My heart.

They sat on a bench at the back of the courtyard and watched the bearded man toss more logs on the fire under the kettle, sending a shower of sparks to join the stars. Sarah yawned and leaned into his shoulder. "Buttons are the beginning," she said in a tired, dreamy voice. "Then spoons and combs, lamp plates, dippers, and later betty lamps and even plug burners."

Duncan grinned at hearing Sarah speak so uncharacteristically of such things, then froze and turned her face toward him. "Did you say plug burners?"

"You know, the new wick plugs for whale oil lamps. Most don't know that a lamp with a two-wick plug burns brighter than two lamps. Dr. Franklin discovered that."

"I didn't know," Duncan said absently, for his question wasn't about the functioning of wicks. Sarah had just recited the list dropped by the killers at the smashed telescope in Lancaster.

Chapter 6

I WILL SEE THE BONES WELL stored on the London ship and then I return to Edentown! That was the bargain!" Duncan said to Charles Thomson for the third time that hour, and the loudest. "We are to be wed at the full of the moon! Mr. Franklin asked for the treasures to be accompanied by Dumont. I have important work on the frontier." He longed to be back in the western forests, walking hand in hand with Sarah and sitting at Iroquois council fires.

Hercules Mulligan, who had just arrived in Thomson's parlor, now cast an uneasy glance at Thomson and turned to Duncan. "These are difficult times, McCallum, requiring sacrifices by many. Do you not wish to avoid hostilities?"

"You really need to ask me that? No one wants war." The Sons of Liberty had never spoken in favor of a violent break with Britain—only for an equal voice in Parliament for the colonies.

"You spent weeks with Pierre. He is an accomplished naturalist but not a man for"—Mulligan searched for words—"taking physical reactions when they are called for."

"Now you speak like a London courtier!" Duncan snapped. He did not understand why these leaders of the Sons were suddenly interested in sending him to London, but he did understand they could say nothing to convince him to leave Sarah.

"Ezra's murderers remain at large," Mulligan observed.

"And yesterday you seemed content to believe they were only interested in finding a secret agreement about Mississippi trade," Duncan argued. "Which they failed to obtain."

Mulligan winced and narrowed his eyes. "You know that is not true. They tried to steal the bones."

"Mr. Franklin's bones will soon be packed on board an Atlantic ship, out of harm's way."

"On their way to London, where the conspiracy against them was hatched. You of all people know whoever is doing this is looking for a stranglehold on the Sons!"

Duncan silently returned Mulligan's stare. "What has changed since yesterday?" he finally asked.

"This list, for one," Thomson replied, and tossed the list that the groom Mathias had given Duncan in Lancaster, left by the murderers, onto his table. "It evidences a broader purpose."

"They apparently have a deeper hold on secrets of the Sons than we thought," Mulligan put in sharply.

Duncan studied the two men, and the way Thomson now looked at Mulligan, as if for an answer. "They knew of Ezra's mission for the Covenant," Mulligan stated. "They knew of your mission for the *incognitum*. Both arranged out of London." The New York tailor fixed Thomson with a troubled gaze. "We have a spy working against us, Charles."

Thomson held his head in his hands. "Many think the Sons drift too far from the king," he said, looking up. "We can't retreat in fear of them, else they will succeed."

"Why do you suddenly think that affects Pierre's voyage to London?" Duncan pressed.

"A rider came from the west, bringing a letter from Reynolds in Pittsburgh, in which he states suspicions that our enemies are moving in coordination against our campaigns for both the Covenant and the *incognitum*, despite great efforts by Franklin and ourselves to keep them separate. And also news from Lancaster that a tinsmith's shop was burned down."

Duncan hesitated, recalling that Mathias had mentioned the fire, which had occurred the night before the murderers' accomplice had left town. "And?"

"Not long afterward, your wagons were set upon." Thomson quickly quieted the alarm on Duncan's face. "All is well. But it may mean you were right, Duncan, that we face the same enemy on every front. Not just fleeing in front of the bones but also following them."

Thomson paced along his broad window with his hands behind his back. "You're not known as a man who retreats, McCallum," he said in a chagrined tone. "Samuel Adams says you were the Sons' strong back along the frontier."

"All the more reason I must return to the frontier. Under no circumstances will I go to London."

"You want to return to the frontier because of an auburn-haired siren," Mulligan groused.

Duncan was on his feet in an instant, struggling to keep his fists at his sides. "You are speaking of my betrothed! Go no further, sir, or I will meet you outside!"

Mulligan raised his hands in surrender. He slowly lowered them, then fixed Duncan with an intense stare. "My mistake. I apologize, sir. She is more beautiful than any siren. Never would I disparage Miss Ramsey. And since you refuse to go to London, perhaps you can help me with other efforts of the Sons. New York is a town of many freedom-loving artisans. And if I could get your intended to New York town I could have her dining with the adjutants, even General Gage himself."

The abrupt change in tone, and subject, caused Duncan to hesitate. "You would use Sarah to cajole the supreme military commander in North America?"

"If he is not soon convinced to pull his troops out of Boston, there will be a catastrophe, I am certain of it. We need more time to appeal to reasonable minds in London. Sarah is more informed about events in what Gage calls the field than any woman I know, and he speaks much more freely with the fairer sex than with men. She is easily capable of engaging, then enchanting Gage. And she has a name."

A shiver ran down Duncan's back. "Meaning what, pray tell?"

"Gage is a friend of her father's," Mulligan explained. "They belong to the same club in London. He has invested in certain of her father's enterprises."

"Sarah has broken with her father."

"I am confident the great lord would not have shared that embarrassing news. General Gage does not know that. But he does know about angry Massachusetts villages building their own arsenals outside of Boston, and his advisers push him to deploy more troops so they can seize the arsenals. The Sons are pressing for a rational political dialogue, not irrational deaths. We need more time. Franklin needs all the help we can give him. You said the killers were probably soldiers. You will never find them here. But Gage may know. In fact, he may have dispatched them himself, in which case we shall discover them all the sooner with Miss Ramsey's help."

Duncan gazed at Mulligan, his heart a leaden weight. The world indeed did not know the details of Sarah's breaking with the pompous, diabolical, too-powerful Ramsey of the House of Lords. Ramsey had so loathed what Sarah had become during what he called her Iroquois captivity that he had once planned to have London surgeons quiet her by excising part of her brain. Ramsey had done everything in his power to separate Duncan and Sarah, and had proven he would not hesitate to have Duncan killed if given the chance. But Duncan would not speak of such things. "Sarah is already helping the cause of the Sons more than you know," he said instead. "She has turned Edentown into a covert post office for the Sons, and hosts the newspaper that is the voice of liberty on the frontier. Now she is embarking on manufacturing to support your Covenant."

Thomson and Mulligan exchanged a meaningful glance that Duncan could make no sense of. Mulligan gave a shrug, as if to reject Duncan's arguments. "I know Miss Ramsey not well, but well enough to know she would not want you to make such a decision for her. And buttons will be made whether she is in Edentown or not."

The only thing preventing Duncan from giving full voice to his anger at the man was the high opinion that John Hancock and Samuel Adams had of the New York tailor. His Boston friends had warned Duncan of Mulligan's acerbic, even manipulative nature, but had encouraged him to get to know the tailor better. "His shop supplies uniforms to every senior officer in Gage's headquarters," Hancock had told Duncan, "and he makes sure he is the personal tailor to every colonel and general. Like a valet. And every gentleman confides to his valet."

Duncan kept his voice impassive. "I shall broach your suggestion to Sarah, and we shall—"

"They are here!" Thomson suddenly cried, interrupting Duncan. "Praise the Lord, they have arrived!" He grabbed his hat and darted outside. Through the open door Duncan saw Ishmael wearily climb down from one of the big blue Conestoga wagons he had last seen in Pittsburgh. His left arm was in a blood-stained sling.

"Bad fall," was all Ishmael would say when Duncan asked about his injury, and the young Nipmuc hurried away to help Dumont down from the second wagon. The French scholar seemed about to drop from exhaustion, and Thomson rushed to escort him inside, calling to his houseboy for tea, then more loudly for brandy. Only two of the three teamsters Duncan had seen with the wagons in Pittsburgh were still with the convoy, though three more escorts climbed down, all strangers in their late teens. They wore dark homespun clothing and straw hats and stared wide-eyed at the buildings surrounding them.

"Sons of farmers, from Lancaster," Ishmael explained. "Palatine Germans, only one with any English. Mrs. McCrae insisted on them, after our difficulties, though she said I had to pay their parents in advance. Ten shillings for each," Ishmael said apologetically. "But steady workers, and happy to do night watch. They pretend to be soldiers, saluting and marching around the perimeter with ax handles on their shoulders."

Duncan raised an eyebrow. "You didn't cut your arm falling down," he stated. "What difficulties?"

Ishmael led Duncan to the far side of the team, to avoid eavesdroppers, then began to remove the harness. "We were followed after the Harris ferry on the Susquehanna. Someone had to have been waiting for us there. The more I think about it the more certain I am of it. It would be the easiest way to intercept us, since the ferry only runs in the daylight and our two wagons would be so conspicuous."

"But they didn't just follow," Duncan guessed.

"That night after leaving Harris Landing, just a few miles from Lancaster, gunpowder starting exploding around us. Not guns or bombs; I discovered afterward it was just pots of powder to make bright flashes to spook the teams. The horses broke their picket line and fled. Dumont and I stayed with the oldest teamster while the others ran after the horses. The intruder seemed to think we all had fled to the horses. He was bringing demijohns of turpentine into the camp when we accosted him."

"Turpentine?" Duncan asked.

"I think he meant to burn everything, though Dumont insists he was a thief since no one in their right mind would destroy such priceless treasures. He's probably right, but I don't see how the thief expected to haul off two big wagons without his own teams. I tried to capture him but he slashed at my arm with his belt knife. A fast brute, with a jagged scar on his cheek. The old teamster drove him off me with blows of a whip, though the fool got himself stabbed deep in the shoulder for his trouble. His spirits rose considerably, though, when Mrs. McCrae demanded that he stay with her for a month to heal the wound. When she learned we were the ones you said to expect, she declined the coins I offered, saying her castle was always open to help a Highlander."

"Where was Dumont during this great battle?" Duncan asked.

Ishmael draped the harness over his shoulder, then turned with a grin. "The professor jumped up on the seat of the nearest wagon, swinging a frying pan over his head and shouting '*On ne passe pas!*' over and over, whatever that means."

Duncan smiled at the image of the Frenchman Ishmael had painted. The scholar wasn't fit for the rigors of the frontier but Duncan admired his spirit. "You shall not pass," Duncan translated. "An old French battle cry."

"Our attacker was fierce but when our fight took him close to the wagon and Dumont bounced the iron skillet off his skull, he had his fill. When the teams came back an hour later we broke camp and went on into Lancaster. Watchmen at the edge of town stopped us and said they were looking for a scoundrel who broke one of the boundary stone markers while riding north. A farmer witnessed it a few days earlier and had just reported it. The stranger was trotting along and suddenly halted as he spied a marker stone in the field, then he dismounted, paced around it several times, then with a big rock shattered the marker stone as if Mason and Dixon had offended him somehow. The farmer marked the position with a post, then brought the pieces to town. The watch asked if I had seen such a man, with a jagged scar on his cheek. I told them of our encounter, though what bones and stones have in common I cannot imagine. Nothing to do with us. Just a mean-spirited bully and highwayman, the watch said, and despaired of catching him. In any event I continued on into town, for by then I was too weary to help them. Then a boy climbed out of a tree and said Mrs. McCrae was expecting us."

"She makes a fine stew. Or perhaps brews it, given all the ale mixed into it."

As Ishmael dropped some coins in the hand of a groom who had arrived from the nearby stable, he nodded. "I was almost jealous of our injured man when he heard he was staying the month with her. Except those working in the tavern began raving about how he could join them in celebrating the transit of Venus, whatever that is. Sounds like some pagan ritual."

Duncan grinned once more. "Yes, one led by an unruly tribe called the American Philosophical Society."

"'His nose like a Hanging Pillar wide / and Eyes like shining Suns.'" The more Charles Thomson read, the more dramatic his voice became. "'His Arms like limbs of trees twenty foot long.'"

Hercules Mulligan noisily set his cup on his saucer to interrupt. "Charles, it's just a fanciful poem," he protested.

The devout, ever-earnest Thomson gave no sign of hearing. "Fingers with bones like horse shanks and as strong," he continued. "'His Thighs do stand like two Vast Millposts stout'!" He looked up with a victorious gleam and pointed to the huge bone Duncan had recovered from the mud pit, now taking up most of Thomson's dining table. "Can you doubt it? The proof is before us! Here sits the very thigh bone!"

"A poem written a hundred years ago," Dumont retorted.

"Never in life!" Thomson shot back. "'Twas but sixty years ago," he corrected, gesturing to the dusty tome he had retrieved from a high shelf. "Written by a renowned member of the clergy and attested to by no less a man than that most pious of Massachusetts governors, Cotton Mather himself! There are precious few who have seen such bones but Mather was one."

The group had spent hours unloading the precious cargo into Thomson's parlor, kitchen, and back stoop. They had agreed that no more than twenty of the relics would be shipped to Franklin, and by mutual agreement Thomson, Mulligan, Dumont, Deborah Franklin, Duncan, and Ishmael had each selected the ones they thought should travel to London with the French scholar. While settling on the final twenty, Dumont had made what now seemed a blunder by suggesting that they apply scholarly criteria to their final choices, to provide for an orderly process in solving the mystery of the *incognitum*. Thomson took offense, saying the mystery had been solved long ago by men of God, then called for his young servant for a stool so he could retrieve the book, which he had passed around the company with an evangelical fervor.

The poem was called "The Gyant of Claverack," and its inspiration had been a huge tooth found in 1705 on the banks of the Hudson, which the leading lights of Boston had declared to be from a member of a giant human race. The biblical scholars, who also ran the most prominent schools, had invoked the tooth as evidence that the native tribes were the remnants of a race of giants which had fallen from grace and been punished by the Great Flood.

"There are those, Mr. Thomson," Deborah Franklin said in a patient, moderating tone, "who are inclined to think these bones came from great beasts such as have been seen in Africa. When brave men finally cross this continent, they will no doubt find them."

Thomson frowned. "When all the bones are assembled we shall see, madame," he replied with stiff politeness.

"Not all the bones are from the same creature," Duncan offered, drawing a vigorous nod from Dumont. Duncan stepped to the skull with two large fangs extending from its upper jaw, then pointed to the great tooth on the table. "That tooth did not come from this jaw," he stated.

Thomson frowned again. "Is it true that the great Bone Lick where you recovered these has plumes of choking sulfur gas?"

"True."

"And nothing grows anywhere on the Lick?"

"Because," Duncan explained, "the springs bring up salt and other minerals. It is what drew these animals there, what still draws buffalo and deer."

"You miss the point," Thomson protested. "Sulfur is the smell of brimstone. The Lick is a reminder from God. Our theologians say He annihilated the original savage giants and the fallen men to start the human race over. But he left the Lick to show us what he had done, and what the entire planet will become again unless we shape ourselves to his will. It is a little sliver of Hades, left to remind us of the narrow path of righteousness. Blessed are those who hear the word and obey."

It was Dumont who broke the awkward silence. "The king of France will be most unhappy," he declared in an oddly mischievous tone. He was gazing with obvious pleasure at a vertebra that was nearly as large as those Duncan had seen in whale skeletons in the Hebrides. Dumont noticed his companions' confusion. "He places great store in the word of his natural philosopher Monsieur Buffon, who heads what the sovereign calls his collection of curiosities. Buffon has long dismissed the Americas as being of no interest to natural philosophy. He claims to have proven that all its species are inferior in size and health to those of the Old

World. But this"—he tapped the vertebrae—"will prove the old fool wrong! I shall confront him and witness his embarrassment for myself."

"Nonsense! It proves nothing!" Thomson's voice thickened. "Have you not listened? The Great Flood washed over the Lick before it was scoured with brimstone. A whale may well have been stranded there."

Duncan was not the only one to see the heat rising in Dumont's face.

"And there you have it!" Deborah Franklin interjected. "A reflection of the exhilarating debates inspired by these amazing objects! No doubt that is why my Benjamin so urgently desires them, for he does so love to keep guests entertained with lively dialogue! Ancient *incognitum* and electricity! How the sparks will fly!" she added, drawing subdued laughter.

They had agreed on most of the London-bound treasures when Duncan noticed that Ishmael was missing. He found the exhausted Nipmuc fast asleep at the kitchen table with his head cradled on a folded arm, his other arm, now bandaged, extended on the table. Duncan had cleaned and stitched the wound, futilely advising Ishmael to keep it in a sling for a few days. Thomson readily consented to have his kitchen boy escort Ishmael to the Preston House, where Sarah would find him a bed as she waited for her shipment from Lancaster.

Dumont posed a question that, to Duncan's surprise, no one in Philadelphia had considered. "What happens to the rest of the collection after I leave for London?" the Frenchman asked.

"The Society shall have it, of course," Thomson asserted.

"Prithee, Charles, to which of the societies do you refer?" Deborah Franklin asked. Her companions were well aware of the friction between the American Philosophical Society and the American Society for Promoting Useful Knowledge, both of which were actively preparing for the coming transit of Venus. She gave an awkward laugh as she saw the cloud she had raised on Thomson's face. "I am a poor arbiter, gentlemen, since my Benjamin founded the Philosophical Society, though certainly the proponents of Useful Knowledge have done valuable work. All have expressed great interest in the *incognitum*."

"Perhaps then our bones will provide the impetus for the two to merge," Duncan suggested.

"The Philosophical Society has earned a place at the forefront of the colony," Thomson declared with uncharacteristic vigor, then darted to his desk, where he extracted a crudely printed sheet. He held up the sheet, with the heading APS AGENDA, and handed it to Duncan, who read it with Mulligan leaning over his shoulder. The agenda items from the last Society meeting were all phrased as questions.

First: *Who is more important to Pennsylvania, the farmer or the merchant?*

Next: *Should colonies print their own money and send taxes to London in provincial currency?*

Then: *Is the electrical phantasm stored in a Leyden jar derived from the air or from the metal?*

The fourth: *Should women be admitted to Councils of State?*

Finally: *Is communication between spirits and the living taking place in dreams?*

"An ambitious undertaking," Mulligan observed judiciously.

"Who else is facing up to such vital issues?" Thomson asked.

Mulligan pointed to the bottom of the paper. "I see you were the chairman of the meeting."

Thomson winced. "I assure you I do not speak out of self-interest."

"And your Society is actively supporting the Proprietary Party," Mulligan said, referring to the new political group that advocated the continued governing role of the Penn family proprietors. "And if I am not mistaken, the Society for Promoting Knowledge is with the anti-proprietors. As is Mr. Franklin." There was a hint of amusement in Mulligan's voice that clearly irritated Thomson. "Philadelphia has become quite a labyrinth."

"I am sorry, gentlemen," Duncan interjected. "I did not undergo our expedition, and Ezra did not give his life, to serve some local feud in Philadelphia. We need to be discussing how to protect the bones. You seem to think those who threaten us have moved on. I am convinced otherwise. These are cunning men we face, and so far they have killed and ambushed with impunity."

His words brought a tense silence. Thomson gave a slow, apologetic nod.

"Messieurs," Dumont said. "May I remind you that I am a member of both societies, engaged solely in the pursuit of knowledge of the natural world with no stake in issues of the colony. The summer kitchen behind my house is seldom used. The bones may be stored there, both those to be packed and those to remain here. I am sure you can find a sturdy padlock after I have sailed, and I suggest you then give the key to the unassailable Mistress Franklin."

Thomson extended a grateful hand to Dumont, readily agreeing. Mulligan offered the services of his Irish attendant as a guard until the bones for Franklin were loaded on their London ship, and they proceeded with selection of the final items for shipment, now giving great deference to the Frenchman. They had completed their task and Thomson was distributing celebratory glasses of sherry when his kitchen boy appeared.

The boy nodded to Duncan, then gave a cursory bow to his master. "Prithee, sir, a message from Preston House for Mr. McCallum." He turned back to Duncan to complete his errand. "Miss Ramsey says she will need your help with her buttons tonight."

Thomson's round face flushed scarlet and he quickly looked down into his sherry. A suppressed giggle erupted from Deborah Franklin. Hercules Mulligan burst out in laughter.

Sarah was standing in a wagon, energetically directing the unloading of the Lancaster barrels into the Preston House courtyard, when Duncan arrived. He stood watching by the gate with a wide smile until she finally noticed him. She straightened her dress and returned his smile, though not before casting a glance at the rear gate, where for the second time in as many days Duncan saw Edwin Jenkins, the assistant blacksmith from Edentown, who was quickly darting away as if to avoid Duncan.

"We have a baker coming for the flour in the morning," Sarah reported as he helped her down. "So we have to extract our secret supplies tonight and reseal the barrels."

She pushed back a lock of auburn hair that had drifted across her face. "Only half of them hold our smuggled supplies. The barrels are numbered. I have the list, the key, from Virginia, showing which ones are meant for us."

Duncan began rolling up his sleeves. "Then let's put the ones not meant for us by the gate and the others by the door of the shop."

"Excellent," Sarah said with a nod and consulted a piece of paper she pulled from her pocket. "First load, then." Duncan saw the barrels were in two groups, no doubt reflecting the two wagons they had arrived in. "Barrels marked 1, 4, 5, 6, 8, 10, 12, 14, 15, and 16 to the shop door, where we can work by light of the wall lanterns. The others to the gate."

When they finished sorting the barrels Mrs. Pratt tied on an apron. "It's going to be messy work," she observed, "and I don't see why ye just didn't say move the ones with the peculiar X on their sides."

"I don't follow," Duncan confessed.

The feisty widow walked along the barrels and pointed out how the four-inch black X mark Duncan had seen in Lancaster were on all those Sarah asked to be opened. He bent over one of the marks. The sign was not simply an X, for at each end of the legs was a small black disc, giving the Xs a bulbous appearance. Duncan half-remembered the symbol from his university days, but he could not put a name to it.

"A cooper's mark," he suggested. "Sometimes they brand their wares with a hot iron."

"Nope," the widow retorted, "it's only on these, not those by the gate. And t'ain't no burnt mark," she added as she rubbed a finger on one of the marks, spreading an oily black smear on the wood. She put her finger to her tongue, winced, then called over the man with the white beard. "That put you in mind of yer early days, Josiah?" she asked the man.

The spindly man dabbed a finger on the black mark. "Lord help me," he muttered as he rubbed the black substance between his fingers and smelled it. "Left face, right face, double-time, and make them shine so I can see my reflection, Corporal."

Duncan suppressed a smile. "You were in the army?"

"Orderly to a colonel in the last war," Mrs. Pratt explained.

"Sometimes they had me make the stuff myself," Josiah added. "I didn't mind if there was good beeswax or lanolin to be had. But usually it was stinking tallow from the bottom of the stewpots. Tallow and lampblack." The old soldier noticed Duncan's confusion. "Dubbin, sir, it's dubbin, used for polishing army boots."

A whispered echo from a long-ago classroom finally reached him. The symbol was an alchemist sign. "Tin?" he asked Sarah. "Do you have tin in these barrels?"

Sarah raised her brows in surprise. "Yes, English tin from Manchester, shipped to a friendly merchant in Virginia. How could you know?"

"That mark," he said, pointing to one of the *X*s with balled feet, "is an ancient sign for tin. Someone knew tin was being smuggled. They marked the barrels to make it easier to follow. The marks can be seen from a distance, then," he explained with new worry. It likely meant that their enemies knew the barrels had arrived, and it could mean there were eyes on the house at that very minute. The fact that they had not been opened in transit meant someone in Virginia had known of the Covenant's secret even before the barrels had been packed with the smuggled tin. Their mysterious adversaries had a copy of Sarah's secret list of barrel numbers. Instead of seizing them, they had followed them to their destination.

The next morning Duncan waited in the shadows of an alley until the short, broad-shouldered man hurried out of the gate of the Preston House yard, casting nervous glances over his shoulder, then followed him toward the waterfront. When the man paused on the wharf in front of a narrow aisle between two rows of hogs-heads, Duncan hurried forward and gently pushed the man inside the gap.

"Mr. Jenkins," Duncan began in a casual tone.

The man sagged as he recognized Duncan. "May as well try to give the slip to a Mohawk warrior," he said.

Edwin Jenkins was the assistant to the blacksmith at Edentown, a reliable, hardworking man who was favored by Sarah for special tasks like retrieving deliveries from port towns. "So you admit you have been trying to avoid me," Duncan said.

"Only because the mistress of Edentown told me to," Jenkins replied. "I meant no offense, sir."

"Prithee, Jenkins, why would Miss Ramsey ask you to hide from me?"

"Don't know exactly, sir. She's a good woman and I take her orders without question. Something to do with the change, I reckon."

"The change?"

"Seeing how I was the one she sent to Philadelphia to bring the button works back, but then she showed up herself. Too important a job for me, apparently." Jenkins looked hurt.

"Is that what she told you?"

"No, no, she would never be so harsh. But what was I to think? Excepting then a few days later she was all upset, and said I had to mind the details after all, that I would be the one to take everything back and set up the new works with Mrs. Pratt."

"You mean she came to take over but something changed her mind?" Duncan asked, raising a nod from Jenkins. "And what are you doing here at the docks?"

"Some days she has me go down to watch the London ships."

"Watch for what?"

"Arrivals and departures. Manifests. Passenger lists."

Duncan tried to fit the report with Sarah's new interest in implementing the Non-importation Pact. "You mean tracking imports."

"Imports and such, yessir. And a week ago she had me tell when a certain ship from Boston arrived. She went on board for a couple hours. Old friends, I reckon. Oh, and berths. Sometimes she has me make inquiries about cabins bound for London."

Duncan recalled that Sarah's brunette friend was visiting from London. "You mean for her friend Miss Faulkner."

"Booked that berth last week. She sails tomorrow. But Miss Sarah still sends me to make inquiries."

Duncan cocked his head in curiosity, but then stepped aside and gestured Jenkins toward the harbor. "Carry on. I do not mean to interfere with your important work, Jenkins."

Jenkins touched his forehead in salute and stepped out of the shadows.

"And, Jenkins," Duncan said with a pang of guilt. "Two things."

"Yessir?"

"No need to speak of this conversation to your mistress. And keep close watch over the Preston House. Find a weapon, a staff or club at least. A battle may be brewing in Philadelphia."

The next morning Dumont let Duncan inside his house before he could finish the coded knock. "Yes, yes," the Frenchman said in rushed greeting and motioned Duncan into his sparsely furnished sitting room. The chamber held only three long benches arranged in a U shape, a trestle table bearing remnants of loaves and sausages, and a writing desk in one corner on which papers and quills lay scattered. The air was tinged with tobacco.

"We worked all night," Dumont explained.

"It looks more like another political meeting," Duncan suggested. He had been up much of the night himself, unable to sleep. He had paced around the empty courtyard of the Preston House, contemplating the mysteries of the past week. It was a puzzle in which new pieces seemed to surface each day. It struck him that if the secret of Sarah's shipment of English tin had been pierced in Virginia, the Covenant was much more engaged and widespread than he had imagined, and just so its enemies. Ezra's killers clearly were not acting alone. They were more like the tip of a spear aimed at the Sons, with invisible agents supporting them.

Dumont sighed, then wiped two glasses with a soiled napkin and filled them with claret. "Sooner or later, Duncan my friend, everything becomes political in Philadelphia and London. If only you and I could have more weeks with the bones, what joy we would have, eh?" He tapped the second glass, still on the table, with his own. "Politics will be the death of us."

Dumont nibbled at a piece of bread, then drained half his glass and stared down at the remaining wine. "It was decided after much debate that a report for Mr. Franklin from the proprietors of the bones should accompany them, and me, to London."

"Proprietors?"

"The colony. Or more specifically the society of scholars. Except we have two societies of natural philosophers, so there had to be a joint report that both the American Philosophical Society and the Society for the Propagation of Useful Knowledge can endorse. And thereby hangs hours of haranguing. We had Mr. Thomson here but also Mr. Biddle and Mr. Rittenhouse, both of whom were more interested in speaking of the coming transit of Venus." Dumont shook his head in frustration. "One would say we hereby present the bones of the *incognitum* and the other says we can't say that since we don't even know the *incognitum* well enough to say what bones belong to it. Another says we must forgo suggestion of an extinct species for fear it will offend the church and still another says which church do you mean, are you suggesting a primacy of churches, which then triggers a discussion about whether we need more Quakers in the societies so we can fairly represent that the report comes from Philadelphia."

"Pierre, my friend, if the bones have any proprietors I think they are you and me," Duncan observed with a bitter grin. "And perhaps some tribal gods."

Pierre conceded the point with an amiable nod and a lifting of his glass, tipped to Duncan. "I had to remind them that our mission is secret, and urgent, so we finally agreed that the best approach is to describe the bones as accurately as possible, and the ground on which they were found, and to offer our warranty that they were not altered in any aspect or otherwise tampered with, and they match no species thus far found on the continent." Dumont gave a weary smile. "I do so relish the notion that such beasts will be found in the great unmapped West. Oh, my life would be complete if I could but be part of that expedition! I pray it will happen before I am too ancient myself."

Dumont emptied the rest of his glass as a rap came from the front door. The Frenchman sighed. "Oh, for the peace of the Ohio again," he murmured. "Mr. Thomson agreed to complete a first draft for further discussion. More hours of debate, I fear," he said before opening the door.

As Duncan hoped, Hercules Mulligan arrived soon after Thomson, with a tall, well-dressed but taciturn man who was introduced as David Rittenhouse, astronomer. Duncan quickly explained the discovery of the secret marks on the barrels. "But McCallum, this is a meeting about the *incognitum*," Thomson reminded him.

"It was the Sons who asked me to retrieve the bones," Duncan said, "not some fraternity of Philadelphia scholars. It is the Sons who are secretly assisting the manufacture of new goods to punish the English merchants and engaging new trade routes through your Covenant organization. All those secrets have been pierced, and by the same group of men, men connected somehow to the British military."

"You must not overreact," Thomson warned again. "We cannot let the *incognitum* be tainted by scandal."

"Become tainted? You mean also ignore the lies, treachery, and murder that have already accompanied it? They will disrupt all the work of the Sons if you do not take measures! These men are ruthless. They mean to bring the Sons to their knees. They will grind every ancient bone to dust if it serves their purpose."

"You are still distraught over the loss of Ezra, Duncan," Thomson said. "We all share that pain. But Mr. Rittenhouse has pointed out that that was the wilderness. You must recall that he married into a native tribe. His death has all the markings of the work of savages."

Duncan turned to Thomson, aghast. Dumont stared down into his folded hands, struggling to keep out of the argument. "Savages, yes," Duncan hissed.

"Savages in powdered wigs. You would prefer to sip tea and blather about Cotton Mather's poetry and your societies and planets while they do their bloody work."

Thomson's anger was instant. His face deepened in color as he glared at Duncan.

It was Mulligan who broke the brittle silence. "What are you asking, McCallum?"

Duncan drained his glass as he collected his thoughts, then stood with his hands on the back of a chair as he addressed his companions. "People say that Highland Scots are the champions of lost causes, the greatest of which was the Jacobite Uprising. That rebellion destroyed my family, destroyed my clan, destroyed the entire Highland way of life. And it failed because honorable but proud men refused to face harsh truths. Instead, every debate of strategy collapsed into bickering. The Camerons couldn't stand by Frasers in battle line. The Chisholms wouldn't bother with muskets or cannon because Highland claymores had been good enough for their ancestors. The Macleans refused to guard the supply train because there was no glory in it, and the McDonalds bristled at taking orders from a Murray. Ultimately no one would stand up to Bonnie Prince Charlie to say Culloden was a profoundly poor choice for a battlefield because it was rude to disagree with the Royal Stuart. They all had the information they needed for success, but they blinded themselves to it. The British troops weren't the cause of the Highland defeat—the bickering and blindness of Highlanders was. I am not going to be destroyed by another cause lost by shortsighted, gullible men."

Thomson looked down into his folded hands. Rittenhouse gazed out a window, stroking his prominent jaw.

"I repeat," Mulligan said in a sour tone, "What are you asking?"

"I am asking that you recognize that we have unseen enemies. I am asking you to recognize that they are playing a game of chess and we have yet to engage on the board."

"We will not let anyone distract us from our course," Thomson said in a simmering tone, as if Duncan was saying otherwise.

"Our course?" Duncan demanded. "All we do is stumble along their course! You want to convince yourselves that our opponents are just uncouth vandals and men being paid to cause distractions. You're wrong. These acts are being orchestrated by a common hand, and that hand is on the other side of the Atlantic.

They knew of the English tin being smuggled to Sarah. They knew of the plan for Mississippi trade devised by Franklin and the Covenant's leader, Hephaestus. They knew of the secret *incognitum* mission. Draw the lines. They intersect on the other side of the Atlantic. Someone in London has pierced the secrets of the Sons!"

"Please, Duncan, the greatest mistake we could make would be to overreact," Thomson said. "There is more at stake than you know. We are not at liberty to divulge all. I accept your point about the danger to the Covenant. If you think there is some threat to our manufacturing plans, then by all means we must discuss how to protect them. For the rest, you have our gratitude. It may be best if you return to the frontier."

Mulligan stepped closer to Thomson. "Charles, Duncan deserves to—"

Thomson interrupted with a raised hand. "We will not sacrifice our noble goals to emotion or to feed someone's misplaced notion of vengeance!" He fixed Duncan with a scolding eye. "Or be cowed by someone else's lost causes!"

Duncan closed his eyes for a moment and pushed down his bile. "I thought your group of natural philosophers stood for advancing civilized society," he coolly replied. "But apparently buttons are more important. I will mind the buttons and ignore those who murder, steal, and smash survey stones and telescopes, even if I may consider them against the interests of civilization."

His words brought an unexpected silence. Rittenhouse, the reserved astronomer, spoke for the first time, with alarm in his thin voice. "Prithee, surely I misunderstand. Did you say survey stones? I heard about the telescope but nothing about survey stones."

"A Mason Dixon marker was smashed. Pieces of it were brought into Lancaster in the hope that it might be replicated. Reports from witnesses say it was the same man with the jagged scar who met Ezra's killers and later tried to stop Ishmael and Pierre with the bones."

Rittenhouse lowered himself onto a bench as if suddenly weak. "Charles, dear God! Perhaps these other acts are not so random as we think! A marker stone! The barbarians!"

Duncan stared in confusion at Thomson and Rittenhouse, both of whom seemed stricken by his news of the survey stone. "The boundary line is still well known," he suggested. "And the incident with the telescope may just have been an impetuous act venting temper on some boys. No business of the Sons."

"No, Duncan," Thomson murmured. "I fear it is part of that chess game you mention. It was an act against all the American scholars working on the transit of Venus. If these are truly related, then God knows what else they have in mind. Smashing precious chronographs?"

"I fear, Charles," Mulligan interjected, "that Mr. McCallum and I are not so well versed on astronomical matters."

Thomson gave a humorless smile. "It's about Charles Mason, you might say. He is the most eminent of the transit scholars. He was awarded the commission to survey the Maryland line because he and Dixon did such an outstanding job of observing the last transit, from South Africa in 1761. There were those in London who were furious that he came to America for the survey commission because it meant training mere colonists for astronomical observation. He created a great appetite here for more learning and soon offered up the precise mathematical calculations needed for the transit. Before he returned to London, he assisted Mr. Rittenhouse and others in preparation for the coming transit. These men wrecked a telescope in Lancaster. The group there was following the chart that we published in the *Gazette*." Thomson reached into his desk and produced the folding chart Duncan had seen on the wall of the shed in Lancaster. "Did you not read along the bottom?" he asked, pointing to the acknowledgement, which Duncan had forgotten. Charles Mason had supplied the chart.

"Smashing that stone was a strike against Mason, against all of those interested in advancing natural philosophy in the New World. If what you report is true, these men are indeed not simply set against Dr. Franklin's bones—they are set against everything the Sons do, and more." Thomson fixed Duncan with a conciliatory gaze and nodded. "Perhaps the Sons do have to stand for advancing civilized knowledge, not just liberty."

While Thomson was speaking, Dumont had, in his pragmatic napkin-wiping fashion, collected and cleaned enough wine glasses for all of them. "Are they not the same?" the Frenchman asked as he presented them, filled, on a tray. "Is not the essence of liberty giving men and women the power to freely pursue whatever knowledge they desire?"

When his guests responded with solemn nods, Dumont raised his glass for an announcement. "Messieurs, if we are to embark in this chess game then I must confess that I have a piece on the board already."

They sipped his claret and listened to the Frenchman, who began with a reminder of how the French adviser to King Louis, Buffon, had loudly dismissed North American flora and fauna, and in so doing had dismissed the contributions of the natural philosophers from the continent. Dumont waved a letter in the air. "This was waiting for me in Philadelphia. I have opened a chink in Buffon's armor." Dumont went on to explain that Buffon had agreed to accept a bone from the famous Kentucky Lick and was expressing an interest in the views of the colonies, accepting Dumont's premise that natural philosophers based in North America should have a voice in discussing the fauna of their continent.

"I am not sure how this plays to our strategy," Mulligan said.

"Convincing Buffon is convincing the French king! If King Louis accepts the advice of Philadelphia's scholars, then King George and Parliament will have to take note! Are we not trying to make the voice of the colonies heard? Nothing will push the king toward us more effectively than competition from Paris!"

Thomson and Rittenhouse were both nodding their affirmation as Dumont held up a finger. "There's more! I have an idea, a brilliant idea, I'd like to think. Once you have shipped the bones and successfully measured the transit, you must finish merging your societies and elect Buffon as a member! The only aspect of Buffon more bloated than his intellect is his ego. We will send him a ribbon or medallion or such to reflect his prestigious status!"

The mood of the room changed instantly. Dumont was praised for his clever insight, Duncan was patted on the back, and more wine was poured before they began reviewing Thomson's draft report.

Duncan retreated half an hour later, going not immediately onto the street but to the summer kitchen behind the house. Mulligan's Irish guard, armed with a long shovel handle, greeted him with a nod and stepped aside to let Duncan in the door. The bones were scattered everywhere, with the smaller ones laid on planks arranged on sawhorses, the larger ones leaning against the wall or lying on beds of straw. They had a strangely calming effect on him as he walked along them, lightly touching their ancient surfaces. When he closed his eyes he was back with Catchoka in the ancient bone shrine, hearing the warning that the gods were following the relics. The very old artifacts could become responsible for something very new in the affairs of men. He recalled Dumont's eloquent words. Maybe it was true. Perhaps the essence of liberty was indeed allowing men and women to freely pursue whatever knowledge they sought.

At Preston House Sarah and her crew were covered with fine layers of flour, looking ghostlike in the moonlight. Wooden crates were being lined with straw to receive the tin plate smuggled from Virginia, being assembled in stacks by the crates. Duncan expressed surprise at the large number of tin sheets.

"Tin is so difficult to obtain," Sarah explained with an authority that surprised him. "Thousands and thousands of buttons can now be made," she boasted, clearly proud of her work. "Our friends can start taking orders," she added, referring to the itinerant tinkers and peddlers who called on Edentown and were some of the most important members of Duncan's network for information gathering.

"I would prefer the crates be gone for Edentown as soon as possible," Duncan stated. "You mentioned a boat?"

"A schooner is waiting on the Delaware, to deliver the crates straight to the landing on the Hudson."

"We should load them and have them dockside by dawn."

"Our people need sleep," Sarah objected.

"No, they don't, not until everyone is safely out of this city. There is treachery afoot, Sarah. We need to be gone. I will help. Ishmael will help, if he ever returns from his wanderings. His curiosity sometimes gets the better of him, I fear."

"Ishmael is on an errand for me," Sarah explained in a tone that brooked no inquiry. "But no doubt he will be back shortly and will soon be covered in flour like the rest of us."

Duncan removed his waistcoat and rolled up his sleeves. "First he should go to the livery down the street and arrange for a wagon to move your crates as soon as they are filled. We should aim to leave the docks in the morning. And, Sarah," he added as she turned to help Mrs. Pratt. "Tell Jenkins to come out of hiding. We need all the strong backs we can find."

She did not offer the explanation he hoped for, only nodded impassively and hurried to Mrs. Pratt's side.

As they packed the last of the smuggled button stock, a fresh idea for evading the killers began taking shape in Duncan's mind. When they had finished loading the crates on the wagon he excused himself, promising Sarah he would return by midnight, in ample time to board the schooner sailing on the morning tide. She grabbed his hand with an oddly troubled expression and seemed about to speak. Then she thought better of it and unexpectedly wrapped her arms tightly around him, as she might when he was leaving on one of his weeks-long journeys.

Mulligan's guard was nowhere to be seen as Duncan returned to the summer kitchen behind Dumont's house. Hearing sounds inside, he lifted a hoe by the door and raised it like a weapon.

"Duncan, *mon ami!*" Dumont gasped with relief as he lowered the pitchfork in his own hands. "You gave me a fright!"

"The guard is missing."

"I told him to get some sleep since I would be here. The poor man was up all last night. And those brigands would never strike in the heart of Philadelphia. No doubt they have fled by now. And after our time with Deborah Franklin today, I felt the need to honor Ezra by honoring the bones, if that makes sense." They had spent an hour at the Franklin house earlier that day to speak of Ezra with Deborah, who had vowed to light a candle on her mantel each evening for a month in memory of the freedman, who had briefly been part of her household.

Duncan had spoken a Gaelic prayer, Pierre a French one, and they had in turns spoken of memories of their lost friend. "Ezra had such a dauntless curiosity about life," Dumont recounted. "*Mon Dieu*, he walked with elephants! When I finally publish, I shall acknowledge Ezra as a hero."

"Miss Sarah came by and left her own token," Lizzie, the scullery maid, reported as she joined the impromptu wake. Duncan went to the mantel, where he discovered a little carved bird, wings outstretched. It was a tribal token, for birds carried news of the dead to the other side, though he was not inclined to explain that to his companions. He was confused not by the bird itself but why she had left it. "Sarah didn't know Ezra," Duncan said to Deborah Franklin.

"Of course she did, Duncan," Deborah replied. "They met in this very parlor more than once, speaking of the tribes and the Ohio and such."

Duncan wanted to tell her that was impossible, but then he realized that neither he nor Sarah always accounted for their days while he was away from Edentown for weeks at a time. Certainly he had been surprised at her manufacturing enterprise for the Covenant. But why would she speak of the tribes and the Ohio with Ezra, as if she knew of the secret Mississippi trade plans?

Dumont interrupted his musings by extending a wooden box for his examination.

Duncan lifted the lid and discovered one of the ancient teeth, packed in straw. "You said you would send a bone to Buffon in Paris," he said, looking back at the tables containing the bones meant for London.

"I'm afraid I secretly excavated one of the large molars for that purpose when I was at the Lick," Dumont replied with a sheepish grin. "I wouldn't presume to diminish the collection for Franklin."

Duncan gestured to a large journal that lay open on a bench by the empty hearth. "You were honoring the bones," he said, and lifted it. He discovered an intricate, highly accurate drawing of one of the giant vertebrae, which now sat nearby under a bright whale-oil lantern. Turning the pages, he found other meticulous drawings of a rib, a tusk, and a jaw with several teeth intact, some drawn of the same relic from different perspectives, with measurements noted for the dimensions of each object.

"These are worthy of publication," Duncan observed.

Dumont shrugged. "I am only interested in creating a record. Eventually you and I will be dust, but these bones will remain. Haven't you wondered, Duncan, why these bones were left, or why the Lick exists at all? I am convinced Providence preserved them for a reason, and not for lessons of fire and brimstone." Dumont grew very sober as he lifted the big vertebra he had been drawing, then sat on the bench to study it more closely. "What fools we are to think that our knowledge of this world, gained from experiencing it for a short span of years, is sufficient to truly comprehend it. There are things we have not even dreamed of. On the canvas of existence, out of all God's creation, our human world occupies a vivid but tiny corner. The rest is a gaping blackness that mocks us. When we solve one mystery, it just leads us to another. But in this momentous year we have both the transit of Venus and the *incognitum*. We are at a crossroads of enlightenment!" He raised the bone higher, closer to his face, to peer down its central cavity. "But do we even know what questions to ask? All we know is from a dark tunnel created by our own ignorance." To emphasize his point, he swung the bone up to peer at Duncan through the long hole in the bone. "How can we presume to know the world when we don't even understand these simple relics? The world of such creatures was a far different one than the one we know." He looked up to Duncan with an oddly distraught expression. "What if it was a better world?"

Duncan had no answer.

"I shall pose those questions to the great Franklin when I meet him," Dumont promised.

"That is a dialogue you must surely record," Duncan suggested, "so you can share it with me upon your return."

Dumont replaced the bone by the lantern, then stepped closer to Duncan. "I shall tell you a secret, Duncan, that only my sister knows. When I am in London I shall ask Dr. Franklin to endorse my expedition to the vast unmapped West! If anyone can cause it to happen surely it would be him. Perhaps I shall yet draw the living, breathing *incognitum*!"

"I very much look forward to seeing your proof of its existence," Duncan said.

"No! No! You must come with me! I know you, Duncan, you are the bold man who makes others' dreams come true, the *chevalier* of the wilderness. You made our Ohio River expedition a success despite our setbacks. We are the perfect team to penetrate *terra incognita*! We shall make our own place in the history books! Christopher Columbus! Magellan! McCallum and Dumont!"

Duncan smiled. He was touched by his friend's fervor. "For now, let's focus on the dream of getting you and your bones safely across the Atlantic. On your return," he added as he paced along the relics from the Lick, examining them from the perspective of his new idea for foiling their enemies, "on your return you must come to Edentown, Pierre. You know that bones of the *incognitum* have also been found up the Hudson Valley. You and I can go on a quest less fraught with danger."

"We shall make it so! We shall discover the rest of that giant of Claverack!" the Frenchman exclaimed. "And I shall interview all your Iroquois friends about their legends of the great beasts. They know chapters of humankind that are obscured to us."

Duncan paused to use his forearm to measure one of the bones. "You are aware, professor, that several ships depart for London each week?"

"Of course, of course. Mr. Mulligan has arranged passage. The bones and I shall travel on a fine bark, the *Galileo*, a commodious three-masted vessel, I am told. And such a propitious name!"

"You are more familiar with this port than myself. But I have often seen timber and lumber for shipbuilding being loaded for England."

"Often, yes. It comes down from the great forests along the upper Delaware." Dumont eyed Duncan. "Why do I sense you are referring to your chess game? But you heard Thomson. The villains have long fled. Do not trouble yourself with unnecessary schemes, *mon ami*."

Duncan examined a flat bone the size of a dinner plate, wondering if the *incognitum* wore it like armor, before replying. "The Sons enlist me in many tasks. But ultimately what they use me for is my intuition, my instincts. And my instincts say the danger is far from over. I need to keep you safe, and keep the *incognitum* safe. Stay close to the bones, Pierre, and to the guard that Mulligan has provided."

Dumont shrugged. "I am a harmless scholar, a threat to no one. And the *incognitum* has survived all these years without a guard. The bones have a destiny. And you have a destiny, Duncan, with Sarah. Go back to your Edentown and rest for our great adventure to the Pacific sea. You and I shall tame two of the great beasts and ride them into Philadelphia!"

Duncan endured a fitful sleep, in which he kept having visions of Catchoka keeping lonely vigil in his shrine, then threw his blankets onto the parlor floor of the Preston House and sat up against the wall. Images of his time with Catchoka still entered his mind unbidden, and in a sleepy daze he wondered if this meant the gods were indeed with him. He slumped, more asleep than awake, thinking of questions he wished he had asked the prophet, until suddenly the peal of an alarm bell lifted his head. Fire was a constant danger in the city, and anyone within the sound of the neighborhood bell was obliged to assist the fire brigade. Rising groggily from the floor, smelling smoke, he stretched, then came desperately awake as he saw the smoke was coming not from outside but from down the passageway.

His heart hammering, he raced up the stairs to the third floor sleeping chambers, pounding on each door, before slamming Sarah's door open. She was already smoothing out the dress she had slipped on. "Where?" was all she said.

"The workshop, I fear. Use the front stairs," he shouted, then ran to make sure the other rooms were being vacated and out into the back courtyard to retrieve the tools left there the night before.

By the time the members of the fire brigade arrived carrying leather buckets and axes, fingers of flame were reaching out of the second-floor windows. Preston House had become an inferno, its old timbers cracking and snapping, the fire so hot the crew could not approach it. A chain of helpers was formed from the nearest town pump to convey buckets of water to throw on the adjacent buildings. After half an hour of the hot work, Duncan broke away to join Sarah, who was comforting a very distraught Mrs. Pratt beside the prostrate form of Edwin Jenkins, who had been found unconscious by the courtyard gate.

"Thank God Mr. Duncan had the crates shipped out early," Mrs. Pratt said, wiping away tears as a burning wall collapsed. "This house was built before I was born. I remember walking by hand in hand with my father, admiring its sturdy elegance. Mr. Preston must be rolling in his grave, God bless him." When Sarah put a hand on her arm, a sob escaped her and she sank her head into Sarah's shoulder. "I guess I am truly destined to start a new life in Edentown," she murmured.

Sarah patted the woman on her back, stared with grim determination at the flaming ruins, then spoke with an odd fierceness. "A warrior must be blooded," she said.

The words had been whispered, as if to herself, but Duncan had heard. It was a phrase of the Iroquois, a reminder that a warrior was not truly ready for the warpath until he survived his first conflict with the enemy. But why say the words here? Why would Sarah say them at all?

She took a deep breath and let it out with a sigh before turning to Duncan. "We should give thanks that you were awake to spread the alarm in the house."

Thank the old gods, Duncan thought to himself, for they had kept him awake. "I can account for everyone but Ishmael," he said, his face lined with worry.

"Who," came a familiar voice behind him, "do you think ran to ring the fire bell, and skinned his knees on the cobbles when he slipped?"

Duncan turned to see the young Nipmuc approaching, tucking a tomahawk in his belt. Ishmael bent to retrieve one of the oak mallets used to beat down barrel lids. "Two men in black cloaks were running away from the flames. Near as I could tell, they threw an oil lantern through the window. I could either give chase or sound the alarm."

"What direction?" Duncan asked.

Ishmael handed Duncan the heavy mallet and pointed toward the city center.

There was no need for further words. "Get everyone on board that Hudson schooner!" Duncan shouted to Sarah, then sprinted away toward Dumont's house.

No answer came from their pounding on the professor's door. With renewed alarm, Duncan ran to the summer kitchen in the back. Mulligan's Irish guard stepped out of the shadows, club in hand, then relaxed as he recognized Duncan. "Professor left for Thomson's place a good hour ago," he reported.

Thomson had not seen Dumont. Learning the source of the conflagration that lit up the north end of the city, he quickly donned a coat and joined the search. They began probing every alley along the six blocks separating the houses, with Thomson breaking away after the first few minutes to fetch Mulligan.

Ten minutes later came Ishmael's call from an alley. "Duncan," was all he said, but Duncan recognized his despair.

Dumont lay in a glistening pool. The gentle, ebullient French professor would never go west to find his living *incognitum*. His throat had been slashed from ear to ear.

Chapter 7

THEY SAT ON A GRANITE step, staring at the body in dazed silence. Duncan had set out for the Ohio with three friends, entrusted with their safety, and now two were murdered. The lives of Ezra and Dumont had been so full of promise. They should have grown old with decades of rich memories, surrounded by loved ones. But they had chosen to join Duncan on the Ohio. He had taken the bones and had to face the consequences, the Shawnee prophet had warned. *There will be blood in the night. You will die, again and again.* Was this what Catchoka had meant? With each death of a friend a little bit of Duncan died.

"You must go back to Edentown, Duncan," Ishmael said abruptly. "Get on that schooner that's leaving for the Hudson." The words almost sounded like an order.

Duncan, numbed by Dumont's murder, took a moment to reply. He was not used to the young Nipmuc speaking so bluntly to him, nor did he grasp why he would speak of such things while Dumont's body was still warm. "We will all be back soon enough," he replied, and gazed mournfully at the dead man. "His sister. What do I tell his sister?" He looked back at Ishmael and realized there was something else the Nipmuc was trying to communicate, something urgent but painful.

"No. We will not. Did you not wonder why I was already awake before the fire, why Sarah's room was empty and she was already dressed?"

"It all happened so fast. No," Duncan said, recalling now that Sarah had been fully dressed and ready to leave when he had run to warn her. "No, I did not."

"She had me take her trunk aboard after midnight."

"Aboard the schooner, you mean."

"Aboard one of the big square riggers. We sail at noon."

"An ocean ship? We?"

"Sarah and I are going to London."

Surely Duncan had not heard correctly. "No. Impossible. She never said a word to me."

"Because she knew you would try to stop her." Ishmael turned toward the sound of running boots. A watchman was sprinting toward them. A soft rain had begun to fall. The dark, expanding pool by Dumont's body began to trickle through the cobblestones of the alley. "But now maybe things have changed."

"This is no time to go off on some lark, Ishmael."

"It's my uncle, Duncan."

Ishmael's stricken tone sent a new chill down Duncan's spine. "Conawago? Is something amiss with Conawago? All the more reason to return to Edentown."

"Sarah swore me to secrecy. While we were gone, he suddenly departed. She thought he was going to Boston, for printing supplies. Weeks later Sarah got two letters from Conawago, the first from on board a ship in New York Harbor, saying he was sailing for England. The second was from London, saying we should not expect to see him, but not to mourn because he had lived a full life. He said do not tell Duncan until he returned to Edentown, then he wrote 'God bless Noah.'"

Duncan looked up into the dark sky. He had thought the death of Pierre had brought all the pain he could bear. He had indeed become a plaything for the gods. "Noah?" he asked in a choked whisper.

Ishmael shrugged. "It made no sense. Nothing makes sense."

A new wave of despair swept over Duncan. Except for Sarah, Conawago was closer to him than anyone alive. The old Nipmuc, born in the last century, was the wisest, most compassionate man he had ever known. At the darkest times of his life, Conawago had been the steady anchor that had kept Duncan on course.

"It isn't possible, Ishmael. Why? He had no business in London. Did he—"

His questions were choked off by a wretched groan from the shadows. Charles Thomson sank to his knees beside the body of his emissary to Benjamin Franklin.

For the first time in Thomson's parlor, no one knew what to say. Thomson and Mulligan sat staring into their cups of tea, occasionally murmuring low epitaphs.

"What an active intellect," Thomson offered.

"He had a prodigious big heart," Deborah Franklin said.

"The best Frenchman I ever knew," Mulligan whispered.

Duncan had gone to help sort through the ruins of the Preston House, adamantly refusing Ishmael's suggestion that he go speak with Sarah at Deborah Franklin's house, where she had taken the unnerved Mrs. Pratt. Instead he had given Ishmael harsh orders that for the first time in all the years they had known each other had brought a look of resentment to the young Nipmuc's countenance.

"A night of such violence. The fire, the murder," Thomson said. "Why last night?"

"Because," Mulligan replied, "as my man reports, a ship for London left at dawn carrying several army officers. That was their plan, to commit these heinous acts just before they would disappear from Philadelphia. McCallum was right. We were played for fools."

Their impromptu wake continued through another pot of tea. Duncan finally rose to leave. He felt shattered, adrift, not sure what direction to go in anymore. Dumont was dead. Sarah was planning to abandon him in pursuit of some impossible news about Conawago. She had known, and she had not only refused to share the news but had purposefully misled him. He rose and took a step to the door. He had to find her.

"Duncan, prithee, wait," Thomson said. "We need you to stay with us. The mission to London must continue. The hopes of the Sons of Liberty ride on it."

"Get on with it, Charles," Mulligan said gruffly, then outlined the preposterous plan he and Thomson had formulated since Dumont's death.

Duncan remained standing. "Sirs, with all due respect, I am going back to the forests. I am not your man. I will serve the Sons faithfully, but on the frontier. And for now—"

The front door burst open and Sarah stormed inside, followed by Ishmael, looking very distraught. "How dare you, Duncan McCallum!" she shouted at him, taking no notice of the others in the parlor. "You have no right to order my trunk off that ship!"

"You are not going to London, Sarah!" Duncan shot back. "And these are private matters best discussed elsewhere." Never in all their years together had he ever spoken so roughly to her. Never in all their years had he been so angry at her. She had deceived him.

"Our friends have an interest in this!" Sarah insisted. "And I am going to London, no matter what you say!"

"Your father is in London. You are conspicuous, very noticeable. Even if you use a different name, your father will learn of you within days. He will lock you up and be certain you never return to America!"

"I don't care!" Sarah shot back. Tears were flowing down her cheeks. "I have to go help Conawago."

"Sarah," Duncan said, pleading in his voice now, "I am speaking of Lord Ramsey, the man who killed your Iroquois father, the man who once kidnapped you so he could have surgeons tame you by slicing into your brain!"

Thomson gasped. Mulligan rose and helped Sarah to a chair. "We were speaking of London just now, Miss Ramsey," the New York tailor said. "Perhaps we have a solution."

"I told you no!" Duncan snapped.

Mulligan ignored him. "With the professor dead, there remains only one man who can deliver the *incognitum* safely to Franklin. Mr. McCallum must go to London."

Sarah went very still, scrubbing at her cheeks as she digested Mulligan's words. "But he mustn't! That's why it has to be me, why I could not tell him. Lord Ramsey has vowed to kill him, has already tried to do so. Duncan has no friends in London. He will have no protection! He will never come back."

Thomson rose and leaned into the kitchen, calling for more tea. "He will have Dr. Franklin," he offered in an uncertain voice.

Duncan didn't speak. He sat and slowly reached to take Sarah's hand. She recoiled at his touch, then her anger broke and she clutched his hand tightly in both her own, as if suddenly he were holding her back from an abyss. He gazed at

Sarah as he spoke. "Miss Ramsey and I have business in Edentown. We are to be wed. Neither of us can go to London."

Sarah gave him a forlorn smile, but another tear dropped. Then she turned to Ishmael. "You must go," she said.

"There is no force on earth, including an angry Highlander, that can stop me," Ishmael vowed, his voice fierce with resolve. "But you need to tell them the rest, everything about my uncle. It concerns Duncan but perhaps also the Sons and Mr. Franklin."

Thomson and Mulligan stared in confusion.

Sarah accepted a cup and gazed into its steam as she spoke. "Conawago said he was going to Boston for supplies. But then notes came in the weeks following his departure. The first was from Sir William Johnson," she reported, referring to their friend the superintendent of Indian Affairs, who lived at Johnson Hall on the Mohawk River. He reported that he had enjoyed his recent chess games with Conawago, and that he was writing to say Conawago need not trouble about returning the traveling trunk he had borrowed, that Sir William was pleased to make a gift of it. He closed by saying it was too bad Patrick Woolford had already sailed for England to attend to his father's estate, but he was pleased that Conawago had been able to spend so much time with Patrick's wife Hannah.

"He lied about going to Boston," Duncan said. "But why go to Johnson Hall before crossing the Atlantic?"

Sarah shook her head. "I don't know. Then more letters came, much delayed, delivered by our Mohawk friends. The first was to both of us, Duncan, written from a ship in New York Harbor before setting sail. In it Conawago apologized for leaving so abruptly but he had known if he had explained in person we would have stopped him. He said he would return in the autumn. It went on to remind us how he had visited Europe many years ago. Royalty in both France and England befriended him." She paused as if for a loss of words.

"Yes, go on," Thomson encouraged her.

She took a sip before continuing, then directed her words to Duncan. "Conawago began having dreams of terrible death, of a new war that is coming." She turned to Thomson and Mulligan, who showed obvious confusion. "To the old tribes dreams are messages from the gods. In his letter he said the gods meant him to stop the bloodshed—that was why they sent the messages. But he could only do that by going to London."

"I don't follow, lass," Mulligan said.

"He said that he knew that if he could only speak with him, man to man, things would be different, that bloodshed could be stopped. He said he had a token from his grandfather, the first one, who had befriended Conawago. He said it was his sacred duty."

"Speak to whom, dear?" Thomson asked. "What grandfather?"

"You mean Franklin?" Mulligan inquired.

"No, no. To him." Sarah clutched Duncan's hand even more tightly. "The Third. He went to London to speak with King George the Third."

No one spoke for a long time. Sarah finally broke the silence, speaking in short phrases as she wiped at tears. "The next message from Conawago was a desperate farewell letter written in London. The last one, written weeks later, was from someone named Noah. It said Conawago had been arrested and declared an insane person. He was condemned to the Bedlam asylum."

Chapter 8

ISHMAEL WAS SO FEEBLE DUNCAN had to help him up onto the main deck of the *Galileo*. For nearly a week the young Nipmuc had kept nothing but watery broth down. The malady had started as a mild case of seasickness, which Ishmael had assured Duncan would soon pass, but then they had encountered a ferocious gale that had tossed their sturdy ship for days.

Now, as they entered the huge natural harbor of Halifax, the ship had at last stopped pitching and rolling and Duncan was able to lead Ishmael into the fresh air to join the onlookers at the rail. Although the *Galileo* had suffered in the storm, losing a topgallant mast and several sails and stays, she was a sound ship with a seasoned crew and had fared vastly better than the other ships limping into the harbor. The crew's only injuries had been a broken arm, a concussion, and a deep gouge in the shoulder of a sailor who had been lashed by a snapped backstay.

"I declare," came the plaintive voice of a seaman. "It be Poseidon's alley. Some of those wretches be that lucky not to be on the bottom already." He crossed himself and pointed to a battered brig that had lost nearly all her yards and her foremast, sitting dangerously low in the water. "And that one will likely never leave these Nova Scotia waters. This place be a shipknocker's dream."

The broad cove before them indeed looked more like a shipbreaking yard than a working harbor. The two ships ahead of them each had only one of their masts left, and beyond them a hulk with no masts was being towed by her crew working the oars of three small boats. Another ship carried the wreckage of her mainmast alongside, listing dangerously as her crew worked to cut away the tangle of line and canvas.

Duncan stopped counting the damaged ships after reaching fifteen. Many would be weeks in repair, assuming the navy yard was generous with her stores. Halifax was Britain's largest naval base in the North Atlantic and no doubt had abundant supplies, but he saw three frigates anchored near the government wharf, all in need of repair, and their needs would come first.

In the distance he saw the tall flagstaff flying the Union Jack at the top of Citadel Hill, reminding him that the killers of Ezra and Dumont were probably army officers and just as likely had been at sea during the storm.

"There's two of the Philadelphia ships," Ishmael said, pointing to a big square rigger missing two of her three masts and a heavy merchant bark with a gaping hole on her port side where a falling mast had hit the hull. He was having the same thought as Duncan. "The bastards are likely over there on one of them, if they didn't sink to the bottom."

"We don't know their real names or even their faces," Duncan reminded him. "There are probably half a dozen ships out of Philadelphia here. And you are in no shape for a confrontation. We'll be well away long before them, which gives us a free hand in London for a week or two. We can rescue Conawago and be back on the Atlantic before they anchor in the Thames." He handed Ishmael a piece of the dry ship's biscuit he had been insisting the Nipmuc chew to get some nourishment in his belly.

Ishmael accepted the biscuit with a grimace, then studied it closely. He carefully plucked a small worm from the biscuit, held the biscuit out over the water, then dropped the biscuit and ate the worm.

"Savage," Duncan muttered and was relieved to see the grin on his friend's face, the first he had seen since leaving Philadelphia.

"Wasn't that friend of Sarah's on a London ship that sailed just ahead of us?" Ishmael asked after studying the repair crews swarming over several of the damaged ships. "What was her name? The frilly one with the curly hair who insisted she had to get back for the annual season of balls."

"Madeline Faulkner," Duncan replied, smiling as he recalled how Sarah always seemed more mischievous in the woman's company, although Madeline had struck him as more of a shallow socialite than most of Sarah's friends.

As the *Galileo* dropped her anchor, Ishmael pointed to one of the ships anchored nearby, a bark missing her foremast. "I recognize that mermaid figurehead," he said. "I saw her in Philadelphia the day before the fire. She was gone the next morning." An urgent gleam came into his eyes. "That has to be the one, Duncan, the ship they fled in. You can go over with one of the *Galileo*'s officers and say you are a friend of Madeline Faulkner and wanted to inquire after her safety."

"She wasn't on that ship, Ishmael. She left earlier."

"They don't know that you know that. It will give you a reason to get on her deck, to see if any military officers are on board. Surely there can't be many with passage on a merchant ship. If there's only two then you can discover their faces, maybe even their real names."

Duncan borrowed the telescope kept on the quarterdeck and studied the ship. It was a tempting suggestion. If the two men were indeed on board, he might even get some notion of when they would arrive in London.

But then suddenly there was a movement of bright color on the deck as figures emerged from a passage. His heart sank and he handed the telescope to Ishmael. "Not now," he said. There were over a dozen scarlet-coated army officers on the ship.

They were awakened shortly after dawn by angry shouts from the main deck. The only time Duncan had heard their Welsh captain raise his voice had been during the storm, to be heard over the wind, but now he raged as loudly as during the height of the gale. "You have no right!" Captain Rhys shouted. "The owners will hear of this, by God!"

As Duncan ventured to the galley for breakfast porridge and bacon, he puzzled over the busy sound of hammers. It was not the sound of repair work in the rigging; it was the sound of carpenters arranging new berths by knocking down bulkheads and erecting new walls, much as was done on warships before and after battle. When he and Ishmael finally emerged into the main deck's chaos of sawhorses, nail casks, lumber, saws, and mallets, they discovered that many in the work party were from the naval yard, under the supervision of a young lieutenant.

Duncan approached the rail to stand beside the bosun, a wiry, compact man named Darby who had been born in Ayrshire, on the shores of the Firth of Clyde.

Darby watched the naval work party with obvious disapproval. "Spit and polish it'll be all the way to the pool of the Thames," he groused. "And pray to God no one recognizes the deserters among our crew."

"I don't follow," Duncan admitted.

"The captain was much put out when that colonel came aboard with his damned orders, expecting us to do his bidding without as much as a by your leave. But then the colonel offers to speak with the port commissioner about supplying all the stores we need to make repairs this very day, with naval carpenters to complete them, then agrees to add officer victuals, not just for the new passengers but for all our own officers and Philadelphia passengers. Plus a case of brandy so long as we can weigh anchor on tomorrow morning's tide. 'Course the captain, practical man as he is, knows it means there'll be no ships from America for days after ours, so the bidding will be high for his cargo. 'So well,' says Captain Rhys with a salute, 'if it's a military necessity then we will do our duty and God save the king.'"

"New passengers?" Ishmael asked over Darby's shoulder.

"Here come the pretty boys themselves," said the bosun, pointing in the direction of the ship with the mermaid figurehead. "Two buckets of damned lobsters."

Duncan's heart sank as he saw the two launches approaching the *Galileo*. They were packed with red-coated officers. His mind raced. He darted down the passageway to the captain's cabin and did not wait for a reply to his urgent knock, then entered to see Captain Rhys standing over a table strewn with charts.

"McCallum," he acknowledged stiffly. The two men had grown friendly during the storm, when Duncan had helped save the ship more than once by ascending the shrouds to cut away torn rigging. But Duncan knew it was a breach of etiquette to intrude so on the captain.

"Beg pardon, sir, but you have men in the sick bay," Duncan observed.

"Regrettably, yes."

"You recall I set a broken arm. It needs close watching, and that gouge from the stay was deep. It could fester if not frequently cleaned and hydrated. Not to mention the concussion."

"I'm not sure I follow. We do the best we can."

"I wish to be assigned as ship's surgeon. I studied medicine at the university in Edinburgh. And if you have need, I can still reef sail as well as any able-bodied seaman. My companion can pass as the surgeon's mate."

"McCallum, why would you suddenly want to—" The captain paused. "This has to do with our new passengers," he ventured.

"I fought in the French War as a ranger, the irregular troops, they called us. Rangers and lobsterbacks don't mix well. We can take mess with the crew and sleep in the infirmary. We ask for no special privileges."

The captain studied Duncan. "You'll want refund of your passage fare," he guessed.

"Not at all. Mr. Mulligan paid full fare for us in Philadelphia and he need never know about this arrangement. You and I will simply be doing ourselves a mutual favor. The crew just needs to call me their surgeon. Let them think perhaps I am a deserter who fears close contact with the soldiers."

The Welshman's bearded face slowly broke into a grin, and he offered his hand. "I just wish I could avoid the prigs as well," he said.

"Bates, Ishmael is going to tie you to your cot if you persist in squirming so!" Duncan railed at his patient, the seaman who had taken a bad fall during the storm.

"But I feel fine, sir. My mates will think I'm a malingerer."

"That fall caused a swelling in your cerebellum," Duncan explained. "Until your headaches disappear and your eyes can focus enough for you to read, you will not go aloft."

Bates reflected his dissatisfaction with an exaggerated grimace, then turned over in his cot to face the wall, pulling the blanket over him. "Don't even think I got one of those cerebellums," he muttered. "And it'd be a miracle indeed if suddenly I knew how to read."

"Thank you, Mr. Bates," Duncan said to his back. "Reading lessons will be given by Mr. Ishmael starting at eight bells on the forenoon watch." It was Ishmael's turn to grimace.

Duncan turned to the Nipmuc as Bates sullenly pulled the blanket over his head. "It will give you something to pass the time."

"I'd rather be aloft," Ishmael said. He had been disappearing for hours at a time, climbing to the maintop or sometimes even the lofty crosstrees, where he tied himself to the mast and read books borrowed from the purser, a literate man who had abandoned his shorebound life as a merchant when his family had all died of the black flux.

Duncan would have greatly enjoyed their long days of fast, fair-weather sailing were it not for the boisterous, haughty officers who dominated the main deck when they were not draining bottles of claret in the mess cabin. He was able to avoid them while performing his duties as surgeon, which he lingered over as long as possible. Several times a day he slipped past them to join Ishmael at his high perch. His grandfather used to scold him good-naturedly for his skylarking, swinging through the rigging of the old Scot's ketch, and he resisted the frequent temptation to swing from mast to mast now.

He lost himself instead in watching the ever-changing Atlantic. Seldom did an hour go by without the sighting of a whale, and sometimes they would spy great schools of the leviathans, too numerous to count. One day they reduced sail to join with an outbound Portsmouth merchantman, learning that French forces had invaded Corsica over British protests and that Parliament was so upset with Prime Minister Grafton for allowing it that he might be swept from office. That night in the crew mess several of the sailors perversely toasted the French victory.

The bosun was able to find some paper for Duncan, and he took advantage of the languid pace of life on board to begin a letter to Edentown.

Dearest Sarah—

Long ago my grandfather introduced me to the nautical tradition of sea letters, composed over weeks and even months so that they read more like a journal than a mere missive. Once he even read to me a thirty-page letter written by his own father who served as mate on one of the early tobacco ships, written to the woman he loved. Now I will write to the woman I love and, if you can suffer it, sometimes express confidences I would not offer to anyone else, for you are my conscience, mo muirninn, *the other half of my heart.*

We endured a furious tempest for days after leaving the American coast, one so severe that I fear lesser ships with lesser captains may not have survived. Ishmael, who suffered greatly but now recovers, says it was brought on by the incognitum, *not to kill us but to remind us that the hand of his ancient world is upon us. He states it was a dire wind populated by demons, but also one that portends momentous deeds of far-reaching consequences. I know not of great deeds but demons do now inhabit our world. We were forced into Halifax for repairs, where a score of army officers joined us, several out of Philadelphia, including the two you encountered at the tavern. My hunter's instinct tells me the killers of our friends are among them—and if true, Ishmael will doubtless say the hand of the* incognitum *brought them to us.*

But enough of the darkness. I am a captive of the Atlantic for a few weeks, and have begun to taste the joys I first felt sailing on my grandfather's ketch. My favorite berth has always been atop a mast, and now that I have introduced Ishmael to the joys of perching in the tops he seems addicted to them. My grandfather used to say up there you grow into the endlessness. When I asked him to explain he said he couldn't, because it was my turn to grow into it. It took me a long time but eventually I knew he meant that although at first you feel tiny and insignificant up there, gradually you become part of the majesty, part of the never-ending power of the planet. The dear old man, who insisted his aunt was a selkie, also said that if you look at it long enough the sea will push back everything that is incomplete in your life. When I look at it long enough, Ezra and Pierre are staring back.

Duncan read over what he had written, the likely first of many installments, before folding it into the oilcloth pouch he would keep it in. There were questions he wanted to ask Sarah, but refrained from putting them into writing. Who did she meet in secret on a Boston ship? Why, he kept wondering, would she meet with Ezra about his mission on the Ohio? Most of all he remembered the way she had recited the words of an Iroquois on the warpath when she had gazed at the ruins of Preston House. *A warrior must be blooded*, she had said, like an angry vow.

The crew were much like the calloused but gentlehearted men Duncan had known from his Hebrides sailing days. Several of them were indeed Scots, and over the simple but plentiful meals they often shared stories of the old life in their beloved homeland. No one acknowledged, though every one of them knew, that their old way of life had been extinguished by men wearing the same scarlet coats as their passengers.

The captain's own patience with his military passengers quickly wore thin, and he began inviting Duncan and Ishmael to join him for private meals in his cabin. "They roister about my ship as if they owned it, damn their eyes," he groused over one of their ample lunches. "Why, my bosun Darby says they are bribing the cook to siphon my best wine into their bottles. Thank God for these winds, for we'll see them off on the Thames soon enough." The flinty-eyed Welshman glared at the door as a raucous laugh rose in the passageway. "Too damned idle, that's the problem. They are from different regiments, just thrown together for the voyage, so there's no one really in charge. Except that strutting Major Hastings seems to think he is running everything, including my ship. They seek out mischief like schoolboys on a holiday." He lowered his voice. "Darby found some of them in the aft hold, exploring the cargo. They said they were just accessing their trunks, but they weren't anywhere near their own baggage, and they had been well instructed that they needed permission to enter the holds."

Duncan exchanged a quick glance with Ishmael. "Why tell us?"

"Because Darby says they were showing unnatural interest in a great curving object wrapped in straw and canvas. I recollect that particular item is yours, McCallum."

Duncan, feigning indifference, gave a shrug. "Probably just trying to capture rats for their competitions." After a week on board, the officers had taken to betting on inane events like whether a seaman climbing the port shrouds would reach the top faster than one on the starboard shrouds, or how long a great whale would stay submerged after breaching. When the galley had caught two rats in a cage, they had taken to staging races across the main deck. "Of course," he added, "I doubt the owners would take kindly to strangers, even officers of the king, rummaging about the cargo. Not to mention how they might shift crates in their quest for new rodent champions."

It was a point that resonated with Captain Rhys. Shifting crates could affect the lay of the ship in the water, which in turn could affect her speed and handling. The Welshman frowned. "Surely they wouldn't be so foolish." He eyed Duncan silently, clearly suspecting there were secrets about Duncan's cargo that were not being shared, and noticed the excitement on Ishmael's face. The news was the closest thing yet to evidence the killers were on board. "I'll have the bosun remind them at their next meal and have him keep a watch on the hatch into the aft hold."

"It was probably that loud artillery officer who's always boasting of his winnings," Ishmael said, catching Duncan's eye. "Perhaps trying to stow some of his new coin." They had been carefully assessing the officers from a distance, identifying five that might fit the vague description they had of the killers.

"No, surprisingly it was that major and his aide, the glib lieutenant who stays at his side like the faithful pup."

Duncan tried not to react to the news. He had carefully avoided the only two men he had encountered previously, the energetic lieutenant and the arrogant major whose wig Sarah had pinned to a tavern mantel.

Duncan's former patient Bates stirred Duncan and Ishmael from sleep early the next morning. "Beg pardon, sir," Bates said to Duncan.

"Are you bleeding?" Duncan asked, pointing to a red trickle along the sailor's temple.

"A scratch, nothing more, but it's why I'm here, ye might say. One came back, and I knocked him good with a belaying pin."

"I am afraid I am a bit dull from slumber," Duncan admitted, rubbing his eyes.

"On sentinel duty," Bates said, "we've been keeping watch on the aft hold from the shadows, like Mr. Darby said."

Duncan gestured Bates closer to examine his wound. "He came in the dark, with a muted lantern," Bates explained. "I gave him a chance at first, since sometimes a man just wants a bit of privacy, but he got right to it, pushing aside the bales of skins we had stacked in front of your crates. When he starts prying at the top one I sprang up and said we brook no thievery on this good ship, and let 'im have it."

"Have what exactly, Bates?"

"Like I said, a hard swing of my belaying pin. Ye can do some damage with a good oak pin. We used them to repel boarders off Madagascar once. Just a glancing blow to the skull, mind. I refrained from crushing his throat or smashing his kidneys."

"And he fought back?" Ishmael asked.

"He just groaned and spun about, then dropped. For a moment or two he lay there like a turbot on ice, if ye get my meaning, then he found his feet and fled.

If he's got one of those cerebellums it be aching something fierce by now." Bates touched the bloody spot on his head. "That I got when I slipped on the ladder trying to catch the bastard. The bosun says we're to hang strands with fresh yellow paint on them tonight, so as to mark the intruders."

"Did you see his face?" Duncan asked.

"It was that dark, sir. Slight in build and young. A thin face. He weren't one of the crew, I be sure of that. Had to be one of those lobsterbacks."

The young lobsterback who showed up at sick call was an ensign from an infantry regiment whom Duncan had treated once before for a particularly intense hangover, which Duncan had suspected was his first ever. He now wore a cap pulled low over his head.

"It's a piercing awful headache, doctor," the nervous officer moaned.

"Ensign Lewis, I recall," Duncan ventured.

"Aye, sir. You gave me willow bark last time that helped considerably."

"I can prepare willow bark," Duncan replied with a nod. His hand shot up to remove the cap.

Lewis just stared down into his hands.

"I wasn't aware we engaged the enemy last night, Ensign Lewis," Duncan observed as he studied the broken skin along the top of Lewis's scalp.

"No sir, yes sir. I mean—I had an accident."

Duncan pushed the young officer's head down. Blood was still oozing from the wound. "Ensign, I will be challenged to know how to treat such a wound if I don't know how it happened. Without knowing what kind of contamination was presented, we face the danger of putrefaction," he declared, working to put solemn warning in his voice.

"Mother Mary! My head? My head might putrefy?"

"I fear it. As it is, I would just shave it and stitch it up."

"Shave my head?" the ensign cried. "Prithee, sir, no! Just some willow bark and I will be on my way. With a shaved head they would mock me all the way to London. I have neither means nor opportunity to purchase a wig."

"Then I will dress the wound the best I can and you must return once a day until I say otherwise. It would go better if you would explain how this happened. Did one of the officers beat you, perhaps? They seem an imperious short-tempered lot."

"Never! I mustn't speak ill of them! I had an urge, sir, in the middle of the night and fell in the dark passage on the way to the head."

Duncan pretended to examine the wound further while he considered the opportunity the ensign presented. He could be a valuable source of information. "Glad to hear that. Some of your companions look like they could handle themselves in a scrape. My sense is they're not just some of those pudgy staff officers who inhabit garrison headquarters."

"Oh no, we have some prodigious warriors among us. Most bore arms in the French War. Major Hastings and his lieutenant trained with the famous rangers, and even fought the savages!"

Duncan had not forgotten that the mate of the *Muskrat* said his passengers had equipped themselves like rangers the night Ezra had died. "If we have to repel boarders, I will be much comforted to have them with us," he said, then directed Lewis to lean over a basin as he poured sulfur water over the wound. He quickly finished his treatment, reminded Lewis he would need daily attention, and suggested that he linger after the lunch mess in the galley, then slip away to the sick bay in secret. Duncan did not want the other officers to know he was cultivating an informant.

"In secret?" Lewis asked.

"I know the army, ensign. I was in the war too. You don't want to appear to rely too heavily on staff officers or medical men."

Ensign Lewis chewed on Duncan's words a moment, then nodded, though the effort caused him to wince again. "After the midday meal then, sir, as you suggest, though I mustn't tarry, since that is when I am supposed to be polishing boots."

Someone had asked Lewis to pay his nighttime visit to the aft hold, and chances were it had been one of Ezra's killers, but Duncan still had no proof. He expressed his frustration to Ishmael as he joined him in the mizzentop, where the Nipmuc was absorbed in reading Defoe's *Robinson Crusoe*.

"But we know three things," Ishmael pointed out. "We know the killers were a pair of men, and that the pair likely served with the rangers, or at least trained with them. And now we know Ensign Lewis is doing their bidding." He gazed down at the deck in silence for several breaths. "Robinson Crusoe developed a whole new perspective on the world, as he studied in solitude," Ishmael observed. "Like being in a mizzentop. It's remarkable how much you can see looking down on the deck from here. Everyone below takes no notice of those above. I count four sets of two and three who regularly speak with each other, as if friends from before the voyage. If the purser is willing, we may discover if they are from the same units, for he would have a log that identifies each passenger."

Ishmael pointed to a familiar figure as he emerged onto the deck. "Ensign Lewis is a popular man, it seems, for he speaks with almost every other officer. Or perhaps it is because he is the most junior, and eager to do the bidding of all. But he seems especially attentive to two pairs of officers." He indicated a pair by the rail, who were watching a school of flying fish traveling alongside the ship, then another pair who sat on kegs playing cards. As they watched, Lewis approached the cardplayers and handed one a small rectangular object, probably a snuffbox. The man who reached for it, snapping what sounded like a complaint about Lewis's tardiness, was the major Duncan had encountered in Philadelphia.

"Hastings," Duncan said. "Major Hastings and his lieutenant served with the rangers."

"Lieutenant Nettles," Ishmael said, then shrugged. "It proves nothing."

Duncan watched in silence for a moment. From the moment he had recognized the major from his encounter in Philadelphia, his instincts had warned him of the man, not because of any specific evidence but because Hastings's combination of loose-limbed prowess and heartless arrogance made him the kind of man who killed easily. "Once your uncle and I found a small brass gear among the stones in a Catskill creek," he said. "My interest was sparked and after a few more minutes of searching I had found a lead disc mounted on a wire, several more gears, and a horseshoe with two bent nails still in it. 'Sometimes truths are constructed of many pieces,' Conawago said, 'but it doesn't make the truth less real. The truth before us is that a reckless settler lost his inheritance.'

"When I confessed my confusion, he said a pack horse lost its load here, which could have been prevented if the man had paid attention to the loose nails. The horse started, shifting a poorly packed load and spilling a clock into the stream, smashing it into pieces. Conawago said, 'A poor settler traveling these trails doesn't have the money to buy a clock, so it would come by inheritance.'"

Ishmael considered Duncan's words. "Tall with black hair, when he isn't wearing his wig. The major matches one piece of the puzzle."

"As do three or four others. But this particular officer trained with rangers and arrived in Philadelphia with his lieutenant just before me, flashing a treacherous-looking dagger."

"Pierre died from a long single slice across his throat. It could have been from a dagger like that," Ishmael added. "The truth is a puzzle of many pieces."

"It doesn't tell how he came to believe the crates were packed on board this particular ship, which he did not even expect to be traveling on."

"The gods," Ishmael whispered. Duncan had not forgotten the haunted way Ishmael had spoken of the old gods that night on the Ohio, nor Ishmael's fear that he would fail them.

They stared out over the endless water for several minutes.

"Our cargo has distinctive shapes," Duncan reminded Ishmael. "If he believes the bones are to be conveyed across the Atlantic, then surely he will be checking every cargo hold he encounters. And if he knows the crates are on board, does he truly believe no one is accompanying them?" He pointed. A stone's throw away from their perch, an albatross glided past. They watched the huge, elegant bird until it was lost on the horizon.

"What if the bones themselves are meaningless to them?" Ishmael asked. "What if they just see the bones as bait, drawing out the secret Sons operatives so they can kill them? They've already eliminated two."

Duncan weighed the words. "The bones are important, or the killers would not have tried to steal them on the Ohio. But we should sleep in shifts, switching when the ship bell rings the change in watch," he suggested. He touched a pocket of his waistcoat, which held a slip of paper that he had been given in Philadelphia. He had long since memorized the address on it. 7 CRAVEN STREET. He prayed the powerful Dr. Franklin could protect them once they reached London.

Ishmael noticed Duncan's motion. He well knew what was in the pocket. "We have nothing to fear," he declared with a hollow smile. "We'll soon have the wizard of lightning on our side."

Sadness had never entirely left the young Nipmuc's countenance since they arrived in Philadelphia, when, as Duncan now knew, he had learned of his uncle's fate. His questions about the place called Bedlam were becoming more frequent.

Duncan had at first professed to know only that it was a famous London hospital, the proper name of which was Bethlem Hospital, itself an abbreviation for Bethlehem. But after a few days in the company of the crew, Ishmael had confronted Duncan in the narrow confines of the sick bay.

"How is it," the Nipmuc had impatiently asked, "that a medical man has no real knowledge of Bedlam when half the crew has tales of its horrors? I can't deal with an enemy I do not understand, but you become a stone wall whenever I ask you. Shall I just accept the stories the crew tells me? That it is really run as a freak show where human oddities can be viewed for a penny? That its long halls echo with screams and insane laughter all night and day? That no one ever leaves except as a hollow shell of a human, driveling saliva and muttering to themselves with no recognition of friends and family?"

"I haven't been there," Duncan explained. "And do you believe all the tales told around campfires of beasts in the woods that shift their shape from man to bear, or of trees whose fruit will grant immortality? Please, Ishmael, we must wait until we reach the Thames and discover the truth for ourselves."

"The bosun had an older cousin sent there. He went to visit him with an aunt and she fainted at the sight of him. He was in a room with bars on the door, stark naked, banging his head bloody against the wall. When the bosun called out to him he just turned and crowed like a rooster."

The words squeezed Duncan's heart like a vise.

"It's Conawago, Duncan! The last great man of our tribe! If even half of what I hear about Bedlam is true, he will be destroyed in there!" Ishmael's voice cracked. "He'd rather die than suffer the horrors I've heard. I don't care about the bones. I don't care about Shawnee gods. I need Conawago."

"All I know is from professors in Edinburgh," Duncan finally said. "So it is not true knowledge, it is second knowledge," he added, using cautionary words they had sometimes heard at Iroquois council fires. "I will tell you what they said." With a chill heart, Duncan explained that Bedlam had been established as a charitable hospital centuries earlier and gained a reputation for its treatment of those who were mentally unbalanced. "There are renowned medical men there," Duncan said doubtfully. He too had heard the terrifying tales of Bedlam, some worse than those Ishmael related.

"The stories make it sound like a living hell," Ishmael said. "We can't even be sure he is still—" Emotion choked his words away. "And you have other business, with the great Franklin."

Duncan gripped his shoulder. "We are going to London to bring Conawago home," he vowed. "Neither the bones nor the king shall interfere."

Ensign Lewis dutifully arrived after the lunch mess, appearing more nervous than the day before. Duncan surveyed his uniform as he pushed Lewis down onto a cot. A faint line of yellow paint ran across his shoulder.

As Duncan washed the wound on his scalp, they exchanged pleasantries about the weather, the spectacular sunrise, and the great shark that the army officers had been taunting with scraps of food.

"I believe we can save your scalp," Duncan declared as he finished, "but I am not certain about your brains." Lewis seemed unaware of the strands soaked in yellow paint hanging from beams of the dimly lit hold.

Lewis looked up, startled. "Sir?"

"You surely must have lost them if you were rummaging around the cargo again like some sneak thief. A merchant ship holds its cargo in trust to the owners. British laws impose severe penalties for tampering with it. But that punishment would pale by that the captain would inflict if he discovered someone stealing or destroying his cargo. That shark would no doubt relish one of your appendages."

The blood drained from Lewis's face before Duncan had finished speaking. "I never—" he sputtered. "I couldn't say nae to—" His face was twisted with fear.

"If you could let me help," Duncan said, "I might soften the captain's temper. Perhaps there is a story, an excuse that could earn his forgiveness."

"Prithee, sir, I beg you! My career would be over before it began! I wasn't tampering exactly. He ordered to me look, said it was just a reconnaissance mission. He's a major! He dwells among the gods in London! The Horse Guards!"

"Major Hastings, you mean," Duncan suggested, then hesitated, considering Lewis's new disclosure. The Horse Guards were the army elite, responsible for the security of the king and for the overall administration of the army.

Lewis did not disagree. "Just look, he said. Find a big curving object, longer than my own height, wrapped in canvas. Look for shipping numbers or names or any other mark, then seek out trunks or crates with the same mark. Note how many there are and where they sit in the hold and what names are on them. That's all."

"And you found what you sought?"

Lewis winced. "There's rats down there, as big as cats. And the stink from the bilge is enough to steal your breath away. I found the big curving thing but it was packed tight between other cargo. I found its mark, a cross with a circle centered over it. It's what they call a Scottish cross, I know because it's the kind of cross my mother keeps over our hearth, from her days as a girl. But I could find the mark on only two crates. He wasn't well pleased, said the rest must be buried beneath other crates and that I had to look harder."

"Why would the major be interested in some civilian's cargo?" Duncan asked.

"He would never trust such a secret to a lowly ensign. His aide Lieutenant Nettles says some of the other officers owe him gambling debts and he's probably trying to locate the assets they pledged to him. I'm just an ensign," Lewis reminded Duncan. "Major Hastings says back at the Horse Guards stables he scrapes ensigns off his boots each morning."

As Lewis turned, one more question occurred to Duncan. "Ensign, one of the crew found a snuffbox, one with a hunting scene etched on it. The major partakes of snuff. Could it be his?" Duncan had remembered that Podrake had mentioned Hastings's snuffbox, adorned with naked Roman women.

"Oh no, sir, the major's snuffbox has women on it, in fine enamel. Gypsies or Italians or such, I guess, for they be all shamelessly unclad."

The Horse Guards. Duncan stared down at Major Hastings from the mizzentop where he sat with Ishmael once more. It explained Duncan's confusion over the ornate uniform the major sometimes wore, for the unit was stationed in London and had not served in the American theater. He had never heard of any of its soldiers even traveling in America, but two had gone in civilian clothes to murder his friends.

"He wants to block the unloading of our shipment," Ishmael suggested when Duncan related what he had learned. When Duncan did not reply, he added, "It doesn't matter what uniform he wears, Duncan. He killed Ezra and Pierre."

"I didn't understand at first when Lewis said Hastings resided with the gods in London," Duncan said. "But he's right. A major of the Horse Guards is well known to the Secretary at War, probably even to the king himself."

"There he is again," Ishmael said.

Misunderstanding, Duncan looked down at the deck. "Who?"

"King George." The name had a strangely chilling effect. "I never really grasped the notion of a king," Ishmael said. "They pretend to have authority over men's lives. But I never gave him authority over me. Conawago never gave him authority. And I know you too well to think you had given consent to be governed by the man who destroyed the Highland clans."

"That was his father," Duncan said in a bitter voice. "And you are sounding more and more like your uncle, Ishmael," he added with a melancholy smile, knowing they might never see Conawago again. "We live in the king's nation, so have to abide by the king's rules."

"Most of them," Ishmael amended. "Elsewise there would be no point to the Sons of Liberty."

"Most of them," Duncan agreed.

"My uncle once told me that kings held public debates over whether Indians had souls," Ishmael added after a moment.

"That was in another century," Duncan said, "in Spain and Portugal."

Ishmael gave an absent nod. "I was thinking that the closer we get to London the closer we are to the other side of the debate, the proper side."

"Other side?"

"Whether the king has a soul."

When Major Hastings finally presented himself, it was without his wig and uniform. He was dressed in a dun-colored sleeveless waistcoat and linen shirt, with a long silver chain extending from a buttonhole into a waistcoat pocket. He was the last of the three men in line for the morning sick call. Duncan quickly dealt with the other two, an infantry officer seeking a cure for his hangover and a seaman with a six-inch splinter in his foot.

"My father suffered from consumption," Hastings declared. "I have a cough at night and thought I might get a renowned medical man to listen to my lungs."

"Renowned in the sense that I am the only one for a thousand miles," Duncan replied, lifting the infirmary's hollow section of horn used for listening to chests.

"Nonsense! The captain from the Buffs says you cured an intimate disease of his."

Duncan spoke in his stiff professional voice. "I gave him blue ointment for his rash and the condition went into relapse, as it is known to do. It will return when he reaches the brothels of London."

Hastings laughed and removed his waistcoat and shirt, leaving only his thin small clothes vest, then studied Duncan's face. "By God, it's true! My lieutenant said he recognized you from the tavern in Philadelphia. I declare, you made light practice of me that evening! What fun we had, eh?"

"I recall that I gave you fair warning about frontier women," Duncan rejoined, and pressed the horn against Hastings's chest.

"I regretted your abrupt departure. I would have gladly shared a bottle of port once I freed my hair from the wall."

"I was weary and the crowd was noisy," Duncan said, and pushed his ear to the curved horn, holding up his hand for a moment's silence.

"What a coincidence to find you on this ship," Hastings said when Duncan rose. "You gave no indication that you were a seafaring man."

"The opportunity arose rather suddenly," Duncan said. "I was in search of new employment and have always been lured by watery horizons."

"But surely an educated man like yourself should be dining with His Majesty's officers. Don't let the uniforms intimidate you, doctor."

"The ship isn't fitted out for so many passengers. The captain asked my assistant and myself to take accommodation with the crew."

"Such a musty, belching lot," the major said.

"I don't mind them. And it shall be a short voyage if the weather holds." He made a dismissive gesture with the horn. "Your chest seems clear."

"But the linen may obscure the sound," Hastings pointed out, and pulled off his vest.

Duncan froze. Across the major's right shoulder and chest was an intricate tattoo. It appeared to have been done by a practiced artisan, in the style of the woodland tribes. It depicted a man in a British army uniform with a sword in one hand and a pistol in the other. Scattered about him were half a dozen bodies, two of which were decapitated.

"You were in the war, I take it," Duncan said as he collected himself and bent with the horn again.

"Here and there. Detached service in the French War. And the Indian War," Hastings added, meaning the short-lived tribal rebellion of 1763.

Duncan gazed at the tattoo again. The figure's uniform consisted only of the tunic. The rest of his accoutrement was the more casual attire of a ranger. "Artists do tend to exaggerate," he observed with studied disinterest. "A good show for London bedchambers, no doubt."

Hastings gave a silky laugh. "You wouldn't credit how they swoon. But this one is most accurate. Lieutenant Nettles described it to the artist just as he witnessed it. Six dead in a matter of moments. What was it he called me? Oh yes, the army's only Oxford-trained Viking." Hastings gave another thin laugh and reached for his clothes. "I must confess that when the blood starts spilling a terrible thrill runs through me. What a day that was. Regrettably, only one Frenchman. The rest were just savages. Although," he added in a contemplative tone, "there is one custom of theirs I learned to enjoy. They take trophies from those they kill. What a collection I got that day. A war ax, a knife with a staghorn hilt, some bulky pouches that hung from their necks, a string of human ears that I threw away for the stench, a couple of old French crucifixes, and some of those belts of white and purple beads they make such a fuss over. What do they call them?"

"Wampum," Duncan said, and instantly regretted it.

"Ah," Hastings said with a narrow smile as he began dressing, "so among the many things you hide is knowledge of the tribes."

Duncan tried not to react. Had Hastings already connected him to the *incognitum*? For a moment he feared that Reverend Podrake had given Hastings his name, then realized that Podrake had not met Duncan until after his meeting with Hastings in Pittsburgh. "We often encounter natives in the colonies," he observed, then shifted the subject. "Detached service, you said. Do you often go to America on your assignments?"

"The main body of the Horse Guards must always remain close to our blessed king. But I go wherever my king needs me. There is greater and greater need in the American colonies. Treason festers, and as you well know, doctor, rotting flesh must be excised."

"Your colonels and generals must put great trust in you."

Hastings laughed again. "We are a small, intimate unit. Just the one colonel, and I hold a stack of his promissory notes representing his considerable gambling debt. Mostly the Secretary at War and I decide with his Council where my very special services are most needed," the major explained as he buttoned up his waistcoat. He made a show of opening his enameled snuffbox, decorated with Roman women, and placed some of the powder up his nostril, then extracted a small purse bulging with coins. "What is the protocol on a private vessel? I feel obliged to compensate you."

"Not at all," Duncan replied. "It would seem disloyal to take the coin of a king's officer."

Hastings raised an eyebrow. "So refreshing to hear such words from a colonial." He nodded before turning away, but paused at the door. "One of the other officers said he thought he had seen you with Deborah Franklin in Philadelphia. I'm not the only one with an interesting life, it seems," he added with another oily smile. "And I've always wondered, is the Scottish cross only reserved for death? I'm not sure I've ever seen it used outside cemeteries."

Duncan watched the brash officer as he disappeared down the passage. Hastings's visit hadn't been a medical call—it had been a thinly disguised threat.

Duncan heard a dull thud on the other side of the wall and found Ishmael in the hold, practicing with his knife. "How much does he know?" the young Nipmuc asked when Duncan reported the encounter.

"Obviously he knows about the *incognitum* bones. Now I know he is aware that I am acquainted with Deborah Franklin, and of course he must have connected the bones to her husband. He spoke mockingly of the Scottish cross, which can only mean he has now connected us to the crates in the hold."

Ishmael stepped forward as if to retrieve his blade, but instead reached up to the beam above, where Duncan now saw the lanyard with the ancient fang hanging on a peg. Ishmael grew still, gazing solemnly at the tooth, his reminder of the ancient tribal gods. He lifted the tooth and touched it to his forehead, then his heart, before draping it around his neck. He too understood that their conflict with Hastings was about to become more personal. "I don't know if I can be the warrior the old gods desire me to be," he said with a dangerous edge to his voice, "but maybe I can be the one the ancient monster needs."

Duncan risked much by confiding in the captain, but his instincts about the stubborn Welshman told him he was a man of integrity, and he knew Captain Rhys felt no warmth toward his military passengers. "Our cargo is marked only with the Scottish cross," he explained. "It is a secret cargo, and death has stalked it from the time we brought it up the Ohio. All I ask is safe passage to London."

"That be bought and paid for already," the captain stated.

"Before either of us knew His Majesty's army would be invading the *Galileo.*"

"There was no arguing with that garrison commander in Halifax."

"There are two men among them who have connected us to the cargo despite our efforts at secrecy. They seemed sworn to stopping us at whatever the cost. I fear they will be greatly tempted to act with violence against us, and the cargo, before we drop anchor in the Thames."

The captain frowned. "I am powerless to act against the army. God knows I'd like to lock the insolent jackanapes in the bilges." He shrugged. "But t'ain't no business of mine if the army has a feud against Philadelphia folk."

"Not a feud, sir. The cargo is secretly bound for the official agent of the Pennsylvania colony in London. And I speak not of the army—I speak of criminals who happen to wear uniforms. They mean to act against the agent."

The captain cocked his head in surprise. "You speak of Franklin? The father of electricity?"

"The same."

Rhys seemed to inflate a bit, clearly proud to be carrying something bound for the famous Dr. Franklin, but as he weighed Duncan's words his countenance took on a more somber expression. He rose and stood facing the windows across the stern, staring at the long wake of the *Galileo*, then spoke toward the sea. "The troubles of strangers from Philadelphia is no concern to a merchant vessel. We are but transporters."

Duncan's heart sank. He and Ishmael would be in grave danger without the cooperation of the captain and the crew.

"But Dr. Franklin," Rhys added a moment later. "All he asks is for those Englishmen in the colonies to be treated like other Englishmen at home. It's like Parliament thinks colonists are only half men." He turned with a solemn, whispered confession. "I am a Wilkes man," he declared. "Tell me what you desire, McCallum."

A relieved smile rose on Duncan's face. John Wilkes was an outspoken firebrand, but his speeches and pamphlets proclaiming that every man had the right to an equal voice in government had resonated with the common man on both sides of the Atlantic. Wilkes, now in prison for criticizing the king, had become a martyr, a symbol for what was now popularly being called the natural rights of man. His pamphlets were often read in meetings of the Sons of Liberty.

"When he was imprisoned," the captain related, "his supporters gathered to chant 'No liberty, no king.' The army fired on them and killed seven. Killed seven unarmed men for invoking the cause of liberty. That was a dark day for the free men of England."

Duncan let the words hang in the air. "I need these particular soldiers to focus their attentions elsewhere, away from me."

"'Tis a close world on a ship, McCallum. Hard to avoid others on board."

Duncan paused a moment, the words of Catchoka echoing once more in his mind. *You will die, again and again.* "So what I desire, Captain Rhys," he declared, "is that you help them kill me."

Chapter 9

THE *GALILEO*'S BROAD MAIN DECK provided ample space for the circuits Duncan began walking twice each day, just before noon and just before midnight. With less than two weeks left of their voyage, he worked hard both to be predictable and to identify a place amidships that could be concealed from the helmsman by some inconspicuous adjustment to the large hogsheads lashed to the deck.

Two days after his conversation with the captain, while the army officers were at evening mess, a line was fixed to the corner stanchion on the port side and inconspicuously dragged behind the ship. The next morning Ensign Lewis awoke screaming, declaring that he had seen the ghost of an Indian hovering over him with a tomahawk in his hand and rats perched on his shoulder. Major Hastings mocked the rattled ensign and ordered him to sick bay for something to quiet his nerves. The next morning it was the turn of Hastings's aide Lieutenant Nettles to dash out of his berth, with shrill, fearful curses. Under his pillow he had discovered a coiled snake. The army officers seemed less inclined to mock this time, and when Major Hastings appeared with a loaded pistol, insisting on dispatching the creature, the bosun apologized.

"Caught the serpent and put 'im over the side," Darby explained. "A bit of seaweed on the tail calms them down ye see, then I grabbed 'im and disposed of 'im. Dreadful poisonous, them sea snakes, though never before did I see one go to the trouble of seeking out his victim," he added with a suspicious gaze at the still-shaken Nettles. The captain had offered his own men the chance to help Duncan, and they had enthusiastically risen to the challenge. None of the military passengers had lingered long enough to see that the snake was a ragged, dried old dead thing that had been quickly returned to the Cape Verde seaman who kept it as a good luck charm.

That afternoon the first mate ordered all the berths vacated for what he called the "regular" scrubbing of wooden surfaces with vinegar, as a precaution against pestilence. The bosun blocked the passage to the army berths as the cleaning crew noisily went about their job.

An hour later Ishmael entered the sick bay carrying a stack of blankets that had been airing on the deck. He set his load down, closed the door behind him, and lifted away all but the bottom blanket, which he unfolded with a victorious expression. "Like the major told you, he likes mementos," Ishmael stated.

On the blanket lay an intricately worked tribal war ax, which ended in a hard, burnished ball with a spike protruding from one side. Beside the ax were two totem pouches, a knife with a stag horn hilt, and two crucifixes. He counted the trophies. "Six. There were six dead men in the tattoo you described."

"So your friend from Liverpool had no trouble?" Duncan asked. When they had asked the bosun if anyone in the crew might be able to open a locked trunk, he had chuckled and produced a sailor from Liverpool who had leapt on board as the anchor was being raised in Dover two years earlier, begging to join the crew. He had waved at the constables who had been pursuing him as the ship drifted away. All sins were forgiven once a ship reached blue water.

"He made short work of it, but was a bit spiteful when I told him he couldn't touch the coin purse inside. The shilling I gave him brought the smile back to his face."

Duncan lifted the items one by one. The war ax had a rich patina, the look of a weapon that had been handed down from father to son, old warrior to young warrior, for many generations. He studied the patterns carved on the handle, glancing uneasily at Ishmael, then reverently touched the totem pouches, each adorned with elegant quillwork.

"The crucifixes we can't be sure of, but the rest is all of the same tribe. They are Mohawk," Ishmael stated in a bitter tone. "Not Abenaki. Not Huron, nor any other Algonquin," he said, referring to the Indian allies of the French.

"Not all the Mohawk fought alongside the British," Duncan said, realizing that Ishmael was suggesting Hastings might have attacked friends of theirs on the frontier. "There were Catholic Mohawks in Quebec who joined the French."

Ishmael shrugged, unconvinced. "But Mohawk nonetheless." With his own tribe nearly extinct, Ishmael's closest tribal friends were all from Mohawk and Oneida clans. "I should slice the damned tattoo off his chest," he hissed.

Duncan extended the war ax to Ishmael. "This belongs with the tribes, not on some London mantel."

"A sign from the old gods," Ishmael said ruefully, but his expression grew sober as he accepted the ax. A new fierceness rose in his eyes when he nodded to Duncan. Neither one gave voice to the conclusion that was becoming more and more obvious. They were two misfit warriors, going to do battle with London.

The next morning, just after the captain announced that they should sight the mouth of the Thames in four days, several army officers burst onto the deck, clearly shaken. Major Hastings appeared bearing new trophies. Ishmael's friends had replaced the war booty in his trunk with a dozen live rats. The major, his face and shirt dappled with blood, coolly paraded onto the main deck holding the tails of three dead rats and two others skewered on his long dagger. He walked to the rail and disposed of them, then turned and silently glared up at Duncan, standing beside Captain Rhys at the wheel, before snapping at Lewis to bring him some water and a towel.

Hastings calmly watched those on deck as he washed away the blood. A moment later when Darby walked by, his eye on the mainsail, Hastings sprang with snakelike quickness, slamming the back of his hand into the man's jaw. The unexpected blow sent the crew chief reeling backward, slamming against the mainmast. Duncan instantly took a step toward the main deck, and just as quickly the captain clamped his hand around Duncan's arm. The captain placed Duncan's hand on the wheel, then darted to the deck himself, just as half a dozen furious seamen closed around Hastings, whose hand was on his dagger. One began wrapping rope around his knuckles. Another was raising a belaying pin like a club when the captain broke through their circle to stand in front of Hastings, shaking his fist in the officer's face.

"If you have a complaint against one of my crew you come to me!" he roared, then lowered his voice so that Duncan could only make out the angry tone and not his words. Hastings listened with an amused expression, then gave the captain a mocking bow that drew jeers from the idle military officers. The captain ordered his men back to work, then returned to the quarterdeck.

"I don't know when you intend to act, McCallum," he growled as he took over the helm. "But if that popinjay isn't dealt with soon, I'll be hauled before the War Board to explain how I misplaced one of their officers."

Duncan was not surprised when he found the bosun waiting in the sick bay. "I'll be fine, sir," Darby said as Duncan examined the bruise on his jaw. "But ye best tell me everything ye plan and what ye need," he said, echoing the captain's sentiments, "'cause if someone don't deal with 'im soon I'll have the damned lobster in a pot!"

The bosun's grizzled face grew long as Duncan explained his intentions. "'Tis why you had us drag that line over the stern," he concluded with a frown. "Don't like it, sir, not one bit, even if you do be a prodigious swimmer. Ye could perish that easy," he said, snapping his fingers.

"Perhaps you could reduce sail an hour before midnight," Duncan suggested. "That would help. And do what you can for Ishmael. I'm more of a fish than he is a bird."

When Lewis arrived at sick bay that afternoon, he announced that it was his last visit. "The major knows that I come here. He ordered me to tell him where I went after lunch," the boyish ensign explained. "I'm sorry, Mr. McCallum."

"You can't disobey an order," Duncan said as he examined Lewis's old wound. "And I declare you healed, Ensign. You're not going to die, at least not from this wound. But you need to pick your battles more wisely," he suggested.

"I don't believe an ensign has much choice in the matter," Lewis replied with a sour expression. He was twisting his cap in his hand. He glanced up, then gazed down at the floor. "It isn't what I signed up for. My ma has had a run of bad luck ever since she was thrown off her croft. We moved to a cousin's house at first but they was poor fisher folk and some days we were living on naught but seaweed pudding, and only then when the cow weren't sick. When we moved to Chester she worked as a scullery maid, a proud woman of the Hebrides just washing other people's dishes all day. I meant to lift her spirits by being a proper soldier."

"Seaweed pudding?" Duncan asked. It was a staple of his own childhood. "Where was this?"

"Why, the isle, sir."

Duncan gazed at the ensign as if for the first time. "The isle of Lewis?" he asked in surprise, referring to the westernmost of the Hebrides.

"Aye, though the old chieftain it was named for died centuries ago."

"My clan was just across the water, Ensign. But you have no island accent."

"Because when I turned ten my ma insisted we move to her sister's in Chester. She said I would get nowhere in the world speaking like a Highland waif. My aunt beat it out of me. She never knew I kept the Gaelic, sir," he added with a small smile.

Duncan was developing a liking for the earnest youth. "I'm sure your mother is proud of you."

"I send her a letter every few months, with as much of my pay as I can manage, so she can save for a new croft." Lewis hesitated. "I guess I'm what they call a broken man in the old lands."

Duncan eyed him more closely. Lewis meant he was a Highlander who had lost his clan affiliation. "Half the Scots I know are broken men, Lewis."

"But you have a clan."

"Aye, though it be quite small. I kept my plaid and have my pipes back at my home in New York province." Duncan was not sure what to make of Lewis's solemn nod.

"There's six now, sir," the soldier blurted out.

"Six?"

"Six in the major's little army. That's what he calls it. The captain from York, the lieutenant from Coventry, the lieutenant from Ipswich, and the older ensign. Plus Nettles and me. The others owe him considerable sums from their gaming. I'm frightened. The seamen spread talk of evil spirits and a ghost warrior haunting the ship. And the major, he wants us back in that hold tonight. If there's evil on this ship that's where it lurks, and tonight we be rid of it, he says." With a forlorn whisper, Lewis added, "I had a coney foot for protection but I lost it in the storm."

"You'll be in London soon," Duncan assured him. "Back with your unit. For now, you need to obey orders." He helped Lewis to his feet, then bent over the small desk of the sick bay and drew a series of images on a slip of paper: a cross, an arrowhead, a snake, and a bird. "A charm of the clans and the tribes," Duncan explained as Lewis leaned over his shoulder. He wrote in Gaelic underneath it and handed it to the ensign.

The ensign's eyes went round, then he puzzled over the words. "I have the speaking of the old tongue but nae so well the writing of it." He stumbled over the first words. "*Mhicheal bheannaichte?*"

"A special Highland blessing for warrior heroes. Blessed Michael defend us from demons, it says."

Lewis gave an appreciative nod as he folded the blessing into a pocket. "So all that's left," he said in an earnest tone, "is for you to tell me who be the heroes and who the demons."

Two hours before midnight, Duncan began helping Ishmael with his preparations, then readied himself just as he had before each of his nightly circuits of the deck. He removed his shoes and stockings, his waistcoat, and the pouches that hung from his waist, leaving only the one at his neck, which never left him. The bosun arrived, producing a dark cloak that he wrapped around Ishmael. "They be rummaging down in the hold, like ye said they would," Darby reported, then slipped away with the young Nipmuc. Duncan gripped his totem pouch, whispering prayers in Gaelic and then Mohawk, and climbed up to the main deck.

As had become his habit, he spent a few moments chatting with the helmsman, who this night had another seaman at his side. By the stern rail an odd contraption had appeared, two casks with a short net slung between them. "Darby," the helmsman said in explanation. Duncan nodded uncertainly, then descended to the main deck to begin his slow promenade.

He heard the muffled steps and urgent whispers before he reached the far side of the hogsheads tied to the deck. As he turned the corner, two of Hastings's accomplices were heaving the great curving bundle from the cargo hold into the sea as the major watched with a smug expression.

"Hastings!" Duncan hissed and sprang forward as three of his crates from Philadelphia were flung into the water by more of the major's men. Hastings stepped between Duncan and his soldiers, ordering them to go for the rest, then bent and leaned forward, dagger in his hand. Duncan grabbed a belaying pin from the rail and crouched on the balls of his feet, ready to spring. "Those crates are not yours to dispose of, Major!" Duncan growled, keeping his eyes on the blade.

"Call it a military requisition," Hastings sneered.

"Didn't you hear?" Duncan asked. "The crates are protected by angry spirits."

"Only old fools are worried about dead gods, McCallum. Old fools and pagan Highlanders."

"What about the fools who feel threatened by old bones?" Duncan shot back.

Without warning Hastings lunged at Duncan, aiming for his heart. Duncan easily evaded the thrust.

Duncan himself lunged now. Hastings did not see that he had shifted the pin to his other hand. The makeshift club slammed into Hastings's wrist, sending the dagger spinning across the deck. But Duncan did not see the man who leapt out of the shadows, seizing one of his legs. Lieutenant Nettles appeared, grabbing Duncan's wrist and pushing him bodily against the rail. An instant later Hastings had his other leg. Duncan had no leverage. He fought for a grasp on the rail, twisting in an effort to shake his assailants off. Then Lewis appeared, dropping the crate he carried and grabbing a foot. With a jubilant cry Hastings heaved upward and Duncan tumbled over the rail.

He had planned to end the fight by falling overboard, but he had intended to stage it so he would be standing on the rail with a clear view of the moonlit ocean as he dropped. Instead he careened against the ship, upside down. His head slammed into the hull before he hit the cold Atlantic water, stunning him. By the time he righted himself and could focus, the ship's stern had passed him.

"Sarah!" he heard himself cry. His heart lurching, he desperately swam toward the retreating ship, his confidence gone. If he missed the dragging rope he would be lost, alone in the vast dark sea with no hope of rescue. He fought his rising panic, taking long powerful strokes, but with increasing dread knew he had missed his lifeline. Hastings had won. "Sarah!" he cried again.

Suddenly a bright lantern flared on the stern and he saw the outline of two bulky objects floating fifty feet away. He reached the casks and with a hammering heart pulled himself onto the netting fastened between them. This only prolongs my death, he thought, shaking off a vision of his parched, withered corpse washing up with the casks on some distant shore. The foolishness of his plan overwhelmed him. Duncan had thrown away his life, had not even written farewell letters to Sarah and Conawago. He drifted in the moonlight, considering how long his body could endure without nourishment and water, and whether he would have the spine to throw himself to sharks if they presented themselves. Then suddenly the casks were jerked about and began moving. The bosun had tied a line to them.

His friends draped a blanket over him as he climbed over the stern, then quickly led him to the port rail. Below on the main deck, Hastings was directing the disposal of the last of Duncan's cargo, cursing at one of his party who hesitated, a small crate in his hand. In the still air Duncan could hear the man's complaint.

"You've eliminated your foe, Major. Must we still flaunt the spirits?"

"You superstitious fool!" Hastings snapped. "Give me the damned box and I'll—" His words were cut off by a terrible wail from overhead.

"It's him, the devil they spoke of!" the nervous soldier cried, and dropped his crate on the deck. "The ghost warrior! God preserve us!"

As the officer backed away, Hastings cursed again. Ignoring the man's gesture to a yardarm on the aft mast, he retrieved a belaying pin from a rack below the rail and raised it to strike his fellow officer.

The act provided the extra moment the warrior needed. The line strung from high in the mainmast was invisible in the darkness, so that as he swung out on it, it seemed the ghost warrior was flying directly at Hastings from the heavens. At the last moment a war ax appeared in the pale warrior's hand, slamming into the major's arm. Hastings screamed in pain as he fell backward, striking his head hard on the deck as the ghost disappeared into the darkness above.

"Damn you to hell!" Lieutenant Nettles shouted at Ishmael. "He is a major of the Horse Guards! Do something!" Nettles had changed into his uniform before coming to the sick bay, as if for added protection.

"Right now he is a patient in mortal danger if he is moved," Ishmael replied evenly.

Duncan smiled as he watched through the small hole the carpenter had drilled in the wall when building the secret berth adjoining the sick bay. Ishmael was play-ing his well-rehearsed role of surgeon's mate perfectly, doing all he could to keep Hastings unconscious and confined to his control.

"He is tied to the cot!" Nettles protested.

"Standard practice," Ishmael explained. "Were he to revive prematurely, he would be too dizzy to remain standing and might concuss his head again. Another blow could seal his fate. And the fracture of his arm means he will need to be restrained for days."

As if to refute Ishmael, the lieutenant jabbed a finger into the exposed flesh of Hastings's good arm. The major did not respond. Before he had set the broken fib-ula, with the bosun guarding the door, Ishmael had administered a heavy dose of laudanum, the tincture of opium, to the still unconscious Hastings. Duncan had instructed Ishmael the day before on how to prepare the doses, to be administered regularly until reaching the Thames.

"The doctor is oddly missing," Ishmael said, "but he will doubtless have more detailed advice when he reappears. Meanwhile your major will be safer here than anywhere in the ship." He pointed to a bundle of leather nailed to the doorframe, containing a feather, a shark's tooth, a length of dried octopus tentacle, and a patch of crocodile skin, the most intimidating charm the bosun could assemble on short notice. Ishmael lowered his voice to a whisper. "There's a Jamaican in the crew who assures me it will repel even the most evil of spirits."

Nettles examined the bundle with a sneer that gradually faded into a sober, worried nod. "What in God's name was that creature?" he asked Ishmael. "I would never have credited it had I not seen the beast with my own eyes. An ape from the clouds, I hear some say, a banshee risen in anger from the deep, said another."

"More likely the latter," Ishmael said in an earnest tone. "I hear he didn't appear until you started throwing those crates in the water." Duncan knew that behind his mask of worried sympathy Ishmael was deeply amused, and he worried that the Nipmuc might break out into laughter. "Though God alone knows why a man of such lofty station as the major would do something to offend the Ancient Ones."

Nettles's face darkened. "A soldier has duties."

Duncan saw the hesitation on Ishmael's face as he considered how far to press. "You mean in the last war."

Nettles's own expression stiffened. "We are the Horse Guards. We are held to a different standard." He seemed to take strength from his own words. He straightened his uniform and spoke more boldly. "We take a vow to protect the interests of the king. We are thus called to a war that never ends." The tinge of arrogance that never left Hastings's voice crept into that of his aide. "No act to preserve the king is ever too bold." It had the sound of a barracks slogan. "Summon me immediately when he regains consciousness," he ordered, and turned to leave.

"I hear that wearing seaweed around the neck helps keep banshees away," Ishmael said to his back. Nettles twisted with a surly expression, but grabbed the dried sprig of kelp that Ishmael extended before marching down the passage.

Captain Rhys had sought in vain to persuade Duncan to take the visitor's berth inside his own cabin, but Duncan would not chance being seen by the army officers. "If you're going to be so stubborn as to decline my hospitality, then oblige me by accepting some comforts," the captain had insisted, and had surreptitiously sent down a quilt, a whale oil lamp, several books, and a fresh baked loaf with a block of cheddar. A note was pinned to the cheese. *If wind holds, then three days.*

Idleness was deeply against Duncan's nature, but he accepted the need to stay out of sight, so he plugged the hole that opened on the sick bay and lit the lamp. He lifted a heavy black tome and saw to his unexpected delight that it was volume one of the *Encyclopedia Britannica*, newly published in Edinburgh. Duncan's gratitude to the captain instantly deepened, for he knew no learned man would lightly surrender such a valuable book. He lay down with an unfamiliar sense of pleasure, bunched the quilt into a pillow, and propped the book on his bent legs. *Aa*, read the first entry, *the name for several rivers.*

The hours raced by as he made his way through the encyclopedia, lost in the wonder of its contents, sometimes drifting away from a passage to consider the immense effort it had taken to catalog the knowledge of the world in such a manner. He recalled now a professor in Edinburgh stating in a lecture that the responsibility of the educated human was to advance the cause of civilization, a sentiment that had been echoed in Thomson's house in Philadelphia. Here surely was a work that advanced civilization. He was humbled by the amazing book and he read entry after entry, lingering long over the thirty-nine pages concerning Algebra and the one hundred forty-five on Anatomy. He began to appreciate why a review he had read in *The London Gazette* had praised it as the second most important book ever published.

When he paused to rest his eyes, Duncan opened the small trunk that contained the few personal possessions he had brought with him and extracted the single biggest object. He removed the linen shirt that had been wrapped around it, not for the first time admiring the intricate natural design of the ancient tooth. He smiled again at the deceptions he had worked on Hastings. Surely in the next edition of the encyclopedia there would be an entry for the *incognitum*. Was he advancing the cause of civilization by bringing it to London? Some seemed to think its essential message was one of religion, others one of natural philosophy. Still others, working for the king, were hell-bent on destroying all evidence of the *incognitum,* as if it were a creature of politics, and a disloyal one at that. He thought of the crates now resting at the bottom of the sea and gave thanks, not for the first time, for the precautions he and Ishmael had taken before leaving Philadelphia.

Alone, quietly studying each crevice and ridge of the molar and the smooth enamel of its sides, which glowed dark gray with swirls of chestnut in the soft light, he again felt an unexpected calm. He felt an odd resonance at the touch of the relic. He had experienced such a sensation before, when he had sat with Conawago beside an aged shaman of the Delaware in a cave shrine built around the skeleton of a massive bear. There had been petroglyphs on the wall, and images of hands that had been painted with ochre and pressed to the stone. Duncan had eventually fallen into a deep contemplation of the ages-old signs, and when he had stirred, the shaman smiled at him and spoke with Conawago in his native tongue. Duncan had asked his friend to translate.

Conawago had rested his chin on one hand. "It is difficult to put into English words, for it is rooted in a world the English do not know. The closest I might come is to say he sees an ancientness inside you. He says you are one of the ones who can touch the ancientness and keep its spark alive. He says nothing else matters, not the wars, not the lives of nations, not kings and queens. What matters is that spark."

The ancientness. Was that what the Horse Guards and their king feared, that the world's ancientness would somehow render them insignificant? He reached to the bottom of the trunk and extracted the little bone he had saved for himself, the small irregular cylinder with a cavity down its center. It was itself ancient and mysterious and he had come to think of it as his personal link to the *incognitum*. He had wondered what to do with it, and had thought about giving it to Charles Thomson or Deborah Franklin, but they had not labored in the mud, carried the body of Ezra, sat in the Shawnee bone chamber, or lingered with Pierre by the pool of his life's blood. He removed the lanyard that held his Mohawk totem, then untied the knot at the top. It was not just in homage to Conawago or the Shawnee shaman that he threaded the lanyard through the hole in the bone and fastened it above his sacred quillwork pouch. It was also to confirm a growing bond he could not put a name to, a link to something ancient and powerful that he had released at the Lick.

He dozed, and was awakened by the angry voice of Lieutenant Nettles on the other side of the wall. "He should be awake by now!" Nettles insisted. "I must speak with him!"

"I told you, Lieutenant," Ishmael replied, "that there was a shock to his brain. If the ship's surgeon were here he might know the treatment, but we fear he is lost. A crewman says he saw you with one of his crates before he disappeared. Perhaps you know the fate of our doctor?"

The lieutenant hesitated. "Of course not, and damn your impertinence!" he finally rejoined. "Everyone knows Mr. McCallum had a reckless habit of walking the deck in the middle of the night. If he was leaning too far over the rail when the ship lurched it was his own damned fault!"

"Ah, well then," Ishmael said. "He was a tolerably fine fellow, our doctor. More than a few will miss him. But here your major lies, a victim as much of the doctor's absence as of the odd misfortune that broke his arm. That fracture is faring well with the splint. But the concussion is troublesome. If you like, I could try to drill a hole in his skull."

"A hole? Surely you jest! A hole in his skull?"

"It's a procedure called trepanning, to relieve the pressures of bad humors pressing upon the brain. I have never done it, but I have read about it. No doubt the ship's carpenter could help me. He has a wide selection of augers."

Duncan grinned at the stunned silence that followed.

"No, no," Nettles finally said, in a much subdued voice.

"Doubtless the army has good doctors in London," Ishmael suggested.

"Yes, yes, in London."

A moment later Duncan heard the door to the sick bay close and he pulled the stuffing from the crack to confirm that Ishmael was alone with Hastings, now lifting him to get a cup of honey and water down his throat.

"Swallow, you damned murderer," Ishmael whispered. "I would have thrown you over the side long ago but your friend Duncan won't have it. We need to tie up all your sins in a neat package for him. How lucky for you. It wouldn't be the Nipmuc way, wouldn't be the Mohawk way. I suspect it may not even be the Highland way. Mr. McCallum grows more English in his sensibilities. He doesn't grasp the great evils you are still capable of inflicting on us." Ishmael's voice had grown louder, and Duncan realized he meant for him to hear. He closed the hole in the wall and chanced a brief dash along the passageway to enter the sick bay.

Ishmael stood and with a wave of his hand yielded his patient to Duncan. Duncan quickly felt the man's pulse, looked at his dilated pupils, and laid his hand on the officer's forehead. "Mr. McCallum," Duncan declared in a chastising tone, "has not succumbed to English ways, he has grown more distrustful of them." Satisfied with his patient's condition, he turned to the young Nipmuc. "This conspiracy was hatched in London. We must sever it at its source or else it will strike at us again. And Hastings is our only link. Better to have an enemy we know and can track than one with no face and no trail."

Duncan prepared another dose, a half vial of laudanum, and as he administered it, they discussed London. Ishmael had identified three crewmen who had lived in the city, including Darby. The bosun had drawn a careful map of the city, responding to his questions, marking the locations of Craven Street, St. Paul's Cathedral, Westminster Abbey, the king's residence at St. James's Palace, and Charing Cross, complete with an odd stick figure with four legs and two heads that Ishmael explained was the famous equestrian statue of King Charles the First. Another sailor had drawn a cruder map with other landmarks pinpointed, mostly around Covent Garden.

"What are these?" Duncan asked.

Ishmael made a rumbling noise as if he needed to clear his throat. "Coffee houses and other establishments."

"Establishments?" Duncan read the names. "Mrs. Wagner's Lodge of Relaxation, the Sauce and Tail, the Garden of Escape." He paused, digesting the names. "These would be landmarks for visiting sailors. Bawdy houses."

"Not at all. Only the low, unhealthy places are called bawdy houses. These are places for making easy friendships, that's how the bosun put it," the young Nipmuc said with an awkward expression. "And he says such places always overflow with secrets of the city." He pulled the paper from Duncan and folded it into his pocket.

Several hours later a rap on Duncan's makeshift door announced the unexpected arrival of the captain, who presented a basket with a jar of ale, several hard-boiled eggs, and a sausage with fresh bread. Duncan nodded his gratitude. "A feast," he observed.

"We are rich in provisions since we took on stores against a much longer voyage," the Welshman explained. As Duncan sat on his cot shelling one of the eggs, the captain lowered himself onto the stool and extracted a sheaf of papers and a writing lead from his waistcoat. "There will be inquiries by the insurance association," he announced.

Duncan took a bite out of the egg. "Inquiries?"

"About your cargo. The ship is responsible. I will acknowledge that mischief on board resulted in the loss of your cargo."

"That would reflect badly on you," Duncan observed.

The captain gave a heavy sigh. "I am well-seasoned in arguing with owners. If I had exercised more authority over the blaggards, your troubles might have been averted."

"I doubt it. More likely you too would have been lost over the side."

"If the army has sunk so low, then it's a wonder the colonies haven't cast off the yoke long ago."

"There are honorable men who wear the king's uniform," Duncan offered half-heartedly.

"Too few, I wager." The captain extended one of the papers to Duncan. "The purser copied a list of your cargo off the manifest. If you sign it, I can begin the process with the association when we drop anchor."

Duncan did not take the paper. "Tell me, Captain," he asked after another bite of egg. "Are you well acquainted with London?"

"Aye, lived there ten years before the flux took my wife. That still sits hard with me, for I fear it may have been the city's foul miasmas that did her in."

Duncan opened the jar to fill the horn cup the captain had provided, then handed it to the Welshman. "Spend an hour with me and do me a small favor or two in London, and I will forgo my insurance claim."

The captain was indeed savvy about the old city, taking in the first map Ishmael had provided and recording a dozen more landmarks on it, even sketching in several streets and the outline of the parks around Whitehall and the site of Buckingham House, which was being converted into the king's new residence. He expressed surprise at Duncan's interest in Bedlam Hospital but readily drew a long narrow building to the northeast of the city's center. "Outside the old Moorgate," he explained, "excepting the gate itself was torn down eight years ago." He added lines around the hospital building. "The grounds are surprisingly spacious inside the great walls, with the southern perimeter covered by a long section of the ancient Roman wall. They built it after the great fire in the last century, and some say it was an effort to match the grand buildings of Paris." He added two short perpendicular lines in the center of the front wall. "There be some right hideous statues over the main entrance.

"And the Moorgate," he sighed, adding another short pair of lines intersecting the city wall. "I was that sorry to see the old gates demolished. Most had been there a thousand years and more. Seemed right arrogant for a gang of quill pushers to decide they must come down to serve their notion of a modern city. Progress comes too fast. Why, I hear there are great ugly steam machines doing work out in the mines. What of the poor men who are put out of work? There's even talk of putting such machines on ships. Who would ever take to the sea if their vessel was banging and coughing up smoke all day?" He shook his head. "There's big changes coming, whether we want or not. You can smell it in the London air, when it ain't choking ye."

Duncan filled his cup again. "And the Horse Guards?" he asked with a nod to the map.

Captain Rhys grimaced. "Ye mean the Horse Guards who tried to kill ye, who think they did kill ye and have been laughing about it ever since? If you love life, McCallum, stay away from them. If ye were smart ye would remain with the *Galileo* until I take her on the Boston run next month."

"Boston?"

"Aye, taking over dry goods from Yorkshire after a stay in the shipyard. The old girl needs her hull scraped and new copper plate installed. And I mean to strengthen some of her knees."

"The Horse Guards?" Duncan asked again.

The captain frowned. "They have a building in Whitehall, more like a small castle." He studied Duncan's map, still laid out before them, and placed a small X beside St. James's Park. "The Angels of Westminster, some in London call them. Not because they are saints but because as far as the king's business goes, they are incapable of committing a sin. That is to say they can commit it but they will nae be punished for it. They just march down the hall and ask forgiveness."

"Down the hall?"

"The Secretary at War and his Council keep their offices there. Some call the Guards their fancy serving boys."

In the middle of the night, seeing light filter through the hole in the wall, Duncan ventured back into the sick bay. Ishmael was carefully sharpening a scalpel, studying Hastings with a hungry eye. "I could fall," Ishmael suggested, "and accidentally cut his throat."

"Then stop carrying a scalpel," Duncan warned, then saw a half-filled vial of laudanum on the apothecary table. "Did you miss a dose? That should have all been used at his last dosing. We can't afford to have him wake."

"I lightened the dose," Ishmael confessed. "Just before the next dose he will become semiconscious. I told him I was Lieutenant Nettles and he responded to my questions."

"Ishmael! It is too risky!"

His Nipmuc friend ignored him. "His club is Boodles on a place called Pall Mall, his games are whist and piquet, and his favorite house of pleasure is Madame Roland's Finishing Academy, where he intends to go directly after we drop anchor."

"You heard all that?"

"In two sessions, with some cajoling. Even in his current state he is most perverse. I had to ask things indirectly, so I dropped the names of bawdy houses from the bosun's map and he cursed and said I should know he was faithful to Madame Roland."

As Duncan studied the prostrate major, Hastings stirred. Ishmael put some of the honey and water mixture to his lips and he drank.

"Christ, that ale is weak, Nettles," Hastings muttered, his eyes still closed.

Duncan jerked back into the shadows but saw Hastings's head loll sideways. Ishmael turned with a grin. This was the semiconscious state he had described. It was a great temptation to use it to their advantage, but also a great danger. The lieutenant might arrive, trapping Duncan in the sick bay. The level of Hastings's consciousness was impossible to gauge.

Ishmael made the decision for him. "What will we tell the colonel?" he asked Hastings.

Hastings turned up in a clownish grin, his eyes still closed. When he spoke his words were slurred. "You know the colonel is useless. It's the secretary and the earl who matter."

"But what shall we report to them?" Ishmael asked.

"Mission on course. So far so good, we tell them, but the campaign is far from over. The fat fool has spun a complex web. He must be stopped at all costs, Nettles. There is clearly more afoot than we estimated. The *incognitum*, the Covenant, the transit. The Council must understand! He uses them like weapons!" Hastings spoke in short, slurred sentences, his eyes still closed. "He is the hub, the rot that must be scoured clean. Too big a risk to ignore." He repeated faintly, "Too big a risk." Hastings's head rolled again and he seemed to have lost all consciousness.

Ishmael and Duncan exchanged a confused glance. "Stopped?" Ishmael ventured.

Hastings did not seem to hear. Duncan took a step toward the door. Suddenly the major's hand flailed the air and he grabbed Ishmael's arm, pulling him close. "If all else fails, Lieutenant, we must kill him! We must kill Benjamin Franklin!"

Chapter 10

B EST TO SPEND A COUPLE hours down in the bilges afore we drop anchor in the pool of the Thames," Darby explained as he guided Duncan and Ishmael toward Fleet Street. The bosun had been loaned by the captain as an escort for their first few hours in London. He gestured at Ishmael, who had been holding his hand over his nose and mouth. "Sort of seasons the nostrils, ye might say."

"If I had known, I would have begged Duncan to sew my nose closed," Ishmael growled. His excitement about arriving in the city had been overwhelmed by its stench. Except along the widest, most heavily used thoroughfares, piles of rotten refuse appeared at regular intervals. The gutters along both sides of the streets held sluggish streams of the excretions of London's residents, both two-legged and four.

Duncan, anticipating the reek, had taken a dozen cloves from the galley and kept one clenched in his front teeth as he studied the crowded streets. Several passing women pressed small bunches of flowers to their noses, sold on the cobbled streets to the hawkers' cry of "nosegay" and "posies." Ishmael, for the third time that hour, declined Duncan's offer of a clove, apparently thinking it less than warrior-like.

"Lobsterbacks," Darby muttered in warning as a squad of soldiers marched around the corner they were approaching. Duncan pulled his tricorn hat low but kept his eyes on the redcoats. He had not expected army patrols in London, but then he understood as an ornate coach-and-four came into view behind them. They were escorting a dignitary through the crowded streets.

"Don't gawk, boy," Darby warned. Duncan turned to see Ishmael staring at the extravagant vehicle, with a liveried driver on the front bench and a matching footman standing on a rear platform. Gilt-edged windows contrasted elegantly with the black enamel of the coach. The gleaming brasses on the harness all depicted the head of a lion.

Ishmael could not resist gazing at the coach, which was no doubt conveying a minor royal, and Duncan pulled him away just as some hard-looking men with quarterstaves began knocking heads to push back the crowd. Darby led them down another fetid alley and they emerged into a small but pleasant square that was the terminus of a paved street with several well-appointed brick and clapboard buildings of three and four stories. They followed Darby up the steps of the large one at the base of the square, scattering a group of youths gathered there with a good-natured cry of "Make way, ye sorry lubbers!" Several of them, clearly recognizing Darby, raised knuckles to their foreheads with suppressed laughs. He tussled the unkempt hair of the nearest. "Why, ye've grown half a foot since I saw ye, Robbie boy." The boy's face broke into a wide grin, and the taller boy beside him swelled up with pride as Darby patted his shoulder on the back and declared, "All shipshape, Captain Xander?"

"Loaded and ready for action, sir!" came the boy's ebullient reply.

"Good lads," he explained to Duncan after tapping a brass knocker in the shape of an anchor. "Link boys and runners," he added, then greeted the maid who opened the door with an exaggerated bow and stepped inside. "Welcome to Neptune's Crown," he announced, then aimed a nautical whistle down the hall that led to the rear of the building. "Most just call it the Neptune."

Duncan and Ishmael shared an amused glance over finding an inn by such a name in the heart of the city, but their expressions changed to wonder as they reached the common sitting room. The walls of the spacious, tidy chamber were lined with nautical charts and shelves that overflowed with books and models of ships. Some of the renderings were skillfully shaped cutaways of hulls, but most were intricate full-rigged miniatures of barks, brigs, frigates, schooners, and even a fat Dutch galliot.

Duncan laid his bag by the door and stepped closer to admire the closest model, that of a seventy-four-gun ship of the line, the main fighting machine of the British Navy, complete down to its tiny anchor chains.

"They call her a Third Rate," came a soft voice over his shoulder, "but that seems such a meager title for such a mighty ship." Duncan turned with surprise to see that the speaker was a big-boned woman in late middle age, whose left leg extending below her skirt was an ornate piece of wood carved with anchors and mermaids, adorned with a pewter cap. "This one's the *Bellona*," she explained with obvious pride, "the prototype, the first of our seventy-fours. Back in sixty-one she captured a French ship of the line. What a glorious fight that was! My Jasper was there, on a frigate off Cape Finisterre, God rest his soul."

Duncan nodded awkwardly. "A magnificent rendering," he offered, casting a questioning glance at Darby.

"Yer landlady," Darby explained. "Mrs. Clementine Laws. She is as seasoned a battle veteran as ye'll find anywhere in the Royal Navy."

Duncan made a respectful bow. "Duncan McCallum. Your servant, ma'am."

Ishmael, however, could not take his eyes off the woman's peg leg until she lifted it and tapped the pewter knob against his shin. "Not polite to gape at a lady's bare legs, son," she chided with a good-natured smile.

Ishmael seemed not to hear her. "Where?" he asked in confused wonder.

"Where's my original flipper? Fish bait long ago. A godforsaken French cannonball knocked it off."

"But the navy doesn't have—"

"Doesn't have wenches manning her guns? I should say not, more's the pity. After my darling Jasper retired out of the navy as a ship's master, he bought hisself a merchantman with his accumulated prize money. He wanted me to accompany him but I said only if he would buy me my very own brass nine-pounder, as a gift of the heart. A small gun, ladylike, ye might say. We was off the coast of Hispaniola when a French privateer came out for us. It was touch and go, I must admit, but I had my brass nine in the cabin set as a stern chaser and I brought her foremast down. The damned frogs took one last shot, the best they got off that day. It took out half of our lovely leaded-glass windows and my leg below the knee. Lying stunned on the deck, I didn't even know it until Jasper picks up my leg and waves it at me. 'Clem,' says he, 'we've had our last waltz,' and he tosses it to the fishes. Right cross I was too, 'cause I would've made a fine knife hilt out of the bone." She shrugged, then called for a scullery girl to collect the spittoons and turned back to the still wide-eyed Ishmael.

"After that we cashed out and bought this place. Mr. Laws spent his last years building them models."

"Extraordinary," Duncan said, now admiring a well-polished ship's bell mounted by the entrance to a simply furnished but commodious dining room.

Mrs. Laws puffed with pride. "Sometimes the navy shipwrights from Portsmouth ask to borrow a model for a spell, to check their own designs."

"A room or two?" Duncan asked. He was anxious to get settled and make contact with Franklin.

The innkeeper nodded. "And didn't the good Captain Rhys send word this hour and more? My two best on the top floor, if ye don't mind three flights of stairs. Quiet and a fine long view of Westminster," she declared, her gaze settling over Ishmael, who had ventured to another model which sat in a pool of light by the front window. "An eighteen-gun corvette, sleek as a cat," she explained as she approached him, then halted, studying the young Nipmuc in the brighter light. She tilted her head in surprise, then with two taps of her pewter knob was at his side, lifting a hand. He froze as she extended a finger toward his jaw.

"Prithee, young sir," she asked as she gently traced her finger along the row of small tattooed fish that ran parallel to his ear and down his neck. "Might ye be an aborigine?"

Ishmael stepped back and bowed. "Of the Nipmuc tribe," he intoned in a solemn voice, then said in his native tongue, "Health and harmony be on this lodge and all who dwell in it."

As Mrs. Laws began a curtsy, made awkward by her wooden leg, a squeal of delight interrupted them from the shadows by the stairway. The landlady rolled her eyes, then called over her shoulder, "Lizzie, come out of hiding and make yer greeting, girl."

A young woman wearing long blond braids, of no more than twenty years, appeared blushing with excitement. She made a quick curtsy to Duncan and a longer one to Ishmael. She seemed to struggle for words, finally murmured a hasty "your honor," then straightened and declared, "I have the top floor."

Mrs. Laws gave the chambermaid a gentle push. "Be about yer chores, lass." The blond maid scurried back into the shadows. "I shall do what I can to protect ye, sir," she said to Ishmael with a businesslike air, then gestured Duncan toward the small desk in the corner where the guest register lay.

"The captain said three weeks and perhaps more," Mrs. Laws said as Duncan sat at the desk, "and he will take a berth here as well after the *Galileo* goes into the shipyard." She glanced up at Ishmael. "No need for ye to wait," she said to the young Nipmuc. "Now where's our pious porter?" She craned her neck toward the kitchens. "Sinner John! Clap on! Action stations!"

Ishmael followed the porter, a stern man with a scarred, lean face and close-cropped hair, up the stairs with the baggage. Minutes later when Duncan found their rooms, however, he was nowhere to be seen. The two small but comfortable rooms connected through a door in their common wall, and Duncan found Ishmael's bags on the bed of the adjoining chamber. He was about to close the gaping door of a narrow closet when he discovered it was not a closet but a low, short passage that led to a smaller hatch-like door that was also ajar, spilling brilliant sunlight.

Duncan's shoulders brushed each side of the passage as he stooped and proceeded down it, discovering that it opened onto a small flat at the base of the roof that provided access for those working on the chimneys or slates. Ishmael was sitting on a small step built into the intersection of adjoining roofs, staring wide-eyed at the remarkable scene before them.

"London," the young Nipmuc whispered as Duncan reached his side. There was awe in his face but also a hint of apprehension. "I never imagined it would be so!"

"Blessed Michael!" The Gaelic exclamation slipped off Duncan's tongue without conscious thought. He had carefully studied the map from the *Galileo*, but the chart had given no hint of the scale or size of the city's buildings. The rooftop perch offered a sweeping view to the south, west, and north. In the distance the majestic twin towers of Westminster Abbey rose over a vast landscape of parkland and elegant stone buildings. Ishmael pointed to a busy square adjoined by a massive three-story building that was only a few blocks away. "That has to be Charing Cross," he said, "with the statue of the old king on his horse and the great Northumberland House beside it."

Duncan extracted the map, and with Charing Cross and the Abbey as reference points they quickly identified the Palace of Westminster where Parliament met, St. James's Palace, Buckingham House, and the long green space known as

St. James's Park. With a chill, his gaze settled upon the slate roof of a long building between the park and the Thames. It was the home of the Horse Guards.

He looked back at the surprisingly plain St. James's Palace, where the king resided while Buckingham House was being remodeled to the tastes of Queen Charlotte. He was a fool to think he might prevail against Hastings. Hastings wouldn't be alone. The major would have the entire Horse Guards regiment at his side. And behind them would be the Secretary at War and the War Council. Ultimately, he wasn't fighting Hastings; he was fighting the king, and this mighty city. It wasn't a fool's errand he was on—it was a death wish. *You will die again and again*, the prophet had warned.

His gaze shifted to his companion, and he saw that Ishmael was now trying to maintain his balance halfway up the steep roof, seeking an eastern view. "Moorgate," the young Nipmuc said. "The bosun said it was by the old Moorgate." He was already trying to find Conawago.

"It's still a couple hours until nightfall," Duncan said. "If we can make contact with Dr. Franklin today, we can scout Bethlem Hospital tomorrow morning."

"I will go to Bedlam now," Ishmael countered. "Franklin is not my concern."

Duncan helped the Nipmuc off the steep, slippery slates, then gently set him on the bench. "You are too young to have ventured into enemy territory, to learn from a raid on Huron or Abenaki camps," he said. "There is no safe place in such raids, no room for mistake, no chance to retreat to nurse wounds or find reinforcements. One misstep and it is over. That's where we are, Ishmael, on unfamiliar terrain with possible enemies at every step. You cannot just walk into the halls of this Bedlam and demand your uncle's release. And Franklin is the concern of every Son of Liberty. We go together or we go not at all."

Ishmael was silent for several breaths, but the defiance that had flared on his face faded. He gazed again over the city, his awe gradually replaced with confusion. "Never before have I looked out over a land and seen almost nothing but buildings. The bosun said hundreds of thousands live here. How is that possible? I can't fathom so many people choosing to live in such a cramped place, walking in their waste, turning their backs on nature. It frightens me," he admitted. "There are no spirits left here." It was his way of agreeing with Duncan. "No wild animals," he added. The tribes kept harmony with their world by considering themselves just one more type of creature in the vast mysterious forest. In his early years with the tribes, Duncan had been chastised more than once for acting as though he were above, or more important than, the forest's other creatures. No wild animals meant there was nothing to keep human humility in check.

Duncan pointed to a flock of pigeons that had appeared from the direction of Charing Cross. "There's messengers at least," he said. The tribes believed that birds and snakes carried messages to the gods, much as the Vikings who had settled the Highland coast believed that ravens went out into the world each day to bring news back to Odin.

Ishmael frowned. "Those fat ugly things? They're like the rest of these city creatures. They probably forgot how to speak with the spirits ages ago."

"Make way! Make way for important personages!" the ragged boy in front of Duncan cried, tapping a man in front of them with the pole on which the boy carried a lantern. When Duncan had asked Mrs. Laws for directions to the Franklin residence on Craven Street, she had fussed over their appearance, ordering Lizzie to brush their clothes, then insisting Duncan hire a link boy. When he had met her request with a blank stare, she had taken him to the front steps and summoned Xander from the throng of adolescent boys watching the lamplighter make his way down the street.

Link boys were apparently fixtures on London streets, hired by those who were afoot to guide them through the shadowy labyrinths of the city. When the porter pointed out that link boys mostly were used at night, Mrs. Laws rejoined that dusk was fast approaching and then, considering the somber man with salt-and-pepper hair for a moment, ordered him to join the party. "Sinner John may look like a chewed-up piece of gristle," she explained good-naturedly, "but he spent nigh fifty years at sea and he's as canny as any on the streets."

"Sinner?" Ishmael asked.

Mrs. Laws sighed. "He spent too much time in Bristol after putting ashore."

The explanation did little to dispel Ishmael's confusion. "Bristol turned him into a sinner?" he asked.

The landlady gave a cackling laugh. "Bristol made him a damned Methodist. It's where those troublemaking Wesley brothers settled for a few years. Put a few drops of rum in him and ye'll likely hear about his wild life on the seven seas. South Pacific tarts and such. He insists on being called a sinner to keep him mindful of his repentance. He's an able-bodied creature, the bosun of my ship ye might say. It's only every few weeks that his evangelical ardor erupts." She put a hand on Duncan's arm. "Please take him, Mr. McCallum. You don't know the dangers of London's streets after dark."

They made an odd procession as the link boy Xander led them out onto the Strand. Ultimately Mrs. Laws had not been satisfied with Duncan's old waistcoat and had brought him a somber tunic with tails that had been used on formal occasions by her husband, saying that Dr. Franklin was a man of high station who would expect finery.

Behind Duncan was a subdued Ishmael, who wore a strip of white ermine tied around his head, also loaned by the landlady, who had insisted that Dr. Franklin would be enchanted if he could just make his aborigine origins more apparent. Ishmael, however, had declined the maid Lizzie's offer to braid his long black hair.

At the rear Sinner John, carrying an oaken quarterstaff, strode in grim silence except for occasional condemning syllables muttered to passersby. "Harlot!" he barked to a woman with a low bodice, then "Papist!" to a man wearing a crucifix. He seemed to have a knack for spotting fellow sinners.

A quarter hour later they came to a halt before an entry in a long row of four-story brick town houses just off Charing Cross. Sinner John rushed forward and took the boy by the shoulder, aiming him into an arched tunnel that led to the stables behind the houses. "Mustn't presume to call all sudden-like at the front door of such a famous personage," he warned. "We ain't been expected or announced. Kitchen door is the path for humble Christians."

When they reached the back door with a numeral seven painted over it, the pious porter arranged Duncan and Ishmael side by side, then had the link boy knock. Duncan had just recalled he had a letter for Franklin written by Charles Thomson and was reaching for it when the door opened. A woman in her early twenties, wearing a gray dress and a white apron, put one foot out the door, then frowned.

"It's past sunset, ye know," she declared in a disapproving tone, then leaned inside and called. "Mrs. Stevenson!"

Moments later a well-fed, tidy-looking woman of mature age appeared and gave them a disappointing shake of her head. "I've seen much better pretend savages," she declared with disapproval as she studied Ishmael. "I can plainly see you're just another of those dark Irish always begging in one disguise or another." She pushed Xander's lantern away, as if steering him back down the alley.

Duncan found himself strangely tongue-tied. On nights floating on the Ohio they had speculated about Franklin and his residence in London, and for weeks he had carefully guarded the slip of paper with the address on it. The reality of at last being at Craven Street, at the house of the great Franklin, suddenly seized him. He had forgotten his rehearsed words and began to fumble for the introductory letter provided by Charles Thomson.

When they did not move, Mrs. Stevenson frowned.

Sinner John began a hymn. "Oh for a thousand tongues to sing," he bellowed in a rich baritone, "my blest Redeemer's praise. The glories of my God and King, the triumphs of his grace."

Mrs. Stevenson rolled her eyes and spoke to the maid. "Wesley men," she said with a sigh. "Too ardent to tolerate, too pious to ignore. Bring whatever's broken, Judith."

"The triumphs of his grace!" Sinner John continued, so loudly his words were echoing down the alley. Mrs. Laws had said his evangelical ardor erupted only every few weeks. Now it was spewing forth like a volcano.

Mrs. Stevenson maintained her smoldering gaze until Judith reappeared, holding a flour sack which she tossed to the link boy's feet. Sinner John had started another verse, so loudly Mrs. Stevenson had to shout. "If you do not vacate my yard at once we shall summon the watch!" She turned and slammed the door. Sinner John, not seeming to hear, continued his hymn.

Ishmael opened the bag, revealing half a loaf, a shank bone with some meat left on it, and two potatoes. Xander reached in with a cry of delight and began chewing a potato. They had been given a broken meal, the proper reward for beggars, consisting of the leavings of the Franklin dinner table.

Forgoing further advice from their new household, Duncan and Ishmael stole out of the inn before dawn and set an easterly course through the shadows of the great city. In the parlor the night before, Mrs. Laws had shared a well-worn map of London, the "famous one published by John Roque," and Duncan had spent an hour supplementing the crude map they had brought from the *Galileo.* They had but to find the old Moorgate, since the bosun had told them once they passed through that gap in the ancient city wall, the "palace of the lunatics" would be impossible to miss.

The slumbering city was quiet but not silent, and a surprising number of its inhabitants were in fact not sleeping. Carts stacked with crates of chickens, slabs of bacon, and baskets of peas and other early vegetables trundled down the streets toward the markets at Covent Garden and Hungerford. Some were pulled by horses and mules, some by heavy dogs, and more than a few by weary men and women. Stern men in dark clothing, armed with staffs, paced slowly along many blocks. These were the watch, their companions the evening before had explained, each responsible to their parish for their assigned patch of the city, and more than once Duncan and Ishmael ducked into an alley to the surly cry of "on wi' ye wastrels!" from one of the patrolling sentinels. Duncan realized that they appeared suspicious, for they neither wore the dandy clothes of late-night revelers nor carried anything that indicated they were bound for work. In one such alley he found a pile of hoes, and after they each leaned one on their shoulders they were challenged no more.

As they came to the quieter streets of Ludgate Hill, Duncan increased his pace to reach a party of laborers ahead of them, then realized Ishmael was not beside him. The Nipmuc had halted a hundred feet behind and was staring, his mouth agape.

"How is it possible?" Ishmael whispered as Duncan reached his side. "Can it be the work of ordinary mortals or did their god just drop it here?"

Duncan followed his awed gaze toward a massive shadow behind the row of buildings before them. The sky was rapidly brightening, making the towering dome glow in the dawn. Duncan did not need to consult his map. "St. Paul's Cathedral," he said and was himself now struck dumb by the immensity of the structure. "Built in the last century by a mere mortal named Christopher Wren."

"We must see it! Look at the stonework! Look at the carvings! We must ascend to the dome! It touches the heavens! Surely up there the gods will take notice of us!"

"We must get to Bedlam," Duncan reminded him.

Ishmael sobered, then clenched his jaw and swung the hoe back on his shoulder. "We must get to Bedlam," he echoed.

Twice Duncan asked for directions, the second time from a more congenial watchman who was whistling in the dawn. "'Tis the gap in the old wall along the next street over," he explained. "If they hadn't tore down the gate a few years ago you could have seen it from here. A good solid gate. Disrespectful to our noble ancestors that was," he added with a frown. "Disturbed many a Roman ghost." He glanced toward the rising sun. "Soon enough you can be guided by the howls from the other side of the old wall."

"Howls?" Duncan asked.

"It's nearly the breakfast hour at Bedlam. Those poor wretches will soon be screeching like hyenas for their porridge and tea."

Their pace slowed as the ancient city wall came into view, each filled with dread of what they would find on the other side. The stories heard on board the *Galileo* and written in London gazettes came back to Duncan, nearly overwhelming him with images of inmates wallowing naked in mud, nibbling their own flesh, and communicating only with the sounds of pigs and donkeys.

"They don't really restrain them with chains and ropes, do they?" Ishmael asked in a tight voice.

Duncan wasn't certain of anything about the notorious hospital, but he would not let his worry show. "Of course not. I hear the establishment is run by trained doctors. It is a hospital, not a stable. Conawago is probably just working as an assistant to one of the learned men. Or perhaps he organized a hospital newspaper," he added, invoking the elder Nipmuc's role as editor of the journal published in Edentown.

Ishmael forced a laugh, then fell silent as they passed through the gap in the high city wall. They walked silently along the newer wall that appeared before them, turning with it at the end of the block, then halting to peer in confusion through a large arched gate that opened onto a gravel drive. "It must be behind the palace," Ishmael suggested, indicating the huge ornate structure with a central tower and faux pillars that sat beyond spacious gardens.

Duncan stepped back to study the elegant gate. BETHLEM HOSPITAL, read the inscription carved into the entrance arch, beneath two hideous sculptures of naked men with tormented faces. One of the figures was labeled MELANCHOLY and the other, wrapped in chains, was RAVING MADNESS. From the long palace before them animallike wails could be heard. They had arrived at Bedlam.

The bushes and trees of the gardens on either side of the wide drive were overdue for trimming, but the lawns were kept short by a small herd of grazing sheep. From somewhere inside the building came what sounded like a trumpet sounding a military call. The cries died away, and to Duncan's surprise a harpsichord started playing what sounded like Bach.

They stepped aside for a hackney cab that dropped off a distinguished-looking gentleman carrying a leather satchel of a size used for surgical instruments. For a moment Duncan wondered why patients confined for mental disturbances would need surgery, then with a terrible chill recalled how Sarah's father had concluded her fierce Mohawk-bred independence was a mental illness and devised a surgical treatment by London doctors.

They sat on a stone bench near the stately portico, each at a loss for words. After two more hackney coaches deposited somberly dressed men carrying medical kits, Ishmael sprang to his feet and, before Duncan could react, entered the building. Duncan muttered a Gaelic curse and followed.

They found themselves in a great hall that at first glance might have seemed the entrance to a royal residence. Large paintings were hung in the three landings of the elegant marble stairs. The massive wings on either side of the entrance hall were built around wide galleries, affording views down the entire length of the building, which Duncan estimated to be more than five hundred feet. An air of reverence had been attempted with a huge painting, hanging over the stairs, of an angel receiving humans who floated up to her outstretched arms. But the humans she greeted were all deformed, grotesque beings with humped backs, misshapen skulls, furry tails, and even some limbs that ended with clawed or hoofed feet. While some of the other paintings were innocuous renderings of pastoral scenes, most had beings that looked like beasts out of Dante's *Inferno*, an impression only increased by the sculptures arrayed along the curve of the rear wall, which included a naked woman with a cat's head, a bull with a man's head, and an ape reading a Bible. More than a few physicians ascribed mental illness to the soul of an animal taking over that of a human.

As if the images were not disturbing enough, noxious smells wafted through the hall. The stench of excrement and urine mingled with those of soap, vinegar, and strong black tea. Men in matching brown waistcoats and britches, apparently staff, were emerging from chambers at the back of the main gallery, shepherding patients out of a dining chamber and opening windows, which created new currents of air that seemed to just circulate the same foul odors. Duncan tried to calculate the number of rooms or cells in the massive building. There had to be hundreds of inmates, and if they were locked in their chambers they were all using chamber pots. Even in the best of hospitals, chamber pots were not always emptied every day.

Duncan realized that Ishmael was pretending to examine the sculptures while inching toward the marble stairs. He had put a foot on the first step when a voice rang out in challenge.

"Wait your turn, young sir," called the man in brown who descended from the first landing of the stairway. His clothing matched that of the other staff except he had an epaulet on one shoulder, which seemed to indicate rank. A silver watch chain ran from a button into a waistcoat pocket. "Visiting hours are posted at the door," he declared, "and they don't start until two o'clock of the afternoon." He blocked Ishmael's path and held up a restraining hand as he saw the resentment in the Nipmuc's eyes.

Duncan moved closer, worried that Ishmael might use force against the man. "But I have family here," Ishmael said instead.

"Nary a difference. Kin or kith, student or pilgrim, all the same to us."

Duncan gently pulled Ishmael away. "Pilgrim?" he asked.

"Well, yes, some are sent by their pastors and such to witness the fate of the fallen. Course, most just come for the entertainment. Sunday's our busiest day, when we allow picnicking on the lawns. Line goes out to the street on holidays." The man worked his tongue around his cheek, assessing the two strangers. "Tickets are required," he said as if in invitation.

"A ticket to visit the sick?" Duncan asked.

"We keepers have steep expenses. Counter opens at noon. One pence apiece," he declared, then glanced around and whispered, "Or half a shilling gets you two tickets now and I'll mark them so no need for you fine gentlemen to wait in line."

Duncan pushed down his bile and handed the man a coin. They received two pasteboard tokens, which the keeper pierced with a little pin hanging from his watch chain, and backed away. Duncan felt a shudder as he left the building and Ishmael rushed past him as if being chased.

"What is this place?" the young Nipmuc asked when Duncan caught up with him. Anguish twisted his features. "Is it a hospital? Or a prison? Or one of those zoological gardens you read about in the journals?"

"Apparently all three," Duncan replied bitterly. He glanced back at the entry, unable to shake the sense that something sinister dwelled deep in the building. He gestured Ishmael toward the gravel path that ran along the east wing. "Focus on what we learned," he urged, trying to calm himself as much as Ishmael. "There are offices past the main hall. They must keep records there, records that will tell us where Conawago is in that great labyrinth."

"If they used his real name."

Duncan ignored him. "Records that will tell us who sent him here. It is a huge, complicated building with scores of staff, which might be to our advantage."

"And the staff is corrupt," Ishmael added.

"The staff is corrupt," Duncan agreed, "and apparently used to accommodating a steady stream of strangers coming and going." They studied the structure in silence before Duncan spoke again. "During the war my friend Patrick Woolford and I walked right into an enemy camp, undetected because there were so many strangers there who did not know each other."

"And later you returned with long rifles and war axes," Ishmael suggested in a hopeful tone.

Duncan had no response. The terrain before them was much more treacherous than that of a French War camp. As they walked along the long wing, he saw figures not wearing the brown of the staff lingering at the windows. Under several windowsills were long stains where the contents of pots had been poured out. At one open window a man urgently pointed into the sky, though there was nothing there but a solitary cloud. At another a middle-aged woman lifted her tunic to expose her breasts to them. At two more, inmates waited until they were close, then with cackling laughs tried, unsuccessfully, to empty chamber pots on their heads.

As they continued along the path, the elegance of the hospital facade increasingly gnawed at Duncan. It had been designed, he suspected, to mimic a French palace, but to house the mentally imbalanced behind it seemed to somehow mock them and those who cared about them. He had heard that one of the grandest structures in King Louis's Versailles compound was the zoological confine where exotic creatures were displayed for the entertainment of the king and his public.

"The stonework has a lot of mortar cracks, all the way up to the roof," Ishmael observed as they reached the end of the building. "And the ivy at the end grows nearly to the top."

"It was built in the last century, after the great fire. It's showing its—" He paused as Ishmael's words sank in. "You are not going to climb the walls of Bedlam." Ishmael was as agile as a spider on vertical surfaces. More than once Duncan had watched him scale heights that he would have been terrified to attempt. "Not yet," he added when he saw a defiant gleam in Ishmael's eyes. "Not until we better understand the challenges we face."

Ishmael raised his token between two fingers. "We must return at two this afternoon. If I don't find him I will hide and pass the night inside."

Duncan's skin crawled at the thought of spending the night in the lunatics' hospital. "We shall watch the building until then." He eyed the side of the building. "There are small courtyards in the rear," he pointed out, "bounded by the old city wall. Perhaps if we can find—"

"No, not we," Ishmael interrupted. His voice was thick with emotion. "You have business on Craven Street. Go consult with the lightning wizard about the Shawnee bones. I will meet you here for the afternoon entertainment," he said and quickly turned away. Ishmael, the sturdy Nipmuc warrior, looked like he might weep.

Chapter 11

B Y THE TIME DUNCAN RETURNED to the Neptune, his best clothes had been aired and pressed. When she learned he had not eaten, Mrs. Laws insisted on serving Duncan a plate of collops, then tried unsuccessfully to convince him to have Sinner John accompany him when he said he was going to explore the grand buildings along the Mall. To his dismay, however, the innkeeper was standing at the front door, arms akimbo, when he finally descended from his room.

"What's the bulky package?" she asked suspiciously, nodding to the bundle under his arm.

"Just an old pair of shoes in need of repair," he answered. "I saw a cobbler on the square." He felt guilty about speaking falsely, but she gave him no choice. His mission was not one he would share. Before she could reply, he offered a quick bow and darted into the street.

The Strand was packed with vendors, sweepers, and hackney cabs. The air rattled with the cries of hawkers. He weaved around men shouting "Socks, fine socks, two pair to the shilling!" and "Chairs to mend, who will have chairs to mend?" Young girls called in oddly mournful voices, "Mackerel, fresh mackerel, who shall eat fresh mackerel today?" He was relieved to turn onto the relative quiet of Craven Street, but then a wave of boyish anxiety swept over him again. Benjamin Franklin was like a star whose orbit he had been drawn into. Duncan had known Franklin's wife Deborah for years, had often been in his house in Philadelphia, had frequented an electrical laboratory Franklin had helped establish, and had even heard a distant Shawnee chief speak of the master of lightning. Did Duncan really presume now to impose on the famous man? Without conscious thought he walked past the town house, desperately trying to remember the introduction he had rehearsed. He touched the letter in his pocket and hefted the bundle in his hand, deciding they would be introduction enough.

Mindful of Sinner John's admonition about arriving unannounced at the front door of such an esteemed personage, he retreated through the arched tunnel into the service alley and again found the steps leading into Number 7. The door was slightly ajar, and he heard activity inside, what sounded like whispers and soft laughter. He decided that he might indeed be better off starting with the kitchen staff, especially if they were in such good moods.

He knocked twice with no response, then twice again, harder. He heard another laugh. "Bring it in, boy," called an amused, distracted voice.

Duncan took a hesitant step past the door that had been slammed in his face the night before. Two figures stood at a high table in the center of the spacious kitchen, making bread. The maid Judith, flour on her apron and face, was assisting the jovial cook, a rotund older man who also wore an apron, as well as a cook's linen cap tilted jauntily on his head. A small circle of flour adorned the tip of his nose.

The cook pointed to a small table by the door without turning. "Just there, son, and tell your master we'd like a fine turkey for the Sunday feast."

Judith, paying closer attention to their visitor, turned and straightened her apron, then made a rumbling in her throat as if to caution the cook. When he finally turned the plump man frowned. "That's no goose," the cook observed, nodding at Duncan's parcel. "I'm fairly confident we can't prepare goose pie without a goose."

"And I am no delivery boy for the poultryman. I was hoping for a word with Dr. Franklin. I've just arrived from Philadelphia."

"Of course you have," the cook said in a disappointed tone, then cracked open the oven, releasing a scent of baking bread before turning to the maid with a chagrined shrug.

Judith stepped between them, as if to shield the cook. "The front door must be used for social calls," she announced, seeming unreasonably irritated over Duncan's arrival.

"I didn't want to impose," Duncan said.

"Front door," Judith repeated, then advanced with arms extended, to herd him out the door. For a second time it was slammed on him.

The reception in the kitchen had done nothing to calm Duncan's nerves, and by the time he reached the Craven Street entrance, he felt like a boy awaiting a dressing down from his schoolmaster. He rapped the big brass knocker three times and stepped back. Footsteps could be heard approaching the door, followed by a long pause before the door was opened. Judith appeared again, her face cleaned of flour and the apron covering her simple gray dress gone. She was brushing away a few particles of flour from her shoulder when he removed his hat and offered a bow, which raised an impish giggle.

"I am but the kitchen maid, sir," she said, then offered a curtsy and giggled again. "The mistress is out, and the doctor's secretary generally doesn't arrive until ten of the clock, but the master will receive visitors in his sitting room." She motioned to the wooden staircase behind her. As Duncan took a step toward it, she darted in front of him. "I should announce you, 'tis the proper way."

Duncan offered a smile and a nod. "Duncan McCallum of Edentown in the New York colony."

She narrowed her eyes. "But you said Philadelphia in the kitchen."

"Edentown by way of Philadelphia," he corrected. "There are many more ships available in Philadelphia."

Judith gave a tentative nod, then gathered her skirts and motioned for him to follow. She cleared her throat loudly when they arrived at the ample sitting room at the top of the stairs. "Mr. Duncan McCallum of—" She considered her words for moment, then with a satisfied nod added "of the colonies." She spun about and disappeared down the stairs.

The heavy drapes on the windows were opened only a handsbreadth, and in the reduced light Duncan thought the room empty, concluding the great man must be in the room beyond. He took a step toward its cracked door, spying a four-poster bed inside, then the drapes on the nearest window were opened a few more inches and he froze.

"You have something from Pennsylvania," came a thin, disinterested voice, and the cook from the kitchen stepped out of the shadows. His apron was gone but the linen cap was still perched on his head. A buff-colored waistcoat hugged his belly, the girth of which seemed amplified by the watch chain stretched tightly across it. He pointed to a large wooden chest under the second window. "We already have ten jars of Pennsylvania honey," he observed, "bolts of Pennsylvania homespun, untold pieces of needlepoint, most of them featuring lightning bolts, as well as deer antlers, a chess set carved from walnut shells, and a walking stick carved with the leaves of every native tree."

The cook stepped forward with a sigh and nodded to the bundle Duncan held. "Prithee forgive me. I sound ungrateful. My gout kept me awake much of the night."

Duncan gripped the bundle under his arm more securely. "It is for Dr. Franklin, sir," he stated, glancing again at the bedroom.

A rumble came from the stairway and a sturdy woman appeared, still wrapped in a shawl from the street, which she tossed into the arms of the breathless Judith, running up behind her. Duncan recognized her as Mrs. Stevenson, who had ejected him the night before, and retreated a step.

"Lord save us!" the woman exhaled. "I can't even go to market but the house is turned upside down!" She hesitated, eyeing Duncan, then gave him a quick curtsy before darting to the cook, who stood stiffly as she wiped the flour from his nose and grabbed the cap from his head, revealing a high balding forehead and releasing long graying hair that fell loose around his shoulders.

"Benjamin, I declare!" she scolded. "Where are your manners? And you have been romping in the kitchen again!"

Duncan stared in disbelief at the man he had taken for the cook. Color rose on Benjamin Franklin's face and he seemed to have difficulty finding his voice. He cleared his throat several times. "Important principles of chemistry can be observed in the preparation of bread, Meg," he declared in his defense. "Why, the yeast alone is—"

The woman rolled her eyes. "Sir," she interrupted, "you have a guest who came across the great ocean to see you. This is my house too and we do not condone inhospitable behavior."

Franklin hung his head in defeat. "I'm sure the gentleman is just paying his respects while out on other business," he suggested.

The woman stared at him, arms folded across her breast with the air of an impatient schoolmarm. Franklin sighed, then retrieved a cold cup of tea from the sideboard, drained it, and turned to Duncan with renewed vigor. "Apologies, sir. I am just a meager printer who has stumbled unprepared into London society." He put an arm across his belly and made an effort at a bow. "Benjamin Franklin. Your servant, sir," he offered. "And this formidable matron," he added with a mischievous grin, "is Margaret Stevenson, my landlady and particular friend. Set your gift on the table and let's see if I can assist in your travels in some small way. Perhaps you want a souvenir signature? I have some cards somewhere," he said, looking back at the desk in the corner. "My secretary Henry will find them. He's most efficient. And meanwhile we shall have some tea," he added to Mrs. Stevenson, with a hopeful uplift in his voice. "The good china?"

Duncan suddenly felt a weariness that went soul deep. All his trials of recent months, the blood, the murders, the Atlantic gale, his own near death had come to this, a bizarre encounter with a distracted man in a London sitting room worried about his porcelain and gout. "No," he said in a tight voice.

Franklin stiffened and stood straighter. Mrs. Stevenson inched toward the hearth, glancing at the tools there, then her brows lifted. "You were at the back door last night!" she exclaimed, and snatched up the poker.

"I mean no, you misunderstand," Duncan continued. "I am here for neither a favor nor a memento."

Franklin moved toward his landlady, who raised the poker. "Explain yourself, sir," he stated.

Duncan silently unfolded the sack he had been carrying, reached into it, and extended the contents toward Franklin. "My name is Duncan McCallum," he answered in a tired voice. "I went down the Ohio for you."

The wizard of lightning gasped and thrust a hand to his chest. His eyes bulged with excitement. "The *incognitum* at last!" he cried. "Can it be true? Margaret, the *incognitum*! Dear God, I had begun to give up hope!" Franklin advanced toward Duncan, groping in his waistcoat pockets. He produced a pair of spectacles, threading the wire temples around his ears as he bent over the ancient tooth. Small syllables of delight escaped him as he hovered over the relic, but he did not touch it.

"Tea," Franklin said to Mrs. Stevenson, "our very best for this hero. And some of the fresh bread and marmalade." He motioned Duncan toward a gaming table set between two overstuffed chairs, then disappeared into his bedroom. He returned moments later with a red velvet pillow that he set on the table. "What a treasure!" he cackled as Duncan lowered the tooth onto the pillow. "The Gift of the Magi! Golconda! El Dorado!" Franklin ran a finger along the dark chestnut enamel of the sides, laughing now, then touched the rippled ridges along the top with a satisfied cooing sound.

"*Incognitum, incognitum,*" he chanted with boyish excitement, then collected himself and studied Duncan with new interest. "You are a student of Pierre's? Is he still resting from the voyage? And that fine man Ezra, did he perchance make the voyage?"

"Perhaps you should sit, sir," Duncan suggested.

"Nonsense, I am too excited. Perhaps the four of us can have luncheon together. So much to tell. I must hear every detail of your expedition."

Duncan stared at the inventor for several silent breaths. "Ezra and Professor Dumont were murdered," he finally stated.

Franklin looked up over his spectacles, his smile lingering but the joy evaporating from his eyes. "I'm not sure I heard you correctly."

"Our mutual friends were killed by men seeking to prevent the delivery of the *incognitum* to you."

Franklin staggered to the nearest chair and collapsed into it. He had trouble breathing, as if the wind had been driven from him. He did not at first seem to see the letter Duncan extended before him. When he finally focused on it he did not touch it, but raised his brows in query.

"From Charles Thomson," Duncan explained.

Franklin took the letter with an anguished expression and rose to go to a wooden chair by the window to read in the sunlight. Duncan watched him briefly, then his gaze drifted around the chamber. A half dozen jars with metal coatings and metal rods rising out of them were lined up on the mantel. He had seen such containers in Philadelphia and recognized them as Leyden jars, used for storing electricity. Large sheets of paper were pinned to the wall beside the hearth, each with an intricate drawing. One was of a great balloon with two men waving from its gondola basket, another of a trestle bridge, and the third of a machine Duncan did not recognize. Bookshelves surrounded the door to the bedroom, packed with scores of leather-bound volumes. In a glass box hung on the wall was a large medal with a plate that read ROYAL SOCIETY COPLEY MEDAL 1753. Beside it were two framed honorary degrees, one from Oxford and one from the University of St. Andrew in Scotland.

Despairing sounds came from Franklin as he read but he did not look up, did not speak. Mrs. Stevenson arrived with a tray and set it on the sideboard at the back wall as Judith collected the dirty dishes that had been left there. The landlady gazed at Franklin with obvious affection, then deep concern as she saw his torment. She poured tea and delivered steaming cups to Franklin and Duncan before shepherding Judith, who had also been studying Franklin with some alarm, back down the stairs. Duncan finished his cup as Franklin still read, then returned to the sketch of the strange contraption. It was beyond his experience, even beyond his comprehension.

He thought he might be looking at some bizarre sculpture or one of the fantastic oddities seen in Bruegel paintings. On the left of the sketch was a post with something fixed to its top that put him in mind of a butterfly with two wedge-shaped wings. Under the right wing was something like an upturned flowerpot with an upside-down demijohn joined to the top of it. In the margin were scrawled the words *heavy gauge steel* and *pressure forty-two*.

"Pierre had a formidable curiosity."

Duncan turned to see Franklin still staring at the letter, but now standing beside the velvet pillow. "He wanted so to share the *incognitum* with learned men," the inventor continued, "saying it was a key that could unlock entire new realms of knowledge. He sent me a letter from Pittsburgh, saying he wanted to take me with him to Paris to debate its meaning with the wise men of his country." Franklin removed his spectacles to wipe moisture from his eyes. "Dear Lord. Pierre," he said, his voice shrunken with grief.

"He planned to take another of these teeth to Buffon in Versailles," Duncan reported.

Franklin turned with raised brows and collected himself. "He confided in you, then."

"We traveled together for nearly two months. He knew some of the professors I had at Edinburgh."

"Traveled to the mysterious Lick of Kentucky," Franklin said with a nod. "I must hear all about it," he added, though without enthusiasm. The news of the deaths had sapped his strength.

"When we are better rested," Duncan suggested.

Franklin offered a grateful nod. "I shall pay for a monument stone for Pierre. He was on the path of becoming one of our greatest natural philosophers. Bougainville. Buffon. Dumont. And poor Ezra. I met him only once but liked him immediately. A giant of body and heart who had been a great help to my wife. Deborah wrote that he was a descendant of great chieftains." Franklin paused and examined Duncan once more. "Duncan McCallum," he said in a low voice to himself, repeating Duncan's name as he stepped to the mantel. He abruptly lifted a hand and lightly touched the rod of the jar at the end of the row. Duncan started in alarm as the older man's body jerked for an instant, and he was about to leap forward when Franklin lifted his hand away, his eyes much brighter now.

"You shocked yourself," Duncan said.

"The jar is not connected to the others and is much depleted," Franklin explained with a slight smile. "Sometimes I need more than Mrs. Stevenson's good oolong for my morning spark." He gestured to the other jars. "If I had them all connected I would be on my back on the floor now, trust me." Franklin straightened his waistcoat and shook his shoulders. His eyes widened. "Duncan McCallum!" he said as if the name finally signified. "The Duncan McCallum whose talents my Deborah praises in her letters? The Duncan McCallum who famously rescued several of our Sons of Liberty from captivity on a Virginia plantation?"

Duncan bowed his head. "Your dear wife has helped me and my betrothed often and has generously entertained us at your Philadelphia table. She still complains about your lightning alarm."

For a moment Franklin seemed to forget the dreadful news from Philadelphia, chuckling good-naturedly as Duncan mentioned the bell Franklin had rigged with wires from a lightning rod, so that it rang whenever lightning was close.

"She says she has to stuff wads of wool in her ears whenever it storms."

Franklin gave a shallow laugh, then stepped to the relic again. "A tooth, you say? Who would have thought that vile assassins would be interested in our old bones? That my friends would fall victim to common banditry? Surely one tooth is not worth so much as a life, not to say two lives. America grows very rough around its edges."

"The hand that directed those particular killers was in London," Duncan said.

Franklin scowled. "Ridiculous. No one here would even know," he protested, but as he considered Duncan's words his face clouded with worry.

"Ezra and Dumont were not the only victims," Duncan continued. "I was murdered as well. Or so the killers think. They are soldiers, sir. And now I fear for you. Before we speak of the bones and our expedition on the Ohio, might I ask if you are well protected here?"

"Here? Craven Street? Of course we are safe. The watch in this parish is very reliable, and my secretary Mr. Quinn is a fine strapping young fellow. But surely you overreact. And as much as I am grateful for this," he said with a falling expression, gesturing to the tooth, "if there is but this single relic my plan is unraveled in any event."

"I traveled with a cargo meant for you," Duncan explained. "But the soldiers disposed of it at sea."

A despairing sound rose from Franklin's throat. "All for naught, then," he moaned. "You said soldiers? The army?"

"But those soldiers didn't know they were disposing of carefully wrapped bricks and pieces of wood. The real relics are due in port any day now."

Franklin furrowed his brow and looked back and forth from Duncan to the tooth. "I sense that my friends were wise in selecting you for this task. And I think, Mr. McCallum, that we will need another pot of tea."

The master of lightning listened with the attention of an eager student as Duncan recounted the tale of the expedition to the Lick, emphasizing the roles of Ezra and Dumont but leaving out his visit to the ancient shrine of the Shawnee. Franklin peppered him with questions about the size, location, vegetation, and soil conditions of the Lick, until Duncan finally asked for a sheet of paper and sketched the site for him, marking where the most significant relics had been recovered. The inventor's eyes sparked with new interest when Duncan described the wide trail made by wood bison, suggesting that the bison were drawn by the same minerals in the soil that had attracted the *incognitum* eons earlier.

"Oh, the glory of such a sight. The great beasts following the hand of the Creator!" Franklin stroked the ancient tooth affectionately, then asked Duncan to describe the other treasures brought from the Lick.

Duncan sketched several in the margins of the paper. "No one must know," he warned. "Not until we understand the nature of the plot surrounding them. And prithee, sir, keep my own presence a secret. The Horse Guards are a formidable enemy."

Franklin went still. "The Horse Guards? You just said the army. The Horse Guards?" he repeated. "Why, they are the elite, the Praetorian Guard, the Janissaries of London. You are surely mistaken. They do not serve overseas, McCallum. These men who opposed you must be impostors. The Horse Guards would never be assigned to America—they are attached to the king. And most certainly they would never trifle with old bones on the Ohio."

"The Horse Guards serve the Secretary at War."

"Technically, yes."

"Meaning they really serve the king's advisers. They are the personal troops of the Court."

"In a sense yes, but you see—" The words died, and something seemed to catch in Franklin's throat. For a moment he looked at Duncan with a stricken expression, then rose and stepped to the window again, as if trying to conceal his sudden distress.

Hurried steps on the stairs broke the silence.

On sudden impulse Duncan grabbed the tooth and pillow, laid them in the back of one of the upholstered chairs, covering the tooth, and sat in front of them.

"Henry!" Franklin said with some relief as an athletic man in his mid-twenties appeared in the doorway. "Just in time to meet a friend from Philadelphia. Mr. Mc—"

"McGowan," Duncan interrupted, rising to shake the man's hand.

"Mr. McGowan," Franklin said with an uncertain glance at Duncan. "He brings news of—of the Quaker City." Franklin nodded to Duncan, then gestured to the lean man wearing an ink-stained waistcoat. "Henry Quinn, my very capable secretary. Mr. McGowan is—"

"A medical man," Duncan supplied. "University of Edinburgh." He rose to take Quinn's offered hand but remained in front of the chair to hide the tooth.

"We never be so healthy that we can't stand a good dosing," Quinn offered with a smile, then looked back at Franklin. "Have you had a complaint, sir?" he asked Franklin.

"Just the usual," Franklin replied, gesturing to his foot. "The price of rich living, I fear."

"We were discussing a case," Duncan said. "An ancient creature who lost a tooth."

"Always difficult to judge whether the elderly are better off without the discomfort of extraction," Quinn said good-naturedly, then opened the hinged top of the secretary desk and pulled one of the wooden chairs to it. "The post will be here soon," he declared as he extracted two goose quills and a small penknife from a narrow drawer. "And we have that letter to Lord Hillsborough to finish."

Franklin made a show of emptying the teapot into his cup, then raised it. "Prithee, Henry, might you get Mrs. Stevenson to renew the brew?"

As soon as his secretary disappeared down the stairs with the pot, Franklin rushed over to retrieve the tooth. "For now I will heed your advice on secrecy, McCal—McGowan," he said, remembering. "If you wish you can use a nom de guerre, though I am sure it is unnecessary." As he darted into the bedroom with the tooth and the pillow, Duncan glanced at the clock. Their conversation had sparked an idea for his rendezvous with Ishmael.

"We must set an hour for more discussion," Franklin said when he reappeared. "Tonight? I have an early supper engagement. We can meet here after."

Duncan nodded. "I will bring a companion who was at the Lick with me. But prithee, sir, take care in the street. Find a reason to be accompanied if you must go out."

Franklin offered an absent nod, then leaned closer and whispered as the sound of footsteps rose from the stairway. "I have been weighing our situation. Even if enemies are afoot, there is much reason for hope. The transit of Venus may still tilt things in our favor!"

Duncan considered his visit to Craven Street as he walked toward Covent Garden. He had been intimidated, awestruck, and humbled by Franklin, but mostly he had been confused. He had expected a somber, intellectual statesman. Instead he had discovered a man of jovial curiosity who drew electricity out of a jar for stimulation and performed jocular experimentation with the kitchen maid. Yet he also clearly harbored secrets about high levels of government that he would not share. Duncan had warmed to the unpretentious man, but he had come away more perplexed than ever about the Sons' mission for the *incognitum*. He chewed on the puzzle for several blocks as he absently navigated around hawkers and horse carts.

He quickly found an herbalist at the large market and bought lavender, oil of juniper, and pennyroyal. The old man expressed regret that he did not have the more exotic items Duncan sought, then suggested he could recommend an apothecary if Duncan could but tell him the direction he was traveling. "There's two apothecaries just inside the wall before the old Moorgate," the herbalist said after Duncan's reply, "and a fine gentleman such as yerself will want the one with the big red door. They supply the best families."

Duncan had a hackney drop him a block from the Moorgate and paced along the street, studying the two shops. The larger one with the big red door was busy with bewigged customers, several accompanied by servants. The second one, with a faded green door on heavy iron hinges, offered no signage but the glass jars of medical oddities in the window seemed advertisement enough.

The proprietor of the smaller shop was a diminutive, talkative German who insisted Duncan recite the bones of the hand before selling medicines to him. "Too many snake charmers and charlatans in London, and oh the cads that see my jars and come in to ask for eye of newt!" he groused in his Bavarian accent, then brightened when Duncan mentioned his training in Edinburgh. As he prepared Duncan's order, he revealed that he had studied medicine in Heidelberg but had been arrested not long after setting up as a doctor, for the allegedly treasonous acts of his brother, and condemned to death. The king had been merciful, however, and after executing his brother had offered him exile if he signed papers forfeiting his family estate.

"*Gnade der Konige*," the German muttered. "Where would we be without such wise men? It was all a game to take over our ancient land holdings and extinguish our titles." He shrugged. "So, fool that I am, I came to London only to have another German king. I have plenty of laudanum and valerian, and can find some rhubarb, but this item," he said, pointing to the next to last entry on Duncan's list, "is very scarce. Coca leaves arrive later in the year, after the harvest in Peru. I may be able to give you a small pouch from last year's harvest, that is all. And this one," he said, indicating the last. "I confess I have never heard of it, and I am familiar with all the herbs of the Black Forest and the remedies of the Romany. Blood root?"

Duncan apologized. "I forgot where I was. It is an Iroquois medicine. Sometimes I find it in Philadelphia or Boston."

The apothecary went wide-eyed. "*Mein Gott*! Medicine of the savage Iroquois?"

"I live among them. And I expect the New World would be less savage if there were more Iroquois and fewer colonists."

A string of excited German syllables erupted from the man's tongue. "I must know all about them! Have a meal with us! I beg you! *Mein frau* can find some sausages and good black bread. You can't speak of living with the Iroquois then just wander back into the streets!"

Duncan smiled. "I have urgent business elsewhere. But I shall do my best to return, Herr—"

"Huber. Heinz Huber," the apothecary answered, stiffening into a short bow. "Heinz Dietrich Huber. Your servant."

Instead of returning the bow, Duncan extended his hand. Huber looked at it, surprised, then grinned and vigorously shook it. When Duncan counted out his payment on the counter, Huber pushed back a shilling. "That's my rebate to a fellow physician," he declared, then pushed another to Duncan. "And this one you will still owe me," he added, "so you are honor bound to return." He followed Duncan's gaze toward a worn satchel of the kind used by doctors hanging on a peg near the counter. Huber lifted it off the wall and set it in front of Duncan. "If you have use of it, I will loan it to you. I seldom need it these days. I am physician only to a few German immigrants." As Duncan placed his purchases inside the bag, Huber reached under the counter and produced a small bundle of dried mint, which he extended to Duncan. "Against the fetor of this world," he declared.

Duncan's quick survey of the Bedlam grounds revealed no sign of Ishmael. Then he spotted a huddle of sweepers and groundskeepers who seemed excited about something in a small grove of evergreens. He found his friend sitting cross-legged in front of a small smoky fire made of branches torn from the cedar tree behind him.

He sat beside the young Nipmuc. "Perhaps, Ishmael, you wouldn't draw quite so much attention if you put your shirt back on," he suggested. Several of the onlookers were pointing at the intricate pattern of tribal tattoos on Ishmael's bronze torso.

Ishmael seemed not to hear. "I spoke with the man who tends the lawn sheep. The top floor is where the most severe cases are housed. Many of the other inmates are allowed to roam the galleries between breakfast and supper. But on the top the doors are kept locked."

"We don't need all this attention, Ishmael."

The Nipmuc still did not seem to hear. "What if he is not in a locked cell? What if he is able to look out one of those windows and see the smoke?" he asked, indicating the rows of windows.

"It will not make things easier to have you taken up as another lunatic," Duncan pointed out, instantly regretting the words, for Ishmael lifted his head as if weighing the possibility.

"What if he thought the gods had forgotten him?" Ishmael asked.

Duncan realized his companion had not been trying to make a spectacle of himself. He had built the kind of fire used at tribal councils, or in the lodges of tribal shamans. Fragrant smoke, especially that of cedar and tobacco, attracted the gods. Duncan extended his arms and with cupped hands drew the smoke toward him, as he would have done at a tribal fire. Then he extended the string of white wampum beads he always kept close and laid them across his open palm.

"I vow that we will find Conawago," Duncan said. The holder of the beads had a sacred duty to speak the truth.

Duncan laid the beads on Ishmael's palm, still clasping one end, and solemnly repeated the words. As he finished, the clock in the steeple down the street stuck the time, a quarter hour before two.

As Duncan extinguished the fire, Ishmael put on his shirt. "Do you really think they will take notice?" the Nipmuc asked. "We traveled the wide Atlantic. Can the gods really be summoned so far?"

Duncan gestured to the clouds, then to a flock of pigeons. "The gods' breath is in the clouds," he said, echoing an old Iroquois liturgy. "And birds whisper in their ears."

Ishmael didn't seem convinced. "The home of the gods is thousands of miles away. Those birds couldn't blunder their way out of the city. And the most important messages are carried by snakes. Snakes bring the dreams in which the gods speak to men. You heard Sarah. It was dreams that brought my uncle to London. And I doubt there are any snakes at all in London."

Ishmael was more forlorn than Duncan had ever seen him. Duncan put his hand on Ishmael's shoulder. "What *is* in London are the two people who are going to save Conawago." He pointed to the line forming at the wide doors into the building. "Now put on your shirt and find your entrance token, and remember this is only a scouting trip. No fires in the hallways."

As they walked toward the hospital Duncan explained that he had purchased medicines and had the loan of a leather satchel similar to what many London doctors carried. "Doctors go in and out rather freely. Once inside I will offer some powders and pills and with the pretense learn more than the average visitor," he said. Ishmael had learned that the brown-uniformed attendants were called keepers, responsible for keeping order in the wards and galleries and supervising the lower staff.

They determined to cover every gallery of the huge building, and so listened to the advice given by a keeper to the first group of guests. They ignored his suggestion that the best entertainment would be found on the upper floor and instead explored the ground floor. They passed offices, examination rooms, and a large dining hall where dishes were being cleared from lunch. The rooms of patients past the dining chamber seemed much as Duncan had seen in other hospitals, with bedbound patients being tended by women in severe gray dresses and white aprons.

"Not so terrible," Ishmael observed as they completed their circuit of the long ground floor and climbed the marble stairs. "Maybe he is truly ill. We could ask a nurse."

"Not yet," Duncan cautioned. "Reveal no connection to him until we understand the lay of this terrain."

They proceeded past the landing of the next floor to the top, arriving in a spartan sitting area where another man in brown was offering suggestions to a growing crowd of spectators. "The House of Lords is always entertaining," the keeper said. "Then there's the hilarious Fairy Queen Court, Chamber of the Immortals, and the Garden of Eden, which may make the ladies blush." He spoke with rote disinterest. "Witness the hand of judgment and the frailty of the human soul. Towels are available for a ha'penny at each end of the halls. And those wearing the tan-colored smocks be patients who need to be supplied clothing. Nothing to fear from them, for they would ne'er be allowed to roam if their physicians considered them dangerous."

As they waited for the crowd to disperse, Duncan and Ishmael settled into a square of chairs and benches where the only other occupants were two well-dressed men who read newspapers, one of them a distinguished-looking gentleman with a doctor's satchel in the chair beside him. Duncan sat on the other side of the satchel.

"Grafton is caught on a pendulum," the man declared in a disapproving tone.

"Sorry?" Duncan replied.

"The prime minister. He is unable to secure votes, so just swings back and forth between his Whigs and the Tories. At this rate we'll never get the budget needed for Bethlem. We must get reconstruction approved, you know, not just another stopgap. Have you seen the back walls lately? The fools in the last century were so bent on quickly mimicking the French that they never dug the proper foundations and now we have walls sinking. You'll not credit it, but I've seen a crack running up from the gardens to the very roof!"

"Prithee, sir," Duncan said, "I am but new here. Do you work with the patients here often?"

"Nearly every day," the doctor replied disinterestedly as he turned the page, then shook his head. "Have you seen the price of tweeds?" he asked. "Scandalous what those Scots get away with."

"I am supposed to examine a patient from America," Duncan ventured. "Do you have many colonials?"

The man lowered his paper, glancing at Duncan, then fixed his gaze on a naked cherub in the faded mural on the wall. "There was a woman from Boston who kept biting her own flesh. But she finally pierced an artery and expired. Then there was the mariner from Connecticut who insisted he was the offspring of a mermaid and refused to leave the baths. It's cold baths every day until winter now. That's the ticket, eh? A great restorative. Focuses the mind."

"It's possible he considers himself an Indian," Ishmael tried.

"Ah well, then the Aboriginal Amphitheater. That's the formal name but most just call it the Savages. Those men love to wait for a visitor with a wig, then reach through the bars and grab it, shouting 'Scalped, scalped!' with a war cry. The keepers sometimes have to apply their quarterstaves to calm them."

"The keepers strike the patients?" Ishmael asked.

"The keepers, the watch, the hall constables they call themselves sometimes, though none has a true badge of authority from the parish. Entirely too enthusiastic at times," the man said, then began rubbing at a dark bruise on his neck.

With a chill Duncan suddenly realized that the man sitting across from them was holding his paper upside down. He looked back to the man beside him as his last words registered. "You were struck? But you are a medical man," he objected.

"We're all medical men in a sense, eh?" the man said. Suddenly he took great interest in Duncan's feet.

Ishmael, growing impatient, rose and before Duncan could stop him grabbed the man's bag and opened it. As he stared inside it, revulsion grew on his face and he dropped the open bag. It was filled with dirty stockings.

The man was unmoved. "I'll pay a good price for yours," he said to Duncan as he lowered his paper. "You have very fine feet. Strong feet. Elegant feet. A full shilling. My credit is good. My family sends a generous allowance."

Duncan shot out of his chair. "Am I to believe you are a patient here, sir? Confined to Bedlam?"

The man sighed. "Are we not all confined in one way or another? I came of my own free will and am at my liberty most days. I had a meal down the road just last week. But at night they lock me up. I asked them to do so because—" The man crossed his legs and hugged his knees, seeming to shrink. His voice grew small and fearful. "Because I get terrible urges in the night. My cell is wonderfully quiet. My cellmate bit his tongue off last year." The man looked back at Duncan's feet. "Two shillings then, but I will need to remove them myself."

They beat a hasty retreat down the gallery, only to be stopped by a hooting crowd that jammed the passage. It formed a semicircle about a set of double doors, opened for a view inside the chamber through a set of barred inner doors. Some of the observers were standing on chairs at the back, calling for the fairy queen. As Duncan and Ishmael pushed their way through the gathering, the hooting rose in volume and an obese woman danced across the opening behind the bars. She wore nothing but a pair of too-small linen britches and a bodice woven of recently plucked plane tree leaves, several of which were also pinned in her strikingly red hair. Two attendants followed her, a tall, stick-thin man and a dwarf, both wearing hoops of wood around their necks that supported wings of brown sackcloth. Behind them came two women with cones over their noses that, judging by the calls from the crowd, made them unicorns. And at the end of the procession an elderly man holding a pail in his teeth hopped like a frog. When his companions had all passed, he stood and hurled excrement at the crowd.

Duncan and Ishmael next encountered a party of workmen patching a series of dents and holes in the plaster of the gallery wall. Beyond them, as the hall thinned of spectators, they came upon more and more inmates sitting on chairs, benches, or on the floor, staring emptily, with no reaction to their surroundings. They climbed to the top floor on the enclosed stairs at the end of the gallery and reached another set of double doors, where a smaller crowd of onlookers lingered. Several of these, in patient smocks, had filthy pieces of cloth on their heads that Duncan recognized to be the remnants of wigs. They had found the Aboriginal Amphitheater. A keeper was at the door and, to Duncan's surprise, was allowing a single-file line of onlookers to enter the room.

Ishmael gave Duncan a grave nod as if to say he was braced against the horror that waited inside. As they joined a line, a loud shriek came from within. It sounded more like a witch's cackle than a war cry. A repetitive knocking sound followed the shriek, and soon they saw it was made by a man in one of the tan tunics beating on a stool with a spoon. He did not seem to notice the drool that dripped down his jaw onto the stool. Three men beside him waved mops in their hands, the handles painted with bright colors, the mop heads tinged with red paint, and Duncan realized they were meant to be spears with scalps at their points. The keepers apparently encouraged the entertainments by providing props. Some of the visitors leaving the chamber were dropping tips in a jar by the door.

Duncan studied each of the other participants in the charade of savages with increasing dread. Several had colorful stripes on their faces, and most, both male and female, had feathers stuck in their matted hair, although these were either from peacocks or the tattered remains of exotic feathers imported to adorn the aristocracy. A plump middle-aged man wearing nothing but a towel arranged as a loincloth spoke in animated gibberish to the onlookers while a woman wearing an inmate tunic painted with birds was arranging half a dozen visitors in a line at the barred door. No one in the Aboriginal Amphitheater was close to Conawago's age.

The woman in the painted tunic handed the visitor at the front of the column a placard labeled MUNRO, then yelled, "Die, ye British bastards!" With hoots and hollers, the Indians set upon the visitors through the bars with their make-believe weapons raised.

"William Henry," Ishmael said in a haunted whisper. In their clumsy, irrational way the inmates were reenacting the most notorious episode of frontier warfare, the massacre of the survivors who had surrendered after the 1757 siege of Fort William Henry by the Indian allies of the French.

No one was injured in the mock melee except for an inmate who accidentally stepped on the foot of a visitor, then collapsed, weeping, with his arms extended through the bars to grasp the legs of the surprised onlooker. After confirming his uncle was not among the inmates, Ishmael, keeping his gaze on the floor now, mutely followed Duncan out into the gallery.

The most obvious opportunity now exhausted, Duncan initiated a more tedious plan, lingering with inmates who seemed capable of rational communication and inquiring after their health. He administered a few powders and pills to inmates circulating in the galleries, though one woman complaining of indigestion accepted his pill and promptly dropped it down her bodice with a disturbing cackle. They varied their questions, asking about Indians, about colonials, about men with shoulder-length hair, keeping only the element of age consistent. None knew of an inmate in his eighties, or of an elderly colonial, a wise old chieftain, or even a well-spoken gentleman of Mediterranean complexion.

As they made their way into the east wing, the crowds grew thinner. Duncan handed Ishmael his medical bag, as if the Nipmuc were his assistant, and spent more time speaking with the patients. As forewarned, they found the barred doors of the topmost chambers locked, although their outer wooden doors were open, allowing them a view inside. A man wearing a soiled velvet dress and bonnet informed them that the oldest patients he knew were all "fine gentlewomen" who spent their time making lace in a locked cell. A well-dressed man seemed quite articulate, but he spoke only in some Slavic language and punctuated each sentence with a whistle.

They encountered a row of the same plaster dents they had seen being repaired downstairs, and they watched two of the brown-suited keepers run past them to apprehend the bald man who had been methodically smashing his head against the wall at regular two-step intervals.

A staff member appeared, ringing a bell and announcing that visiting hours would conclude in a quarter hour. "We can return tomorrow," Duncan said, unable to disguise his disappointment. Ishmael gave a mute nod but pushed on down the hall. The only people ahead of them were gathered around one more set of iron-barred doors. As they approached, a woman in a plain dress who might or might not have been an inmate put a finger to her lips for silence, but made room for them to see inside. A hand-painted sign over the entrance announced IMMORTALS in uneven letters. A badly chipped marble bust of Julius Caesar sat on a four-foot-high pedestal just inside the door. Everyone inside, all older men, wore only sheets, most of them wrapped like togas. One man had tied his around his waist and wore a placard around his neck stating HOMER. He mounted an upturned wooden box and began reading from a book in Latin, interrupted every few moments by a severe twitch that drove his head toward his shoulder.

Duncan listened. The reading was uneven, and he had the sense that the man was only reading the words phonetically, without any grasp of their meaning, but he caught the pronunciations well enough that Duncan made out that it was a poem. After hearing a reference to Daphne being turned into a laurel tree, he realized it was Ovid's *Metamorphoses*. The reader was allowed a few minutes for his performance before a large man in a soiled toga came forward to replace him on the box. He had a noble bearing and wore a circlet of dried leaves over his shaggy hair. He began speaking in an eloquent bass voice, but his words were entirely gibberish. A stout man with double chins took over the box and announced times for chariot races and the defeat of the Carthaginian army, then proclaimed, "Let the games begin." At that cue two men in togas began tossing a wooden globe back and forth like a ball, calling out nonsensical syllables each time they caught it. "Siga," one said, then "quin" cried the other, followed by "mond" with the syllables repeating afterward.

A bell rang. The crowd rapidly thinned out. A keeper tapped Duncan's shoulder. "Time, mate," he said.

Ishmael held up Duncan's satchel and the keeper hesitated. Duncan fixed him with a sober gaze. "Observations on acute dementia require quietude and assiduity," Duncan scolded.

The keeper held up his hands. "Pardon, doctor. Weren't familiar with ye." He glanced down the hall. "I recommend no farther, though," he warned. "But if ye do, there be towels on the table at the end."

They listened to a man wearing a Cicero placard shout observations about government, facing his fellow inmates. Duncan realized the participants were not performing so much for onlookers as for themselves. It was the reality they had created for themselves, locked into daily repetition. The half-naked man shouted "*habeas corpus!*" and the speaker sullenly walked away, then helped pull an old man to his feet, handing him a crutch. The lame man recited several verses of the *Iliad*, then stopped mid-verse and bowed toward a shadowed corner, where someone had coughed. Two men reverently helped the frail figure there to his feet. He wore a long mop head on his skull, which threw his face in shadow. Ishmael began pulling Duncan away, but he resisted. The frail man tightened the waist cord that bound his toga over his skeletal body and began speaking in a voice so hoarse that Duncan could not understand. One of his attendants handed the man a ladle from a bucket. He drank and started over, then paused as one of the others lowered a placard over his neck that was labeled PLATO. The man with the twitch approached and flipped the placard to show ARISTOTLE. The aged man's voice was louder now. "The ultimate value of life depends upon awareness and the power of contemplation rather than upon mere survival," he said, his voice cracking with the effort. It was indeed a quote from the great Greek philosopher. The voice strengthened and offered a new recitation. "There is no great genius without some touch of madness," the inmate said, and looked up in surprise at the applause from both inmates and audience.

Suddenly Duncan's heart leapt as he recognized the features in the shadow of the mophead. The frail man was Conawago. Ishmael gasped and pushed past Duncan to clutch the bars. "Uncle!" he cried. Conawago did not react, just kept speaking toward his cellmates.

"Conawago!" Duncan shouted. The old man gave no sign of hearing. Duncan tried the name he used when passing for a European. "Socrates! Socrates Moon!"

Conawago still did not respond, but both his attendants did. They tried to turn him toward the door but he refused, clearly irritated at the interruption. The Nipmuc continued his performance, though now he switched to Shakespeare and began mixing up his words. "Alas your question, poor Yorick? To be or not to be?"

"Uncle!" Ishmael shouted again, and the old man very slowly turned. Duncan's heart soared as he stared straight at them. But Conawago's face remained empty. Tears began streaming down his cheeks and as one of his companions escorted him away, he was wracked with a sob. As he shuffled to the bench in his corner, he tossed off his filthy wig, then sat and buried his head in his hands, weeping. The half-naked man approached and with a distraught expression reached through the bars to pull the heavy doors shut.

Duncan and Ishmael walked to the end of the hall in a daze. Nothing in this bizarre place seemed real. They had found only a weak, empty shell of the man they had known as Conawago. As they reached the last cell, oblivious to how close they were to its door, an inmate threw the contents of a chamber pot on them.

Chapter 12

ISHMAEL SPOKE NO MORE. FOR the first time since Duncan had met him as an orphaned youth, his deep reservoir of strength seemed utterly drained. Duncan hailed a hackney at the gate and they rode in silence through the busy streets, the hubbub of the city providing a welcome distraction to their despair.

"He heard me," Ishmael finally said as they pulled onto the Strand. "He saw me. I know he did. He saw me and turned his back. It was a mistake to come, Duncan. Conawago has already left us. That was but his ghost."

"He saw us and didn't see us," Duncan countered. He too had been reliving the nightmarish scene in his mind. "We don't know what that place does to a man's brain. He's fragile. Many of the inmates clearly have visions and illusions. It may become difficult to know what is real and what is not."

"Meaning what?"

"I think he didn't believe what he saw. He was looking at phantoms. Perhaps he has decided his senses can no longer be relied upon. He retreated to the corner. Maybe the fact that he wept meant that deep inside the man we know still exists. It's what you have to do in such a madhouse, push the essence of yourself down into a hidden place inside."

It took a long time for Ishmael to reply. "It wasn't Conawago, only the husk of what was Conawago," he said in a voice that shook with emotion. "You would have me believe a spark of him still burns despite what my own eyes told me."

Duncan revisited the scene again, and again, then turned with a glimmer of hope. "Do you recall the men tossing the globe? Do you remember what they said?"

"Just more nonsense."

"No. One said *siga*, the other said *quin*, then next *mond*. Ishmael, it was a Nipmuc word! But we heard the sounds out of order. Quinsigamond."

Ishmael hesitated then slowly repeated the syllables, all together. "Quinsiga-mond!" he exclaimed. "The original home of the Nipmuc!"

Duncan nodded, recalling the heart-wrenching night, months earlier, they had spent in the ancient seat of the Nipmuc, now called Worcester. "I think it is a way for Conawago to keep a grip on reality. He taught them the word, and devised a way to keep hearing it. He may be slipping but he is not gone."

The excitement slowly faded on the young Nipmuc's face. "But that hospital is like a fortress. No way to raid it. How can we ever get him out?"

"The key that locked him in will be the key that opens his door," Duncan said as they reached the Neptune. Xander the link boy leapt up from the steps to open the cab. Inside, Sinner John greeted them, then blocked their passage as they headed for the stairway, with a nod toward the parlor.

" 'Tis a fine representation of the *Yarmouth*, third rate, before she had her guns reduced," came a familiar voice. Captain Rhys was bent over a model of a fighting ship, speaking to Darby, but straightened as he recognized his former passengers. "Your golden-haired angel from Philadelphia has arrived," he announced with a twinkle in his eye. "Her ship anchored next to the *Galileo* this afternoon and she paid me a visit. Said to tell you she has a monster waiting for you."

Duncan and Ishmael tried not to run on the way to Craven Street, wary of drawing the attention of the watch, but still they wove in and out of the throngs at an urgent pace. A vendor with a basket of handkerchiefs stepped in front of them, waving one of his wares in Ishmael's face, and the Nipmuc nimbly stuffed it in the man's mouth. A recalcitrant mule with a cart of hay blocked the street until Duncan pushed through the crowd and twisted its tail, producing a bray and a lurch forward.

The ship from Philadelphia had anchored shortly before noon, Captain Rhys had reported, meaning she had been in London for several hours. The passenger dispatched by the Sons of Liberty had only one address in London, and Duncan was painfully aware of how strangers could be dismissed by the Craven Street staff. He had a horrible vision of Olivia Dumont being turned away and left to roam the streets of London, with no notion of what to do with her special cargo.

He pounded the heavy brass knocker until the rather cross landlady opened it. "Mr. McCallum, sir, we run a quiet establishment here!" She hesitated, glancing at Ishmael. "McGowan. Pardon, I mean McGowan."

"I have no secrets from Ishmael," Duncan said, "and beg pardon, Mrs. Stevenson, but I must see Dr. Franklin at once! He must be prepared for an unexpected visitor!"

He did not understand her wry smile. As she stepped aside to offer a polite curtsy to Ishmael to introduce herself, Duncan dashed up the stairs.

Seeing the sitting room empty, he called out toward the bedroom. "Dr. Franklin! Forgive me. I have vital news!"

A girlish laugh rose from the hearth, where the two large stuffed chairs had been moved, their backs to him.

"That particular news, Mr. McCallum," came Franklin's amused voice as he rose from one of the chairs, "has already arrived."

Olivia Dumont rose from the other chair and with a joyful cry rushed forward to embrace Duncan. Franklin seemed highly entertained by her show of affection. Duncan returned the embrace of Dumont's sister, then gently pushed her away, hands on her shoulders.

"Is it safe?" he asked urgently.

She nodded. "Under guard and awaiting your instructions."

"Thank God," Duncan exclaimed, and gave her another, more brotherly embrace. "Now to decide where," he said, looking at Franklin.

"Mrs. Stevenson has an idle chamber on the top floor," Franklin suggested.

"The *incognitum* cannot come here," Duncan warned. "There's been too much violence accompanying it." He did not give voice to his increasing worry that Franklin himself was in danger.

Franklin cleared his throat. "I was thinking of lodging for the enchanting mademoiselle, Duncan. After the tragedy she suffered in Philadelphia and her arduous journey, it's the least we could do."

Duncan was inclined to reject the suggestion, but as he chewed on Franklin's words it struck him that she might be safest in this very residence, in plain sight of a busy household. He nodded. "Assuming the landlady consents."

"Of course she will!" Franklin replied, then made a clumsy bow to the mademoiselle. "Welcome to the Craven Street family," he said.

As Olivia began to recount the adventure of her voyage across the Atlantic, Franklin disappeared and returned with the landlady and Judith, carrying trays of tea and small cakes. The genteel landlady was pleased to accommodate the Frenchwoman, and when Duncan neglected to do so, she introduced his companion to Franklin. "This is Mr. Ishmael, of the Nipmuc tribe," she explained.

"An aborigine!" Judith exclaimed and took an eager step forward to examine Ishmael more closely.

"Judith!" Mrs. Stevenson scolded.

The maid halted and made a curtsy to Ishmael. "Pardon me, sir. No offense intended. We never had a genuine Nipmish Indian as a guest."

"Nipmuc," Ishmael corrected, then bowed to Judith and made a graceful leg to Franklin. "Your servant, sir."

Franklin glanced quizzically at Duncan.

"Ishmael journeyed to the Lick with me," Duncan explained. "He has been with me for the entire ordeal."

"The amazing epic of the *incognitum*," Franklin murmured. His face clouded and he turned to Olivia Dumont. "Beg pardon. I shouldn't speak so with your brother's tragedy still overshadowing you."

Olivia offered a sad smile. "Pierre would not want it any other way. Recovering the *incognitum* was the greatest achievement of his career." Her smile faded, and she stepped to the tooth, now back on the gaming table. "Of his life." She touched the relic and sighed, then looked up with new energy. "Oh, Dr. Franklin, you will not credit the amazing treasures we have brought you! Why, the rib alone will—"

"Rib?" Franklin exclaimed, looking now at Duncan. "You brought me a rib? But that was not in your sketches."

"A surprise, but one which Olivia deserves to share with you."

"*C'est magnifique*," the Frenchwoman said. "It takes two men to carry it. We could all fit inside its curvature."

"I could not have dreamed of such!" Franklin was almost unable to contain his excitement. With a sudden impulse he hastened to the sideboard and extracted a bottle of port.

"Your gout, sir," Duncan warned him in a low voice as Franklin poured out the glasses.

"Damn the wretched gout! We must celebrate!"

"Oh, and I neglected the rest," Olivia said as Franklin extended a glass to her. She bent to a bag embroidered with fleurs-de-lis lying against the wall by the hearth and extracted a bundle of papers tied with blue ribbon. "Mr. Thomson calls it a gift to the Royal Society. But Mr. Rittenhouse, who stayed up all night copying it all before I sailed, said it was Philadelphia's gift to the world. Both made me promise to give it only to you."

"My dear?" Franklin asked, clearly confused.

"Why, the transit, sir. The complete observations from three American locations."

Franklin stared disbelieving for a moment. "You stun me, mademoiselle!" His hand went to his chest. "Lord, how my heart races! Your visit," he said with a gesture that took in all his guests, "why, it is the completest thing!" He took a long drink of his port, nearly draining his glass. "No one else has reported complete observations yet. We only have those done by himself at his new Royal Observatory at Kew, which he built just for June the third."

Olivia's blond curls tumbled as she turned quickly. "He?"

Franklin's voice dropped to a whisper. "Himself. George Rex. The king."

After several minutes of excited conversation, Mrs. Stevenson offered to show the exhausted Olivia her bedroom, stifling the Frenchwoman's protests that all her baggage was still on the ship by saying she would send someone with a note in the morning.

Franklin's gaiety slowly subsided, replaced with a quiet awe as he untied the ribbon, put on his spectacles, and surveyed the astronomical observations. Finally he set the packet down beside the ancient tooth. "All these years I have dreamed of such an opportunity. The *incognitum*! The American transit! How tongues will wag! Divine Providence shines on us at last!"

Duncan and Ishmael shared a troubled glance, and Duncan knew the young Nipmuc was having the same reaction as Duncan to Franklin's behavior. "I explained how two good men, and a woman and her child, died because of the bones," Duncan reminded Franklin.

"I am not likely to forget such terrible loss."

"Surely they did not just die for some ornaments to be boasted of at a London party."

Franklin's eyes flared as he recognized the challenge in Duncan's voice. "I have more respect for them than that," he replied stiffly.

"Them?" Duncan shot back. "Meaning the bones of the *incognitum* or the bones of our friends?"

The fire that lit the older man's eyes left as abruptly as it appeared. "You shame me, McCallum." He was silent for several moments, staring into the glowing embers of the hearth. "I will honor them in my own way," he said at last.

"Let me honor them," Duncan replied, "by making sure their purpose is achieved."

Franklin's gaze hardened. "You have delivered the *incognitum*. That was your mission. You are, I have no doubt, an adept agent for our endeavors in America. But this is London. I have lived here for more than a dozen years. You have been here for what, two days?"

"The *incognitum* is a creature of the wilderness. That tooth and claw world has accompanied it. Ishmael and I are also creatures of that world." Franklin studied Duncan with eyes that had grown cunning. "My instinct, sir," Duncan continued, "is that the path you mean for the *incognitum* strikes more into that world than the one you are accustomed to."

The learned inventor sighed and gazed again into the hearth. "You're a Highlander, I take it. I spent three of the happiest months of my life in Scotland. I have entertained the notion of retiring there. I love the Scots. So intelligent, so educated, so affable. But they tend to rub the truth raw." He paused, not speaking, while he retrieved a pipe from a box on the sideboard, filled it with tobacco, and lit it. "I would welcome such strong souls at my side, but it cannot be. Highland Scots still stir strong feelings in London." His words triggered a new thought and Franklin lowered his pipe. "You haven't told me how you were bred in the Highlands but found yourself in America, McCallum."

"Like a few hundred others, I was found to have assisted in rebellion. Some were executed, some were transported."

Franklin puffed on his pipe in silence, examining Duncan with new interest as Ishmael studied the drawings on the wall. "How could that be?" he asked. "You would have been but a boy during the uprising."

"The British army captured all the McCallum men who survived Culloden and hanged them at the toll house in Inverness. I was at a boarding school in Holland when I heard the news. The government and I both thought all had been dealt with, but years later my great-uncle found me at the college in Edinburgh. He had been a fugitive all those years. I felt obliged to give him shelter, but stipulated that he stay out of sight whenever I was away at school. He did, except on his birthday he found a bottle of whisky I had been saving as a gift to a professor on my graduation day. He proceeded to get drunk, and when he began singing Highland songs of his youth the other tenants complained. The watch arrived and he cursed them for abandoning the Scottish king. He was hanged, and I was convicted of harboring an enemy of King George."

"That was a different George," Franklin observed.

"George the Second," Duncan agreed. "I was sentenced to seven years hard labor, which was converted to an indenture in America. I served that term and now I sit with the tooth of the *incognitum* in the parlor of the wizard of lightning."

Franklin stared at his pipe with a chagrined expression, then rose and stepped back to the sideboard, from which he returned with a dusty green bottle and three fresh glasses. He uncorked the bottle, releasing a rich peaty scent, and poured out the whisky. "I am more inclined, my friend," Franklin said as he distributed the glasses, "to say that a very inadequate public servant sits here with the heroic survivors of the battle of the *incognitum*." He touched glasses with Ishmael and then with Duncan. "And I am exceedingly grateful to you for supplying a reason to uncork this Highland nectar."

Duncan closed his eyes against the flood of memories brought by his first sip. It was the best whisky he had tasted in years. The scent of heather and peat released more smells and even sounds, long hidden in the back passages of his mind, of shaggy cattle, damp wool, and the laugh of his long-dead sisters as they played with the calves. When he opened his eyes, Franklin was rubbing the crust of dust from the whisky's label. He pushed the bottle toward Duncan and gestured to the elegant calligraphy. PUT IN CASK 1744, it said, then ALEXANDER MACGILLIVRAY OF DUNMAGLASS.

Ice touched Duncan's heart. He looked up at Franklin.

"You're wondering if I understand the poignancy," the older man said. "I am aware that Alexander MacGillivray was killed at Culloden two years later. A nephew of his took me to the graveyard at Dunlichity where he and many others who died there are interred. Afterward he presented this bottle to me, saying it was to help me remember all those good men who died fighting tyranny."

Duncan stared into the smoky liquid amber as another wave of emotion washed over him. The hands that had put up the whisky had known the joys of the old Highland culture, had not known of the apocalypse that was coming to destroy it. "You do us honor, sir," he finally said. He drained his glass and sat down. "Like many, MacGillivray died for his clan, not for his prince, who was but a stranger from France. 'Tis the burden and the honor of the clans."

Franklin fixed him with a quizzical expression.

"We commit our blood to our brothers," Duncan explained. "Ishmael and I have survived the battles thus far. And our mission changed when our brothers Pierre and Ezra were murdered. We are honor bound to our lost brothers to see this war through."

Franklin took a moment to grasp his meaning. His voice hardened. "I told you this is London business now."

"And I tell you we are honor bound. Need I remind you we control the bones right now?"

Franklin glanced at Ishmael. "We?"

"Yes," came a gentle voice from the shadows by the stairs. Olivia Dumont stepped forward. "We. The bones are here for the American cause." She stood between Duncan and Ishmael and put her hands on their shoulders. "I too am honor bound. For Pierre's sake, we must not be quarrelsome. So let's decide together where we shall deposit our treasure."

Franklin filled his pipe again and paced along the hearth, then looked up with sudden excitement in his eyes. "Where better to hide bones than among other bones?" he asked, then with a flourish of his pipe gestured them closer.

They were reviewing the rough map Franklin had drawn for them when Mrs. Stevenson appeared. "He came to the back door," she said apologetically. "I tried to deal with him by offering a piece of meat pie and a disapproving gaze, for he looks every bit the scoundrel, but he insisted on seeing Mr. McCallum."

Darby, the bosun, stepped from behind the landlady, looking deeply worried. "The lap dog of that damned major," he began, looking only at Duncan, "the one who carried him out of the sick bay when we anchored, who always smells of bergamot and gunpowder and helped toss ye in the drink."

"Yes," Duncan said slowly, not understanding. "You mean Lieutenant Nettles."

Ishmael, whose warrior instincts were often sharper than Duncan's, went to the side of the nearest window to steal a gaze at the street.

"I wouldn't trouble you fine folks," he said, putting a knuckle to his head as he nodded to Franklin and Olivia Dumont in turn, "excepting that very lieutenant and another man wearing the same tall black boots be just outside, watching this Craven Street house."

Sarah—Ishmael says he believes the city drains the soul out of men, for it cuts them off from the true things of this world. He is worried that the old tribal gods will become lost trying to find us in such a place. When I consider the noise, the filth, the greed, and the violence that dwells here I fear he may be right. Yet I have also found charity and kindness. It is as if the city were one of those old gardens where for reasons we may not ken, many plants shrivel into gnarled ugly things but still we can find small patches where beauty reigns. Within the confines of this city are the extremes of the hand of man. I have seen buildings whose grandeur would take your breath away but in their shadows lurk human vipers and inside their walls acts of great depravity are committed. It is as if the city were put here to remind us of the heights, and the depths, of humankind.

That the *incognitum* had made it from the Ohio to the Thames was a victory that Ezra and Pierre Dumont would have been proud of. Duncan couldn't help but think of his lost friends as the crates were transferred from the big square-rigged merchantman from Philadelphia to the river barge. When he had at first been reluctant to include Captain Rhys in his planning, the Welshman had fired questions at him. "Do ye know where the revenue agents linger to watch for goods coming up river?" he had demanded. "Do ye know which of the stairways on the upper Thames are closest to your destination? Do ye know what bribes to pay when the watch shows an interest? Do ye even know how to retain the services of a black barge crew experienced in stealthily moving cargo in the night?"

When Duncan had been unable to respond, the captain had looked around to assure there were no eavesdroppers in the inn's sitting room, then made an impressive confession. "You're a lubber from America, lad, but after what those coves did to ye on my ship I mean to see things right. I had my start on the sea smuggling whisky from Cork to Cardiff and London. Let me help. You were murdered on my ship after all."

Duncan grinned. "And resurrected with your help."

"Which makes me feel an obligation of a kind," Rhys said. "I sense you still may need friends to throw ye a rope from time to time."

Captain Rhys and the bargeman did indeed seem to be old comrades, and as they coasted up the Thames with a light breeze on their black sail, the silence was often broken by the soft laughter of the two as they stood at the helm. The captain had brought the indomitable Darby and three of his crew, insisting that Duncan would be glad to have the use of them and that otherwise they all would just be losing their coin in some bawdy house.

"Not a murmur, lads," the captain cautioned at they passed the Billingsgate customs wharf, "and nary a light." They glided by a handful of men in dark cloaks huddled under a streetlamp, who were busy speaking with two women in bright red dresses.

"Excise men." The bosun spat the words like a curse. "They'll be glad not to take your shilling for the king so long as ye put a half shilling in their own pocket."

Duncan felt an unexpected thrill as they glided along under the black sail. His grandfather had been a smuggler's smuggler, gathering whisky from small boats in his sleek ketch. For an instant he could hear the old man's deep guttural laugh as he patted the rail of his beloved boat and outsailed one more revenue cutter.

A north wind had cleansed the air and the moon now escaped the clouds, reflecting off the river, revealing the small wherries, the river cabs, that hauled late-night revelers and others on dark business.

"There they be," the bosun announced as a low stone pier appeared below a set of steps. "Temple Stairs. The captain knows his business. The excise men stay away from the Temple Stairs because above here be the Inns of Court, where the lawyers be thick as rats."

The two wagons Rhys had promised were waiting at the top of the stairs. Duncan had somehow not been surprised when the captain had solicited the help of Mrs. Laws's pious porter. Sinner John now paced by the wagons, holding his quarterstaff with a stern, hungry expression, as if hoping someone would interfere.

The atmosphere was that of a midnight raiding party, with lookouts from the *Galileo* posted and each man carrying a weapon in his belt. They worked with silent efficiency and soon they had the bones loaded in the wagons, their only interference being a drunken man in a long barrister's wig who arrived in a wherry and expressed irritation at having the stairs so crowded as to impede his passage. Sinner John politely asked the men to pause and bow for the noble knight of the law, then escorted the tottering lawyer up the stairs and summoned him a link boy.

Captain Rhys insisted that his men accompany the wagons to their destination, which Duncan appreciated until the bosun renewed Ishmael's London education by calling out descriptions for the surprising number of working women they passed. "A Genteel," Darby said of a woman in a stylish dress being escorted by a watchman. A woman standing in front of a pub with a pint in one hand and an umbrella in the other was a "Bunter."

Duncan learned, with Ishmael, that the apparently popular profession of what some just called women of the night actually had a complex structure, with ten categories of "particular specialties," with the lowly Bulkmongers at the bottom rank and well-heeled Women of Fashion and Demi-reps, who would never be seen at this time of night, at the top. Duncan was beginning to believe reports he had read in *The London Gazette* months earlier: that what was termed the "companionship industry" was the largest in the city.

Sinner John led them down empty alleys and did not let the wagon party cross larger thoroughfares until he had checked them, twice handing coins to watchmen who seemed too interested in their party. Duncan was beginning to admire the talents of the taciturn porter, suspecting that he too had once found profit in evading excise men.

Franklin anticipated Duncan's annoyance at seeing him as soon as the wagons arrived at their shadow-strewn location. "I have written repeatedly of the importance of getting a full night's sleep," Franklin announced in a self-important tone. "The entire city knows I retire early. No one would waste time watching Craven Street at this hour. I am safe, I assure you."

Duncan was not convinced. "It is not just your safety that concerns me," he replied, "but that of every man here and whoever lives in this house."

Duncan could see Franklin's frown in the light of Ishmael's dimmed lantern. The inventor glanced at the house with the open cellar doors, and with an awkward rumble in his throat gestured to the hooded and cloaked figure behind him. "Mademoiselle Dumont insisted on coming. Surely you understand I could not let her go out unescorted."

Duncan fixed the colonial agent with a skeptical gaze. "I see. And how would you defend her if assaulted? With witty predictions of the weather?"

Franklin raised his walking stick. "This is good Irish blackthorn, with a hard knob at the top. A rap on the skull with my shillelagh will stop any assailant," he added tentatively.

"It was very noble of the esteemed doctor to join me," Olivia interjected, breaking the tension. "And since he is here, we can show him his treasures this very night!"

All chance of arguing the point was banished as Franklin gave a cry of delight. The men were lifting the huge rib out of the first wagon. "Oh, the joy! Bless me! Bless me!" He repeated the litany as he followed the rib down into the cellar.

As Duncan carried another crate down the stone steps, he heard a frightened gasp. Olivia took a hasty step behind him as if for protection. A row of human skulls was staring at them.

"Deepest apologies," came a refined voice from the darkness. The speaker lifted the screen from the lantern he held, though the increased light only seemed to add to the macabre scene, for it lit a fully assembled skeleton hanging from a rafter peg, looking very much like the remains of a prisoner in a dungeon. Beyond the first row of skulls were more skulls on shelves along the cellar's stone wall. Most of these were human, but several were apparently of apes. Assorted arm and leg bones dangled from the ceiling.

The stranger stepped forward. "I conduct anatomy classes here. These represent, you might say, my curriculum." He made a slight bow, then introduced himself. "William Hewson. Dr. Franklin and I share both a deep affection for the daughter of his landlady and a deep interest in the natural world. When he described his particular problem, I was more than happy to offer a solution." Hewson nodded to Duncan. "I am honored to serve the cause of—" He hesitated, glancing at Franklin. "Natural philosophy," he finished. "Bones come and go from my residence on a regular basis. Those of the *incognitum* will not be particularly conspicuous to the untrained eye, especially once we cover them with canvas and stack my other bones on top. I found that even the most curious of watchmen tend to shy away from questioning my specimens."

"But no canvas yet, William," Franklin put in, unable to contain his boyish excitement. "Tonight the *incognitum* shall reveal itself!"

Duncan tipped their helpers generously and the wagons soon disappeared into the darkness. When he returned to the cellar, a trestle table had been erected in the center, and Hewson had brought wine and bread. Ishmael, Duncan, Franklin, Olivia, and Hewson opened the crates in a spirit of lively celebration, Franklin proclaiming each one a "priceless gem" or "the key to unlocking the ancient world." Words finally failed the effusive Franklin when Olivia produced her brother's journal, which included the drawings he had completed in Philadelphia. The lightning wizard donned his spectacles, then energetically matched each bone with a drawing, reading aloud Pierre Dumont's description before offering his own speculation about the creatures they derived from.

Franklin paused over the Frenchman's description of the tooth. "The *incognitum* is a member of the elephant family?" he read, lifting his voice to turn the sentence into a question. "A sizable leap for Pierre to make based on one tooth."

"The evidence is more than just a few molars," Duncan said. He picked up an iron crowbar and opened the last of the large crates. Ishmael helped him lift a long tusk onto the table.

Franklin sighed. Hewson's eyes went round.

"The jewel in the crown!" Franklin cried in his astonishment.

"It was to be my brother's surprise to you," Olivia explained to Franklin. "A vital piece of the *incognitum* puzzle, he called it."

"I put great faith in the testimony of Ezra," Duncan explained, "who grew up among elephants. He had been to great funeral grounds where elephants go to die and would have seen dozens of tusks and jaws like those we found."

"Will you ever stop taking my breath away?" Franklin exclaimed, reaching out to stroke the cool, enameled surface of the tusk.

"How extraordinary!" Hewson exclaimed. "The rarest of things!" He too ran his fingers over the smooth, ancient ivory. "Imagine, from a living creature," he whispered in an awed tone.

Franklin looked up, breaking his reverie. "Tell no one!" he instructed Hewson. "I must keep the surprise for the—" He caught himself. "I must keep the surprise."

Once more Duncan resisted the urge to press Franklin for his intentions, but instead answered Hewson's questions about the nature of the Lick and how the bones had been situated when discovered. An hour had passed, much of it taken up in completing measurements in various dimensions of the tusk and the great rib. "Pennsylvania can at last offer up a solution to the mystery of the *incognitum!*" Franklin exclaimed as he poured himself more wine.

Hewson looked up from the curvature of the rib, which he was now measuring with a pair of calipers. "You could fit a team of horses inside!"

"If all these came from the same creature, what a wonder it must have been," Franklin observed. "Why some of the bones seem to indicate the sturdy strength of an ox, others the nimbleness of a cat."

As if on cue Duncan lifted the last crate, an iron-bound cube. "One thing we know for certain," he said, "is that not every bone in the Lick came from the same creature." He gestured for Ishmael to open the crate. The young Nipmuc clearly relished the drama, slowly releasing the latch, then withdrawing handfuls of straw and crumpled paperboard. When he finally withdrew the fanged skull, Franklin was capable of only a surprised whimper. He sank onto a stool.

"Pierre and Ezra died," he said in a choked whisper, overcome with emotion again. "Warriors lost in our war for knowledge."

At last they painstakingly hid the Lick's treasures and a weary Franklin bid farewell, but only after making Ishmael and Duncan promise to be at Craven Street later that afternoon when he returned from meetings at Whitehall.

"You've been most generous with your time, Dr. Hewson," Duncan said to their host, "but I wonder if I might beg a bit more."

"Only if you join me for an early breakfast," Hewson replied. "No hope of sleep this night. I have patients to call on, and I asked my housekeeper if she might cook up something with eggs and last night's leftover ham."

Duncan liked the man's good-natured, modest intelligence and was impressed to learn that the physician was engaged in detailed research into the lymphatic glands. When Hewson learned that Duncan had studied at Edinburgh, he erupted with fresh questions about professors of mutual acquaintance, then eventually turned to the practice of medicine in the colonies.

"I am honored to say I have learned much from both the wise medical men of Edinburgh and the wise healers of the Iroquois," Duncan declared, raising new wonder in Hewson's tired eyes.

"I beg you, sir, prithee, you must speak to me of this! The miracles of the human body can be interpreted in so many ways. How wonderfully rare it would be to hear of how an entirely different world interprets them."

The reaction brought a smile to Duncan's face. "I confess that if I were suffering a battlefield wound I would much prefer to be under the care of an Iroquois healer than that of an army sawbones. But to explain in any meaningful way would take hours, which I fear neither of us have at present."

"Then we must set a time to do so!" Hewson said, then paused. "But I have usurped our breakfast with my own questions and I believe you had a request of me."

Ishmael, who had quietly consumed several servings of the delicious breakfast, put down his teacup and gazed pointedly at Duncan, who was not sure how to make his request. "As a medical man," Duncan began, "I thought perhaps you might offer insight into—"

Ishmael would not let him finish. "My uncle is incarcerated at Bedlam," he blurted out.

The lingering joy on Hewson's face evaporated. "Then I am most sorry for your uncle," he replied in a tight voice.

"I was hoping you might give us some insight into the working of the hospital," Duncan ventured.

"Those who run Bethlem Hospital have the best of intentions," Hewson offered flatly.

"But?" Duncan asked. "But they can't resist the temptation to run it as a public entertainment?"

Hewson clamped his jaw, then sipped at his tea, weighing the unwelcome shift in their conversation. "The government encourages all the physicians of London to provide support for those unfortunate souls. I did attend some patients there, but after they passed away I never took on new ones. I stopped going." He turned to Ishmael with a melancholy air. "What floor?"

"The top floor."

Hewson's face twisted in a grimace. "What wing?"

"East wing."

The doctor hesitated over the news. "That seems unlikely," he said.

"We saw him there."

"But those rooms are quite different from most of the others. Some are reserved for truly deranged criminals. And others are"—Hewson searched for words—"under the authority of Whitehall."

"I am not sure I follow," Duncan confessed.

"Patients usually undergo review by a panel of physicians before being committed. But some are reviewed instead by a committee of officials, though they must evidence some degree of mental instability."

"You're saying lords and ministers can just send their enemies to Bethlem Hospital?"

"No. Not exactly. Only a handful of very senior men, men entrusted with very substantial responsibilities for the safety of the government, I assure you."

"Meaning what?"

Hewson was growing uncomfortable and now carefully chose his words. "Meaning their decisions take into account factors not always obvious to those on the outside or to medical men. If a high-ranking lord were showing signs of mental stress in a way that could harm the government, Bethlem might be a convenient way to deal with the problem."

"If I gave you my friend's name, could you discover who sent him there?"

"You don't understand, McCallum. These are men who do not react well to anyone looking over their shoulder."

"Don't react well?" Ishmael asked in a heated tone. "You mean someone might get sent to Bedlam for doing so?"

The question hung in the air. "If a medical man asked in a suspicious way," Hewson replied, "the War Council might suddenly need a doctor in the fever isles and soldiers would escort him onto a ship." He sipped his tea. "I assure you, all of those special patients do have a genuine infirmity of some kind."

"Then you could at least check to see if my uncle is one of those," Ishmael pressed.

Hewson just stared into his empty plate.

"We have imposed too long on the doctor's hospitality," Duncan said, pushing back his chair and rising.

Ishmael slammed a fist on the table. "He is not insane!"

Duncan pulled the angry Nipmuc up and gently pushed him toward the door. "We will disturb you no further," he said to Hewson, offering a short bow in farewell.

The doctor forced a lightless grin. "It is only fair that I reciprocate for the lessons you will give me on Iroquois cures." He gestured to a paper and writing lead on the sideboard. "Write his name and I shall see what I can discover. But do not build hopes of welcome news. Men are sent to those chambers to be forgotten by the world, but soon they forget themselves." He watched as Duncan wrote on the paper, then accompanied him to the door, where he spoke in a near whisper.

"On my first visit three years ago I was eagerly trying to diagnose patients, believing that some suffered from mere physical disorders. One of the senior doctors cautioned me, saying that if a patient is in Bethlem more than two or three weeks then the diagnosis is fulfilled in any event. I asked him to explain, and he said by then they are lost, and all a medical man can do is make them comfortable. He had been attending Bedlam for thirty years, he told me, and that if I sought a diagnosis for the hospital itself it was that Bedlam is where the human soul goes to rot."

Chapter 13

"DEAR LORD, LOOK AT THE grime!" Mrs. Laws declared as they tried to pass the parlor to reach the stairs. She softened as she noticed their grim expressions, then herded them toward the chairs by the hearth. "Whatever calamity has struck ye, the world will be brighter tomorrow," she insisted. "And meanwhile there's tea!" She headed toward the kitchen, her peg leg rhythmically tapping the floor.

Duncan and Ishmael were too drained to resist when she summoned them into the kitchen to apply towels and a basin of hot water. With matronly chuckles, interspersed with mild nautical curses, she wiped the dirt from their faces. By the time Lizzie arrived with a tray of tea, Captain Rhys had descended the stairs.

"Why the long faces?" the Welshman asked. "The bosun says all went as planned."

"It's my uncle who's gone missing," Ishmael replied in a hollow tone. "He is very aged and I fear for his health." He caught Duncan's eye. They had learned to be careful in speaking directly of Bedlam.

"Well now, for a missing boat I find that following its anchorages serves well," observed the captain. "A vessel leaves a trail in its anchorages, and the anchorages themselves give their own clues. A man's just the same. Who did your uncle know in London, lad?"

"No one," Ishmael replied.

"He would have made arrangements, to sleep and eat and such. There's your trail."

"No one," Ishmael repeated. "No trail."

But the Welshman's words lingered with Duncan. They desperately needed to know more about the path Conawago had taken in London, for that path would likely offer the best hope of saving their friend. Something about Sarah's description of how she received letters had been nagging him. He turned to Ishmael. "Sarah said there were letters delivered by Mohawks. Why Mohawks? If Sir William Johnson had received them, he would have forwarded them by fast post rider."

"Because," Ishmael suggested in a contemplative voice, "Sir William didn't receive them."

"Delivered by Mohawks. Patrick Woolford had already sailed to England to some unknown estate in the countryside, but he and his wife Hannah live near Johnson Hall, and Conawago is well acquainted with Hannah, the daughter of a Mohawk elder. What if Conawago didn't go to Johnson Hall to see Sir William? What if he went to see Patrick's wife, because Patrick knows London, even has an office here when he visits."

"Or because Hannah herself has a connection," Ishmael ventured, and saw the query on Duncan's face. "She has a china cup from London on her mantel, and Patrick always laughs about it, saying what need do they have for such a frivolous thing in their cabin?"

"As if," Duncan mused, "he were not the one who gave it to her."

Ishmael nodded. "Patrick would be a connection to London, but so may his wife. She does work with the Disciples."

"The Disciples?"

"One of those old charities for the tribes. The Disciples of the Wilderness, or of the Trees or such. She goes to Albany sometimes and brings back blankets and pots, saying when she passes them out to thank the kind hearts of London."

"Hannah has a friend in London," Duncan concluded, "one whom Conawago would trust. But we know nothing of who it is," he groused. Another door had creaked open, only to be slammed shut again.

Sarah—I was talking with Xander, one of the link boys who carry lanterns to guide citygoers in the night. He says he heard on the streets about the Sons of Liberty in America, but he can't grasp what they are. He says if you have to claim your liberty then you have lost some of it, and that the only way to have real liberty is to be sure the king has no idea of who you are. I can't explain the American view of liberty to people here, perhaps in part because there seem to be so many differing views in America. I would never make them understand how my new friend Daniel Boone gave up all his life in the settlements to find unfettered freedom in the wilderness, or how the tribes give up nothing for that freedom, for it has always been theirs. I tried to explain it to the porter here, Sinner John, and he said that it's not the way things work in England. When I asked him to explain, he just said that liberty is meaningless for a man if that man doesn't know his true self, and that maybe this is what's happening in America, that people are discovering who they really are.

Duncan awoke from a fitful afternoon nap after writing to Sarah again to find a note on his nightstand. *Coffee shop, Craven Street*, it said in Ishmael's handwriting. The small shop, half a block down from Charing Cross and not far from the Franklin residence, was not yet crowded and Duncan paid his penny for a chair and a steaming mug without any sign of Ishmael. He sipped his brew and watched the flow of passersby, imagining Conawago arriving alone in the unforgiving city. The aged were treated with contempt by many on the streets, and he had seen more than a few huddled at night under the bulks, the tables set in front of shops to display wares. On the Strand he had watched in despair as an old man struggled with a dog over a bone.

"If you are up for stalking some game," came Ishmael's voice from behind him, "you are welcome to join me in the chase. Dr. Franklin scoffs at the notion that soldiers are secretly watching him. Wouldn't you prefer to say you have proven it?" Ishmael had acquired a large tricorn hat which he had pulled low to obscure his features. "The relieving watch has reported and the off-duty man is leaving," he declared, nodding across the street. "He wears high black boots," he added, indicating a man who had begun moving at a brisk march in the direction of Whitehall.

"I see no boots. He wears long trousers."

Ishmael gave a small laugh. "Like the cavalry and dragoons wear. That link boy Xander and his friend Robbie ran by him and spilled a chamber pot on his foot. He cursed them but did not chase them, because he could not leave his assigned station. But he went to the horse trough and put up his leg to clean his foot, lifting his trouser leg to do so."

"And exposed his boot in doing so," Duncan surmised with a grin. He drained his cup and followed Ishmael onto the street.

As they walked, Ishmael explained that Xander, Robbie, and the other link boys had accepted his challenge of playing the stealthy Indians stalking an enemy soldier. They had soon reported that the watchers worked on four-hour shifts with one or two on duty at a time, and they had a link boy from a different parish who ran messages back and forth. Sometimes they sat in the coffee house, sometimes at the small bake shop across the street; otherwise they sauntered along the street or lingered in one of the shadowed alleys.

"Soldiers recruited from other duties," Ishmael said, voicing the suspicion they had shared since hearing the bosun's first report of men in high boots. "Not accustomed to ground maneuvers or subterfuge. They stand too erect, and usually look like they are marching when they walk. A couple have legs bowed from long hours in the saddle."

A knot grew in Duncan's belly as he watched the man walk through the gate of the large parade ground, returning the sentry's salute despite being in civilian clothes. A sign with gilded letters proclaimed the compound to be the home of the Horse Guards.

It came as no surprise, but seeing a place filled with men in the same uniform as Hastings made their danger more real, and more grave. Ishmael was gazing not at the soldiers but at Duncan, and Duncan realized the real reason they had come. Ishmael was not simply performing the warrior's duty of reconnoitering the enemy—he was chastising him for not confronting the danger to Benjamin Franklin more directly.

"The major made good on his threat," Ishmael observed. "Poor lad. I do feel sorry for him despite his red coat."

Duncan followed his nod toward the east side of the parade ground, where a line of high-prancing horses was being ridden in a pattern around barrels. "Poor lad?" he asked.

Ishmael answered with a quick gesture beyond the exercising mounts to the stable itself. Duncan didn't understand until the forlorn soldier hauling a barrow of horse manure emerged into the sunlight. It was Ensign Lewis.

Ishmael having departed for Bedlam, Duncan was a block away from the Craven Street house when a figure dashed out of an alley, grabbed his arm, and pulled him into the shadows. "It's true!" the man said. "I never would have credited it if I had not seen with my own eyes!"

"Henry?" Duncan asked, surprised to be accosted by Franklin's secretary Henry Quinn. "What's true?"

"The men who creep about! The watchers! Dr. Franklin was cross about you suggesting it, Mr. McGowan, saying you didn't understand the comings and go-ings of the city, but I do believe you are right. I saw some rough-looking fellows studying the house yesterday and they are back today, lurking in the shadows. When I saw you approaching, it occurred to me that you might help me."

"Help you?"

"Convince the household of how important our secrecy is. They speak so freely, sir. I have been with Mrs. Stevenson in the market and heard how she prattles on about the doctor and his experiments. And his visitors," Quinn added, nervously glancing around the corner of the alley as he spoke. "And he treats Polly like a beloved daughter, tells her everything. I suspect she keeps no secrets from Dr. Hewson. Then there's Judith, who goes out to the tavern down the street once a week with three or four women in service with other houses. The market gossip, the parlor games, the tavern tales—who knows what confidences can be breached in friendly banter! Why, if it were a ship, the Stevenson house would have sunk from all the leaks long ago."

Duncan eyed the earnest clerk uncertainly. "Why reveal this to me?" he asked. "I am little more than a stranger."

"You brought Dr. Franklin something, something precious it seems," Quinn said, then held up his open palms. "Don't tell me what it is. But if you value it, take precautions, I beg you! I only want what is best for Benjamin. He is a man of little guile. Too trusting, I fear, and his health troubles me. It would be a cruel shock to him if someone in his household betrayed him, even inadvertently. And he needs to be more careful with his mail. Why, he often just finds the nearest link boy or runner to send a message to Whitehall. The seat of government! It is his colonial way to be so trusting and I admire that, truly, but there must be a limit, especially in these troubled times."

Quinn abruptly spun about, his face in the shadows now. A man in high riding boots was pacing along the opposite side of the street. Franklin's secretary pulled Duncan deeper into the alley.

"I have already set myself the task of reminding him of the dangers," Duncan said.

"Then I am truly grateful. And perhaps mention what a bad practice it is to be so negligent with mail. If necessary, I myself can run messages to Whitehall." Quinn leaned closer. "These are precarious times. Government is shifting. It is not proper for a secretary to speak up to his master, but if Benjamin's friends fall from power, he could lose everything. You and I have to protect him from himself."

"Preposterous! I tell you again, you are mistaken, sir!" Franklin protested when he heard Duncan's report. "I assure you the Horse Guards have no interest in me! Those men that sailor saw, why, they were just some toughs looking for easy prey. Some of the houses here are just the city dwellings of families who spend most of their time at country estates. 'Tis not unusual for them to attract footpads and burglars. What you suggest is beyond right thinking!"

"You live in a world of diplomacy," Duncan said, "in which you must pretend to believe the best of everyone. Just because you don't openly express support for the Sons of Liberty doesn't mean you have not been connected with the Sons by men who live in a different world. Ishmael and I are trained for reconnaissance and war, where we must seek out bitter reality. These men are not watching this house because they think it is easy pickings or because of me, for they believe I am at the bottom of the Atlantic. I tell you, you are in danger, sir, and you will put the entire household in danger if you do not take more precautions."

Franklin made a small harrumphing noise and sipped his tea. "I am a diplomat, agent not just of the Pennsylvania colony but for New York and Massachusetts as well. There is an etiquette to be observed in the government's treatment of an official representative." He paused, then searched his pockets and produced a slip of paper. "I have something for you, my friend," he said, seeming keen to change the subject.

Duncan accepted the paper and gazed in confusion at its words. *Oal hiumun biings ar born fri and ikwul*, it read.

"It's my new alphabet!" Franklin explained. "You are one of the first to see it! My dear friend the landlady's daughter and I use it for now just to correspond but soon it shall be embraced by the masses. Much easier to pronounce and spell."

Duncan studied the words again. "All human beings are born free and equal," he read.

"Precisely! You prove how simple it is to assimilate! Soon I shall breach the secrecy and tell the world."

Ishmael took the paper, quickly scanned it, and handed it back. "It looks like a code," he observed.

"At first glance perhaps, but soon it will quickly become second nature." Franklin leaned forward as if to answer their questions about this, his latest invention.

Instead, Duncan folded the slip into his pocket and said, "I believe we were speaking of your diplomatic world, Doctor. You are not a member of Parliament."

"No," Franklin said, clearly deflated. "That's rather the point of my efforts with Whitehall, to try to attain proper influence for the colonies despite that sad reality."

Duncan pressed on. "You are not appointed by the king."

"Of course not."

"In fact, you are appointed by the colonial assemblies, whose very existence is an annoyance to the king."

"An annoyance to the king's advisers," Franklin said, as if correcting Duncan. "The king shows due respect to the colonial representatives."

Duncan did not remark on the hollowness of the assumption by so many that the king was ever a virtuous and reasonable man. "I recall reading something by a great man," he observed instead. "Half a truth can become the greatest of lies."

Franklin's expression softened into an ironic grin. "Unfair, McCallum, to use my own words against me." He turned with a contemplative gaze toward the low fire in the hearth. "But truly I have done nothing to offend the king's elite troops," he said after a moment.

"It is not the army pointing these secretive men at you, it is members of the

War Council. And if it is not something you have done that offends them, then it must be something you intend to do," Duncan suggested.

His words stiffened Franklin, who rose and paced along the hearth, hands folded at his back. Duncan remained silent as he stepped to the giant tooth, again on his gaming table. The tooth had clearly taken on a deep significance for him. He touched it the way Duncan touched his own totem pouch.

When he finally looked up his eyes were heavy with worry. "If what you say is true, then it is difficult to maintain hope for peace," he declared. "I must—" He broke off at a commotion in the entry below. Clearly grateful for the interruption, Franklin moved to the sitting room entrance as steps sounded on the stairs.

"Polly!" he cried in greeting and threw out his arms as an attractive woman of perhaps thirty years left the arm of Dr. Hewson to embrace him. "Ever a reviving sight for weary eyes," Franklin said, and introduced Mrs. Stevenson's daughter to Duncan and Ishmael.

"Adventurers from the New World, I hear!" Polly exclaimed. Her eyes sparkled with deep intelligence, and Franklin was clearly delighted at the way she still held his hand as she spoke. "I tortured William terribly when his housekeeper told me of secret goings-on last night. But no confidences breached, for I was already in the *incognitum* cabal, so to speak."

Franklin's smile faltered as if Polly were about to expose a layer of his secret world he did not wish to share. "Tea! More tea, Margaret!" he called out. "And let's try the almond cakes and madeira!"

Hewson cast a grimace toward Duncan as if apologizing for the interruption, then carried an empty tray from the sideboard down for renewal in the kitchen. When he returned, he was escorting the final member of the *incognitum* circle, energetically speaking with her about the workings of the lymph glands.

Olivia Dumont had left Hewson's house the night before with great reluctance, for she had been fascinated by his own bone collection and mention of his research. "Dr. Hewson has a great cobra in a jar of alcohol!" she exclaimed to Duncan as Hewson and Polly poured tea. "And over a dozen dried lizards!"

The afternoon had grown cool and Franklin added more fuel to his hearth, then stared at the flames intently. Duncan had begun to realize that Franklin had certain habits for his contemplations, one being consulting the smoke of his pipe and the other being studying the flames of his hearth. Duncan recalled from conversations with Franklin's wife in Philadelphia that he had first lived in the Stevenson house a dozen years earlier, and now with the long rays of the sun shining through the windows he could see the faint discoloration and indentation in the floor indicating the track of such musings through the years. Franklin was a man who could burst into ebullient exclamations and explanations but who could just as quickly sink into deep, brooding silences. When his focus finally returned to his companions, he gestured with a forced smile toward the little blue crystal crescent moon hanging in the top sash of the nearest window. "Have you forgotten, Polly dear?"

Polly glanced at the moon, clearly not understanding. "Benjamin?"

"The treasures. The blue moon. My message."

"But I've received no message from you this week and more," Polly replied. "Nothing about a moon, blue or otherwise."

Franklin cast a puzzled expression at her, then rose and stepped to his desk, where he rummaged through papers stuffed in the pigeonhole compartments. "It's not here, dear," he concluded, then paused as he perused what seemed to be a stray letter. "Oh. Oh my," he muttered, then looked up sheepishly, holding the letter out. "It's my original report to Prime Minister Grafton on the debates in Philadelphia about a new Pennsylvania currency." Franklin's expression slowly shifted from embarrassment to amusement. "Henry was away the afternoon I sent it. I stuffed your message, Polly dear, in the envelope for Grafton. Won't the prime minister be entertained, receiving a missive about pearls in a blue moon, although I am not sure he will be able to decipher my alphabet." Franklin chuckled, then pointed to the moon again. "For you, Polly dear."

Mrs. Stevenson's daughter approached the window, then with a polite gasp of surprise extracted two pearl earrings draped over the center of the crescent moon. "Treasures from the heavens!" she exclaimed with a laugh, then rewarded Franklin with a kiss on his cheek. "Truly you do too much for me, Benjamin," she said. "I must find a way to reciprocate. William," she added to Hewson, "perhaps we can find another front-row seat for Guy Fawkes Night?"

Hewson offered an affirming nod, then stepped closer to Duncan and began to explain what he had learned at Bethlem Hospital that afternoon.

"There is no record of any patient named either Conawago or Socrates Moon," Hewson reported, mentioning the second name Ishmael had given him. "So I asked for a list of the patients in the so-called Chamber of the Immortals." Hewson saw Duncan's question and shrugged. "I said I was studying the pathology by which ancient Greek and Roman mentalities mysteriously surface in the inhabitants of Bethlem, which is curiously built in the shadow of the ancient Roman wall. That clearly intrigued the keepers, so they complied, with knowing nods and more than a few mutterings about Roman ghosts that have been seen on the grounds." He produced a piece of paper. "Fifteen names with estimated ages and descriptions, the best the keepers could manage. Eliminating those clearly under the age of sixty, a man estimated to weigh over twenty stone, one with a red beard, and the one so pale that he poses as a marble statue, leaves five." He handed the list to Duncan with five names underlined. "The keepers added the personages they have adopted."

Ishmael looked over his shoulder as he read:

Jacob Quimley, Homer and sometimes Moses
Charles Postle, Athena and sometimes a naked king of Spartan
Oliver Anderson, Crier of decrees and sometimes Bathsheba
Thomas More, Plato and Aristotle
Thomas Wolsey, Zeus and Dionysus

Nothing stood out except the odd coincidence of the last two names. He pointed to them and looked up at Hewson. "Our friend was wearing a placard labeling him as Plato on one side, Aristotle on the other. He has always been a great student of their teachings. Why call him Thomas More? Why Thomas Wolsey, for that matter? Why reach out for historical names?"

"No one questions what the admitting doctor writes," Hewson tried to explain. "And this one was Doctor Granger, physician to the royal family."

Polly Stevenson had joined Ishmael at Duncan's shoulder. "They are both men who died after being charged by the king with treason," she pointed out.

"That was King Henry the Eighth, dear," Hewson confirmed, "though I doubt many keepers would make the connection."

"As if they were suppressed by the same man," Polly continued, "who thought himself so very clever, creating a record that chums at his club would laugh at."

"Or the sovereign," interjected a troubled voice. Franklin was listening now.

"Dear God," he said, and gestured for the list. Duncan handed it to him and he walked to his chair by the fire, his feet strangely leaden.

"If I knew more about your friend's activity here, whom he met with, where he visited," Hewson said, "I might have some notion of how this happened. Without knowing what was done, how can we undo it?"

Duncan offered a grateful nod. "If only I had access to those who oversee Indian Affairs, those who deal with Superintendent Johnson and his deputies or their friends, I might turn up a clue as to his activities in London before his confinement. Perhaps someone with that charity, those Disciples who help the tribes."

Unexpectedly, it was Olivia Dumont who spoke up. "Oh well, Madeline then. She is always genteel, and although sometimes lightheaded, she seems to be a good friend of Sarah's and her family had a connection to some such charity. She told me it was de rigueur for young society women to adopt a benevolent cause."

Duncan eyed her uncertainly. "Madeline from Philadelphia?

"Madeline Faulkner, yes. I carried a letter for her from Sarah." The Frenchwoman paused, then flushed. "*Pardonnez-moi*! I was to give you her address here. It's in my room in my jewelry case. I shall retrieve it this instant," she said and hurried toward the staircase.

A moribund whisper broke the silence that followed. Franklin had been contemplating Duncan's words. "The *incognitum*," the inventor said, still facing the fire. "If I credit what you said, McCallum, it means there are those in this city who fear our monster could rip the higher circles of London apart. The Royal Society. The War Council. Secret committees of Parliament. The Privy Council, even. There are jealous men in each who consider the lives of common men to be little more than those of pawns on a chessboard, and whom would never tolerate plebeians such as ourselves interfering with their affairs."

"I must confess I don't entirely comprehend, Benjamin," Hewson said. "At times you speak as if there is a feud among natural philosophers, at others as though matters of state were involved."

The doctor's words brought a heavy sigh from Franklin, who rose to pace along the hearth again, hands clasped behind his back. "I fear you have struck upon it."

"A feud or a matter of state?" Polly asked.

"Until Mr. McCallum spoke I had not recalled what happened to poor Mason, sent into exile in a bleak Greenwich office. He should have been offered a knighthood. If these are the same persons who persecuted him, then God help your friend. God help us all."

"Perhaps we need to better understand the context you speak of, Ben," Polly observed. "You have lost me. Shall we have some madeira and start over?" The landlady's daughter guided him back to his chair and handed him a glass of wine, then invited the rest of the party to gather by the hearth.

"I should have seen it from the start," Franklin confessed. "The attack on the *incognitum* expedition, the use of my letter to choke poor Ezra to death. Pierre's murder. The attempts to suppress our transit observations, and the campaign against Mason."

"Prithee, sir," Duncan said, "perhaps we should hear more about this man Mason."

"Why, you must know of him, McCallum. Everyone in America knows of Charles Mason and his partner Jeremiah Dixon."

"The Mason-Dixon Line!" Ishmael exclaimed.

"Exactly. Perhaps the greatest astronomical feat of the century. Do you have any idea of the scale of that accomplishment? And of course he was chosen for that honor by the Royal Society because of his own work on the 1761 transit of Venus. He had been dispatched to Sumatra then, with Mr. Dixon at his side, but they were so slowed by attacks of the French along the route that they were unable to progress beyond the Cape of Good Hope. So, blessed man, he had the resourcefulness to set up his equipment for observations from the Cape, which became the best of all those done around the globe, although we hope the recent work out of Philadelphia may prove his match, eh?" Franklin added with a twinkling glance at Duncan.

"Of course, while in America for all those years, Mason made many close friends among the natural philosophers of the colonies. He was forced to end his survey by some difficulties with the tribes less than two years before this year's transit, so naturally he helped train the members of our community of scholars in Philadelphia to make the necessary observations. It was the most generous, selfless of gestures, solely to advance the scholarly cause. But when he returned to London, certain members of the government, even some of the Royal Society here, reviled him for doing so, saying London and Edinburgh were the centers for learning and no good would come from advancing the minds of shallow colonials. Instead of crowning him with laurels he was sent to lunar chronicle oblivion in Greenwich, poor soul."

"But surely you put in a good word for him, Benjamin." Mrs. Stevenson said. She too had drawn up a chair. Her relationship with Franklin was clearly more than that of landlady and tenant. "After all, you also are a fellow of the Royal Society."

"Margaret, I am but a second-class citizen in the Society. The only one who can change Mason's position is the Astronomer Royal, and Nevil Maskelyne is the last person on earth I can alienate right now. The situation is very delicate. I need to have him build anticipation for the Philadelphia transit observations or all may be lost. If we are not careful, our seeds will be cast on barren ground."

Mrs. Stevenson rolled her eyes. "I am at a loss to understand this sudden fascination with astronomy."

Franklin turned his gaze from her to stare into his own folded hands, then sighed and looked toward the sideboard. "Ah! Bavarian creams!" he exclaimed, and stepped with renewed vigor to the plate of cakes brought with the tea.

Polly saw the confusion in Duncan's eyes. "The Astronomer Royal," she explained, "is the natural philosopher closest to the king."

Duncan did not miss how Franklin, his back still turned toward them, froze for a moment at her words. As the inventor walked with a plate of sweets toward the teapot, he took notice of a blank space on his wall. "Meg," he asked his landlady in a peeved tone, "did you move my drawing of the—" He paused. "Did you move my drawing?"

It was Olivia Dumont, rushing to his side, who answered. "Oh! Dr. Franklin! *C'est moi!*" She put her hand on his arm and his mood instantly softened. "I awoke at dawn and recalled the fascinating image of that machine. I was going to ask but you were asleep. Your secretary Monsieur Quinn saw me studying it yesterday and said I should feel free to examine it more closely. I took it up to my bedroom to study in the early light of the sun and neglected to return it." Duncan was at a loss to understand the knowing glance that passed between Franklin and the Frenchwoman.

"Nonsense, my dear, no need to apologize," Franklin replied. "Of course. It is a fascinating image, is it not? You must allow me to explain it in more detail," he added, offering Olivia one of his cakes.

Ishmael, taking no interest in the exchange about a strange drawing he had not even seen, gazed fitfully into the hearth. "None of this gets us closer to Conawago's trail," he groused.

"I nearly forgot," Hewson said, and reached inside his waistcoat to produce another list. "The board of governors for Bethlem Hospital. No one at the hospital would decline a request made by any one of them."

Duncan took the list and read it out loud:

Lord Pennington
Duke of Westmoreland
Earl Aylesford
Duke of Portland
Earl of Milbridge
Baronet Darnel
Lord Wolfington
Lord Oxley

He searched the faces of his companions. "None of these signify to me," he said but nodded his gratitude to Hewson. "A clever notion, doctor, but if we can find no signs of Conawago's trail into Bethlem, then we need to just focus on procedures there. Like which doors are locked, who has keys, what access there may be through the rear of the building, when laundry is exchanged, and whether the inmates from the top floor are ever permitted exercise outside."

"Not exercise as such," Hewson replied, "but there are the daily baths. The governors are quite convinced of their efficacy."

"I don't follow."

"There is a device with a chair and a harness. Patients are lowered into very cold water for thirty seconds. The chief doctor swears by it."

Duncan recalled mention of such baths on his visit to Bedlam. He closed his eyes against the image of his gentle friend being forced into a harness and soaked each day. When he opened them he saw that Ishmael's fists were clenched so tightly his knuckles were white.

"Major Hastings and his men must answer for what they have done," Duncan said in a smoldering voice.

"But, Duncan," Olivia protested, "as horrible as the Horse Guards have been, surely they can't be involved with Conawago's confinement."

"In war," Duncan replied, "to survive you develop an instinct, an extra sense that tells you where enemies lurk before having actual sight of them."

"Surely you overreact," Polly Stevenson said. "All the Horse Guards do is protect the king."

"Except for travel to America to commit murder," Ishmael shot back. "And my uncle traveled across the Atlantic to see the king."

Franklin's hand, lifting another cake, froze halfway to his mouth. The inventor looked up with sudden interest.

Polly's brow creased. "But why would a simple member of the tribes think he could reach the king?" she asked.

"My friend Conawago," Duncan said, "is anything but simple. He lived in France as a boy, being educated by the Jesuits. He speaks more languages than, I wager, anyone in this room. He was a friend of Louis Quatorze, who begged him to join his court, and even visited old Queen Anne. Later, with French diplomats, he visited the first King George. He is capable of cutting a most impressive figure, I assure you."

"But why?" Polly pressed. "What was so urgent?"

Ishmael and Duncan exchanged a glance. Conawago had had dreams. No one else in the chamber would possibly understand the primacy, and urgency, of such messages from the gods. "I believe," Duncan said, "that he had cause to expect an approaching catastrophe and felt honor bound to do something about it."

"What cause?" Franklin pressed. "You mean the murders in America?"

"No. He was underway to London before those occurred. About armies. About thousands dying. About the destruction of nations."

"Ben!" Polly called out and rushed to Franklin's side. He had grown quite pale, and was suddenly so weak he accepted her arm to support him to the nearest chair, by the gaming table. He put his hand on the *incognitum* tooth for a long silent moment, as if for strength, then turned to Polly. "Paper, child, and writing lead."

When she complied, he bent over the table, writing feverishly as all the room watched. When he finished he extended the paper to Duncan. "William gave you the board of governors for the hospital," he said. "This is another board, the king's

War Council. The Horse Guards are directly under them. I don't say I agree with your theories, McCallum, but I accept that there is a certain perverse logic to them. Anyone seeking to see the king is likely to fall under their attention. They have almost as much power as the Privy Council and work almost entirely in secret."

Duncan read the list out loud, quickly, not understanding Franklin's point.

Lord Barrington

Lord Paxton

Duke of Cornwall

Lord Salisbury

Earl of Milbridge

Lord Abercromby

Lord Lincoln

Lord Paisley

"Why such a coincidence!" Mrs. Stevenson cried out. "The Earl of Milbridge is on both bodies!" Her look of curiosity faded as she saw the hardened reactions of Duncan, Ishmael, and William Hewson. "Oh," she whispered in a deflated voice. "That's the point."

"It all rests with the Horse Guards and the War Council," Duncan said. "I think they stopped Conawago from seeing the king. And now," he said to Franklin accusingly, "they want to stop you from seeing the king."

Duncan's words seemed to finally pierce the shell of Franklin's resistance. The wizard of lightning looked stricken. Polly put her hand on his shoulder, for suddenly he seemed in need of comforting. His breath caught several times as if he were about to speak, but then he seemed to lose his words. When he finally spoke it was in a near whisper. "The bones are the only way in," he said. "The old aristocracy loathes me. But George has a keen interest in natural philosophy."

"Which is why you are so beholden to Astronomer Royal Maskelyne," William Hewson suggested.

Franklin nodded. "If Nevil recommended it, the king would meet with me. But none of his other advisers must know. The lure will be that we will tell George he will be the first to receive the official transit results from Philadelphia, which may not be entirely unexpected, but doing so out of the public eye so he can control their use is still a sign of great respect for him. And then he shall behold the astonishing secrets of the American *incognitum*. His perception of the colonies will be transformed!"

"But surely, Benjamin," Mrs. Stevenson interjected, "if it causes all this fuss with the Horse Guards it can't be worth it."

"I am afraid it is, dear Meg," Franklin said with a sad smile. "Worth my life, if it comes to it."

"But Ben, it is only bones!" Mrs. Stevenson said, new worry in her voice.

"The transit and the bones are the admission to the meeting," Duncan said. "The purpose is something else."

Franklin nodded to Duncan. "My new friend is most perceptive," he said, and sighed. "No one else can know this, I beg you, and God knows how your Conawago reached the same conclusion. Five months ago, the War Council surprised the king with an extraordinary proposal. They said sparks had to be suppressed before the fires broke out. He said he would decide before he departed on his hunting trips in the fall, after the social season. So the calendar is nearly run out. The War Council is so confident that they are already making preparations. Ships are being provisioned in Portsmouth as we speak."

"Preparations, Benjamin?" Mrs. Stevenson asked.

Franklin said to Duncan, "Your friend Conawago is right. It would be brother against brother. Untold thousands would die. Your old Nipmuc and I somehow came to the same decision. The only way to stop the nightmare is through an unguarded discussion with the king." He silently looked into the eyes of his companions and sighed again as he surrendered all pretense. "The War Council intends to dispatch troops to occupy Philadelphia and New York. They will have orders to send all those who speak against the government to London to be hanged."

Chapter 14

D UNCAN PAUSED AS HE CLIMBED out of their wherry to admire the elegant building on the hill above the Thames. He had been so obsessed with the conspiracy against Franklin and Conawago that he had not truly focused on their morning destination. But now, as he stood on the pier, a sense of awe seized him. His reaction had nothing to do with the stately building along the riverbank, the Naval Hospital, but rather with the sturdy, templelike structure at the top of the hill. He recalled that the site had once held the castle where Henry the Eighth and his daughters had been born, but on those ruins Christopher Wren had built the center of the world. Everywhere on the planet mariners paid homage to the site, knowingly or otherwise, but few had the honor of visiting it.

Here was where time began. Here was the anchor of place, without which every mariner would be lost. Since before history sailors had been able to fix positions up and down on their maps, fixing the north-south movements of their ships. But it had taken the ingenious men in this temple of knowledge to reconcile the movements of time and stars so that east-west positions could be fixed. Here was the shrine of navigation. Here was zero degrees longitude.

Duncan had learned from Franklin and Hewson that the celebrated strides of the astronomers of Greenwich meant that the site had also become the center of the government's efforts to advance natural philosophy. The Astronomer Royal had thus become the king's natural philosopher and the general of the small army of dedicated mathematicians, astronomers, and surveyors housed in the hilltop complex.

Captain Rhys had insisted on joining Duncan and now, realizing that Duncan had not kept pace with him, waited at the end of the busy dock. He seemed to recognize the expression on Duncan's face. His weather-beaten countenance widened in a grin. "I felt the same way on my first visit, son," he said. "I was a young lieutenant with the sailing master from our ship. Here, says the master, is the place where distance begins. I remember him saying that ye can't really know something unless ye can measure it. So ye might say that it was the sages who labored on that hill who truly introduced us to our planet."

The Welshman led Duncan up the path to the observatory complex. As they climbed, the din of the waterfront receded. A door in Duncan's memory opened unexpectedly. He recalled being with his mother as a young boy on a pilgrimage to the cathedral in Edinburgh, when his usual clamor of questions had died away as he was struck dumb by the immense, uplifting architecture. He sensed Wren's building too was a cathedral of sorts, and felt a humble reverence as he walked through the high double doors into a gallery lined with shelves of chronological devices and portraits of famous mariners and astronomers.

The captain, in a dark blue waistcoat and britches adorned with brass buttons down the legs, struck an authoritative pose with the functionaries they encountered. No one challenged them as they walked up the central stairway to what appeared to be the primary working offices of the observatory, where earnest, mostly bespectacled men bent over charts. Halfway down the corridor the captain stopped a young clerk with several rolled charts under one arm and more balanced in the crook of the other.

"I thought Mr. Mason's office was here," the captain said with the air of impatience often heard on quarterdecks.

The clerk took notice of Rhys and straightened, dropping some of his load. "No sir. Yes sir. I mean 'tis the other end of the corridor, sir."

The corner office overlooking the forest of masts on the Thames was lined with tables covered with charts, and the clutter overflowed onto the large desk in the center of the room. A telescope on a tripod was aimed downriver, toward the larger ships anchored in the Lower Pool. Rhys gave a sigh of disappointment at finding the office empty and was turning away as the mound of papers in one of the deep windows moved. The window was half-obscured by an easel to which more charts were pinned, but a leg now revealed itself from under the papers. A moment later, a disheveled man emerged, wearing what looked like a baggy scholar's robe.

"Oh," was all he said when he saw them. He looked about and located a cold cup of tea balanced on the edge of the desk. "I wasn't expecting anyone." He stood up straight and pushed back his long hair. "Was I?" He stretched his arms, revealing a rumpled linen shirt under the robe, then drained the cup.

"Gentlemen?" he asked then, in afterthought, apologizing for his appearance. "I was up most of the night with the new telescope. A two-inch apochromatic! Not as good as the reflector in Edinburgh but I still found three moons of Jupiter!" With new energy he pulled off his outer garment, straightened his shirt and britches, and donned a waistcoat that was draped over the desk chair. "Charles Mason. May I be of service? Did Nevil send you? Is this about Tahiti? I thought that wasn't until next week." He shrugged. "I am so immersed in the world of lunar tables I tend to lose track."

"I came from Philadelphia," Duncan said. "Charles Thomson and the philosophers' society."

The announcement ignited Mason's countenance. He hurried to the door, looked into the hall as if for eavesdroppers, then closed it and leaned against it. "It is rumored that they were successful on June third," he said, question in his tone.

"Very successful. Three sites."

Excitement lit Mason's eyes. "The city, the farm, and the Henlopen peninsula? David Rittenhouse? Mr. Biddle?"

"Yes to all, I believe. The captain and I were on the Atlantic on June third, but I heard them speak of their readiness before I left, and have had confirmation since."

Mason looked upward and briefly closed his eyes as if in prayer. A smile rose on his broad, earnest face. "At last!" he exclaimed. "My greatest hopes have been realized!" He glanced back at the door and his happiness seemed to fade. "And you, sir, Mr.—"

"McCallum. Duncan McCallum. And this is Captain Rhys of the *Galileo*."

"Bark from Philadelphia," Mason acknowledged with a nod, then approached Duncan and spoke in a low voice. "Prithee, McCallum, be sparing of this news for now. Who has the numbers? Where are the blessed results?"

"In the hands of the agent for Pennsylvania."

"Benjamin?" Mason considered Duncan's announcement, then nodded with satisfaction. "He understands the volatility of such news, for he is himself a fellow of the Royal Society. Or, as he and I sometimes call it, the club for inflated mirror gazers." Mason nodded more vigorously and pumped Duncan's hand. "It was kind of you to bring word, sir."

"We were coming in any event," Duncan said, "to speak of the War Council and its battle with natural philosophy."

Mason jerked backward as if physically struck. He glanced nervously from Duncan to Rhys. "The War Council serves the best interest of the country," he said, his voice grown brittle. "May God preserve the noble gentlemen."

"I have a friend who came to England to reason with such noble gentlemen," Duncan said. "He now wastes away in Bethlem Hospital despite being the sanest man I know. I think the War Council put him there."

Mason's gaze shifted to his feet. He did not look up as he spoke. "They serve the best interests of the country," he repeated. From somewhere down the hallway a clock chimed the hour, followed closely by another timepiece, then a third. "I have important work, gentlemen," he said and moved behind the big desk. He seemed frightened. "The lunar tables are tedious, but in the hands of a trained navigator they can save lives. The proper chronometers are finally being produced, but should one prove defective nothing but the lunar tables will serve. Captain Cook's survey of the Pacific relied entirely on lunars." He seemed desperate to change the subject.

"Mr. Mason," Duncan said. "I am familiar with the challenges of sine and cosine and am convinced the world owes a great debt to you and your colleagues."

"It is a heavy burden, sir, but I dedicate my very soul to it. The War Council is well served here, I assure you, for the first to get the new tables will be our naval ships."

"Perhaps you confuse me for an emissary of Whitehall. I am no friend of the Council, sir," Duncan declared.

Mason seemed to think Duncan was trying to entrap him. "We all should be friends of the War Council," he said with an uneasy glance at Rhys, who had positioned himself to block the door. He cast about nervously, then saw his hat hanging on the wall and retrieved it. "I have an engagement," he said, his voice cracking. "I forgot I had an engagement." He would not look Duncan in the eye.

"A few weeks ago," Duncan ventured. "I was in Lancaster, in the Pennsylvania colony. I met some of those who were emulating your preparations for the transit of Venus, following your very helpful chart. Your good work was bringing out the nobility in them, sir." Mason hesitated, and finally looked into Duncan's face again. "A farmer there brought in the fragments of one of your marker stones," Duncan continued. "It had been purposely shattered by an agent working with the Horse Guards."

Mason's eyes flared. "Dear God, no! They go too far! The stones were to be perpetual! What stone? What number? A five-mile marker or a single-mile stone?"

"I do not know. What I know is that you and I both have enemies among the Horse Guards. I am convinced two of their officers committed murder to suppress certain efforts of Dr. Franklin."

Mason seemed to weaken. He steadied himself on the corner of his desk, then settled into the chair. "Do not antagonize them, I beg you! If you love life, sir, do not antagonize the fiends."

Duncan cleared the chair on the opposite side of the desk and sat. "I only wish to discuss the fiends with you, sir. In the way one man speaks to another of mutual enemies."

As Captain Rhys entertained himself with the telescope, focusing on the war ships on the Thames, Mason slowly revealed his tortured experience with the Horse Guards. He began tangentially, speaking first of his surveying commission and the hardships he and Jeremiah Dixon had endured. "The marker stones," he said, "they made it all seem permanent, as if indeed our work was for the ages, that people might recall it decades from now. They were all mined and carved in England, you know." The astronomer was clearly disturbed by the news that one of his precious stones had been destroyed. "Three years and nine months. Such a labor. Living rough. Taking over a thousand star fixes, checking timepieces, sighting lines across rivers, through thickets, over high rocky ridges."

"It was a labor of Hercules," Duncan offered. He was ashamed to have made the man so uncomfortable. Mason's work in America had been an extraordinary accomplishment.

"We weren't permitted to finish," Mason confessed. He sounded broken-hearted yet somehow relieved to speak of it, as if Duncan had become a long-sought confessor. "When we started west of the Alleghenies the tribes had to be placated. The superintendent of Indian Affairs, the great Sir William Johnson, got involved, and had to convince the tribes that we were not seizing land, simply measuring it for the good of all. It had not been all that long since the Indian uprising, so it was agreed that we would have an escort of Iroquois warriors."

Duncan was well aware of the tensions with the tribes over the survey, for William Johnson and Patrick Woolford had asked for his help, and more importantly that of Sarah, in convincing the Iroquois Council to support the effort.

"We had a terrible scare that last summer when an Iroquois war party intercepted us. We were sure we were to be set upon, but they were only passing through to pursue some feud with the southern tribes. Still, several laborers deserted after that and half of our own escorting warriors decided there was more glory in the war party and left us." Mason shrugged. "We pressed on. What an ordeal. But then on October ninth our enterprise was terminated. Our Iroquois friends had spied enemy tribesmen of the Leni Lenape across a creek and insisted we could go no farther."

It was an exaggeration to say the Iroquois and Leni Lenape, the Delaware, were enemies, but the Leni Lenape did have a deep resentment of the Iroquois for giving away huge tracts of their ancestral lands to the Penn proprietors. Duncan had heard of the incident at council fires, and knew the Leni Lenape party had far outnumbered the survey crew. Lives had indeed probably hung in the balance, and the Iroquois had made the right decision.

"Two hundred thirty-three miles," Mason said. "It might have felt better if we had terminated on some majestic mountaintop, but it just ended at some nameless muddy creek." He hung his head a moment. "Destroying a marker. It is sinful. It is a crime against civilization."

"Help me, Mr. Mason, and I will ensure a proper replacement stone is erected. The farmer preserved the location with a post."

"Pennsylvania stone can be very soft," Mason pointed out.

"I know of good granite in the northern mountains," Duncan said. "I vow to you that I will do this. But I need to know more about the Horse Guards."

Mason lowered his face into his hands for a moment. "Not here," he said when he looked up. "Walk with me outside."

They left the building and climbed to the topmost ruins of the old castle, with Rhys following a few steps behind, and sat on a slab of stone fallen from the ancient walls. "They called this a castle but it was really a hunting lodge with a tower, built for Henry the Fifth. The Eighth liked to bring his mistresses here, they say, and would joke about yearning for a good hunt. It's all dust now. The Henrys, the mistresses, the castle, all dust. Worlds come and worlds go. Looking back now I can see that to the tribes it was as if we were laying cornerstones for new castles in their ancient homeland. But if Jeremiah and I hadn't done it the Royal Society would have found someone else."

"The Royal Society? I thought it was the colonial governors who sent you."

"They asked the Royal Society to select the leaders of the expedition, and determine the protocols for measuring. It felt unifying somehow, the way relations with the colonies were meant to be, answering a political problem with the application of scholarly knowledge."

"The Society must have been overjoyed upon your return to London."

"Most members were, the ones who are true scholars. Several said I should be the new Astronomer Royal. But others were furious when I reported that I had helped the colonials prepare for transit observations. They said I had exceeded my commission, that if the king desired to advance such knowledge among colonials he would have so decreed.

"I admit I didn't take them seriously, Mr. McCallum. By what right does one man tell another that he is not permitted to acquire knowledge of the world? Isn't the process of acquiring knowledge the very essence of human progress? I continued my efforts to help the colonists, assembling and shipping equipment to them. Three telescopes, two sextants, tinted glass lenses, plumb bobs and levels for setting up the equipment, even special bound ledgers for recording the observations and performing the calculations.

"One day months ago a horrid man appeared in my office wearing high boots and a uniform so overdone I thought it might be a costume. He said, 'Sir, you must stop presuming on the king's affairs.' I thought he was gibing me, and laughed. Then he picked up one of my lenses and dropped it, shattering it, and repeated the words. I called for the house stewards to escort him out, saying that the army had no authority here. He sneered and said he was not the army, he was the king, as far as I was concerned. He named himself Major Hastings and said that if I did not respect his word, I would learn about the power of the king well enough.

"I put the miserable man out of my mind, for I was busy preparing our presentation to the Royal Society about the survey line. I kept up my transit work, though, and was corresponding with astronomers in France and Germany. I always thought natural philosophy was the best unifier between nations, the structure to build common ground with others despite political differences."

Mason quieted. He picked up a piece of stone at his foot that Duncan saw was the carved head of a bird broken off a statue or wall carving, and spoke to the bird. "I came into my office one day to find Hastings in my chair. He dragged me to the window. Another officer stood outside with a basket filled with papers. It was all the correspondence they could find on my desk, including important letters from the continent and several calculations that had taken days to complete. Hastings didn't say anything, just clamped a hand around my neck to force me to watch as his man—a Lieutenant Nettles, I learned later—ignited my papers. They reduced all that valuable work to ash and then laughed about it.

"I was furious. I complained to the Astronomer Royal, who was strangely subdued in his reaction and just told me that with dedication to prayer I would find the right path." Mason shrugged. "Nevil started out as an Anglican minister. So I complained to the Society. I complained to the commander of the Horse Guards."

"Their colonel?" Duncan asked.

"A man who is as genteel as he is worthless, a mere figurehead. He offered me brandy and explained very solemnly that Major Hastings was on long-term detachment to the War Council, engaged in matters vital to the security of the kingdom."

"The War Council is eight men. Hastings works for all of them?"

"I doubt Hastings and the Secretary at War would worry about anyone less than an earl."

"So you gave up your efforts."

"No. Ignorant, proud fool that I was, I redoubled them. Surely, I thought, a few bullies cannot be allowed to interrupt the pursuit of knowledge, for that is the God-given right of every man. I printed instructions for observing the transit and dispatched them to Philadelphia through the Pennsylvania agent."

"Dr. Franklin?" Duncan asked in surprise.

Mason nodded absently. "I began to give lectures on the transit observations in church and guild halls. It was so gratifying to see how the common man was uplifted to learn about the workings of the heavens. In the words of poor Mr. Wilkes—may he find peace in his captivity—the masses are a great fallow field waiting for the seeds of knowledge to be planted. At one hall a man actually shouted out 'Wilkes and Liberty' at the end of my talk, as if I were speaking for Wilkes. I though it somewhat droll at first, but later it scared me.

"One day Hastings and his men appeared at the back of one of my lecture halls. He waited until I finished, then informed me that I hadn't sufficiently grasped his lesson, then just left." Mason's face twisted with pain. "I had an assistant, a bright young student from Oxford. The next day he was bringing some instruments for us to calibrate. He never arrived. His wagon was found on a bridge with no sign of him. The instruments were gone. Of course we thought it was highwaymen. But two days later his body was found in the river. I don't know that they meant to kill him, probably just threw him off the bridge. But he drowned, and I don't think they cared. A day after that, Hastings and his man Nettles were waiting at my door with the missing instruments stacked in the hall. It hadn't been highwaymen—it had been the despicable Horse Guards.

"I stopped my lectures but they somehow intercepted letters Benjamin and I had written to friends in Philadelphia. Later Benjamin warned me about the Black Chamber of the Post Office, which intercepts certain mail to the colonies. One day my ten-year-old son went missing. We were terrified, had the whole neighborhood looking for him for hours. I was out all night searching the alleys and riverbanks. The next day Hastings arrived here in a coach and told me to get in. We drove up here. My son was with Nettles, who was cheerfully showing him how to fire a pistol.

"Hastings didn't say anything to me, just exclaimed about what a fine lad my son was, and what a great soldier he would make, said that young orderlies were needed by the king in the fever islands. Then he pulled out a heavy hammer, a sledge for pounding rocks, and took me to the ruins over there—" Mason pointed to another pile of stone slabs. "One of my best telescopes was there, on its tripod. He kicked it over and handed me the sledge. 'Destroy it,' he said, 'and we will let you have your son back, for so long as you behave.'" Mason wrung his hands and for a moment Duncan thought he was going to weep.

"I can still hear the ring of the crystal as I shattered the lens, the groaning of the brass tube as I flattened it. It was one of the finest instruments in England, in all of Britain, and the king's ape made me destroy it."

"Surely there could have been avenues of redress," Duncan suggested. "There are reasonable men, perhaps some who are fellows of the societies in Philadelphia and London, who could set things right."

As Mason studied Duncan, fear flickered in his eyes. "Did Dr. Franklin send you? I can have no contact with Franklin, don't you see? They will take my son, McCallum, maybe next my wife."

"Franklin did not send me," Duncan stated truthfully. "It's just that—I mean, surely the king can't resent your telescopes, or oppose scholarly pursuits."

A bitter laugh escaped Mason's lips. "That's the trap, isn't it?"

"The trap?"

"Thinking that the cause of reason is a shield, that if you can but reach the king he will understand. I'm not sure if he will understand but it doesn't matter, for men like Hastings make it impossible to reach him. They seem to think that the work of natural philosophers borders on treason, for it cannot be controlled by the king. It has an authority and logic all its own. That is what they resent. They form an invisible force around the king, made up of child snatchers and killers and thieves, for whom no act can be a crime, because all they do is in the name of the king. They won't think twice about committing the most hideous of acts, for in them they take a perverse delight. They will even take your mind and twist it into a shriveled, raving, useless piece of gray tissue."

Duncan felt ice in his belly. "Why would those words come to mind, sir? How do they twist minds?"

"If they but call you insane you are insane."

Duncan leaned closer. "Do you speak of Bethlem Hospital?"

Mason winced. "Such a horror. I barely know how to speak of it. It is as if they have devised a special kind of torture for men of intellect. He was an acquaintance of mine, a professor from Cambridge. A nephew of his, a student, had been taken up by a press gang for the navy. The professor was outraged. He sent letters of protest to the War Council. When they did not respond he went to their offices. He waited for hours without being seen and then lost his temper, saying he would see the king, that the king would understand if he could have but five minutes with him. We know all this because there was a witness, an army contractor from Cambridgeshire who saw the confrontation and reported it to the professor's wife. Some officers of the Horse Guards dragged the professor away, and one of them laughed and said we must call Dr. Granger for such an illness. His wife never saw him again. She made inquiries at Newgate Prison, at all the prisons, then thought of Bedlam. They discovered that this Dr. Granger was a senior physician for the royals, and eventually bribed an attendant there who reported that her husband had been there, in one of the lunatic wards on the top floor, with instructions for him to be dosed heavily with medicines from this Dr. Granger."

Duncan was numbed by the words. Mason was describing Conawago's fate. He wanted him to stop but just stared, stricken, at the astronomer.

"He had screamed and raved," Mason continued, "then taken to reciting long scenes of Shakespeare. But he hadn't lasted. In the end he took to hitting his head on the walls. He died after a week of smashing his skull and was buried in one of those mass graves for paupers."

Sarah—Every night since arriving in London I have dreamed of Conawago. At first it was nightmares, of the king having him drawn and quartered, of him smashing his skull on the walls of Bedlam, of his head on a pike outside some castle gate. But lately my dreams have been like lenses on times we have spent together. One night he and I walked among a herd of wood buffalo we found in Seneca country, speaking comforting words that kept them from spooking. Another night we were gliding in a canoe along the moonlit shores of Lake Ontario. Last night it was the first time I camped with him on one of the treeless mountains in the Adirondacks. We spoke about the mysteries of the stars and afterward he went to the highest point, arms outstretched, and spoke toward the night sky. When I asked him what he had been saying he said he could not tell be-cause that was between him and the heavens. Then he put his hand on my shoulder and said what a man whispers to the stars is the truest reflection of his soul.

The house on Chesterfield Street looked like a small version of one of the city's palaces, far too opulent for the residence of a friend of Sarah's. Realizing there had been a mistake in the address, Duncan crossed the street to wait for Ishmael in the shade of a plane tree, then whistled as the young Nipmuc stepped out of a hackney cab a few minutes later.

"I bribed one of the keepers to get in before visiting hours," Ishmael reported. "I went to the barred door of the Chamber of the Immortals and called my uncle's name. He looked up at the ceiling as if the sound was coming from the heavens. I spoke to him in our tongue. He held his head in his hands and wept. I stayed for his performance. He was wrapped in a sheet again and spoke loudly in what I think was Latin, though he was faltering from time to time as if forgetting what he was saying.

"When he finished I shouted '*Quinsigamond!*' He cocked his head for a moment toward the door and I thought at last I had reached him. He threw his arms into the air." Ishmael hesitated, and for a moment Duncan thought he might offer a glimmer of hope. But then his face twisted in pain again. "Then his sheet fell off and he stood naked except for a short loincloth. People thought it was part of the show and threw pennies at him." Ishmael leaned against the tree as if needing support.

"The keeper I had bribed, Taggart is his name, said they had hauled one of the inmates away from the chamber the day before because he was showing his companions exactly what part of their heads they needed to slam on the wall to cause death."

Ishmael seemed incapable of further speech. Duncan put his hand on his shoulder. "We'll walk back. We can find the right house tomorrow." They had taken half a dozen steps when the black enameled door of the palatial house opened and a woman in an elegant dress the color of claret appeared, holding a fan of peacock feathers. It was Madeline Faulkner, waving her fan to summon them inside.

Madeline had been perplexed to receive a note from Duncan that morning since she had not known that they were in London. When she suggested that they must all come, including Pierre Dumont, for a dinner the next evening, Duncan said nothing, waiting for the maid to finish pouring their tea. He recalled that Madeline had departed Philadelphia before the catastrophic night of fire and death. Duncan closed the door of the parlor as the maid left. The words grew more difficult each time he spoke them. "Pierre Dumont," he announced, "was murdered in Philadelphia."

A small moan escaped Madeline, and her fingers went to her throat, touching the cameo that was fastened tightly around her neck with a wide ribbon that matched the color of her dress. "I only met him once," she said after a moment, "but he seemed a kind, gentle man, and most intelligent. He encouraged me about mankind."

Duncan studied the woman with more interest. He had not taken her too seriously when he had met her in Philadelphia, for she had seemed just another frivolous socialite. "He was coming to help Dr. Franklin," he said.

"To give him those big bones you collected," Madeline replied.

"To stop the army from occupying the colonies."

Madeline's cup stopped in midair as she considered his words. "I am not sure I follow, Mr. McCallum."

"Another wise, gentle man came to London earlier. From the Nipmuc tribe."

For a moment Duncan thought Madeline was going to pretend to not understand, then her rigid expression broke into one of chagrin. "I never had the honor of meeting Conawago," she said.

Duncan leaned forward with new interest. "I didn't mention his name."

"You might say I met the gentleman indirectly. I first heard his name in a letter from Johnson Hall."

"My uncle and William Johnson have spent long nights playing chess in Johnson's manor house," Ishmael ventured.

Madeline gave a small sad smile and examined Ishmael with new interest. "Two Nipmucs in London. Did you leave any of your tribe in America?"

"Are you saying William Johnson asked your family to help Conawago?" Duncan asked, not bothering to ask how a woman like Madeline would know anything about the diminishing Nipmuc tribe.

"Not at all. Requesting the hospitality of one of London's great families would seem impertinent, since Sir William does not know my father."

"Miss Faulkner," Duncan said more stiffly, not able to get the measure of the woman, "I am not clear on your involvement with the tribes."

"Dear Sarah asked me to revive our old family charity. We send books and blankets and missionaries and other useful things to the suffering savages." She made a fluttering, dismissive motion with her hand. "It gives me something to talk about at society affairs. The Disciples of the Forest they were named, decades ago. Such an earnest, Quaker name. Perhaps you have heard of it?"

"I believe it has an office in Albany," Ishmael said.

"So I understand. What a lot of silly paperwork it takes to help poor heathens." Madeline was sounding more like the featherbrained woman he had met in Philadelphia. Duncan was more confused than ever about her. "You don't strike me as particularly evangelical."

She smiled. "My family in the past were all strict Quakers. Now we are burdened not so much with religion as with riches. I am not married. My father believes I need to be campaigning for a husband, as he puts it, which means being more socially engaged and living in London. He is right, of course. The dressmakers are *tres courant* here. And the charity becomes such a wonderful game, charming lords and ladies out of gold for the exotic tribes. Perhaps you two have some advice on how to play it?"

"Right now we are interested in helping one particular Indian," Duncan said, losing patience. "If you're saying no one asked you to help Conawago, then we thank you for the refreshment and we shall be leaving."

"No, Duncan," Ishmael interrupted, keeping an appraising eye on their hostess. "I think Miss Faulkner is saying it was not William Johnson who asked her to do so. My uncle had other friends at Johnson Hall."

Duncan blinked. "The deputy superintendent? Patrick Woolford? Or perhaps his wife?"

Madeline gave a bored sigh. "Yes, yes. Henrietta or Hetty or some such name. It's been ages and ages since we met, but she sent a letter to me in Philadelphia saying their friend Conawago was coming to London and might I help. No doubt she knew I had a connection to the old Disciples."

"Help how?"

Madeline sighed again. "If only Patrick had been in London. All his fussing with land agents and solicitors over the family estate surely must be over soon. And why did your uncle have to come during the social season? Does he understand nothing about London?" She shrugged. "The house sits vacant for much of the year. It's too modest for my father's tastes, and his is too ostentatious for mine. And I have so little time during the season. One ball after another, and never may I wear the same dress twice. Do you have any notion of what a burden that is?"

Duncan struggled to maintain his forbearance with this pampered woman. "Are you saying you assisted Conawago?"

"Perhaps we should go upstairs, if I can be so bold as to invite two gentlemen into the sleeping quarters. The servants will carry on so," she added with a mischievous smile, then rose, opened the door, and summoned the maid.

"We require the groom," she instructed the woman, "and a bucket of strong vinegar water."

"He is busy polishing the coach for your father to use," the maid pointed out. "Should I send the footman?"

Madeline seemed to puff up at the impertinence. "Did I not say the groom? You shall instruct the footman to put on an apron and take over the polishing. At once!"

Duncan was surprised that Sarah would befriend a woman who could put on such airs, but then saw a hint of amusement on the maid's face as she turned away. He thought again that he did not fully understand Madeline Faulkner. He silently followed her up the wide stairs, pausing with her as she explained the portraits of venerable ancestors.

Ishmael was less patient. "Are we to understand that you secretly made arrangements concerning my uncle without involving us?" he asked accusingly.

"Prithee, sir," she coolly replied, "surely you understand I knew nothing of your presence in the capital until this past hour. When I left Philadelphia no one had mentioned you were coming to London. I had briefly met Mr. McCallum in Philadelphia, but that was just ships passing in the darkness, as they say. When I left your very Quaker city," she reminded them, "Sarah was planning to come to London, to stay with me. And that charming Pierre Dumont was still alive." She indicated a portrait of an elderly man wearing a broad lace collar and holding a terrier in his lap. "They say Sir Humphrey was a friend of the gallant Francis Drake," she said with an expectant gleam.

Duncan nodded and spoke in a flat voice. "I believe I had an ancestor who stole cattle from a landlord named Sir Humphrey."

A suppressed giggle rose from the maid, who had arrived with a pungent bucket.

"Why, Mr. McCallum!" Madeline rejoined, amusement in her eyes. "Shameful! I suspect if we investigated we would find that some of my ancestors hanged some of yours." She turned down the hallway, missing the flash of resentment on Duncan's face. It was indeed possible that her noble family had hanged some of his kin, but in his own lifetime.

As Duncan and Ishmael followed Madeline down the hallway, the maid busied herself in what was obviously a familiar routine, rolling up the long hallway carpet and spreading a generous layer of the vinegar water on the floor, then attacking it with a mop. She seemed oblivious to the biting scent of the vinegar, which was used often to scour what most called lingering miasmas, though Duncan was surprised to see it used so liberally in such a mansion, and with guests present. He saw the same questioning reaction on Ishmael's face, then caught up with Madeline, who had opened what Duncan had taken for a closet door. A narrow winding stairway was revealed, and he realized he was looking at a hidden passage for servants.

Madeline glanced briefly down the hallway behind them. "The rest of the staff do so hate the smell of the vinegar," she said with a quick, wry smile, then gathered up her skirts and mounted the stairway.

Duncan looked back at the maid before following Madeline. The maid was middle-aged and carried herself with some authority. Why was a woman who was obviously a senior member of the household staff doing the work of a chambermaid? Madeline had only called for vinegar water, but the maid had instantly understood where to take it. Was it possible she was using vinegar to assure their privacy? But why would the flighty Madeline even care about keeping the rest of the staff away? Did some of her servants share news of her household with her estranged father?

"I sent instructions that a guest bedroom be made available," she said as she climbed, speaking over her shoulder. "But apparently he was more comfortable with a less pretentious accommodation, which upset the household to no end since he was here as my guest."

They arrived in what Duncan took to be the top floor, emerging into the servants' quarters. At the far end of the hall, past a doorway that divided the floor in half, a maid in a shift, her hair negligently flowing to her shoulders, darted to the door and shut it. At the near end, illuminated by a small window at the end of the corridor, a well-built man, taller than Duncan's own six feet, stood outside the last door. He began a deep bow to the mistress of the house, which Madeline forestalled with a wave of her hand.

"This is our groom," she said without further explanation as she lifted the door latch and gestured them inside. It was a bright corner room with windows on two sides and walls made of fragrant unfinished planks.

"Duncan!" Ishmael cried, and darted past him to a familiar cartouche bag lying on the narrow bed. He clutched the bag to his breast, then sat and gazed forlornly at its quillwork pattern of deer and birds.

"You be family then," came a deep voice over Duncan's shoulder. The groom was gazing at Ishmael with a profound sadness on his face. Duncan stepped aside to let the tall man enter, and the groom approached the bed and put a hand on Ishmael's shoulder. "The Nipmuc tribe," he announced. "My friend spoke proudly of a nephew named Ishmael, and said if I ever met him I would be allowed to learn his nephew's tribal name."

Ishmael looked up in surprise. It was a hidden message, meaning that Conawago trusted the big man.

Madeline, still in the doorway, made a sound of clearing her throat. "Your uncle apparently shunned being treated like a proper guest of the household," she explained. "I am told he preferred to spend time in the mews, with the horses. I take it Noah and he formed something of an attachment." She glanced back down the hallway. "I must go select my jewelry for tonight," she declared airily, "but Noah may provide some small comfort."

Duncan and Ishmael exchanged a glance. "Noah?" Duncan asked, trying to recall where he had heard the name.

"In Conawago's last letter!" Ishmael said. "He referred to his friend Noah!" He faced the groom. "And you, Noah, sent the letter with the news about him being in Bethlem!"

The groom gave a melancholy nod of affirmation. As he settled onto a stool by the window, Duncan could see he was of mixed blood. His skin was a light almond color, his hair black with small, tight curls. He watched Ishmael stroke the quillwork on the cartouche, then spoke in a slow, articulate voice.

"Your uncle was the first from the American tribes I had been able to speak with in over eight years. Such a pleasure it was to meet him. Such an honor to get to know him." His speech was refined, his accent hinting of Yorkshire. Noah saw the curiosity on their faces and began to explain.

"I was born on a sugar plantation where many years earlier captives from the old New England wars had been sent in chains, tribesmen turned into slaves. Conawago saw that blood in me right away, said I reminded him of a Narragansett or maybe a Wampanoag, though I told him I knew only that my mother was a high mulatto, herself the offspring of a French overseer and one of those native slaves who worked in the kitchen. I never knew my father, but just before she died of fever my mother told me he had escaped when I was just a year old and gone back to the Massachusetts home of his people, where he fathered another son." A smile flashed on the groom's broad face. "Conawago said it was wonderful, to think of all the worlds embodied in me. It was the kind of thing my mama would say, when she gave me lessons at night instead of sleeping. She had great learning, and in her prime was one of those the overseers called a fancy."

Noah's expression grew sadder as he studied Ishmael. "You are the one, then. He was so proud of you, with the love of a father for a son." The groom tilted his head, his eyes widening as if in sudden recognition. "And the other he spoke of like a son was a Highlander. A man with straw-colored hair, a huge heart, and an overactive mind, he said. Duncan. Duncan who wears McCallum plaid." He saw Duncan's nod, and nodded himself. "Both his sons. It's right that you came. He would have liked that, would say that the old spirits summoned you." He gestured to the cartouche. "Miss Madeline and I weren't sure what to do with his things. She said she would take them back next time she went to America." He gestured for Ishmael to open the bag.

With a slow reverence the young Nipmuc laid the bag on the bed and lifted its leather flap to reveal Conawago's personal possessions. He pulled out strands of beads, a wooden spoon with a dark patina of age, a tattered cornhusk doll, and a tiny, tattered buckskin bag, sewn shut, cherished because it held a coin given to the old man's grandfather by one of the settlers at Plymouth. Finally he withdrew a rolled piece of black broadcloth. With a rush of excitement he unfurled the cloth, then groaned as he saw what lay inside. He was staring at the little quillwork leather pouch that had hung from Conawago's neck for decades, his totem, the home of his protector spirit.

"No! He cannot—" Ishmael began in a choking voice. His emotions overwhelmed his tongue.

"He did. He said it was yours now," Noah explained. "He said it will see you into the next century like it saw him into this century."

Duncan had to push down his own emotion. "Are you saying he knew beforehand what awaited him?" he asked the groom.

"I don't know. He was frightened. He had gone to the Department of Indian Affairs in Whitehall, but no one was there but clerks. They sent him to the offices of the War Council, where some military man spent hours questioning him. He had been ordered to return there the next day, and he said he had to comply because he still had a chance to convince them to let him see the king. This was the last time I was able to speak with him. That last night I heard him speaking in here in his old tongue, for hours. I think he was praying, though sometimes it sounded like singing. It put me in mind of a funeral. The next day he disappeared."

"Disappeared into the oblivion of Bedlam." It *was* a funeral, Duncan almost said. His old friend had been singing his death song.

Ishmael looked into the cartouche and withdrew the last object, wrapped in a tattered velvet pouch. He opened the pouch and emptied it onto the bed. "It's real!" Ishmael exclaimed. "He talked about it but I had never seen it."

They were looking at a round medal rimmed in gold and blue enamel, encircling a shield of white on which a red cross was centered. Underneath in inlaid lettering was *George Rex*.

"The cross of St. George," Duncan said, not sure why he was whispering. "And just George Rex. Not the second, or third."

"He said he was given a gift by the first George, which he was going to share with this George," Ishmael said.

"It's the emblem of the Order of the Garter," Noah said. "Not a gift given lightly."

"He left it here," Duncan said in a sorrowful tone. "He didn't really expect he would be seeing the king that day." They stared in silence at the decades-old medal, until Duncan finally turned to Noah with another question. "Why would you send that note about him being imprisoned to Philadelphia?" Duncan asked.

"I sent it to Miss Madeline in Philadelphia, thinking she would know who to give it to. Someone should know, I thought."

"But Noah," Duncan asked, "how could you know where he was?"

"I didn't, not at first. I asked the parish watch, then those in the adjoining parishes. I asked at the prisons, and began to despair that he had taken his own life." He shrugged. "Then when I realized what had happened, I found some of my friends who work at Bedlam, some cleaning the building, others working the laundry. They let me in and they went from room to room with me. There was no sign of him, but they would not enter the east end of the top floor. They were frightened of it. So I paid for one of those tickets and went in with the visitors. That's when I finally found him, with those Immortals, but watched over closely by a cruel keeper who was missing part of his ear. The man spoke harshly and told me to be on my way when I showed an interest in your uncle. The next night I went in with the laundry men and I was able to get inside his cell, to sit beside him for a few minutes. He didn't recognize me at first. He was becoming untethered from reality. He spoke gibberish, and then when he made sense it was only a few words at a time, like he could not focus his mind. That's when he gave the totem to me, saying someone had tried to eat it the night before. He said that Ishmael must have it. Ishmael the last Nipmuc."

A silent sob wracked Ishmael and he wrapped his hands tightly around the totem.

"He said the totem wouldn't work in there, that everyone there had their souls ripped open, and their souls were shrieking so loudly that his gods would never hear the groans of one worn-out old Nipmuc."

Ishmael lowered his head into his hands. Duncan stepped to the nearest window. The world outside blurred through his tears. He balanced himself with a hand on the wall as he fought a despair so wrenching he feared he might collapse. When he finally spoke it was a whisper. "How did you know?" he asked the groom. "How did you realize he was in Bedlam?"

"Like I said," Noah replied, "it took me a long time, nigh two weeks. But then a man came."

"From the Horse Guards?"

"A man in high riding boots and a flash waistcoat. It was a day when Lord Faulkner was having a banquet and all the staff was over at his big house for the preparations. They would never have me mind the house otherwise. This flash fellow pounds on the door. He demands to know whether the man named Conawago had lodging here. I think he had come to take away Conawago's belongings, to wipe out any trace of him. But when need be I can play the cringing servant. 'No, master,' I said. 'This be a proper house. Lord Faulkner would ne'er allow nobody with one of those disturbing foreign names to cross his threshold, 'cause Lord Faulkner is a proper Englishman, God save the king.' He quieted then, and I said maybe look down around Charing Cross or Covent Garden where the bawdy houses and coffee shops are, 'cause that's where disreputable foreigners linger. He nodded and said there must have been some mistake, then gave me a penny and left.

"But then I saw he was waiting across the street for a hackney, so quick as I could I changed into old stable clothes and followed him. On a busy afternoon a cab goes no faster than a man can briskly walk. It took him to the Moorgate, where the hackney waited while he met a man in brown clothes in a tavern. He gave the man some coins, then got back into the cab. I was right tired by then and worried about chasing him all over the city but I didn't need to, 'cause he yells out 'Horse Guards barracks' plain as day to his driver. So then I followed the man in brown, though I thought I recognized his clothing already."

"He worked at Bedlam," Duncan suggested.

Noah nodded. "A keeper, they call them."

"A keeper who spies for the Horse Guards," Ishmael said. "Would you recognize him?"

"Of course. He had gray and brown hair cut short, and his left ear was missing its lobe, like it had been bitten off. Made it that easy when I went in during visiting hours. He walks around the top floor like a soldier on guard, especially watching those chambers at the end."

"And the officer's name?" Duncan asked.

"Briggs. When I answered the door he says he was Captain Briggs and he demanded to see the master of the house. That's how I could make inquiries."

"Inquiries?" Duncan asked.

"I have friends who sometimes work the coaches for the Horse Guards, 'cause sometimes we are together tending fancy coaches at banquets and balls and such. This Captain Briggs usually works in civilian clothes, even some old tattered ones he wears when he wants to blend in on the streets. He boasts to those in the stables that he does loyalty patrols, saying his job is to redress the loyalty of those closest to the king and dissuade those who seek to impose on the king. Like natural philosophers, if you credit the rumors."

Duncan, now intensely interested, sat on the bed, facing Noah. "I do indeed credit them. Speak to me about them."

"They say while his commanding officer was out of the country, Briggs was stalking the Astronomer Royal and members of the Royal Society. But Briggs was the one who took my friend—our friend—to Bedlam, I am sure of it. Conawago had been making his visits to Whitehall, and he wouldn't have tried to hide his intentions. Briggs was the one. Sometimes in the visitors' registers in Whitehall they ask for an address. That's how he must have found this place. He came to eliminate any evidence that Conawago had been in London. Once I knew it was Briggs who sent our friend to that living hell, I could at least act with a clear conscience."

"A clear conscience?"

"He had a morning riding routine. Very rigid, very predictable, the same path every day in Hyde Park, out where the Guards have a stable for the training of their mounts. One day when he dismounted to pass water in a clump of bushes, I placed a stalk of thorns under his saddle. His horse threw him against a tree and broke several of his ribs. He still can't get on a horse. And I don't feel a bit guilty," Noah declared with a defiant gleam. He looked down at the stable yard and muttered about the fool mixing up the harness, then excused himself. As he lifted the latch to leave the room there was a sound of hurried footsteps in the hall. Someone had been listening.

Noah hesitated before he stepped into the corridor. "Don't do it, son," he said to Ishmael. "Don't throw your life away trying to beat the Horse Guards and Bedlam. You think you owe that to your uncle—I can see it in your eyes. But what you owe him is survival. Do him that honor."

"Honor?" Ishmael asked.

"The way you honor Conawago is by leaving now, by going home and living a long life as the last of the Nipmucs."

Chapter 15

D
UNCAN SAT IN THE CAVERNOUS sanctuary for over an hour, distracted
at first by the carved faces, the tombs, and the impossibly high arches built
centuries earlier. Soon enough, however, all he could see were scenes of Bedlam.
He felt no less helpless now, in the great abbey near Whitehall, than when he had
sat under the bone arches of the Shawnee shrine. He searched the shadows as if
for answers, but everywhere he looked the ghastly faces of gargoyles and long-dead
knights mocked him. The image of Conawago's empty face and drooling words
gnawed at his consciousness, as did the conjured image of his wise old friend bash-
ing his skull against Bedlam walls and the thought of Conawago's frantic soul
being drowned out by the shrieking souls of other inmates. The assured denial
by Franklin when Duncan had warned him that he was on the same track as
Conawago was almost as distressing as Noah's description of a Conawago who
had given up all hope.

He had passed the late afternoon of the previous day with Franklin at Craven
Street. As if by unspoken agreement, they had spoken of Franklin's experiments,
his travels in Scotland, his house in Philadelphia—anything but the treacherous
intrigue that surrounded them. As he grew more familiar with the inventor, Duncan had begun to discern a profound innocence in the man, a stubborn tendency
to see only the good in others. It was surprising to find such qualities in a man of
Franklin's years, and Duncan could see it endeared him to those in his makeshift
family, but it meant others had to protect him. He recalled a bitter day in Philadel-

phia when he had called the leaders of the Sons of Liberty gullible, but Franklin was more so, and now Duncan wondered if the inventor himself was endangering secrets of the Sons.

Failing to find the peace he had so desperately wanted, Duncan made his way out of Westminster Abbey and then to the rear of the complex that housed the Horse Guards. In sternly warning him away from the compound, Captain Rhys had emphasized that although the small Department of Indian Affairs office was indeed based there, it also housed the Horse Guards officers, the Secretary at War, and a mix of officers and civilians, used by the Council, who advised the secretary and administered the army. He wasn't merely in enemy territory; he was in the enemy headquarters.

Duncan had reconnoitered the perimeter, confirming through the signage and the busy traffic of well-dressed civilians that the main entrance was off the parade grounds, where the elegant coaches that called on the building had ample space to maneuver and await their passengers. He had discovered a familiar face among those exercising horses at the side of the large grounds. Ensign Lewis was one of those leading a string of horses at a slow trot along the walls. For a moment he felt a twinge of sympathy for the awkward young Scot, but it was quickly banished as he recalled that Lewis had been among those who had tumbled him into the Atlantic.

Duncan discovered an inconspicuous door at the rear of the building, at the end of a shadowed alley, where men in civilian clothes briskly came and went without being challenged, some of them in clothes no better than Duncan's own worn waistcoat and britches. He had begun to understand that the War Office managed information to suit its purposes, and was not above using secrets like weapons. It meant the office would have many informers and watchers, some of whom would be dressed to blend with London's street traffic. He screwed up his courage, waited as two men busily engaged in conversation entered the alley, and followed them inside.

He pushed in close behind the pair and the sleepy guard at the door gave them a cursory nod. Knowing that Indian Affairs would be a small, less prestigious office, he had decided it was likely to be relegated to the top floor, so he mounted the first stairway he found. After the first flight he peered out into the hallway, seeing a noisy collection of uniformed men gazing out a row of windows overlooking the parade grounds, commenting on the riders and coaches. He quickly continued his ascent, emerging into an alarmingly busy hallway where bewigged men in starched collars walked alongside senior officers in the uniforms of several different army units. Duncan selected the direction with the fewest officers and soon found them thinned out to just a handful lingering on a bench outside a chamber with a double set of doors. Past them the furniture and paintings on the walls seemed to grow less elegant. He reached the end of the hall only to find another hallway joining it from the left, then followed this corridor past doors with small neatly printed placards declaring CORDAGE, EQUINE, GUNPOWDER, VICTUALS, and other supplies requisitioned by the military.

Encouraged by a painting of tribesmen standing with officers around a captured French banner, he quickened his pace and entered the double doors at the end of the hall. Over the head of the inquisitive clerk who sat inside was a portrait of Sir William Johnson, superintendent of Indian Affairs.

The clerk assessed Duncan with a skeptical eye. "Yes?" he asked.

Duncan simply stated, "The deputy superintendent."

The clerk frowned, glancing at a set of inner doors that were slightly ajar, where two more clerks anxiously lingered, each holding thick journal books. "All appointments were cancelled today. The secretary convened an urgent meeting and everyone—"

A chorus of voices interrupted him, followed by the scraping of chairs. The two clerks retreated with deferential backward steps. Grinning at what he took to be a confirmation that he would soon know how to reach the deputy superintendent, Duncan stood by the doors as they opened and richly attired men began filing out. The first man in a uniform froze as he saw Duncan, then darted to him, shoving him into a nearby office.

"Patrick!" Duncan said, not understanding the furor on his friend's face. "I came just to learn how to contact you but now—"

His friend Patrick Woolford replied only with a sharp curse. He seized Duncan by the edge of his waistcoat, half dragged him to a tiny chamber at the back of the office that seemed to be an unused water closet, and pushed him inside. "Not a word! Not a movement, if you love your life!" Woolford snapped and pushed the door shut. Duncan heard what sounded like a bench being drawn across the floor and pressed against the door. Then he heard the office door being shut, followed by muffled, unintelligible voices.

Duncan at first grinned, remembering the early days when Woolford and he played pranks on one another, but then he recalled the rage on his friend's face, and when Woolford did not reappear after several minutes, all possibility of amusement evaporated. He strained to make out what the muffled voices from the outer office were saying, then began to worry he might next hear the heavy boots of provosts coming to arrest him.

In the dim light that seeped under the door, he made out a row of pegs that held an old uniform tunic, an empty sword scabbard, and a crescent-shaped piece of brass that he recognized as an officer's gorget. On a shelf above the pegs leaned a cornhusk doll, a plaything of Iroquois children, and an intricate piece of quillwork showing two hands reaching across a tree to clasp each other, no doubt done by his wife Hannah. In London Woolford probably did not advertise that he had a Mohawk family.

The longer he waited the more apprehensive he became. He was holding the scabbard like a club when the barrier was finally pulled away and the door opened.

"You damned fool!" Woolford growled. "You came within an inch of your life! That was the War Council!"

"Patrick, I had to find you."

"The War Council, damned you! Do you not understand?"

"But I don't know anyone on the War Council."

His friend cursed again, then grabbed Duncan's arm and pulled him to the window at the side of his office. To Duncan's surprise, they were looking over the parade ground. Opulent coaches with teams of four were being loaded in the courtyard below.

"The coach with green enamel and gold trim, the one pulled by the four black Friesians, belongs to the Earl of Milbridge!" Woolford said.

Duncan leaned forward with new interest, remembering that the Earl of Milbridge was the one name on both the War Council and the board of governors for Bedlam. "I don't know the Earl of Milbridge, Patrick."

"You are reckless beyond belief! The Earl of Milbridge," he snapped again, then pointed as the team of elegant black horses pulled up to the palace entrance.

Duncan looked down as a footman positioned a stepping stool, then opened the coach door. An overweight aristocrat emerged from the palace, speaking with a more simply dressed somber-looking man, then shook the man's hand and strutted toward the coach.

"That's the Secretary at War he left at the door," Woolford explained. Duncan glanced at his friend in confusion. "Look harder," Woolford pressed.

As Duncan watched, the corpulent man turned and the sunlight hit him full on the face. Duncan's gut instantly turned to ice and he jerked to the side of the window.

"The king awarded him a new title and estates a few months ago. Something to do with arranging new borrowings with Dutch bankers."

Over two years had passed since Duncan had seen the man who had vowed to kill him, the man who had tried to kidnap Sarah in order to remove part of her rebellious brain. The Earl of Milbridge was Lord Ramsey, Sarah's ruthless father.

Woolford retreated to the desk in the center of the office, extracted a bottle of gin and two glasses from a drawer, and poured an inch into each glass. "Welcome to London, my friend," he said ruefully and toasted with one of the glasses. His hand trembled as he drained his glass. "By Christ, if he had seen you, your life would be forfeit! What in God's name are you doing here?"

Duncan drained his own glass, trying to keep his own hand from shaking. "Trying to find you," he repeated.

"I mean in London!"

"Trying to save the lives of two good men."

"I've been away. As I told you, my father died. The estate is tied up in a tangle of solicitors, creditors, and land men. I returned only two days ago to find a note from Madeline Faulkner with the news of Conawago. I had no idea you were here. I have contacted a lawyer who says we can file a writ."

The words stirred Duncan from his paralysis. "Patrick, no judge will act to save him. He is in Bedlam on a sentence of slow death, in the name of the king."

Woolford studied Duncan uncertainly, as if not sure whether to believe him. "Two. You said two lives."

"Those who condemned Conawago also have Benjamin Franklin in their sights."

The deputy superintendent frowned, clearly not believing the announcement, then poured more gin. "It won't be safe for us to leave for at least a couple of hours," he said. "I can either labor over piles of dusty correspondence or be entertained by your tales."

Duncan was still struggling to collect himself after seeing the earl, who embodied evil more intensely than any creature he had ever known. He drained his glass again. "Then first you must hear of an ancient monster I retrieved from the Ohio country."

Woolford gave a weary grin. He was changed from the former captain of rangers Duncan had parted from in the Mohawk country months earlier. His weathered skin had grown pale, and the intense energy that had always burned in his deep-set eyes had dimmed to a dull glow. "Sounds like a Highland fairy tale," he said after Duncan had spoken of why he had gone down the Ohio. "Are you honestly going to tell me that Conawago is in Bedlam because of some long-dead creature from the Ohio?"

Duncan's reply died on his tongue as he weighed Woolford's words, then looked back toward the window over the parade grounds, visualizing again the powdered demon who had become the Earl of Milbridge, advisor to the king. A cold blade was slowly piercing his heart. He knew now the odds against him would be nearly insurmountable, but he forced himself to consider again the parallel paths that Conawago and Franklin had taken, converging on the same goal and attracting the same enemies. "Yes," he said, "maybe I am. Or better to say because of the same men who have shrouded the *incognitum* with death."

They lost all sense of time as Duncan recounted the events after his arrival at the Lick. Woolford recognized Ezra's name but had never met the freedman, though he knew that his agent Reynolds in Pittsburgh was fond of him. "We had a council with some Shawnee near Fort Pitt last year," he said. "They were excited because the prince of a distant tribe had married a princess of their tribe. They boasted of a new alliance between the tribes," he added with a sad, ironic smile. "But it became an alliance of tragedy."

He listened intently as Duncan described his journey to Philadelphia and why he had been forced to unexpectedly make the voyage across the Atlantic.

"Pierre Dumont was an acquaintance," Woolford said with a sigh. "He visited Johnson Hall once, asking to speak to tribal members there about any strange animals they had seen, said he would return in a few months to record their stories. He was a congenial man, I recall, dedicated to his sister almost as much as to his studies. I remember one night he asked Sir William and me what is the point of a man's life if he cannot advance the knowledge of this mortal sphere. That's what he said, the knowledge of this mortal sphere. I remember because Sir William toasted him, saying it was a noble sentiment spoken by a noble man."

Duncan went on to explain their subterfuge with the false crates on the *Galileo* and how Pierre's sister Olivia had secretly escorted the real bones to London. Finally, he revealed how Major Hastings and his aides shadowed those connected to the *incognitum*. He finished with the statement Hastings had made about the need to kill Benjamin Franklin.

"But Hastings was drugged, you said," Woolford pointed out. "You cannot put much faith in words spoken under such conditions."

"I placed much credit in them after we discovered that the Horse Guards' secret hunters were stalking Franklin." Duncan paused. "You did not react like everyone else has when I said the Horse Guards were involved."

Woolford's face tightened. "The difference is that I actually sit in meetings of the War Council. I hear of certain Guards going on detached duty. I know what some of them are capable of doing."

Duncan accepted more gin, then recounted what he had learned from Charles Mason.

"Mason," Woolford said with a sigh. "His name came up in a War Council meeting two days ago. I sit in the back of the room in case there are questions about the tribes. I had just returned from Wiltshire and didn't understand at first. Apparently the Council had been receiving reports about the transit of Venus. Today Major Hastings angrily reported that Franklin had engaged in a subterfuge, then was sternly rebuked by the Secretary at War for speaking so openly of something that was the affair of only a few members of the Council."

"Why would Venus be the business of the War Council?" Duncan asked.

"Not because they are natural philosophers. Nearly every man on the Council owes his wealth and position to the king, and their continued enjoyment of their status requires endless currying of favor with George. They are very jealous of those trying to communicate with the king through channels not under their control."

"Violently so," Duncan agreed.

"If someone outside their circle gets secret news to the king, they consider it not merely disrespectful but an attack upon their own authority, upon their own position with the king. They would not get their own hands dirty, but those who do their bidding are ruthless."

"Why," Duncan pressed, "is distant Venus so important to the War Council?" He still had difficulty accepting that the king so coveted the transit records that he would agree to a secret meeting with Franklin.

"It took me quite a while to fit the pieces together. Do you know that King George built his own private observatory in his deer park?"

"So I've heard."

"And he personally made observations of the transit on June third. The paramount observations, the palace has called them, the primary observations, demonstrating the genius of our sovereign. Apparently they were sound, although of course he had a small army of astronomers to assist him, including the Astronomer Royal, none of whom shall receive credit. But now there is an astronomical twist that has both the Privy Council and the War Council most upset. George had not fully grasped that a single observation is useless. It is an exercise in trigonometry. No one observation site, not even a royal one, can provide the solution. There must be at least one other reliable one to compare it to, so the angles and distances can be calibrated and the parallax defined."

Duncan shook his head, not understanding.

"Duncan, rumors are rampant that the next best observations are from the colonies, from Philadelphia! The War Council loathes the leaders of the colonials even more than the royal governors do. One of the Council members actually went so far as to say a new front of resistance has been opened up by the colonials, conducted by astronomers and mathematicians. The king has not been told. It has become a conundrum, for they know the king takes his own philosophical work most seriously. He would dearly like to have those observations, especially if they were confided to him so that he could publicly declare the results, as if they had come to him by some divine right. He is deathly afraid the French will be the first to announce the final calculation of the distance to the sun."

"And?"

"The Council intercepted a message to the Astronomer Royal. Franklin proposes to give the observations to the king, but only in person, so he might also present the king with a priceless gift from the American colonies."

"The *incognitum*," Duncan whispered. "They're committing murder to keep the bones from being given to the king."

Woolford's expression grew tormented. "Duncan, surely no one is killing over old bones. You must be—"

Duncan interrupted, his anger rising. "Sarah's father would. Major Hastings would. Three murders plus that of an unborn child already. They can't stop now. If their treachery is exposed they will have all those deaths to account for. So one more death, or one after that, means little to them. But as far as they know for now, they threw those priceless bones into the sea, along with me."

"God's blood, Duncan—" Woolford clutched his glass so tightly Duncan feared it would break. "It would be a perversion of the truth. A crime against—"

"Against knowledge," Duncan said, nodding, "against civilized progress, Franklin says. If there is such a thing," he added, exchanging a pointed glance with his friend. They both knew the tribes might consider the phrase a contradiction.

Woolford rose and stepped to the window, gazing onto the parade grounds. "But if they believe they destroyed the bones, why would they not withdraw? The Philadelphia scholars can just publish their observations and let the world judge the quality of their work."

"Then Franklin would lose his leverage, his opening to see the king. Were it not for—" Duncan dared not speak of the secret plans for more troops to be sent to America, not in the very headquarters of the army. "Were it not for matters of state Franklin would likely just turn everything over to the Royal Society."

"He must not!" Woolford snapped. "Several members of the War Council and the Privy Council are in the Society. Franklin's safety depends on his secrecy. Surely he knows there are those in the aristocracy who despise him. He has foolishly allowed himself to become a declared enemy of the Penn family, and they are one of the most powerful families in Britain. His speech against the Stamp Tax was called traitorous by the Penns and many of their circle. He may have strong support among the Whigs, who sympathize with the colonies, but Lord Hillsborough loathes him, and Hillsborough is not only the Colonial Secretary, he is also head of the Board of Trade which regulates all commerce with America. The Duke of Grafton does his best as prime minister to keep the policies moderate but he is no favorite of the king. And the proprietor, Thomas Penn, spreads poison about

Franklin whenever he can, ever since he sought to have Penn's charter revoked. The latest is that Franklin arranges secret shipments of cranberries so he can gift them to attractive young women, knowing they are a native aphrodisiac."

"I'm sorry—cranberries?"

Woolford paused and stepped to his desk, opened a drawer, and extracted three sheets of expensive paper, extending them to Duncan.

"You want me to read a report on army food stores?" Duncan asked after scanning the first page.

"The embossed mark of crossed swords at the bottom is that of the small press used by Whitehall for official business. Forget the official business, just look at the bottom of each page." He pointed to verses in small type above the swords. Duncan quickly read the couplets:

Little red pearls from the cranberry bog
Given to tarts by the fat colonial dog

Ye ladies of London heed my words well
Ne'er visit Ben in the morn, he's au naturel

That rogue's the inventor who plays the Norse god
Seeking to pin all London with his stiff lightning rod

"I'm not sure I understand," Duncan confessed.

"They are about Franklin's eccentric private life! The printer receives these little mocking pieces and sometimes inserts them into documents for the War Council, which is highly amused by them. I have heard them read aloud and sometimes the Council breaks into laughter for minutes at a time, I assure you."

"But why show me?" Duncan asked.

"Because you need to understand. The War Council has Franklin in its sights. He is not infrequently discussed in meetings. They are not enemies to trifle with. And the Earl of Milbridge is the most insidious of all. Publicly it is said he was elevated for his role in saving the government from financial ruin, but behind closed doors it is said he procures for the king certain pleasures not otherwise available to him. The earl has a new palace, a hunting lodge, he calls it, close to the king's own lodge in the old deer park, and George is known to have taken late-night carriage rides from one to the other."

Duncan was silent for several long breaths. "But where do these couplets come from? Franklin is covetous of his privacy."

"His life is not nearly so private as he thinks. For some at high levels he is the symbol of the protesting colonials they have come to loathe. His veil has been pierced."

Duncan returned his friend's pointed gaze. Henry Quinn had warned of the loose lips at Craven Street. Someone had known about the tin Franklin had arranged to be smuggled through Virginia. Someone had known about Ezra's mission for the Covenant. Someone had known about his mission for the *incognitum*. The spy working against the Sons was likely someone in Franklin's own household.

Woolford reached deeper into his open drawer and extracted several small gold and silver pins, each like a little shiny brooch. He dropped them in front of Duncan. "The men of the War Council have immense wealth, which they seek to display like strutting peacocks. One of the ways is to present lavish tokens and favors at balls and banquets. I've seen diamond bracelets handed out to every lady in attendance, and silver-mounted walking sticks to every gentleman. One of the common devices are these, pins of gold and silver, always with some image that glorifies the benefactor. An image of a newly purchased ship or castle is common."

"Why do you—" Duncan began.

"Because such pins are a favorite of the Earl of Milbridge," Woolford explained, nudging three pins, all in gold, closer to Duncan. "All from Milbridge. His renowned race thoroughbred Achilles," he said, pointing to a pin with an image of a horse and the Latin phrase ACHILLES FORTIS EQUI arching above it. "His new Scottish castle," Woolford continued, indicating a pin bearing the image of a turreted building. "And this one," he said, pointing to the third, in the shape of a horseshoe with what appeared to be a tombstone inside it. Engraved around the horseshoe were the words PARS LIBERTATIS.

"Fate of liberty?" Duncan asked as he lifted the pin to more closely examine it.

Woolford nodded. "This particular pin was distributed to the staff at all his many estates, and to attendees of a War Council meeting last year, where several members considered it very droll, as if it represented some private joke. It was mysterious enough that I made inquiries with his coachmen. Only one would talk, and he just said to take a lens to it. I did. Inscribed on the tombstone in tiny letters is the name Barrett. I asked more questions. Barrett was a groom at the earl's Merseyside estate. He had organized a meeting in support of John Wilkes. The barn was ringing with cries of 'Wilkes and Liberty' led by Barrett when the Earl of Milbridge unexpectedly arrived, a day before his planned visit. Milbridge loathes Wilkes and his movement. He dismissed the steward on the spot, and Barrett's body was found the next morning in the stall of a stud horse, made frenzied by placing mares in heat in every nearby stall."

Duncan dropped the pin on the desk.

"Don't give him a chance to make a pin for you, Duncan. Go home. Let me work with solicitors to help Conawago."

"The Sons of Liberty trusted me to secretly deliver the bones. I will see them through to their purpose. I made a vow, for Ezra and Pierre."

"There are ships leaving most every day for the colonies. Ezra and Pierre would not want you to die on their account."

"The Sons of Liberty," Duncan whispered, "will take it quite ill if I allow Dr. Franklin to be assassinated."

Woolford gave a slow, reluctant nod. "As I expected you to say."

"Ishmael and I are not going to retreat."

Woolford offered a bitter grin. "This city wears on me. I need a good battle. You, me, and Ishmael. Two rangers and a Nipmuc warrior against the War Council, the Horse Guards, and the castle keep of the lunatics. And if Milbridge gets the slightest hint that you are still alive and in London, he will rip the city apart to find you."

Woolford was increasingly uneasy as they approached Bethlem Hospital. When they had finally climbed into a hackney by St. James's Park he tried to make small talk about Sarah, about Duncan's beloved orchards at Edentown, about his wife Hannah and their expanding family. But Duncan did not miss his anxious glances out the window or his tight grip on the leather seat as they passed under the statues of Melancholy and Raving Madness.

"I was here once before, Duncan," he said, "many years ago. It gave me nightmares for weeks. I vowed never to go back again. I will wait for you on one of the benches outside."

"When Conawago decided the gods wanted him to go to London, he went north to Johnson Hall, to see your wife, Patrick. If Sarah or I had known we would have found a way to stop him, even it meant locking him in his room. But your Hannah helped him, and I suspect she wrote to you of it. You never told Sarah or Ishmael. You never tried to stop it, to intercept Conawago. Your wife and Madeline secretly made it possible and now he is locked inside what you so aptly call the castle keep of the lunatics."

"I had no idea what had happened, you must believe me," Woolford protested. "I wasn't even certain Conawago had gone through with his plan to cross the Atlantic. Hannah made me promise to say nothing. Conawago had insisted on secrecy because he knew what you would do. It was Conawago! When have you ever said no to him?"

Duncan ignored the question. "You are going up to the top floor with me."

Woolford sighed and pulled his cloak tighter over his uniform. "I'm going to the top floor."

When they met Ishmael at the back of the throng by the Chamber of the Immortals, the young Nipmuc gave the deputy superintendent a cool greeting.

"I'm sorry, Ishmael," Woolford said. "I only recently returned to London. I did not know until today. I thought that if he was in London he would be safely encamped at the Faulkner House. I was planning to go for a visit."

Ishmael's eyes narrowed. "If he was going to see the king it was to stop the bloodshed of English brothers fighting each other," he said.

Woolford recognized the accusation. His face twisted in torment. It was not a sentiment Duncan had heard before, but Ishmael had spent long hours in the hospital thinking about his uncle and the path that had taken him there. He meant the old Indian had come to London to help the colonists more than the tribes. It was a particularly poignant point to make to the deputy superintendent of Indian Affairs, who himself was married to a Mohawk. Woolford was well aware of how the tribes had been treated by colonials and the British government.

"Your uncle has the most generous heart of any man I know," Woolford replied. The words did nothing to soften Ishmael's expression. Woolford clenched his jaw and looked toward the barred doors, now blocked by the afternoon audience. He fixed each of his two friends with a sober, determined expression. "We will not let him die here," he murmured.

Ishmael impassively studied the Englishman, who still held a commission as captain of rangers, then pulled his totem pouch out from under his shirt and extended it. "Say it again," he instructed.

Woolford, understanding the tribal gesture, solemnly touched the pouch and complied, then gazed in mute astonishment at the huge fang that hung next to the pouch. Ishmael chose not to explain.

When they finally pushed their way through the crowd to glimpse Conawago, Duncan thought Woolford was going to be physically sick. A low groan escaped the lips of the ranger and he clutched his belly. Conawago had been staring blankly at the onlookers, but as they watched he began smearing something brown on the far wall. His linen drape was slipping and his left buttock was exposed.

"Praise the Lord, I've seen Aristotle's breech," a man quipped, raising guffaws. Duncan wanted to pummel the man.

Ishmael, whose daily visits had steeled him against the horror, commented that his uncle's color looked better and his hair was clean. "They say he seems to enjoy his morning treatment of being submerged in the cold water," Ishmael recounted in a hollow voice, and nodded toward a gaunt keeper on duty at the edge of the barred door. "His name is Taggart," the Nipmuc whispered. "On the second day I gave him half a shilling but made no request, just mentioned I was interested in the welfare of the old man they call Aristotle. The next day I gave him another coin and he said it was a shame, for the old man seemed a gentle soul except he had the wrong eyes. The next day I asked Taggart what he meant and he said Aristotle's eyes had been deep and defiant at first, so he had to be treated. I asked him to explain, and yesterday he gave me this"—Ishmael revealed a small muslin pouch clutched in his palm—"and said Aristotle and most others in here, as well those in several other wards of the top floor, get a strong brew of this tea with their porridge each morning." As they watched, another of the Immortals joined Conawago and to Duncan's surprise the random smears began taking on a shape.

"It calms them, Taggart says, and helps with the entertainments."

"The entertainments?" Woolford asked.

"That's all he said. He says he can speak with me only once a day, or otherwise the other keepers will grow suspicious and ask to share in his fee. But he did say that fat one, the town crier, has been agitating the other inmates and hounding the keepers, inflaming them even, by insisting that Conawago doesn't belong in Bedlam. Taggart told the crier to shut his mouth for once or he would truly have something to cry about. There's another keeper, the one with a piece of his ear missing, who scares Taggart. He warned me to stay away from the man, says he works for men in high places, that he has a squad of toughs he calls out whenever there's trouble in these wards, and afterward there's always blood to wash up."

Surprised laughter rippled through the crowd. The shape had become a temple, a crude representation of the Parthenon. Conawago finished by writing symbols beneath the building, then straightened his toga to cover his nakedness, raising ribald laughs, and turned to address his fellow inmates.

One of the inmates responded with hoots like those of a monkey, another with the bleats of a goat. Conawago ignored them and earnestly continued with his speech. "Got to hand it to the old cracked pot," someone behind Duncan said. "He can spout out gibberish like he really means it, and at such a pace." The man reached past Duncan to throw a penny into the cell.

But then Conawago stepped aside and Duncan saw more clearly the smears below the temple. They weren't random smears. They were letters in Greek. Alpha, Beta, Gamma, Delta, Epsilon, Zeta, Eta, Theta. One of the inmates began wiping at the marks of the crude temple on the well and Conawago pointed a chastising finger at him. "*Min enochleite tous kyklous mou!*" he shouted at the man.

Woolford grabbed Duncan's arm. They had both understood. The Greek words were from Archimedes, spoken when a Roman soldier attacked and killed him in Syracuse while drawing geometric shapes. Duncan had never learned Greek, but many students studying the classics were taught the memorable sayings of famous Greeks. *Do not disturb my circles.* The lunatic "Aristotle" had not been speaking gibberish. Conawago had been speaking in eloquent Greek, taught to him by his Jesuit teachers as a boy.

They were about to turn away when the obese crier stepped to his makeshift podium and loudly intoned toward the audience, "*Felix, qui potuit rerum cognoscere causas!*"

They left together, walking in silence. It seemed that by wordless consensus they had decided to walk off their despair. The revelation that at least part of

Conawago's mind still held a bright spark had unexpectedly deepened Duncan's melancholy, for it seemed to underscore Conawago's suffering. The man speaking gibberish might be so confused as to not understand his surroundings. The man reciting perfect Greek perceived the hell he was living in. The final words of the crier gnawed at him. The man had recited Virgil, a motto over the door of Duncan's boyhood school. *Fortunate is he who is able to know the causes of things.* Duncan understood the cause of nothing.

Woolford seemed even more troubled than Duncan. At last Duncan suggested they pause at a tavern in an effort to lift his friend's heart. The stealthy, confident ranger, renowned for his deep forays into enemy territory during the French War, said nothing when the barmaid asked his preference. Duncan ordered strong ale for the three of them, then had to push Woolford's tankard against his folded arms before the deputy superintendent took notice.

"You're not to blame, Patrick," Duncan said. "I spoke too hastily earlier today."

"I could have warned him. I could have interceded had I not been away all these weeks."

It was Ishmael who responded. "No, you could not have, Captain. It's my uncle. The depth of his gentleness is exceeded only by the strength of his will."

Woolford's face lifted into a bitter smile. "It's Conawago," he whispered. "The wisest man I know. Possibly the best educated man I know. He has been the anchor that keeps hope alive in more than one tribe. But for the intolerance of the War Council he should have been made the superintendent of Indian Affairs himself. For him to end up like this—" He didn't finish the sentence. "Even if he does leave Bedlam, what hope is there that he will ever find his right mind again?"

"The man we saw today was created by Bedlam," Duncan said. He lifted the little medicine pouch Ishmael had given him. "Maybe this is how they did it," he said.

"If Milbridge was responsible for sending him there," Woolford said, "there is no hope of getting him released."

"Milbridge?" Ishmael asked.

"He is Sarah's father."

The news took Ishmael several long breaths to digest, then new alarm rose in his eyes. "You mean the man I am ordered to keep you a mile away from, Duncan?" He saw Duncan's questioning look. "Sarah made me promise."

Duncan grimaced. "There is no longer any real hope of getting him released," he said. "So he will have to escape, and soon."

"Impossible!" Woolford exclaimed, not noticing Ishmael's vigorous nod. Duncan knew the Nipmuc had always assumed that his uncle's freedom would have to be won by warriors.

"Says the man who once spirited half a dozen British captives out of the heart of an enemy camp," Duncan said.

"That kind of war I understand," Woolford replied. "This is a terrain we don't understand, with deadly vipers at every step. We need much more time to plan."

"I have a friend with a ship that soon sails to Boston," Duncan said. "We are going to be on that ship, with Conawago."

Woolford frowned. "Or dead."

Sarah—Benjamin Franklin now names me friend. I am not certain he even thought about his choice of words but it means much to me. I felt like an awkward schoolboy when going to his Craven Street house the first time, for he had become so much bigger than life to me. You might say I have been in his shadow for years, befriending his wife, visiting his Philadelphia home, meeting his Philadelphia friends. He always stood on such a high pedestal as the wizard of lightning, the father of electricity, the inventor of so many useful objects. I had been moved years ago by Immanuel Kant's description of him as the Prometheus of the modern age. Yet it was hard to be frightened of him when he presented himself with flour on his nose, and I found him quite affable. The lines of his round countenance are uplifted by frequent laughter, and I begin to realize that his rumored ardor for the fairer sex is mistaken for his larger lust for life. His prodigious intellect is not that of some erudite scholar but that of the energetic schoolboy. He told me that a long time ago he decided that the world was much more interesting if he approached everything with a sense of wonder. Life, he says, is more fulfilling if you understand that it consists of a series of miracles. I want very much to believe so but miracles are hard to come by in King George's city.

Dr. Hewson was clearly fatigued from a long day of calling on patients when he returned to his house at dusk, but he brightened when he saw Duncan waiting for him. After sharing a pot of tea he gladly took Duncan into his cellar workshop, where bones and medicinal jars were scattered over a workbench.

"I must confess," Hewson confided, "I came down here last night and took out some of the bones from the Ohio." He glanced uneasily at Duncan. "With no ill intention, I assure you."

"I sat with them for hours at a time while coming up the Ohio," Duncan admitted. "I understand. They are a wonder. There was a shrine built by the tribes near the Lick where the ancient animals died. An old chieftain told me the bones gave him visions of huge creatures unknown to humans today. At first I felt a strange fear when I heard that. But I have long wondered whether the people of the forest, the people who live embraced by nature, don't see and hear and feel things that the rest of us cannot. After a while I was envious of that old Shawnee. I pine for such visions."

Hewson gave a knowing nod. "So old, old as the mountains as far as we know. What did the earth look like when these creatures lived? What plants did they see? What did the sky look like? What stars did they look up to? They are so humbling," Hewson mused, in a physician's matter-of-fact tone. "Despite the arrogance of this modern world, a few years after we are gone, you and I will be dust. But these bones were preserved, as if the creatures of that ancient world were sending us a message." Duncan felt the pang of a sudden memory. Pierre Dumont had voiced almost identical words when they had sat together with the bones in Philadelphia.

"If Dr. Franklin can raise that sense of wonder in the king for even an instant," Hewson continued, "I know the king will listen to whatever Benjamin has to say." The doctor spoke earnestly, almost pleadingly. "There are things greater than we mortals, greater than politics. Isn't that what binds us all? In the end maybe that is really what Benjamin is trying to achieve, to strike that chord with George Rex."

Duncan smiled. "Maybe you should be the one speaking to the king."

Hewson gave a self-deprecating laugh. "The Astronomer Royal holds that key and he would never give me the time of day. He dwells in much higher altitudes than I."

"But Dr. Franklin is no aristocrat."

"Benjamin Franklin is a species apart. The wizard of lightning, the holder of honorary degrees from famous institutions, and American Fellow of the Royal Society."

Duncan suppressed a grin as he recalled Franklin in the kitchen with the maid, smeared with flour. "A species apart," he agreed, then motioned to the muslin pouch he had laid on the bench. "Brewed into a tea for patients at Bedlam."

Hewson hesitated. "Surely you know I cannot interfere with a regimen prescribed by another physician."

"I only want to know if you recognize it."

"You mean, physician McCallum, can I confirm your own surmise?"

"I studied at Edinburgh but never received a diploma. I had a few months remaining when someone else decided my lessons should be those of a prison."

Hewson's expression turned cold and he fixed Duncan with an intense stare.

"I gave a long-lost uncle shelter. Only later did I learn that he was a fugitive from charges of treason, stemming back to the uprising. We were both arrested. He was given a noose and I was thrown into a cell and sold in indenture."

Hewson relaxed and was silent for several heartbeats. "I am sorry, Duncan."

"If it had not been so I never would have gone to America, never made this new life and found the woman I love. What happened in Edinburgh is long behind me." He motioned to the granules from the pouch, which Hewson had poured onto a sheet of blank paper. "Do you have some tinctures for testing?"

His companion moistened a fingertip and lifted some of the granules to his nose, then sampled them on his tongue. "An alkaloid," he suggested. "Mandrake perhaps, or nightshade. In mild doses they have a strongly calming effect."

"Mandrake smells like tobacco," Duncan said, "and nightshade tastes like tomatoes. There is bergamot and ground cloves in this mixture, but I suspect only because the foul taste would be overpowering."

Hewson frowned but did not disagree. "Henbane, then," he said with a shake of his head. "Very dangerous. In strength a powerful hallucinogenic which numbs the senses. We tend to stay away from it."

"We?" Duncan asked.

"The physicians of London."

"Not all. This is being administered to certain patients at Bethlem, including my friend Conawago. Most patients may come in as lunatics, but for anyone else, this would assure they become lunatics after they arrive."

Hewson ran his fingers through the coarse powder as he weighed Duncan's words. "A hideous suggestion," he said.

"But what if it were true?"

"Surely no doctor would do such a thing. We take oaths. There are ethics."

"No honorable doctor. Perhaps only an apothecary or herbalist, though I tend to doubt it. The men who confined my friend were very highly placed. They would prefer a physician."

"Henbane!" Hewson spat the word like a curse. "There's stories of men overcome with henbane who climb steeples and jump, convinced they can fly."

Hearing the words spoken, the articulation of the fear that had been eating away at Duncan for hours, somehow made it real and nearly unbearable. Conawago had been living in a world of hallucinations, probably for many weeks. He recalled their first visit, when his friend had stared at him as if not trusting his eyes.

"Do you know the Earl of Milbridge?" Duncan asked.

"I know of him. He dwells on in the clouds with London's other gods."

"Do you perchance know his physician?"

Hewson frowned. "I have named him to you before. He is one of Bedlam's managing physicians, who sits in meetings of the board of governors. He will never be denied any request, for he is also the royal physician. Dr. Granger."

Chapter 16

Duncan and Ishmael watched from the shadows half a block away as Olivia Dumont descended the front steps of the Craven Street house. She handed a coin to Xander the link boy, who had so relentlessly dogged them the past few days that they had agreed to Sinner John's suggestion that they put the boy on a shilling-a-week retainer as "an extra pair of eyes and for such grimy tasks as ye may choose," in the porter's words. During their time at the inn they had begun to grasp that Sinner John had great affection for the flock of link boys he watched over, giving them scraps of food and shelter in the stable on foul nights.

Sinner John seemed especially fond of Xander, and had said a blessing over their clasped hands when Xander had spat on his palm and extended it for Duncan to reciprocate. The link boy had already proven his worth by running several errands for Duncan, including buying more ink and paper for his letters to Sarah, and had glowed with conspiratorial excitement at Duncan's instructions for Mademoiselle Dumont's foray.

The shadowed figure positioned across the street from the Stevenson house waited until the pair was fifty paces down the street before following. The Frenchwoman and her young escort moved slowly, engaging in lively conversation, with Xander, his clothes cleaned and his shaggy hair brushed and tied, apparently explaining each of the shops that bordered Charing Cross. As they passed a hat merchant, Olivia lifted a nosegay which Xander had purchased earlier that day and waved it overhead as if to perfume the air around her. It was the agreed signal, and Duncan and Ishmael entered the side door of the coffee shop by the gate of the Royal Mews. The proprietor was a great friend of Dr. Franklin, who sometimes lingered into the night speaking of the wonders of electricity, and was amenable when Duncan asked to rent his back meeting room for an hour. "This be a respectable establishment, mind," he cautioned when Duncan mentioned that Mademoiselle Dumont would be arriving with a link boy, then pocketed Duncan's coin.

With the door slightly ajar, Duncan was able to watch as Olivia played her role with an efficient grace, pausing in the main chamber to exclaim over the provocative Hogarth prints of *Gin Lane* and *Beer Street*. She made no hurry of following Xander into the back room, but when she did she quickly dropped the nosegay on the table and dashed out the rear door, which opened into the kitchen.

They had only one lamp lit in the windowless room, with the baffle set low so that it sent out only a small flickering beam onto the discarded nosegay. The slight figure in black pushed the door with a tentative hand, then saw the flowers and rushed forward, realizing his prey was trying to evade him. Ishmael, standing along the wall, closed the door behind the man. He froze as Duncan stepped into the light, then turned deathly pale. A terrified, choking cry escaped his throat just before he fainted.

Ishmael hauled the limp soldier into a chair, bracing his head on the table, then took the pitcher from the sideboard and dribbled water on his face. Ensign Lewis revived, coughing, then saw Duncan again and with another abject cry shot up out of the chair, tipping it over. When he saw that Ishmael blocked the door, he pressed into the corner and with fearful moans collapsed onto his knees.

"Dear sweet God, no! It is true! The murdered come back to haunt!" He raised his clasped hands to beseech the heavens. "Oh blessed Jesus, protect me!" he gasped in desperation. "A Highland ghost! Forgive me, shade of Duncan McCallum! I am too young to be taken to the other side!"

Lewis was so shaken that Duncan was beginning to regret taking Ishmael's suggestion that he dab flour on his cheeks. "You admit, Ensign Lewis, that you were among those who killed me," Duncan said in a slow, lugubrious voice.

The ensign took a drink from a jar of ale Ishmael pushed toward him. "The major said we was just going to give you a bad scare by dangling you over the rail!" Lewis paused to collect himself. "He said you were to be shaken enough to not complain about the loss of your precious cargo! I actually joined in to be sure you didn't fall, then Lieutenant Nettles elbowed me away and over you went. Please! I beg you! I have tried to live a virtuous life! My mother! Oh, my blessed mother!"

"Stand up," Duncan instructed.

Ishmael had to help the ensign to his feet. He gave a mournful groan as Duncan grabbed his hand, then quieted as Duncan pressed it against his chest. Lewis grew very still, then extended a finger, jabbing Duncan's shoulder, then his arm. "You came back in the flesh?" he asked in an agonized whisper. "It's a miracle!"

"I did not die that night, Ensign. I am a good swimmer."

Lewis still seemed unconvinced. "You swam to England?" he asked, more astonishment than fear in his voice now.

"I swam enough to save myself," Duncan replied, then righted the upset chair. "Sit."

Duncan lifted the baffle from the lamp to brighten the room, then took the chair opposite Lewis at the table and wiped at the flour on his face. "I read that there are two hundred capital crimes in England," he began. "Attempted murder is as good for a noose as murder itself. The ship was an English ship. English laws apply. I have half a dozen witnesses including the captain who will testify you were part of the gang who tried to kill me."

Lewis hung his head. "All because of that storm off Nova Scotia. My ship was badly damaged. I lost my coney foot, I told you, and all my luck with it. That's why I was thrown in with the major. I didn't ask for the Horse Guards, he forced me." Lewis twisted and looked at the rear door with a forlorn expression. "And now I've lost the Frenchwoman. Lieutenant Nettles will beat me."

"If you prefer prison to your work, we can have you arrested now."

Lewis grimaced but appeared to hear the invitation in Duncan's words. He seemed years older than the naive ensign Duncan had first met in the mid-Atlantic. "Why did Hastings force you to join him?"

"Because he thought I would be one of his thralls. He has his own special squad and calls himself the shadow general. They get extra pay, in silver from his own hand, and sometimes he arranges special pleasures for them. But they don't behave the way proper soldiers should, sir. They are more like highwaymen for the king."

"Why you?" Duncan pressed.

Lewis hung his head again. "I wanted to be a farmer, that's all, just wanted to keep a croft with my ma. I told her if I did well maybe someday I might even be a schoolteacher." He turned his gaze to the nosegay on the table as he spoke. "I drank too much ale those nights on the *Galileo*. Hastings insisted one of the artillery lieutenants pay him a gambling debt. The artilleryman said his purse was in his trunk and damned if he would unlock it for Hastings. I said I could open it, and in my drunkenness boasted that I had been a picklock when I could not afford another loaf for my mother, and when I was arrested my uncle bought me the cheapest commission he could find to keep me out of jail."

"Picking locks would be a preferred skill for one of Hastings's dark warriors," Duncan observed.

"I had repented of that life! I just wanted to be true to my uniform and the vow I made to the king when I signed my army papers. I wanted my mother to be proud of me again."

"But here you are, wearing no uniform and performing favors for a murderer."

"I have no choice! I told you, they beat me, even threaten to confine me in their dark dungeon. I know it is wrong. I can't sleep at night. I stay up and pray."

"There are always choices, Lewis. Help us and maybe you don't have to be included when Hastings falls. Help us and maybe you can sleep better at night."

"What do you want?"

"I want you to talk. About Hastings. Who he meets with, where he goes. But first, why follow this woman?"

"Mademoiselle Dumont?"

Duncan glanced at Ishmael. "How did you know her name?"

"Major Hastings knew it. Far be it from me to ask how he came by it."

"Why follow her?" Ishmael echoed.

Lewis shrugged. "She is French. The major seemed to think that was enough. He did say that the French reopened the old war by invading Corsica and that France's most important spies were beautiful women. He says the prime minister is going to fall because of Corsica, and pushing the damned Whig out with evidence of French perfidy in London would be that much better for the king." Lewis paused, seeming to consider what he had just said. "His words, sir, not mine."

Duncan considered Lewis's news. The Duke of Grafton, the Whig prime minister, was indeed being excoriated in Parliament for having allowed the French to invade Britain's ally Corsica. It gave Hastings a plausible excuse to watch Dumont, and would make a good tale for the War Council though he knew it was not the major's real reason for doing so.

"But then there was her journal," Lewis added. "After that he assigned more men to watch her, though who knows why old bones upset him so."

Ishmael and Duncan exchanged an alarmed glance. Ishmael pushed a chair close to Lewis and sat. "Old bones?"

Lewis nodded. "She has a drawing book, you know, with blank pages, that she carries and consults sometimes when she sits in coffee houses. Lieutenant Nettles has one of those link boys who's really a cutpurse, one of those can steal from your person without you knowing it. The lieutenant went out with this boy, Bertie, and had him steal the book out of Mademoiselle Dumont's bag while she drank coffee and read a newspaper. Then he looked through it and had Bertie put it back in her bag. He had taken me along, for training, he said, and told me we were seeking evidence for the king. They were just some drawings of old bones, though I don't know why a woman with Miss Dumont's charms bothers over such. The lieutenant was confused at first and said something about Frenchwomen and their surprises, but then he laughed and said, 'Lewis, you and I know they don't signify anymore,' which I guess means it's true what the men on the ship said, that your boxes were full of old bones.

"But then three days ago we did it again, 'cause the lieutenant wanted to see if she had anything new in the book. It was all the same drawings, except now many of them had measurements, like she had been studying the bones here in London, which was impossible, of course. The lieutenant went real quiet. He touched the pin on his waistcoat, then began cursing something awful. He told me training was over for the day and he ran out to catch a cab back to the Horse Guards Palace."

Duncan stared into the shadows, digesting Lewis's report. On his first look at the journal, Nettles had discovered that Olivia was unexpectedly part of the *incognitum* scheme. But on his second he had realized that the new markings meant the bones were not on the bottom of the Atlantic after all.

"Pin?" Ishmael asked. "You said he touched a pin?"

Lewis nodded. "Not long after we got back there was one of those secret meetings in the war room. When the major and the lieutenant came out they were laughing and fastening these little gold pins on their lapels."

"What sort of pin?" Duncan asked, recalling the collection of small pins in Woolford's office.

The ensign shrugged. "Far be it from me to be studying their ornaments up close. But my sense is that it was a medal for a victory of sorts. From some earl—I heard them talk of the earl's token and his sense of humor. The lieutenant touches it and still laughs sometimes."

"Tell me, Lewis, where do you go at the end of your duty?" Duncan asked. "Whom do you report to?"

"The major, or sometimes just Lieutenant Nettles. Sometimes we go up to a chamber by the War Council rooms, where gentlemen sit in the shadows and listen. Rich gentlemen, I take it, for they wear silver buckles and velvet waistcoats and great quantities of powder in their wigs. They smell of too much lavender and rosewater. There's earls, and even a duke sometimes."

"Members of the War Council," Duncan suggested.

"Don't know, for they hardly would introduce the likes of me."

"What do you report?"

"Where Franklin goes. Where the mademoiselle goes."

"And where does Franklin go?"

"To a doctor named Hewson. 'Course everyone knows Franklin suffers the gout, so that's no surprise. To dinner at a club by St. James's last night. The lieutenant was angry when I said I didn't know whom he ate with. But the major said it was all right, that the steward there was a friend of his from a place called Madame Roland's and he would know."

Duncan rose and paced along the table as Ishmael cracked the door and surveyed the coffee shop. "Tell me, Ensign, who else do Major Hastings's men watch?"

Lewis grimaced. "I'm not sure I should be—"

"I'm not sure the army should be spying on loyal subjects," Duncan interrupted. "I *am* sure the prime minister would like to know about it."

Lewis stared down into his folded hands. "I'm a soldier," he said. "I just want to stand in battle line and do my mother proud."

"And your mother would be proud of you now?" Ishmael asked.

The words unlocked Lewis's tongue. "The men talk a lot in the barracks. I hear they spent much time in Greenwich these past months."

"You mean Charles Mason," Duncan stated.

"Sometimes, but they said mostly Mr. Maskelyne, the Astronomer Royal."

Duncan tried to recall what he had learned about Nevil Maskelyne. "The Reverend Doctor Maskelyne."

Lewis seemed crestfallen at the news. "No one said he was a man of the cloth."

"Why Maskelyne?"

"They never said. But that all stopped, no more after the dinner he had."

"What dinner?"

"The men of the shadow squad, for that's what they call themselves, talk about it and laugh sometimes over their ale. The Astronomer Royal met Dr. Franklin at Billingsgate, at a low kind of place more suited for sailors and smugglers, and the shadow men remembered 'cause they were betting on which of the fancy tarts there would leave with the gentlemen. But all they did was talk about the king's schedule, the Venus observations, and the king's new observatory near his new lodge in the deer park. Then everything changed again a few days ago, when Hastings returned and made a miraculous recovery from his injuries. His head seemed fine after a day or two, and he even stopped wearing his arm in that sling. He ordered the men to stop watching the Astronomer Royal and start watching Craven Street. Then two days ago an urgent meeting with some of the War Council was called."

"After Lieutenant Nettles saw Mademoiselle Dumont's journal the second time," Duncan suggested.

Lewis nodded. "We could hear the shouting all the way down on the parade grounds. When Major Hastings came out he was furious, cursing about colonial tricksters and the sons' sleight of hand."

Duncan leaned closer. "Whose sons?"

"Don't know. Some sons across the ocean, I took it, for he said, 'How dare the damned colonial sons practice so on us!' The major was like a mad dog in his frenzy. 'They'll soon have more dead bones than they ever dreamed,' he shouted."

Mrs. Laws, steadfast in her nautical tradition, started breakfast at six bells, announced by three pairs of strikes on the ship's bell mounted by the dining room door. Duncan let Ishmael sleep and joined Captain Rhys over platters of sausage and boiled eggs in a discussion of the *Galileo*'s overhauling at the Blackwell Yard that ended with Rhys railing over the owners' reluctance to pay for new copper plate on the hull.

Franklin had boasted of being an early riser, so Duncan felt comfortable arriving in the Craven Street kitchen door while the sun was just rising over London's steeples.

No one answered at his knock, and though its hearth was lit no one was in the kitchen. Recalling that Mrs. Stevenson had talked of buying food for breakfast each day at the nearby Hungerford Market, he ventured into the hallway. Then, still finding no one, he cautiously proceeded up the stairs, pausing at each step to listen. His hand went to the knife concealed behind his waistcoat. Hastings's bravado knew no limits. Duncan knew he was perfectly capable of ordering his teams to surreptitiously enter the house if given the opportunity.

His knife was in his hand as he entered Franklin's sitting room. The hearth was freshly stoked. Beams of the early sun were streaming in through the wide windows. Duncan stayed in the shadows along the edge of the chamber, moving stealthily toward the bedroom, until a floorboard creaked.

"In here," came a languid voice from the bedchamber.

Duncan straightened and returned his knife to his belt. "It's Duncan McCallum, sir," he called.

"Duncan, my friend, do come in."

Not sure how he felt about entering the great man's bedchamber, Duncan took a tentative step inside and froze. Franklin was seated on a chair by the open window, reading one of London's newspapers. He wore nothing but his spectacles.

"Such an excellent morning!" Franklin exclaimed and rose to greet him. He laughed as Duncan pivoted to avert his gaze. "No need for embarrassment, Duncan. This is my daily air bath. Been doing it for years. An hour every morning in the fresh air, no matter what the weather. So salubrious! Have I told you my theories of how contagion travels in foul air? Bathe away the noxious fumes! Join me and we can read the papers together. Leave your earthly restraints on the chest at the end of the bed."

Duncan still did not face Franklin. "I—I have already taken my morning ablution, sir." He recalled now one of the couplets Woolford had shown him. *Ye ladies of London heed my words well, ne'er visit Ben in the morning, he's au naturel.*

"But you're a medical man! No false modesty here! There is nothing so invigorating as fresh air on the liberated skin. Every gust is a shilling in the bank of health!"

"My account is well funded, sir," Duncan offered, struggling to find a way to delicately disengage.

Franklin laughed amiably. "The younger generation is not so bold as they think. I have another twenty minutes before I am finished. Pull up a chair on the other side of the door as my secretary Henry does sometimes and we can continue to converse." Duncan, hearing Franklin walking toward him, darted out the door, to more laughter.

"The Duke of Grafton continues to struggle as prime minister," Franklin observed after Duncan had arranged his seat by the door. "And there is a great debate on whether the rains in the north will harm or benefit this year's wool production," he continued, then summarized more of the news in the morning papers.

"The Tories are bent on neutralizing every possible obstruction to their goals," Duncan observed after the inventor spoke of the battles in Parliament.

"They are relentless," Franklin agreed.

"You are one of their obstructions."

"Nonsense. This obsession of yours over my safety is unhealthy. You really should try an air bath. It will relax your nerves. If you are shy, just strip down in there. Open the window. Let the dawn wind massage you."

Duncan refrained from replying that the London air seemed more apt to choke him than renew him. "I do not know how I could face your Deborah in Philadelphia if harm came to you during my visit," he said instead.

Franklin laughed again. "The only threat to me here is scalding my tongue if the tea is too hot or taking so much port it excites my gout."

"You recently had a secret meeting in Billingsgate with the Astronomer Royal. Except it wasn't so secret. The Horse Guards took news of it to the War Council."

The rustle of the newspapers stopped. The sound of a chair creaking, then footsteps, came from the bedroom. "You astound me. How could the Horse Guards know this?" came Franklin's voice, just inside the bedroom door. "How could *you* know this?"

"The Horse Guards were following the Astronomer Royal. You met at one of the sailors' taverns, no doubt considering it safe for a confidential discussion. You spoke of the transit of Venus and the king's observatory. After that the Guards switched to watching you. As if they had been waiting for the Astronomer Royal to lead them to some secret and you turned out to be the secret. You had been under suspicion, but after that you were a target. There are those who think clandestine meetings about the king are only conducted by traitors."

"Dear God, dear, dear God," came Franklin's worried reply. The floorboards in the bedroom creaked again and Duncan tensed, worried that Franklin would walk into the sitting room.

"Benjaaamiiin!" came a lighthearted cry from the stairs. Mrs. Stevenson appeared with a tray of tea. "Breakfast in a quarter hour!" She greeted Duncan with a surprised smile. "We shall happily set an extra place for you, Mr. McCallum." She caught herself and looked over her shoulder. "McGowan," she corrected herself.

Duncan could hear Franklin clearing his throat. "Still time to join me, Margaret. Release your skin! Dare to be a renewed woman!"

She rolled her eyes as she set the tray on the sideboard. "Every morning the same silly joke," she whispered to Duncan, then raised her voice. "I am quite comfortable with the woman I am, Benjamin."

The landlady did not seem to notice that the jovial laugh from the bedroom was forced. She paused at the head of the stairs. "A quarter hour!" she reminded her famous tenant.

"McCallum!" Franklin pressed as the sound of her footsteps receded down the stairs, then he muttered under his breath and Duncan heard the rustle of fabric. "I have my linen on. Now come in and talk while I ready for breakfast. I am always famished after a good air bath."

Duncan quickly explained that Ishmael had discovered, among the Horse Guards spies, a man who was obliged to them, then recounted how Olivia Dumont had helped trap him.

Franklin looked up from buttoning his britches. "Olivia? What does she have to do with any of this?"

"They learned she is French and are trying to posture her as a spy against the king."

"Sentiment grows hot against France over the Corsican affair."

"Allegations of a French spy operating out of the house of an official agent from the colonies—"

"Would undo me!" Franklin finished. "And dear God, not to mention the danger to dear Olivia!"

"They know she helps with the *incognitum*," Duncan said.

"She knows much more than—" Franklin faltered, reconsidering his words.

"They know the *incognitum* is in London," Duncan added.

Franklin closed his eyes and murmured something that sounded, uncharacteristically, like a curse before looking up. "The death of her brother is burden enough for her—we cannot add to her troubles." His voice was shaking. Duncan pointed to the buttons of his waistcoat, which he had misaligned. "Look at me! I am already being undone!" He steadied himself and paced into the sitting room, reached up to touch the solitary Leyden jar, jerked with a quick convulsion, then breathed more deeply. "They shall not prevail, Duncan," he said in a steadier voice and began rebuttoning his waistcoat. "I see now why the Sons put such faith in you. I am afraid you are with me now, until the end."

"Then there must no longer be any secrets between us."

Franklin solemnly nodded, accepting Duncan's point. "It's very simple, really. I've told you much already. The king's advisers have us on a path to war. They are blinded by their arrogance and lust for power, thinking they can treat the colonists like the serfs of old. As I've said, if the course is not corrected soon there will be troops occupying Philadelphia and New York, and the colonists will not stand for it. That will be the end of compromise. It will mean war, a bloody civil war of the like not seen since Cromwell. There is only one man who has the power to alter that course."

"George Rex."

"Exactly. But he is protected, sealed off from those who would reason with him, who would be willing to share difficult truths with him. There is only one approach possible, to reach him through his interest in natural philosophy. He takes that interest most seriously, has said he wishes to stand for the advancement of learning. His political advisers are all ambition and envy and no intellect. They don't understand this deep root that nourishes him. Nevil says he was like an energetic schoolboy on the day of the transit."

"So you will offer up the American observations of the transit and the American *incognitum*."

"You are seized of the essence, yes."

"With all due respect, Doctor, I have known these secrets for days. The Horse Guards know them as well now."

"There you go again, suggesting dishonesty in my circle of friends. I refuse to credit such a suggestion."

"The slender reed of hope left is the secrecy of the final arrangements," Duncan said. "That is what the Guards so desperately seek. You must take greater precautions. Don't use runners for messengers."

Franklin nodded reluctant agreement. "Secrecy in implementation is everything. And the king's other advisers would cut me off in an instant if I attempted it through them."

"But Nevil Maskelyne is his trusted natural philosopher."

"Yes. The others consider Nevil harmless, sort of a lapdog scholar. But the king respects him, always responds to him. That is the key. We will—" Franklin searched for words.

"You will secretly meet with the king and his Astronomer Royal so you can recalibrate the sovereign's thinking on America. But where? The details are all."

"Just so! It will be a defining moment, don't you see? If he can only accept that the colonials are equal to those here in intellectual pursuits, I am convinced all else will fall into place. Intellectual parity, that's the hinge we can pivot on. The Horse Guards still don't have the final pieces of the puzzle. They don't know where the bones are hidden, don't know when or where the momentous meeting will occur."

"And if you would protect those vital secrets, sir, you must share them with me."

Franklin, slipping on his shoes, gave a tentative nod, then inserted his ever-present silver watch into a waistcoat pocket.

"The writer of *Poor Richard's Almanack* always struck me as a complex man," Duncan observed, "but what came through most of all was his tenacious optimism."

Franklin smiled, seeming to take the comment as a compliment. "I accept your offer to see the bones achieve their destiny. Our meeting will be at the new Royal Observatory in the old deer park, as close as possible to his departure for his hunting tour, so as to give his advisers no time to react."

Duncan considered Franklin's revelation. "So all we have to do is keep the bones protected now that the Guards know they are in London, secretly transport two wagonloads of them into the heavily guarded royal estate, find a way to hide them there, and protect the details of your secret meeting date from the hordes who make it their business to know all the king's secrets. If this were a military campaign a general would give it maybe one chance in ten."

"Now you're the optimist," Franklin said. "More like one in twenty. But prithee, Duncan, tell me again why your friend Conawago came to London?"

Duncan sighed, conceding the point. "To persuade the king not to start a war."

Franklin raised his eyebrows expectantly.

In answer Duncan stepped to the mantel, raised his hand, and held his cupped hand over the rod of the Leyden jar. He extended his other hand. Franklin solemnly accepted it. Duncan grasped the rod and the shock rippled along his body, down his arm, and into Franklin's hand.

"I think they call that a binding," Franklin said, grinning, when Duncan released the rod.

"If we were in Iroquois country," Duncan said, returning the grin, "we would have cut our palms and shared blood."

Franklin seemed deeply moved. He opened his mouth and seemed about to say something profound, but then the landlady called up the stairs. "Scones are leaving the oven, Benjamin!"

For the third time since departing the inn, Duncan ducked into an alley to watch the street behind him. It was hard to put a name to the persistent nagging in the small of his back. Patrick Woolford called it the battle instinct, acquired from his years in the war. Conawago called it the hunter's sense, acquired from years with the Mohawks. But Duncan suspected it might have been more to do with the smugglers, reivers, and warriors of his own Highland ancestry. Whatever the reason, he could not escape the sense of being followed, although not once on any of his stops did he see any sign of a stalker.

When he arrived at the big house in Mayfair, he passed it and circled the block, slipping into a narrow alley a few doors down. He pressed himself into the deeper shadow of a recessed doorway, touched the hilt of his knife, and waited.

The wiry man made no sound as he entered the alley, using it himself as cover as he surveyed the street. Duncan relaxed and sat on the marble step before him. He heard a low, nautical curse, then the man looked back up the street as if he had missed something. Duncan kicked a pebble at his foot.

The man spun, hand on his own blade, then sighed. "Why, look who it be," he said. "You too must have thought it prime weather for a walk."

"Darby," Duncan said. "You have been following me since I left the Neptune."

"Well, apparently we be going in the same direction, sir."

"So you have business at one of these Mayfair palaces, do you?"

Darby winced, then sat beside Duncan. "Gig's up, I see. It's just that the captain be that worried about you. Says when a man dies on his ship he has a certain responsibility to him."

"But I didn't die."

The bosun sobered for a moment. "Well now, there might be different views on that particular question. I'm thinking maybe you died a little bit that night, like maybe you invited the shadow of death to hover over ye, and he knows he has unfinished business." He shrugged and brightened. "Plus our cargo's been delayed in Yorkshire and the shipyard has banished us from looking over their shoulders every other minute." Darby gestured toward the blue sky. "It do be a right pleasant day for exercise."

"That's what the moth was thinking the instant before it hit the spider web," Duncan said, but heard the determination in the man's voice. Darby had the bit firmly in his teeth. "You might as well walk alongside me."

"No sir. That would defeat the purpose."

"Tell me, Darby, is someone following Ishmael as well?"

"No need. We did, for two days, but it was always just the same. Don't think a man is likely to get hurt in a hospital."

Duncan gave a reluctant nod. Ishmael insisted on going to Bedlam every day, to study the terrain, as he called it. Each day he still gave a coin to the keeper named Taggart, who was gradually growing more talkative. News from Taggart was, in fact, why Duncan had returned to Mayfair.

Duncan stood. "Very well. I am going to the big house in the center of this block. I won't be more than an hour."

"I'll give ye until the clocks strike through an hour, then. After that I'll get worried," the compact Scot said, tapping a knuckle to his forehead.

Duncan went straight to the gate that led to the courtyard behind the house but to his dismay found it locked. Reluctantly he stepped to the oversize front door and knocked. It was instantly opened by a maid holding a broom, who made an awkward curtsy, supporting herself on the broom. "Thought ye was the post, sir. I fear Miss Madeline is out."

"I came to see Noah. Might I just walk through to the stable?"

"Mr. Noah won't be found in the stable, sir. He's repairing loose bricks in the library hearth," she said, then turned and beckoned for Duncan to follow her.

The groom was on his hands and knees inside the fireplace, and hit his head when the maid spoke. "Don't be putting on airs, Noah, but ye have a caller," she said, then returned to her labor in the foyer.

Noah backed out and stood, greeting Duncan with a broad smile, then wiped his hand on a sooty rag before taking the one Duncan offered.

"It's about Conawago," Duncan said. "About Bedlam, really."

Noah nodded. "How is our friend?"

"Not good. His mind is—" Duncan fought a new wave of emotion as the empty face of his friend once more appeared in his mind's eye. "I fear he is being drugged."

Noah pressed him for details, his expression growing grim as Duncan described the Chamber of the Immortals. "Please, McCallum," the groom said. "Let me help."

Duncan looked at the open door, then stepped past the big desk in the center of the book-lined chamber to confirm the hall was empty. Noah sat in one of the wooden chairs in front of the desk. "You said you know some of those who work at Bedlam," Duncan began.

Noah nodded. "At least half a dozen. The board of governors tries to help freed men and women." He anticipated Duncan's next question. "Some in the laundry but in the kitchen mostly. It's a big place. Hundreds of meals three times a day."

"Do the same kitchens serve both the staff and the patients?"

"I don't know. Probably, yes. I will find out."

"Good. And when are the keepers served, who serves the tea for their breaks, and when are the breaks?"

"I can have answers in a day or two."

"And the laundry," Duncan started, but then his gaze fell upon several complex drawings on the desk. He paused, recognizing the strange contraption he had seen in the sketch on the wall of Franklin's parlor. But these drawings were much more detailed.

"The laundry?" Noah asked.

"Yes, the laundry," Duncan said absently. Why would Madeline Faulkner have such drawings, he wondered, and why would they be similar to those of Franklin? He was not even aware they knew each other. One of the expanded drawings had lists of materials in the margin. He glanced up at Noah, who watched him with an uneasy expression.

"The laundry is taken in wagons to a big washhouse just down the street that belongs to the hospital," the groom offered. "Inside the hospital it is collected in baskets, then transferred to big wicker pallets that take four men to carry."

Duncan collected himself. "All on one day or is the work rotated so wagons go every day?"

"A portion each day, I suspect, but I will ask," Noah confirmed. "Do you talk about that of only the patients or of the keepers' uniforms as well?"

"All of—" Duncan was interrupted by a girlish laugh.

"Why, Mr. McCallum!" Madeline Faulkner entered the library, followed by an attendant carrying two bolts of cloth. "Whatever are you doing, arriving without announcing your intentions to the lady of the house?" She removed her cloak, draping it on a chair, then took one of the bolts of cloth and flung it over the desk, spreading out a deep green silk. "But such propitious timing. You must help me decide!"

Duncan held up one end of the silk to expose the papers underneath. "I was admiring your drawings, Madeline."

She hesitated only a moment, touching the tight yellow ribbon around her neck. A choker of some kind seemed to be a permanent feature of her wardrobe. Some women used beauty marks to set themselves apart. Madeline apparently used chokers. "Oh, those boring things. Just the work of some of the men in my father's enterprises. They use the library sometimes, to hide from competitors or some such nonsense. I haven't time for such silliness. It's nearly the end of the season and I am simply immersed with the dressmakers. The king is throwing a royal ball to cap it all off." She gestured her attendant forward with the second bolt of cloth. "Prithee, Duncan, is it to be the green or the blue?"

Not for the first time Duncan wondered why Sarah would have befriended such a frivolous woman. But he was grateful for her help to Conawago, and he had long ago learned that the servants of a household often reflected much about its master or mistress. He could not reconcile the gentle, intelligent Noah with his mistress.

"The blue," he declared. "A royal color for a royal affair."

"Of course!" she exclaimed. "Such a blessing to have the view of a worldly man." She turned to her maid. "Run the blue to the dressmaker. We'll barely have time for a second fitting as it is." She left the green cloth draped over the desk. "Now let's leave this stuffy old book closet and find some tea. I am simply parched!"

Duncan caught Noah's eye but the groom quickly looked away, then stood and backed toward his work at the hearth. Duncan hesitated until Madeline had stepped into the hallway.

"Most days I am in the stable after the luncheon hour," Noah said, lowering his voice, "brushing down the horses."

Duncan lingered still, sensing that something had gone unexplained, but Noah turned and crawled back into the fireplace without another word.

The block below the old Moorgate teemed with last-minute customers as shopkeepers began bringing in the goods they had displayed on their bulks. Ishmael, who had increasingly assumed the wary air of a warrior in enemy territory, was now distracted by a watchmaker's shop where two apprentices sat in the window, polishing gears. "Mrs. Laws says London makes the best watches in all the world," the young Nipmuc said. "She has her husband's watch and unscrewed the cover to show me the works. There were jewels!"

Duncan was pleased that Ishmael had forgotten his despair, however briefly, but found himself studying the street. A wiry figure leaning against the wall of a nearby alley caught his eye for a moment and nodded. Duncan had begun to feel grateful for the bosun's dogged determination to shadow his movements.

He had to pull Ishmael away from the watchmaker's shop, with the Nipmuc casting regretful glances over his shoulder at the apprentices, but as the apothecary shop came into view he gasped and darted forward to Huber's dusty window. When Duncan reached him, he began pointing to the glass jars, each filled with alcohol. "A giant centipede! A scorpion! And, Duncan, a tiny alligator! There," he said, indicating a large jar on an upper shelf. "Could that be a vampire bat?"

Duncan pointed to the most exotic item, a two-headed snake, then pulled his companion inside. Huber greeted him enthusiastically and went round-eyed as Duncan introduced Ishmael as a member of the Nipmuc tribe. The German darted to the open door behind his counter and called out, "Greta! *Hier ist ein wilder!*"

Moments later a weary-looking middle-aged woman emerged from the rear of the building, pulling off her apron and straightening the blond hair placed in a bun on top of her head. A wonderfully sweet, yeasty scent seemed to cling to her. Greta was as affable as her husband and good-naturedly announced that she had just taken a strudel out of the oven and she would not permit them to leave until they sat for tea.

Huber smiled fondly at his wife as she hurried away to make preparations, then turned to Duncan. "I take it your curiosity about Bethlem brings you back."

"I might still have need of that satchel, Herr Huber."

"Please, it is Heinz. And keep it so long as it is of use to you."

"Even more useful may be your knowledge," Duncan said.

Huber's brows rose.

"You said you were a physician by training. In my experience it is difficult for a physician to simply abandon his calling."

"If I can be help to someone in need, yes. But most don't want a foreign doctor, at least not unless you ride in a grand coach and speak with a thick accent," Huber said with an ironic smile.

"It's different at a hospital," Duncan suggested.

Huber shrugged. "I help in Brideswell and Bethlem from time to time, yes."

"And you serve them as both doctor and apothecary."

"More the apothecary, but yes. Where to draw the line? The apothecary needs to know the human body, the doctor the medicine."

"I have questions about doctors at Bedlam."

Huber frowned. "You know a patient's confidences to his doctor are sacred."

"Not about a patient. We know our patient, an old man who is unjustly confined there."

Huber sighed. "Kin and kith almost always say the confinement of a loved one is unjust."

"It's my uncle," Ishmael interrupted. "The last chieftain of our tribe. This is not his land. He cannot die here. His soul would be in eternal torment."

Huber seemed confused for a moment, then as Ishmael's words sank in, his face grew pained. The silence was broken by an insistent voice from the doorway. "We will have strudel now," Greta Huber announced. She had been listening. "You will ask your questions, Mr. McCallum," she declared with a peeved glance at her husband, "and Heinz will answer them."

They sat in a small but comfortable dining chamber, around a table adorned with lace and linen. Greta moved back and forth from table to sideboard, offering a matronly pat on Ishmael's shoulder each time she refilled his plate. Huber's resistance disappeared as they ate, and he readily confirmed that medicines at Bethlem Hospital—he never used the colloquial name—were often administered in teas. Patients drank them with relish, and the staff would never have time to separately administer pills and powders to hundreds of patients.

"Laudanum?" Duncan asked.

"Never in tea. It requires much more precision in dosing."

"Henbane?"

Huber looked down, suddenly very interested in the crumbs on his plate. "You know what's good with strudel?" he asked. "Cheddar cheese."

"Mr. McCallum shall have cheese if he desires it, Heinz," Greta said, exasperated. "But he asked you a question."

"I don't approve," Huber said.

"Heinz! Mr. McCallum is our guest!"

"*Nein, nein, mein liebchen.* I mean I don't approve of the practice he refers to." Huber ran his hand through his long graying hair and fixed Duncan with a troubled gaze. "Henbane is a very dangerous substance. We don't understand it well enough to use it. In small amounts it can be a useful sedative, but some of the doctors use it to other purposes, you might say."

"Including Dr. Granger," Duncan said. "Who advises the board of governors."

"And is physician to half its members."

"Are you suggesting he is fond of using henbane?"

"Do you have any idea of its power in higher doses?" Huber asked.

"Hallucinations. Seizures. Coma even."

"In the northern lands," Huber related, "there are tales of Viking warriors who rubbed on a salve made of henbane before battle. It transformed them into monsters of battle. God knows how it affects those poor souls in Bethlem."

Duncan chewed on a piece of Greta's pastry, considering Huber's distraught tone. "You supply henbane," he suggested.

It was Greta who answered. "We run an apothecary. Supplying medicines is what we do. It is our bread and butter."

"Not so often as the shop up the street," Huber amended. "But yes, Dr. Granger asks for henbane from time to time. We usually have it available."

"And you have some now?" Duncan asked.

"We just received a shipment from our man in Bremerhaven, yes," Huber replied. "Why?"

Duncan replied with another question. "When you examine patients at Bethlem, are you summoned to do so?"

"Sometimes. But physicians who would contribute their services are generally welcomed at any time."

"Are patients ever brought to you in an exam room?"

"Never. There is no time nor staff to deal with private exams. We go to the wards. Sometimes I will set up a station in one of the galleries for the patients who are permitted freedom of movement."

"But sometimes you go inside the locked wards?"

"Sometimes, yes."

"And do they give you a key?"

"Never. A keeper accompanies me."

"There must be so many keys to mind."

"There are many locks at Bethlem. The entrances, the supply rooms, the offices, the special wards. The lower-ranking keepers have the keys to their assigned wards. The more senior keepers have master keys."

Ishmael lowered his fork. "Tell us more about master keys."

The German doctor's face clouded. "I don't think I am at liberty to do so," he said, and fixed the Nipmuc with a stubborn gaze.

"Heinz!" Greta snapped. "You will speak of keys, *mein liebchen*, or you will be eating nothing but cold sausage for a month!"

"We take this coach," Ishmael said, lifting a salt bowl from the chart spread on Mrs. Laws's dining table, "down the road to the old deer park, then, to what they call Kew."

Darby swatted at his arm. "Don't be daft! Didn't we say five minutes ago the salt is the Horse Guards Palace! Ye can nae move a building, lad. I told ye, coaches are the walnut shells!"

The dining chamber of the Neptune had been turned into a war room. Captain Rhys had contributed some old charts, which they had reversed and pinned down with books. Lizzie the chambermaid had joined in with a conspiratorial gleam to find various markers in the scullery while Duncan sketched in streets and marked with preliminary *X*s the Horse Guards Palace, Craven Street, the Neptune, Hewson's house, and Bethlem Hospital. Ishmael added another mark near the last one and wrote *Bethlem Laundry*. Mrs. Laws's small salts were deployed to mark buildings, then Darby had arranged a dozen peas around the Neptune.

"The second company of watchers," he explained. "Good lads every one."

"Whose lads?" Duncan asked.

"We ain't got enough sailors to go around, especially seeing how three got thrown in a parish cell for public drunkenness. So Sinner John volunteered his link boys. You know, Xander, Robbie, and the others he lets sleep in the stable, the ones he leads in songs at the noon bell."

Duncan didn't know many of the boys, but he did recall hearing songs from the stable. He gave an appreciative nod.

"Link boys make pennies a night," Darby explained. "As Sinner John said, give one a shilling and he's yours for days. And who notices link boys? They're everywhere, the poor little buggers. People pay as much attention to them as rats and squirrels. The fools from Whitehall are so arrogant they even keep their long boots on. If a boy sees any of the boots near here he'll come running to tell his boss, ye might say." Darby motioned to someone out of the shadows of the adjoining room. Xander, wearing a new shirt and beaming with pride, gave a bow to the company. "Xander is captain of the link boy brigade," Darby declared. A second boy, his freckled cheeks pink from scrubbing and his usual thicket of hair brushed and tied at the back, emerged from behind Xander. "And young Robbie is his sergeant." Robbie gave a quick, shy nod and edged closer to Xander.

Duncan threw the boys a salute, which they eagerly returned, with a joint "Your servant, sir." Xander took a tentative step toward Duncan, extending a small piece of metal on a cord. "We'd like ye to have this, sir," he said to Duncan. "Robbie and me found it in the Thames mud, where we sometimes lark about at low tide." Duncan accepted the token and studied it. "It be Roman, I warrant, 'cause we found it with pieces of old Roman glass. We put a good strong cord on it to save ye the trouble."

The little bronze amulet was of a leaping dolphin and had an air of great age about it. It could indeed have been Roman.

"Fish be good luck," Robbie blurted out. "Everyone knows fish be good luck. Good luck for our Highland gladiator!"

Duncan smiled and thanked the boys, then considered them for a few heartbeats. "Do you know a boy named Bertie?" he asked.

"Oh aye, if ye mean the scrub who's taking coin from them soldiers," Xander confirmed with a scowl.

"The very one." Duncan produced a shilling. "Have a talk with Bertie," he said.

"I can stop him from working for them without a coin," Xander said, rubbing a fist in his palm.

"No. Not all battles are won by shedding blood. Give him the extra coin," Duncan said, pushing the shilling into Xander's hand. "I want him to continue but I want him to tell you what he does for them. And there's a little added task. Lieutenant Nettles wears a little gold pin on his lapel. I want to see that pin. I'll give it back. Bertie can replace it so that the lieutenant may not even miss it."

Xander's eyes lit with excitement. "I will have it later today!" he declared, and with a whoop he and Robbie sprinted away.

As the boys disappeared, a figure in a heavy cloak entered from the kitchen, then threw off the hood to reveal radiant curls. "Is there another seat at this table?"

Olivia Dumont asked. "What game is this? Who has the peas and who the walnuts? And oh," she added, touching a bowl at the edge of the table, "there's raisins!"

They sat in council until midnight, proposing plans and discarding many of them, discussing how the *incognitum* might be secretly delivered to the location chosen by Franklin and the Astronomer Royal Maskelyne. An hour after Olivia arrived, Sinner John appeared with two new members, their cloaks dripping from a summer shower. Captain Rhys and Patrick Woolford had met on the steps of the Neptune and were already chatting warmly as they reached the dining room.

Woolford appraised their map with the eye of a seasoned ranger as Duncan explained the plan they had devised. The deputy superintendent listened with a skeptical eye, then dropped three raisins on the road leading out of the city, shaking his head. "The three of us won't be enough. We need watchers surrounding the block around Hewson's house and runners connecting the watchers with us."

Sinner John stepped forward. "Which will be my brigade of link boys," he declared, and repositioned several peas near Hewson's house. "Peas be the young soldiers, raisins the older ones," he explained. He added a raisin by the peas. "That be me, may God protect us."

Darby added several more raisins. "Myself, and my stalwart *Galileos*."

"With the blessing of Saint Joan, *moi aussi*," Olivia chimed in, dropping another raisin.

Another hand appeared but was quickly intercepted by Mrs. Laws. "Not you, dear," she told Lizzie firmly. "You are fully engaged in the battle of mops and brooms."

Duncan pushed a smile onto his face, trying not to think of the disaster that might await any of them if they fell into Hastings's hands. "Enough for the main campaign," he said. "Now we must look to our first skirmish, that of the magicians who are going to make the lightning wizard vanish into thin air."

Chapter 17

THE PATCH OF BATTLE FOG, as Patrick Woolford called it, was a block where a narrow street led off Pall Mall and then became little more than a crooked alley that connected to St. James's Street with a sharp turn. For the past three days Franklin had played his part well, emerging from Craven Street to climb into the same hired coach, then instructing the driver to take him on his prescribed "touring circuit" to Whitehall, a circular route that took him up to Piccadilly on St. James's Street, then back through Green Park, where he called on the driver to pause while he admired a particular bird or tree. Once he even got out to retrieve, with exaggerated exclamations, a huge plane tree leaf. The watchers in black boots, some wearing cloaks, some in workman's clothes, had no trouble keeping up with his leisurely pace, including down the alley identified by Woolford, a common shortcut to avoid the congestion around St. James's Palace, where the king was still residing while Buckingham House was being rebuilt.

Today Franklin had continued his routine, with one watcher following on horseback and two others on foot, but as soon as the driver made the turn for the shortcut to St. James's Street, a farmer's cart stacked high with cabbages turned into the narrow pathway. Moments later the cart driver seemed to lose control of his mule. The cart made an abrupt turn, stopping at an angle that blocked all traffic, and half the cabbages tumbled out. Darby had intercepted the farmer before dawn and offered him double his market price for the load if he threw in the use of the cart for the morning. The farmer had been hesitant until Darby pointed out that he was merely paying for the loan of the cabbages, which could still be sold at Covent Garden or Hungerford Market.

The rider on the black horse spat a curse at the chaos of cabbages, then wheeled about and went back onto the main street. By the time Franklin's coach emerged, Franklin had leapt out and Xander and his friend Robbie had jumped in, laughing over the trick and the free ride they were taking to deceive the followers. As the coach emerged onto St. James's Street, Duncan, Franklin, and Woolford were riding in another direction in a sturdy nondescript vehicle of the kind that often served those traveling to and from the towns and villages outside London.

Franklin had a hard time controlling his mirth until they had crossed the Westminster Bridge. "Fresh air! Fresh air!" the Philadelphian called out as he rapped his cane on the coach roof, and for a fearful instant Duncan thought he might be suggesting he was about to take one of his air baths. But then the coachman opened the screen behind his bench and Franklin settled back in his seat, gesturing for Woolford and Duncan to roll up the leather flaps covering the windows.

Fields of crops appeared on either side of their road, and as the breeze brought the sweet scent of newly cut hay, Duncan looked out to see half a dozen men with forks pitching hay into a wagon drawn by two heavy Shire horses. Beyond the field, rows of fruit trees extended toward the horizon.

Franklin closed his eyes and breathed deeply. "Two or three extra miles at least, but who can complain on such a fine summer day? An excellent suggestion, to conduct this reconnaissance."

"Extra miles?" Woolford asked.

"The King's Road runs directly to Hampton Court and the deer park, a fast, well-maintained road, but of course it may only be used for royal business. Years ago I was a guest at a banquet at Hampton and so my coach was allowed on it after I showed my invitation," Franklin explained, bouncing as the coach lurched over a rut. "A fine road, and considerably smoother than this," he added good-naturedly. "The Astronomer Royal and I discussed whether the *incognitum* might travel on it but decided that was too risky." Franklin leaned out the window. "Just look at this scenery! Industrious agrarians! Breathe in the green, growing scents! And orchards! Nothing like a good apple for avoiding the physicians."

Duncan and Woolford exchanged an awkward glance. While waiting for Franklin that morning, Woolford had handed Duncan a piece of paper bearing the crossed-sword printer's mark, torn from a document. It held another mocking couplet, this one about the special apples Deborah Franklin sent to her husband, which he insisted were better than any available in England:

Newtown Pippins, Pippins of Newtown
From over the sea to fatten the clown.

The apples, Duncan had learned from Judith the maid, were sent secretly because they were in very short supply and Franklin chose to share them only with the household. Duncan could not help but wonder if there were any secrets of the Craven Street household that had not been compromised. In the night he had recalled Darby's warning, that the shadow of death hovered over him, and every compromise brought that shadow closer. *You will die, again and again*, Catchoka had warned.

As Franklin leaned out the window, studying the countryside, Duncan extracted a slip of paper and handed it to Woolford. The sketch on it was of the small pin Xander had shown him the night before, temporarily removed from Lieutenant Nettles's waistcoat. It was in the style of the other pins from Milbridge that Woolford had shown Duncan, but he could not make any sense of it. The image was of a lightning bolt with a bursting star superimposed over it. Along the edge of the golden pin were the Latin words POMPA FULGUR VINCERET. Fireworks conquer lightning.

Woolford studied the sketch, then took a lead from his pocket and quickly scrawled on the bottom of the paper. *Famous racehorse named Lightning*, he wrote. *M. must own horse named Star or Starburst or such that beat Lightning.*

As their vehicle settled into a more even gait, Franklin settled back in his seat and addressed Woolford. "Deputy Superintendent. Most impressive. How is my friend Superintendent Johnson? We have corresponded for years, though I have never had the pleasure of meeting him face-to-face."

"Very fit when I bid him farewell four months ago."

"And his Indian bride, of such famed beauty?"

Woolford exchanged an uneasy glance with Duncan. They both were well aware of Johnson's ambiguous relationships with tribal women. "The Mohawk princess Molly Brant is the bright star of Johnson Hall, the superintendent likes to say, illuminating all who visit with her brilliance." Woolford brightened, thinking of a change of subject. "I was at the ceremony for the naming of your son, sir."

Franklin stiffened. "I don't follow."

"Your son the governor of New Jersey. It was to honor him for bringing murderers of several tribal members to justice. He was granted a tribal name. The Doer of Justice, the Mohawk called him, a great honor."

Duncan puzzled over the sour expression on Franklin's face, then recalled that Deborah had told him that Benjamin and his son, born to another woman before their own marriage, had fallen out years earlier and almost never spoke with each other. Though they had both spent years in London, they lived in different houses. Franklin's son had in fact penetrated the social circles of the high aristocracy, a feat that had always eluded his father.

Woolford seemed to sense his blunder. "Superintendent Johnson has an avid interest in electricity," he ventured, and Franklin's expression thawed as the deputy superintendent explained that a whole room at Johnson Hall was filled with equipment for experimentation. "One of his great joys in recent years had been reenacting the experiment he read about in which a cork connected to a glass tube with a hundred feet of wire was electrified by rubbing the tube with a piece of silk. Extraordinary. A tribal chief saw the spark at the end of the wire and said Johnson was another wizard of lightning, but the superintendent declared no, there can be but one wizard of lightning, and that is Dr. Franklin."

The tale banished Franklin's dour expression and soon he was explaining to Woolford how Johnson should set up a lightning alarm at Johnson Hall, with a proud description of the alarm he had rigged in his own Philadelphia home. They passed another quarter hour in pleasant conversation about Franklin's latest observations on the currents of the Atlantic, based on measurements taken on his last voyage, then the inventor sobered as he recollected news for Duncan.

"I had unsettling news from my old friend, Joseph Priestly. Half a dozen of the Horse Guards came to his house and roughly searched through the upper floors, cursing him and abusing his belongings, demanding to know where the American bones were. They found nothing, of course, but he thought I should know. The American bones," Franklin repeated.

"Is he near Hewson's house?" Duncan asked with sudden worry.

"Not at all. He lives in Mayfair on Blue Moon Street. They were most quarrelsome, those soldiers. He is thinking of filing a complaint."

Duncan gazed out the window, trying to make sense of the news. "Blue Moon?" he asked. "You have a blue moon in your window," he reminded Franklin.

"Why, yes, but that hardly signifies."

"You sent a message to Polly Stevenson." Duncan extracted his writing lead. "Can you recall its words?"

"Of course," Franklin said, then found a scrap of paper in his pocket and began writing. "A test," he said with a smile as he handed the paper to Duncan. "Polly is a quick study, and I think she has mastered it."

The note to Polly was in Franklin's phonetic alphabet. *Myi spyi*, it said, *mor pyyrlz amyng iur trezhyrz. Luk thru thi mun hwen it is blu, upsterz, and fyind iur harts dizyir.*

"My spy?" Duncan asked. "You actually began with 'my spy'?"

"It's a game we play. We pretend we are a secret army. We call Mrs. Stevenson the field marshal."

Duncan read the message to Patrick. "My spy, more pearls among your treasures. Look through the moon when it is blue, upstairs, and find your heart's desire," he recited, then explained it was about a pair of earrings before turning to Franklin. "Your friend lives on Blue Moon Street. And the Guards searched upstairs."

"Yes but it was all a misunderstanding of some kind."

"They found nothing because they were looking for the *incognitum*."

"Yes, but—"

"I was there when Polly found her pearls in your blue moon, upstairs. You said this message was misdirected to the prime minister."

Franklin's brow furrowed. "Yes . . ."

"Your message referred to a treasure you would present. It was upstairs, connected to a blue moon."

"All perfectly harmless," Franklin argued.

"No. Someone is intercepting the prime minister's mail. And what they saw was a coded message referring to your spy. Joseph Priestly is a renowned natural philosopher and a friend of yours. Your note led them to that connection."

"Duncan! Surely not!" Franklin protested, but Duncan saw the surrender in his eyes. "Dear God. I did put Polly's message in the envelope addressed to the prime minister. If only Henry had been there—such a mistake would never have happened."

"The Guards will consider it further proof that you are working against the War Council. If you were not going to present the bones to the king then the prime minister would be the obvious alternative."

Franklin sagged and spoke no more until they reached their destination.

Although the king's new observatory was in the royal deer park, Sinner John, who was proving a rich source of information about London's secrets, knew of a hidden access road for the construction crew. While the observatory had been complete enough for the king's observations of the transit, the small castle-like structure still required much finishing work, and the masons, carpenters, and other tradesmen would never be allowed to clutter the King's Road. Thus it was that Franklin, Woolford, and Duncan stood a hundred yards away from the building in a construction yard, wearing the long tunics of tradesmen, borrowed at the cost of a few pennies.

Woolford studied the building and its grounds with the eye of a stealthy ranger. "The king won't come without a bodyguard," he observed.

"If he comes," Duncan said, "it will be knowing it is for a secret meeting with Benjamin Franklin, a meeting neither side will want to publicize. Many in the court would oppose it. The king won't want a lot of witnesses."

"A small bodyguard, then," Woolford concluded. "Two or three men."

"The danger isn't after the king arrives," Franklin said. "I will be here alone, with only the Astronomer Royal as a companion. Neither of us is too intimidating."

"The danger is before," Duncan agreed. "From those who seek to block any conciliation, those who do not want the king to meet the *incognitum*. That danger is why we came," Duncan reminded Franklin. "To discover how we will conceal the bones once here."

Woolford pointed to canvas-covered piles of materials. "They must be disguised as construction stores."

"Patrick," Duncan protested, "we have a great arcing rib and a long tusk. How do you propose we disguise those?"

Woolford studied the piles, then pointed to the roof of the building. A compact dome-shaped structure lay at one end of the roof, the seat for the king's telescope.

The frame for another was being erected at the opposite end. He then gestured to a pile near the tree line, which contained several arcing struts of wood. "They can hide among the arches for the second dome, wrapped with canvas so they just look like more struts."

Duncan weighed Woolford's suggestion, then slowly nodded. "We will have men of the *Galileo* watch over them. If the king comes, it will mean he is curious about what Dr. Franklin has to offer. He will tolerate the unexpected appearance of goods brought from his construction yard, especially once he sees the massive rib and tusk."

Franklin nodded. "But can you really arrange for dependable guards?"

Duncan smiled. "They will compete for the privilege. For months they will be telling their shipmates how they stowed away in the king's own park."

Speaking so matter-of-factly seemed to calm their nerves, so much so that as a party of workers set off for the observatory, Franklin pulled his hat down and joined them. Woolford gasped and seemed about to call out when Duncan grabbed his arm and pulled him to the rear of the column of men. As they passed a pile of sand, he borrowed two shovels and laid them on their shoulders.

Newly emboldened, Franklin let his mischievous nature take over, telling the men he was an inspector and asking how deep the foundations had been laid and whether there were sufficient resting places for the king at the stairway landings. One of the older workers mentioned that the marble rubbing crew was off that day so he could take the inspector inside. Woolford muttered a curse and Duncan pushed forward to join Franklin.

Suddenly the atmosphere seemed to shift. The workers stiffened. Those few sitting back by the stacks of materials shot up and grabbed tools. A ringing sound came from a gravel road leading into the forest. Woolford, recognizing it instantly, darted to Franklin and pulled him from the column.

Six riders in the uniforms of the Horse Guards were trotting down the road, each leading two riderless horses. The jingle of the harnesses echoed through the woods.

"Exercising the mounts," Woolford whispered.

Franklin, his bravado gone, accepted the shovel Woolford thrust at him. Duncan had to hold his arm a moment, for he seemed about to run in the direction of their waiting coach. "Steady on, sir. Show them nothing suspicious and they will just focus on their task."

Franklin's protest came out in a hoarse whisper. "If we're found here I will be ruined!"

Woolford caught Duncan's eye. "If we are found out we will all be ruined." The horses seemed to veer toward them. "Do not show your faces," the deputy superintendent warned.

The ground shook as the eighteen horses trotted by, so close Duncan could hear their heavy breathing. When the three men reached the partial cover of the construction yard they all turned to look at the wooded road where the soldiers had disappeared.

"There's ancient chambers under the Horse Guards Palace," Woolford said suddenly, "said to be part of the old Palace of Whitehall. They say it is haunted by the ghosts of knights killed on the tilting ground where the Horse Guards parade ground is now. King Charles was beheaded just outside and is rumored to roam those halls at night. And they say that Henry the Eighth had dungeons there that the Horse Guards still use. Dungeons and machines used to coerce Henry the Eighth's prisoners when they were reluctant to confess. God knows those would be particularly vengeful ghosts."

"Surely they would not dare to misuse me in such a place," Franklin said, his voice still hollow.

"I wasn't speaking of you, sir," Woolford replied. "They would find something less physical for you. But they wouldn't hesitate to take Duncan or me down to meet those Tudor phantoms."

Franklin flushed with color as he recognized the callousness of his words. He studied the former captain of rangers for a few heartbeats. "I sense more anger than fear in your words."

"I'd be a fool not to fear the possibility," Woolford answered. "But yes, sir. Even greater is my fury that we need worry about Englishmen doing such things to other Englishmen. If King George allows such things right under his nose, then think how little he must care about what happens to distant colonists."

Sarah—I recently passed a memorable hour with Dr. Franklin. As his secretary Henry, quite the genteel and efficient fellow, transcribed some letters, the great inventor took me to a rear room on the floor he rents, which he called his experimentation chamber.

Oh the wonders, Sarah! It was strewn with papers and experiments, all the products of his extraordinary imagination. There was his famous armonica, which is twenty-five glass bowls mounted on a spindle rotated by a treadle, which in vibrating can be modulated by the fingertips. There were plates from his stove, which he is trying to have manufactured here, and an amazing three-wheeled clock that he claims is more reliable than any other except those made for Greenwich. On one table he had parts of spectacles and lenses, and he explained that he is looking for an artisan who can make a lens with different properties on the top and bottom, for close and far seeing.

We spent a quarter hour at a long table with several battery jars and a maze of wires. He is attempting to devise a simple method to demonstrate how electrical flows have positive and negative charges and how they always seek equilibrium, though I confess his zealous description was beyond me. At last he showed me the workbook for his remarkable phonetic alphabet with reformed spellings that are such simpler than the ones we use, and which he and the landlady's daughter employ in letters to each other. A pox on those who would call him too awkward, too much the rogue, or woefully absentminded. The man is the Da Vinci of our age!

At Bedlam a small crowd had gathered under a second-floor window at the west end of the long building, from which tin cups, articles of clothing, towels, small stools, chamber pots, and other random items were being tossed. Ishmael lingered near the entry, watching as onlookers braved the rain of objects to snatch up anything of value. "I've seen this before," he observed. "When the keepers stray away too long, the patients roaming in the galleries like to express their frustrations."

"The keepers can't be everywhere at any given moment," Duncan observed.

"Not what I mean. I speak of the crowds outside. Whenever something interesting happens here, dozens of people materialize to take advantage, in just minutes, as if they are keeping watch."

Duncan nodded absently and then Ishmael's meaning struck him. "A distraction, you mean," he said. A crowd of people from the surrounding neighborhoods would provide cover for the work of a few men trying to evade the keepers.

Ishmael rolled his eyes as if disappointed in Duncan's slowness, then led him up the stairs.

Duncan's business had kept him away in recent days, and he longed to see

Conawago, to try again to break through the spell he was under. The visitors were not so numerous as before and the benches before the Chamber of the Immortals were empty. The heavy double doors were closed and the nearest patients in the long gallery were keeping their distance, casting nervous glances at the doors.

Ishmael began asking what had happened. The first two inmates turned their backs and hurried away. The next one just vigorously shook his head and cried, "No, no, no!"

The fourth one pointed at the closed doors. "Those who are not in the book of life shall be cast into the lake of fire!" he shouted, causing a woman near him to burst into tears.

Ishmael advanced to the chamber and tried the latch, only to find the doors locked. He knocked on it, to no avail, then kicked in frustration at a pile of towels leaning against the wall. The blow dislodged the clean towel on top. All those under it were soaked with blood.

The young Nipmuc began pounding on the door now, so furiously he did not react to Duncan's insistent cries that he stop. The patients in the galleries stopped and stared. Two of them began clapping. One ran for a keeper.

Duncan dragged Ishmael away, then pressed him against the wall at the end of the corridor. "Attracting attention does neither us nor your uncle any good!" he told the frustrated tribesman, then pushed him toward the narrow stairway. "We will go down and come up again so you can collect yourself. Look for your tamed keeper."

Ishmael spied Taggart finishing tea with his colleagues in a small hall off the central stairway. They followed him as he set off for his assigned chambers. "There's an audience gathering for a performance of the Immortals," the Nipmuc said when he caught up with the careworn man in brown.

"Delayed," the keeper said. "The doctors say we should call such things a spasm of mental disease. This morning one of them laughed and said we should call this one the Peloponnesian War, though Christ knows what that means." He paused and eyed Ishmael expectantly.

Ishmael handed Taggart a coin. "What happened?"

"Took me all morning to clean up, and didn't it take four of us to carry the old fool out on a laundry pallet."

"The old fool?" Duncan asked uneasily.

"The crier, that's what most called him. The fat one who called out the news from the wooden box, like yesterday he declared that Julius Caesar had been assassinated and Socrates had committed suicide, though I'm right skeptical that those things happened on the same day. And then before closing up he started shouting that they must stop drinking the tea." Taggart lowered his voice. "Then as we was closing he starts calling out, 'We must purge ourselves of Dr. Granger.'"

"An accident of some kind?" Duncan suggested.

"Or another keeper could have come in here in the night," Ishmael said accusingly and glanced at Duncan, reminding him there was a senior keeper who worked for Dr. Granger and the War Council.

Taggart shrugged. "I locked the doors myself last night. When I opened them this morning the blood was all over the floor. They say he liked sleeping under that cracked bust of Caesar. The bust was on his head this morning. The cracked was on the cracked, if you get my meaning. Skull split like an egg."

"And the others?"

"Most were terrified, cowering in the far corner. A couple were happily drawing on the wall with his blood. The overkeepers said wash it all off, bad for business."

"So the business goes on," Duncan said, trying not to betray his bitterness. "When do the doors open?"

The keeper pointed to the big key on his belt. "As soon as I get there. They gave me a master key today, to keep things efficient," he added, raising an interested gleam in Ishmael's eye. The day before he had shown Duncan a slab of beeswax he had procured, to make an impression of a master key should he ever get one in his possession.

The occupants of the chamber were indeed subdued when the doors creaked open, huddled in the corner like a frightened flock. The metallic scent of blood hung in the air but there was no sign of it other than a pinkish stain on the wall. The bust of Caesar, a pink smear on its ear, was back on its pedestal.

"How did the death happen?" Duncan asked Taggart.

"I told you. The bust crushed the man's skull. No sense in calling it anything but an accident," he muttered. "How are we to tell what goes on in the night behind the locked doors?"

"Or whether a murderer with a key found his way inside," Duncan suggested in a low voice.

The keeper's eyes flared. He looked about as if for eavesdroppers. "Never in life! An accident, I said! The fool nudged the pedestal in his sleep and down came Caesar." As if he needed to defend himself, he added, "These ain't the criminally insane, mind, just regular lunatics."

Duncan searched the man's face in vain to detect any sign that he was making a macabre jest. As Taggart carried the pile of bloody rags down the hallway, the frightened flock began to disperse and Duncan finally saw his old friend. Conawago had not set the mop head on his skull yet, so Duncan had an unobstructed view of his face. He had aged shockingly. His leathery countenance had new wrinkles, his eyes were locked in a mournful expression, and as he tightened the knot that held up his makeshift toga, his hands were shaking.

Ishmael's hand pressed against his waistcoat pocket. At dawn Duncan had found him out on the rooftop perch by his room, whispering into a small smoldering mound of tobacco set on a roofing slate. Duncan had recognized the words, had seen the feathers and strips of fur and linen laid out by the fire, and had backed away. Ishmael was assembling a medicine bundle, a charm of sorts.

Now the young Nipmuc slowly extracted the charm and held it out for Duncan to examine. "The demonslayer," he said. "That's what my mother called such a charm, though I made some alterations since I couldn't find a snake fang or owl and woodpecker feathers."

Among the half dozen feathers arranged in a fan, Ishmael had included those of a pigeon and a seagull, and at the center was a beautiful iridescent feather, that of a kingfisher, that Duncan suspected had come out of the cherished totem pouch that hung around Ishmael's own neck. Such brilliant feathers were favorites of the gods, and Ishmael had probably been given this one by his mother or father when he was a boy. The feathers were fastened with a strip of dark fur and a red ribbon. Duncan cocked his head at the charm.

Ishmael recognized the question on his face. "Lizzie found an old fur cap, and she untied one of her stockings to give me the ribbon."

Duncan recalled Ishmael's earlier anguish in questioning whether their gods would even hear them from distant London, but then he understood. "Pigeon, gull, kingfisher. Bird of the city," Duncan said, "bird of the ocean, and bird of the gods' own home. A map of sorts, for a prayer to reach from London over the ocean to the American forests."

Ishmael nodded solemnly. "Maybe it will bring my uncle back. But I don't know how to get it to him."

As Duncan gazed at the old man, his heart ravaged, a door opened in the back of his mind, unbidden and unexplained. He removed his waistcoat and pulled out the tail of his linen shirt, the closest he could come to a toga, then planted himself in front of the bars and spoke in a loud voice. "*Diffugere nives, redeunt iam gramina campis arboribusque comae.*" He had not recited the Latin poem for years, but his Dutch teacher had hammered it into his students, insisting that this, Ode Seven of Horace's Book Four, was the most beautiful poem ever written. "*Mutat terra vices et decrescentia ripas flumina pvaetereunt,*" he continued.

"It's working!" came Ishmael's excited whisper. Conawago had looked up toward the door and taken a step forward. The last time Duncan had recited it had been under a full moon on a mountaintop near the Susquehanna River. Conawago had been so taken with it he had insisted that Duncan teach the poem to him.

As Duncan continued, the other inmates slowly approached. "*Gratia cum Nymphis geminisque sororibus aud ducere nida choros.*" The words had been pounded into him so deeply that they came out now without conscious thought. It was about spring, the cycle of the seasons, and the need for men to embrace life before winter overcame them. One of the inmates who had on a prior visit recited poetry began weeping and pushed one of the circlets of dried leaves through the bars and placed it on Duncan's head. Others gathered around for another verse, but then fell away. They had a strange deference to Conawago, who now stepped forward with feeble, shuffling steps to stand directly opposite Duncan, only an arm's length away. The old man's eyes repeatedly dimmed and brightened; his mouth seemed to try to turn up in a smile, but failed. He lifted a trembling hand to reach through the bars, and he touched Duncan's chest, as if challenging the illusion before him. As he drew it away Ishmael reached out and folded Conawago's fingers around the feathered charm. The aged man seemed to take no notice, but kept the charm in his grip as he turned and shuffled back to his corner.

"*Magis! Magis!*" one of the other men cried out, and the request for more of the poem was taken up by several other inmates.

Duncan offered a few more lines but then let Ishmael pull him away. More spectators had arrived and were pressing close for the afternoon entertainment.

"Darby, you blasphemer!" Sinner John growled. "Stop chewing up the horses!"

Duncan's map was back on the inn's table, strewn again with salts, walnut shells, peas, raisins, and now also currants.

Darby withdrew the hand that hovered over a set of four currants arrayed in front of a walnut shell. "Don't see why ye got two extra berries anyhow!"

"'Cause a wealthy gentleman's got a coach of four, ain't he?" Sinner John groused. "Who ever heard of a fine coach pulled by only two nags?"

Darby hid the offending hand under the table, muttering something about overbearing Methodists, then cast a jealous eye at the small cone of sugar that was marking St. James's Palace.

Sinner John whispered an impatient prayer and then, with Woolford hovering beside him, returned to sketching on the chart. Duncan was surprised at their knowledge of the alleys between Hewson's home and the Westminster Bridge, and of the gated entrances to the King's Road, which the porter was depicting with small cramped rectangles on Duncan's chart.

Lizzie was contributing too, whispering into Ishmael's ear with a somewhat dreamy expression as the young Nipmuc impassively drew triangles along the river to mark the locations of landing stairs. Duncan knew he would rather be planning the rescue of his uncle than the secret delivery of the *incognitum*.

His head shot up at a frantic knock on the inn's front door. A moment later a breathless Olivia Dumont rushed in. "We need help to get him inside!" she cried, then unexpectedly turned to Captain Rhys. "Captain, your man—" Rhys and Darby shot up and darted out of the room. By the time Duncan and Woolford reached the entry the two were on the front step, bracing a limp figure between them.

It was a *Galileo* sailor who had volunteered as one of Darby's watchers. They laid him on the divan in the sitting room. He was breathing regularly but had a swollen lump on his left temple. Duncan leaned over him, checking his pulse, then lifting an eyelid.

"He'll have a nagging headache, nothing more serious," Duncan concluded.

"He was attacked?" Olivia asked.

"He was neutralized," Woolford said grimly. "They wanted to take out a watcher, make a gap in our line!" He asked Darby where the man's station was.

"The block behind," Darby reported. "There's an alley that connects to the mews road behind the houses."

"Lizzie!" Mrs. Laws cried. "Check to see if the lanterns are lit at the back, to discourage any intruder."

As Lizzie hurried away, Sinner John, seemingly oblivious to what was happening, called out. "Finished, Mr. McCallum, including all the alleys to the bridge. No need to worry about traffic on the main streets 'cause ye won't even need to—"

His words were drowned out by a shattering scream from the back door.

Duncan darted into the kitchen as Lizzie staggered backward from the doorway. She turned and raised blood-covered hands, then stumbled to Ishmael, now beside Duncan, and threw her arms around him, sobbing.

The boy sprawled across the back step had been beaten so badly Duncan couldn't make out his features. For a terrible moment Duncan thought it might be Xander, but then he came running through the night, frantically shouting the boy's name.

"Robbie! Robbie! Robbie!" Xander cried, then collapsed on the step, weeping, as he reached his friend. It was the young boy whom Xander had called his sergeant, the playful youth who that morning had ridden just for fun in the decoy coach.

Duncan knelt beside the boy, searching vainly for a pulse. Robbie was dead.

Chapter 18

"THEY HAD HIM FOR HOURS," sobbed Xander. "Look what they've done!" He shook the boy's shoulders. "Robbie, Robbie, it's me, wake up!"

"He'll have no waking in this world, lad," a mournful voice said. Sinner John pulled Xander off the body to allow Duncan and Ishmael to lift it. "He's rising with merciful angels now."

They carried Robbie to the scullery table as Olivia and the porter took the stunned Xander into the dining room. Duncan clenched his jaw and began to examine the body. The boy had been cruelly used. The inch-wide abrasions on his forearms showed where he had been bound by straps. His shoes had been removed and the bones of one foot were broken, smashed with repeated blows of what looked like a hammer. His head had been beaten with a cudgel or narrow club, leaving indentations in the scalp. His face bore raw slashes from the blows of what he guessed to be a riding crop, which had reduced one eye to a bloody pulp. The blood around the injuries was congealed and drying, meaning they were hours old. All but one. The single piercing of the boy's heart still oozed blood. It had been done only minutes earlier.

"Poor lamb couldn't have been more than eleven or twelve," Mrs. Laws said as she brought a basin of hot water and some towels.

"He would have been ten next month," came a voice choked with emotion. "I promised to take him fishing on his birthday." Sinner John stepped forward and took Robbie's hand in his and began to stroke it as if to comfort the boy. "His ma died of consumption last year. He never knew his father."

"He was so happy today." The trembling words came from the kitchen doorway, where Xander stood with tears streaming down his cheeks. "He was keen as mustard about our ride. He'd never been in such a grand coach before. He was laughing and saying how the other boys will be so jealous when he told them he had been in the coach of Benjamin Franklin. When the driver finally stopped at Whitehall, like Mr. Franklin said to, I told Robbie we didn't need to get out but he did anyway, 'cause he said that was what the gentry would do, step out of the fancy coach in front of the palaces. So he did get out, and I figured I'd join his playacting 'cause it made him smile so.

"We had gone maybe thirty paces down the street when those soldiers shouted for us to stop. He laughed when I said we gotta fly, 'cause didn't he love a good run. I thought he was keeping up with me but when I turned he had stumbled on the cobbles and they were on him, dragging him back to the parade grounds."

With a shudder Duncan recalled the tale of dungeons below the Horse Guards Palace. "You mean to the Horse Guards?"

"They put him in a coach by their stables. The driver protested and took a riding crop on his cheek for it, then one of them got up on the seat beside him and pointed out the gate."

"Any idea of where they went?" Woolford asked.

"I know for certain, sir, 'cause didn't I leap on the back of the coach down the street and hold on. They went into Hyde Park, to a horse ground full of soldiers and young horses."

"Their training field," Woolford said. "I know the place."

"There's barns and sheds and such. They took him into a big shed past the barns. A workshop for the farrier and saddlemaker I reckoned, for I saw racks of saddles and harnesses and a forge at the far end when I lifted myself up at a window. Then some soldiers spotted me and called out 'thief!' and I had to save my own skin. I watched from the trees for a while but then they brought out dogs and I knew they would have me if I stayed." He stared forlornly at the boy's ruined foot. "There was tools in that shop," he said with another sob.

"But how," Duncan asked, "how did you know to come looking for him here?"

"I didn't, but I was spreading the word and one of the other boys said he saw a couple of those brutes in black boots two blocks from here, and one had something rolled up in a blanket over his shoulder."

Xander watched with silent sobs as Duncan finished his examination of the dead boy, then began helping Mrs. Laws wash the body. "He didn't tell 'em anything, Mr. Duncan," Xander blurted out, as if he had to defend his friend. "He wouldn't. He didn't know anything he could tell 'em anyway, 'cepting he met the great Mr. Franklin."

Duncan and Woolford exchanged a worried glance. The boy had also known about the Neptune, and obviously had revealed it to his captors, or they wouldn't have known to bring the body there. Duncan tried to recall whether Robbie had known his name, or those of Ishmael and Woolford.

Mrs. Laws cleaned the blood from the boy's face, then gently patted his forehead. "There, there," she cooed, "we'll see you have a proper Christian burial. No pauper's grave for you, Robbie boy."

Sinner John, still standing by the body, had his eyes closed and hands clasped in prayer. "Amen," he murmured, then with a look of cold fury turned to whisper in Xander's ear. The link boy's face lit with fierce determination as he listened. He followed Sinner John out into the back courtyard.

"Poor man takes it personal, I fear," Mrs. Laws said. "He cares so for the boys. Last year he formed a choir and had the boys sing along the streets during Yuletide."

Lizzie appeared with more towels and handed the proprietress a hair brush, which she used to straighten Robbie's hair as Duncan cleaned the boy's mangled foot. "Why, Mr. McCallum," the maid asked with a sob, "why did poor Robbie have to die?"

It took him a moment to recognize the accusation in the maid's words. Robbie would still be alive if Duncan hadn't brought his troubles to the inn. "He wanted to ride in the coach," he said, immediately shamed by his words.

"Don't be impertinent!" the landlady snapped, punctuating her words with an angry knock of her pewter foot that brought Ishmael and Olivia back to the kitchen door. "This waif died because of you, all of you! You owe him the truth!"

"He died because of us," Duncan admitted, the anguish tight in his throat.

"Because of a silly feud you started with some damned soldiers! And now look at him! All his years are forfeit!"

"Because of some devils who would stop men from voicing their freedom, Clem," came a deep voice. Captain Rhys had appeared at the innkeeper's side. He put a calming hand on her arm.

"So this poor child died because colonials can't get the respect of some starch-necked fools in Parliament?" she asked, her voice breaking.

"Well," Captain Rhys answered, "it's complicated, woman. You know the political men can be—"

"Yes," Duncan interrupted. "That's exactly why he died. Because Parliament would rather strap the yoke on the common man than listen to him."

A tear streamed down the cheek of the woman who made light of losing a leg in battle. "Then a pox on Parliament and the cowards who inhabit it!" After a moment she collected herself. "Lizzie dear, go take a look in my Jasper's old trunk. There may be a pair of shoes there. We can't let the boy go barefoot to St. Peter."

Olivia volunteered to help the maid. As they left, Patrick Woolford nudged Duncan's arm and motioned him toward the parlor.

"I was in my office this afternoon," Woolford confided. "Just before the tea hour there was a great hubbub on the parade ground. I looked out to see the big green coach with the matching Friesian horses."

"You mean the Earl of Milbridge's conveyance," Duncan said.

Woolford nodded. "Lieutenant Nettles ran out to get inside it, but it did not move. After a few minutes he ran back, then returned with the Secretary at War, who climbed inside. The Secretary at War is not a man accustomed to being summoned, believe me. When he climbed out he seemed shaken, but before he reached the building he was shouting orders. The guards at the doors were doubled. The sleepy guard at the back door where you entered was replaced with two men with swords and pistols."

"I'm not sure I understand, Patrick."

"Duncan, they began torturing that poor boy this morning. Nettles must have sent urgent word to Milbridge afterward. Milbridge arrived midafternoon and began giving urgent orders to the Secretary at War, who called for more guards and then summoned Major Hastings to his office." Woolford paused, seeing the question in Duncan's eyes. "It pays to be friendly with all the clerks," he added.

"I still don't follow," Duncan confessed.

"There is only one thing that would get Milbridge so excited. The boy gave up your name."

For a moment Duncan seemed to have trouble breathing, then he pushed back his fear. "Surely there could be another explanation. Matters of war."

"I did not tell you before, Duncan. When I first returned to England months ago, the earl summoned me to accompany him to the chambers of the secretary. He asked if I knew of a man named Duncan McCallum who resided on the frontier of New York province. I said the frontier was a vast place, that the name sounded only vaguely familiar. He frowned and said that Superintendent Johnson had responded the same way to his inquiries, but that we must make greater effort against such renegades, for this McCallum had been engaged in acts against His Majesty's government. He said if the outlaw was still at large when I returned, it was my duty to apprehend him. There would be a large bounty paid. He pays bounties just for information about you, Duncan. You know he has spies in the colonies.

"There was a man at Johnson Hall last year." Woolford shook his head and looked away from Duncan but kept speaking. "An ex-soldier. You were away and Sarah didn't want you to know. He came looking for you. In a tavern he got drunk and boasted he would soon collect the rich bounty on McCallum's head. Sarah found out and had some Mohawk friends capture him. They tied him to a tree and made as if to kill him. Then Sarah appeared and told him that if he ever was seen within a hundred miles of Edentown the Mohawks would burn him alive. Then she cut him free. He fled, never came back."

Duncan clenched his jaw. He had lost track of the number of secrets Sarah had been keeping from him. "You are saying there is an order for my arrest?"

"No. I asked to see such an order, on the pretense that it should be distributed on the frontier. As I expected, there is none. The secretary said this was more in the way of a private matter for the earl, that some outlaws must be dealt with discreetly for the sake of the government, and the earl had authority over those who handle such things for the king. I wasn't going to tell you. As far as I knew you were safe in Edentown surrounded by Mohawks and protected by Sarah. But Milbridge is a merciless devil enamored of his own powers, which the king sees fit to keep increasing. There is talk that he will be the next Secretary at War."

"And now I am in his city."

"No one will challenge what he does. If his tentacles wrap around you no one will ever see you again. What he feels for you is beyond loathing. His hatred is an obsession. You took his daughter. You took his dream for his own colony west of New York. Then you took away one of his plantations and his title in the Virginia militia."

"He made a very poor admiral of the Virginia sea," Duncan said.

"This is nothing to joke about. He has estates now in the Carolinas, in Yorkshire, in Kent, in the West Indies. He has so many palaces and lodges he probably can't remember them all and so many kept women he doubtless forgets their names. He's had three wives who suffered terrible accidents when he grew weary of them. He has only two obsessions that will never fade. His never-ending lust for power and his never-ending lust for your head on a spike."

"Sarah's father is not my business here. I will avoid him and be gone soon."

"My God, Duncan, you are not listening! If he wants them at his command, Hastings and Nettles and their black-hearted company are his! Now that he has reason to believe you are here, everyone connected with you will be targeted. Do not force me to have to tell Sarah her father killed you. I will stand by you. I will continue to lie to the War Council to protect you. But do not be dismissive of the threat, I beg you. You put Ishmael at risk. You put Olivia at risk. You put this poor boy at risk. If you keep going without more care, you will put Franklin and his household at risk."

"And Conawago?" came an anguished voice from the shadows. Ishmael had been listening. "Was Conawago at risk?"

"Ishmael," Duncan said, "you shouldn't—"

"Is my uncle in Bedlam because of you, Duncan?"

Duncan turned to Woolford, who grimaced and looked away.

"Was he in Bedlam because he was a friend of yours? If Milbridge had agents making inquiries on the frontier about Duncan McCallum, then surely he would have learned that your closest companion was Conawago!"

"Ishmael," Duncan said, struggling for words. "I can't—I won't—I don't know," he finally admitted.

Ishmael's face clouded with rage. He stormed past Duncan to the inn's front door, slamming it behind him.

Duncan worked in morbid silence over the body of the link boy, cleaning the wounds and sewing up a long gash in his upper arm where a blade had pierced him. He pushed down his emotion as he worked but it welled up with a silent sob as he tied a knot in the thread and looked at the ruin of Robbie's face. The boy was dead because of him. The grief ripped at his heart, and he slipped outside, bracing himself against the wall as he took in deep gulps of the cool night air to steady himself. When he finally returned, Mrs. Laws was using the needle and thread to repair the dead boy's ragged clothes. He murmured a farewell to Woolford, who agreed to escort Olivia back to Craven Street, and silently followed them onto the front steps. Ishmael was nowhere to be seen. He had lost Robbie and now might be losing Ishmael.

The Nipmuc's words bore down on him with a terrible weight. He believed it unlikely that Milbridge had known of his connection with the tribal ambassador who had arrived in London but he could not entirely dismiss the possibility. He knew that Sarah's father had lawyers, minor officials, magistrates, and more nefarious agents in his pay, in both England and America. He had invested much in an effort to double the term of Duncan's indentured servitude, frustrated only when John Adams stepped in at Sarah's request. He had killed Sarah's Iroquois father. His men had enslaved Duncan and many natives and Sons of Liberty on his tobacco plantation in Virginia. There were no depths to which he would not stoop, and the more Duncan considered the torment Conawago was suffering, the more he knew it could be true that his friend was being punished because of Duncan.

He helped carry Robbie's body into the stable, where a trestle table covered with a sheet awaited him. The dead boy would be visited by his friends in the morning, then sewn into the sheet. Mrs. Laws called into the shadows for more lanterns and stools, but no one replied.

"Mr. John's gone, this hour and more," Lizzie explained. "He and Xander gathered a dozen of the boys and they stole off into the night."

"I'll stay with the boy," Captain Rhys offered. "Someone should keep vigil."

"We'll take watches, Captain," Darby said. "I'll relieve you."

"We'll fetch some tea for you," Mrs. Laws suggested, "and in the morning Lizzie and I shall set out food for a proper wake."

"And the choir," Lizzie said. "The boys will want to sing him something. Robbie dearly loved to sing, such a soft gentle voice."

Duncan slipped away, out into the street, making a circuit around the block, then climbing up to their rooms when he still could not find Ishmael. The young Nipmuc had not come back. Ishmael's bed was still made, and Duncan sat on it for several brooding minutes before venturing into the cramped passage that led to the roof. The little flat at the base of the roof was empty. Knowing Ishmael's propensity for climbing he studied the roof itself, confirming no one sat on the peaks of the gables, then descended to the street.

He was sitting on the inn's front steps when the city's steeples struck midnight. The deep voice of a parish watch called out from a block away. "Mid of night and the sky is fair," came the hourly call of time and weather that would be echoed by watchmen all over London. He looked into the sky, painfully recalling the many nights he had discussed the stars with Conawago, then turned toward the east, toward Ludgate Hill.

He stayed in the shadows along the edge of the Strand, then Fleet Street, politely declining offers from link boys and night women. Twice he ducked into alleys and watched the street to confirm there was no one to worry about.

St. Paul's chuchyard held several sleeping bodies covered with blankets or cloaks. To his surprise a beggar was stationed by the entrance, wearing a tattered cassock. "Alms for poor," he chanted, "alms for your soul." Duncan suspected the alms would be going to a local alehouse but still dropped a ha'penny into what looked like a church collection plate.

He felt insignificant as he stepped into the cavernous nave. Huge lanterns hanging along the walls cast flickering shadows, lending movement to the pious statues below them. A woman sat in a pew, weeping. A cleric knelt on a prayer bench in a small chapel to the side. Duncan paused in the crossing, the centermost point under Christopher Wren's massive dome, and looked up toward the narrow, silvery windows high overhead. He recollected an enjoyable meal at the Neptune during which Mrs. Laws and Sinner John had described the remarkable features of the building.

The narrow, curving stairs grew darker as he climbed, lit only by the moon's rays that seeped through the windows at the landings. He reached the walkway around the base of the dome, called the Whispering Gallery, then climbed ever upward to a narrow door that led out to the narrower Stone Gallery. He made one circuit of the walkway, then located yet another even narrower stairway and climbed again, emerging onto what the innkeeper had called the Golden Gallery, the small topmost level at the base of the lantern-like pinnacle. His despair deepened as he found this walkway empty as well. Then he noticed a small ladder built into a sliding track for workmen needing to access the lantern-shaped cap of the dome. He stretched high to pull the ladder down and climbed up, discovering a surprisingly wide ledge that was invisible from below.

The solitary figure sat with his legs dangling over the edge. Regretting that he was not as fearless about heights as his tribal friends, Duncan sat against a column near the Nipmuc, but did not speak. A cool breeze had cleared the haze over London. The gibbous moon washed the city with its metallic glow, silhouetting the steeples, towers, and high palace roofs above the densely packed houses. In the distance, two miles away, he could make out the towers of Westminster. The lonely call of a nighthawk echoed below them. From the river came the sound of distant bells as ships marked the watch.

"London seemed a miracle when I first saw it," Ishmael suddenly said, "a wonder of the modern world. But it doesn't feel like it anymore. I never would have believed men could banish nature the way they have here. In America, in Philadelphia or Boston or New York, you are always close to trees and a quarter hour's walk can always take you to farmland or forest. We shouldn't be surprised there is so much cruelty in this place. Men are adrift here. They've cut their roots to the land. It is the earth that gives strength to a man's heart, that enriches his spirit. Without that what is a man? An empty shell, kept busy with coffee shops, gossip, and fancy ribbon sellers."

Duncan had no reply. He followed Ishmael's gaze to the long, ominous-looking structure several blocks away, bifurcated by a tower.

"If these English had not cut their roots to the true things," Ishmael said, "there would be no need for a place like Bedlam."

"That sounds like something Conawago would say," Duncan offered, regretting the words as he saw the pain they brought to Ishmael's face. Neither spoke for several minutes. An owl glided past on silent wings and disappeared in the shadows of the shorter tower above the west portico. Ishmael twisted his head, trying to make it out. Owls were sometimes seen as harbingers of death, but they were also potent messengers to the spirit world. The young Nipmuc seemed troubled by the sign. "We can't just rescue my uncle," he said. "I know you agree. Not after what they did to Robbie. It proves they are devil walkers," he said, referring to an old myth of his tribe about demons who stalked men and killed them to eat their souls.

"You must rescue Conawago and get on the *Galileo*," Duncan said. "I will make the devil walkers pay."

"And know I was a coward for the rest of my days?" Ishmael snapped. "Not me. Not now. I didn't tell you. I went out to Charing Cross two nights ago and sat with those link boys. Robbie was there. He asked questions about the tribes. He asked what the pouch was I always carried around my neck, and I said it was my protector spirit. He asked if he could touch it, and when he did he jerked his hand away, saying he felt something like a spark. I said it meant the spirits were speaking with him, that they would protect him now too. He rejoiced and said the tribes were calling him, and since he had no family here could he could go back with us to be with the tribes. But now I know I lied. The spirits couldn't be with him. I don't think they have even taken notice of us."

Duncan had trouble speaking past the lump in his throat. "I will find another place to stay," he said. "If Milbridge truly knows I am in London his men will be like wolves on the hunt. I can't put those at the Neptune in danger."

"Noah can find a place for you."

Duncan nodded. "Tomorrow. I promised Dr. Franklin I would go to a textile works with him. I don't like him traveling unprotected. Tonight I will sleep in Mrs. Laws's hayloft." Duncan thought a moment, then reached inside his waistcoat into the secret pocket he had sewn there. As Ishmael watched he touched the white wampum beads, the sacred beads, the truth beads, to his forehead, then to his heart. He held them out toward Ishmael and then extended them toward the brilliant moon.

"By the gods of the forest," he intoned loudly, "by the gods of the sky, by the gods of the water, I swear that I will not leave London without Conawago, even if I must give my life."

He heard a sharp intake of breath. Ishmael was watching as the owl approached again, swooping close now as it swiveled its head toward them. It then flew directly toward the moon.

"Duncan!" Ishmael cried with sudden excitement. "That's a forest owl! He's finally arrived. Your beads brought him close, and now he's heard you, now he knows we are here. He came from the west, flying low over all those Englishmen before coming back to us. He heard your words and saw the beads! He knows his duty now. Sometimes the old ones fall asleep."

"I'm not sure I follow," Duncan admitted.

"An owl can be a bad omen, Duncan, but this one is bad for the English. He is rising to the moon now to wake the old gods. They have a lot to answer for."

Dr. Franklin was not well pleased that his household took Duncan's view and insisted he not go out unescorted. "I am proceeding to the textile mill and I shall have my blackthorn shillelagh," he argued when Duncan arrived, now wearing a cloak with a hood borrowed from Captain Rhys.

"And I will see that he has an escort," a soft, impish voice declared. Olivia Dumont appeared at the entrance to his sitting room. "Benjamin, *mon cher*," Olivia exclaimed with an exaggerated French accent. "You are too important a personage to take casual risks. Mr. McCallum is a great frontiersman who wrestles bears and lions and the *incognitum*! You must heed his advice." Duncan rolled his eyes at her. She decided she had won her argument and hooked her arm through Franklin's. The inventor paused at the door to speak to Henry Quinn, who was unobtrusively transcribing letters at the desk in the corner of the room.

"Those three letters to Whitehall will also need copying, one for our records here and one to be sent back to the colonies. Oh, and if you have a moment, remind Mrs. Stevenson that the new shower bath is due to arrive any day now, the one of Mr. Feetham's patent. We will need to make room for it in the bath closet. Our expedition should conclude by noon, though we shall take luncheon before returning. Maybe the shower bath will be here when we return!"

Quinn gave a cheerful wave. "And don't forget to give me last week's notes later for me to organize."

Duncan had no idea why, in the middle of all his intrigues and work for the colonies, Franklin would devote half a day at a new textile mill. As their coach rattled along Old Bond Street toward the northern edge of the city, Duncan decided it might just have been a gambit for Franklin to spend a few hours with Olivia, who always seemed to become more French in his presence. Then he chided himself as he heard Olivia ask about warp threads and shuttles. She shared her brother's insatiable curiosity and sounded as though she knew more about the production of cloth than either Duncan or Franklin.

The coach took them into a labyrinth of alleys between low sturdy buildings, most of them made of brick, then finally halted in a wide alley that ended at a simple door marked HAMPSTEAD TEXTILE WORKS. They were greeted in the entry lobby by a genteel man who introduced himself as the superintendent and then opened an inner door, releasing a rattling din caused by scores of turning shuttles as weavers bent over their looms.

"We use Mr. Kay's new flying shuttle," the superintendent boasted, then gestured to the nearest loom. "One weaver can do what four did before, and we can produce much wider fabric!" he declared with obvious pride. As if to explain, he approached the loom and pointed to a board under the threads that ran from side to side, creating a track to carry the shuttle and thread. Olivia exhibited great enthusiasm for the machine, which was duplicated at all the looms spread over the broad oak floor of the factory. As Franklin fired questions at the man, Duncan was reminded that the inventor was secretly helping the Covenant by finding new industry for America. On another day Duncan might have been fascinated himself, but his spirit was heavy with Robbie's death and Ishmael's words of the previous night. He hung back, seeing that Franklin and Olivia did not seem to notice his absence, and retreated to a water butt he had seen by the entrance. As he was dipping in the ladle for a second drink, one of the clerks he had seen in the offices burst through the door. He paused near Duncan, straining his neck as he searched the aisles before turning back toward Duncan.

"There is a disturbance outside. I am sure that the superintendent will want to know."

"A disturbance?" Duncan asked.

"Probably some alley ruffians waiting for some coins before they move on."

"Let's not disturb Dr. Franklin's visit," Duncan said. "You and I can deal with a few ruffians."

The clerk straightened his waistcoat with new self-importance and led Duncan out the front door.

A green enameled coach sat a dozen steps away, blocking the view down the alley. As recognition burst upon Duncan, a brocaded arm extended from the coach's window and pointed at him. Six men darted from around the coach, each holding a drawn cavalry saber. Lieutenant Nettles appeared, leveling a cocked pistol as the others slowly converged. "The earl ordered us to take you alive, McCallum," he declared. "But I'd be happy for the excuse to put a bullet in your knee."

Duncan froze as Nettles lowered the pistol toward his leg. They stared in brittle silence at each other. "We have already killed you once," Nettles reminded him with an icy smile, then nodded at someone behind Duncan. He turned barely in time to see the saber being raised, then the heavy hilt slammed into his skull.

Chapter 19

THE CEILING IRONS," A HARSH voice growled. Duncan's hearing was as blurred as his vision. He struggled to keep his eyes open for more than a few seconds at a time. "Dangle 'em from the arms for a few hours and they whimper like babes."

"The major said he must keep his wits fer now," came a gruff reply. "It's his way. First he tortures 'em with words, then the messy stuff follows."

"There's King Hank's old rack down the end of the hall," the first man put in. "A little stretch might clear his wits fine."

"Which I wager ain't been used since the last century. Probably fall apart when we start the winding. And the earl says he wants to build a new one using that as a model, so we can't be breaking it."

"Worth a try, I'm just saying," came the disappointed reply.

Duncan finally was able to keep his eyes open. The cell door and the wall adjoining the next cell were of rusty iron straps riveted together, which meant it was very old. He was in the first of a row of cells. What had Woolford said about the cellar of the Horse Guards Palace? It held the dungeons of the sadistic Henry the Eighth.

The realization stirred his senses, and he studied his musty surroundings. His two guards were at a table a few paces from his cell, the lantern between them the only light except for a guttering candle on an iron sconce on the wall behind them. He took advantage of the shadows, and his guards' distraction, to touch the throbbing lump on the side of his head. Blood still seeped from it. The rest of his body seemed intact, though his ribs and thigh ached where someone, probably Nettles, had kicked him.

A smell of mildew, tobacco, and night soil hung in the dank air. Duncan recognized something else, the faint scent of stomach bile. He probed the front of this shirt and pushed his tongue around his mouth. Someone had vomited and it wasn't him. Not wanting to draw the attention of his jailers, he stayed prone and twisted wormlike along the stone flag floor until he could see into the adjoining cell. Through the shadows he could make out the shape of another man leaning limply against the rear wall, asleep or unconscious.

Duncan twisted again to look back into the corridor that led to where the jailers sat. He had been a prisoner before, and knew that the more information he possessed the better his chances for survival. He saw now that the men wore high black boots, though they were worn and not polished to a military sheen, meaning they were probably employed as grooms or groundskeepers but that he was still in the custody of the Horse Guards.

Patrick Woolford's offices were in the building above him. Would he be there now? Did he know of Duncan's abduction? Duncan had no idea of the hour. His head spun. Surely by now Franklin and Olivia would know of his capture, but they were powerless to help him. How had Nettles known that Franklin was going to the textile mill, and that Duncan was with him? Ishmael would help, he told himself, then recalled that Ishmael was probably at Bedlam, and after Duncan had vowed to find accommodation elsewhere the Nipmuc would not miss him for hours, perhaps for a day or more. King Henry was known for leaving his prisoners to starve and rot. Was this forlorn hole where he would breathe his last? Would Sarah ever know of his fate? He had never finished his letter to her. He held her image in his mind as he drifted back into unconsciousness, hands around his totem pouch.

"Rise, ye worthless lump!"

Duncan sat up gasping, shaking off the water being poured over his head. As he thrust out an arm to knock away the bucket, the point of a cavalry saber pressed against his thigh.

"Like I said, McCallum," came Lieutenant Nettles's oily voice, "just because we have to keep you alive doesn't mean you can't be damaged."

The guard with the bucket laughed and emptied the rest of its contents over Duncan.

"How did you find me?" Duncan sputtered. He knew they had not simply followed Franklin and discovered Duncan in attendance. They had sprung a carefully planned trap.

"The king knows all," Nettles quipped, then turned. "Don't neglect our other guest," Nettles said to the jailer, who laughed again and retrieved another bucket by the cell door. The second prisoner woke gasping, clutching his side as the bucket was upended over him. The man turned toward Duncan, then guilt darkened his face and he looked away. It was Ensign Lewis.

Nettles edged his sword under Duncan's chin and pushed upward, forcing him to his feet. "He's hurt," Duncan said.

Nettles grinned. "In another unit he would have been brought up on charges. But dear God, imagine the tedious paperwork, the military lawyers, the damned judges, the endless delays. Why put the poor ensign through all that torture over months when we can condense it all to a few hours down here?"

"Charges for what?" Duncan asked. He glanced back at Lewis and saw that the second cell's door was ajar. It had not been locked.

"Insubordination. Lying to an officer. Defiance of orders. Dereliction of duty. Not reporting the ghost of an enemy. Embarrassing the major and me. That one alone should be five hundred lashes. And my God, the king's horses could have been lost. As it is, the new geldings will be skittish for weeks."

Duncan had no idea of what Nettles spoke of but knew every minute of distraction meant delay for his own torture. "The king's horses?"

"Tell him your shame, Ensign," Nettles instructed Lewis.

"I was on duty at the Hyde Park paddock last night," Lewis said in a low, fearful voice. "I allowed a building of the king to be burned to the ground."

"The smith's shop is gone," Nettles snapped. "The harness shop is gone. Twenty good saddles gone!"

Nettles glared at Lewis as the words slowly sank into Duncan's consciousness. Sinner John had left with Xander and a group of vengeful link boys, after Xander had explained that Robbie had been tortured at the Guards' Hyde Park paddocks. "That would be the barn where you tortured and killed a nine-year-old boy," he said to the lieutenant.

Nettles tilted his head in surprise. "No, McCallum," he replied with a chilling grin. "He wasn't killed until we approached the inn. Quite the little fighter. Squirmed right up to the end."

Duncan fought the impulse to spring on the soulless lieutenant. "You put your stiletto into his heart."

"I would have sliced his throat, but I had on my uniform. The heart is less messy."

Duncan clenched his jaw. "You're the one who tortured him as well?"

"My role was more in the capacity of field commander for that particular exercise. Sometimes it is more fulfilling to just watch. And do you have any idea how hard it is to remove bloodstains?"

"He did you no harm!" Duncan spat.

"We are taught to improvise, Highlander," came a new voice from the darkness. Major Hastings stepped out of the shadows. "The boy was a weapon to use against our enemies. And the training grounds are always so convenient. Out of the way, yet only a twenty-minute trot from here. Horses at the big barn—throwing a man into a stall with an angry stallion can be most effective—and then there was always the smithy and harness shop with all those interesting tools." Hastings spoke in a cool, disinterested tone as he lifted a pair of manacles from the guards' table. "Hammers, nails, hoof clippers, trimming knives, leather straps, awls. The lieutenant even found a way to use an old bridle and bit last year, though it finally broke when the man was hoisted to the ceiling." He turned to Duncan. "Did you actually set that fire?"

"Small price for the death of a young boy. His name was Robbie. He loved to sing."

Hastings greeted the news with one of his lightless smiles. "Thank you for that. If anything runs amiss we will take that as a confession. We can always just hang you for destroying the king's property, though sometimes we find ways for the king's enemies to disappear, to avoid all the public fuss. If we let the king know, he might even vie with the earl over the joy of killing you." Hastings shrugged.

"But promises were already made. The earl is most adamant in his claim over you. I have never seen him so animated. I had no idea there was a history between the two of you."

Hastings turned for a moment to speak to someone in the shadows. Duncan heard footsteps retreating, then the creak of heavy hinges down the corridor.

"Ensign?" Hastings said, and swung Lewis's cell door open. "The cell was never locked, you know. But you were told to stay and you stayed. Bravo!"

Lewis was in obvious pain. He gazed dully at the major, then gripped his side and left the cell with small, mincing steps. Hastings offered mocking applause then gestured to the guards' table.

"Tea! Get the ensign some hot tea. Nothing like hot tea before battle!"

Lewis spat blood on the stone flags, then with obvious pain lowered himself into one of the chairs by the table.

"For God's sake, let me help him!" Duncan cried. "He needs a doctor."

"Nonsense. Just part of his training."

"Training? This is nothing but cruelty."

Hastings produced the long dagger Duncan had first seen in Philadelphia and lifted it to sight along the blade. He cast an icy smile at Duncan, then with sudden quickness threw the knife, embedding it in the table inches from Lewis. "What an extraordinary opportunity it is, to kill someone twice," the major declared with amusement. "Obviously we were negligent the first time." He looked at Duncan. "So seldom do we get a second chance. So seldom do we need it. What a game we shall have. I recall reading somewhere that there are two or three organs that can be removed without causing immediate death, though I'm not sure I remember which ones," he added, raising a laugh from Nettles.

The lieutenant moved behind Duncan and pressed the point of his saber against Duncan's spine, pushing him out of the cell.

"Was it only yesterday we discovered McCallum was still alive, James?" Hastings asked his lieutenant, then turned back to Duncan. "I was furious at first, of course, but later quite excited about the opportunity it presented. I could hardly credit it when you were among the names the boy gave us. I even struck him for lying. Then Mr. Lewis said, 'No, it's true, McCallum is alive.'" Hastings swiveled his head toward Lewis. "Did you honestly think we would spare the boy by making that confession, Ensign? It only made me put more energy into the lessons we had to give you. How could you withhold such vital information from your cherished commander?" Hastings gave a cackling laugh. "McGowan, McCallum." He shrugged. "I should have known that if the *incognitum* could resurrect itself from the ocean floor, then so too could its Scottish curator."

As Duncan desperately tried to recall those who had known him as McGowan, Hastings stepped aside for two men carrying a heavy device. It was a wooden armchair made for torture. Thick straps lay open on the arms, the front legs, and on a panel that extended upward, apparently as a way of stabilizing the head. Hastings produced a handkerchief and carefully wiped dust from the arms. "My favorite Tudor heirloom," he declared, then smiled at Duncan. "If at first you don't succeed at death, try, try again, eh? You should be honored, McCallum. I believe some very prominent members of Tudor society experienced this chair before you. You are about to join the ranks of the martyrs."

"Killing a child was not much of a challenge for a king's warrior," Duncan said in a seething voice. "But then, slashing Pierre Dumont's throat in an alley wasn't exactly up to Horse Guards standards."

"I am proud of my Italian steel," Hastings retorted. "One quick stroke was all that was required. '*Mon Dieu!*' the Frenchman cried when I grabbed him, as if he were making a final discovery. That's all, just *mon Dieu*. I would have thought a scholar would have offered something more eloquent for his final words. You know," Hastings added with a sneer, " 'I gladly sacrifice my mortal being for the glory of the dusty *incognitum*,' or such." Nettles laughed again.

"So you admit to murdering him," Duncan said. "Then there was killing an unarmed man in a mud pit and slaying his wife and unborn child."

Nettles uttered a victorious cry. "A double to me!" he exclaimed to Hastings.

"So you are the one who murders innocent women and children, Lieutenant," Duncan said, letting his anger burn away his fear. "Thank you for clarifying that."

Hastings gave another haughty laugh. "Bravo, McCallum, living up to the Highland reputation. As dense as one of those shaggy cows. You need to grasp your situation. You did die in the Atlantic. It was in my report to the War Council, so it must be so. That makes you nothing but a piece of meat for us to carve. A practice dummy such as we use for our lances." He gestured to the two big men who had been at the guards' table. They seized Duncan, one on each arm. He resisted only an instant, then Nettles's saber pressed against his breastbone. The guards slammed him down into the chair, strapping in his legs, his arms, and his neck.

The major turned to Ensign Lewis, who now stared down at the table as if willing himself not to watch. "Ensign, congratulations. Tonight you matriculate from cleaning up horse dung to cleaning up Highland dung. Prove yourself here and you will become apprentice to the lieutenant and myself, which carries some amazing privileges." Hastings extracted his dagger from the wood of the table and dropped its hilt into Lewis's hand. "Where would you like to start?"

Lewis finally raised his head. "Sir?"

"Just preliminaries. To make the point, so to speak. By the end of the night we will slice his tendons so he can't walk. Lieutenant Nettles will teach you with one foot, then you can do the second. But for now, just something simple, to get McCallum's attention."

Lewis's face drained of color. "Sir, I cannot. I joined the army to meet the king's enemies on the battlefield."

"And Mr. McCallum is our enemy. Conspiring to gain the king's secrets. Concealing treasures that rightfully belong to the king. Aiding and abetting the traitor Franklin and his lovely French spy." Hastings closed Lewis's fingers around the hilt of his blade. "By all rights McCallum's kind should have been exterminated on the battlefield at Culloden. The Bonnie Prince was never captured, so if it makes you feel better let's say we are still in that battle. Scratch him and you will see Jacobite venom spill out."

"Sir, please! Let me return to the stables!"

The amusement left Hastings's face. "Scratch him or we'll fetch another binding chair for you!" he snapped, then seized Lewis by the collar and hauled him to his feet.

Lewis stood frozen.

Hastings shouted, as if instructing a company of recruits on the parade ground. "Do we have to beat the weakness out of you, boy?" The major grabbed the ensign's hand with the dagger and drew the blade across the back of Duncan's hand.

Duncan jerked at the sudden pain, but could only watch as the blood welled up along the shallow cut. Hastings gestured, and one of the guards began pulling Duncan's right sleeve past the binding strap.

"That wasn't so hard, now, was it?" Hastings said in a low voice. The sight of the blood clearly excited him. "Do it again, Lewis," he ordered.

With a trembling hand Lewis placed the edge of the blade on Duncan's exposed forearm, but he went no further.

"Again!" Hastings shouted.

Duncan flexed his muscle, raising his forearm so the razor-sharp blade sliced into his skin. Another line of blood seeped out of the cut.

"No!" Lewis moaned. "Duncan, no!"

Hastings laughed. "This is going to be quite the entertaining evening! We'll have to find some farrier tools, Nettles, and in the rack room there is a—"

"Enough, enough, enough!" came a high voice from the corridor. "What is it you men of arms say? Stand down. Yes, stand down, Major. Rest on your laurels. I am forever in your debt and all that." The voice was coming from a party of men now emerging from the corridor. The front rank parted to make way for the Earl of Milbridge.

A look of great contentment settled on the earl's corpulent face as he studied Duncan. "What an unexpected joy, Hastings, to have this Scottish mongrel in my grasp after all these years! You can't imagine the difficulties he has caused me. I have long suffered from the inability to reach him, and now at last to have him surface under my nose, why, my suffering is rewarded." He turned to one of his men with a sudden impulse. "What do you have? A riding crop? A cat-o'-nine? Quick, man!"

The attendant, unprepared for the request, shrugged. "Nothing, my lord. There's a whip on the wagon."

"Your belt, then!"

The man fumbled with the buckle of the belt he used to carry a short sword, then stripped away the weapon and handed the belt to Milbridge. A heavy scent of rosewater wafted toward Duncan as the earl approached, his eyes wild with cruel desire.

Everyone seemed to hesitate, not understanding. Everyone but Milbridge, who wound the buckle into his palm and with surprising quickness slashed the belt at Duncan's head. It cut into the flesh of his cheek, but for the next two strikes Duncan twisted, letting them break their force on his head board, though Milbridge did not seem to notice.

Milbridge closed his eyes and made a small mewing sound. "Oh, to at last reach the itch that could not be scratched!" He sighed deeply. "I will take him now, Major."

Hastings seemed confused. "Lord?"

"I will relieve you of this Scottish rubbish. A wagon and a cage await behind the building."

"But he is a prisoner of the Horse Guards."

"Who do the bidding of the Council, of which I am a senior member."

Hastings seemed unconvinced. He too had plans.

Milbridge rolled his eyes. "Dismiss your men, Major, so we may speak freely. The lieutenant and the boy who drew first blood may stay."

Hastings frowned, obviously unhappy, but snapped orders. His attendants disappeared down the corridor.

The earl lowered his heavy body into one of the chairs and straightened his long wig. "You may know I have a new hunting lodge, Major."

"I hear it is the envy of all the nobility."

"I never appreciated the versatility of such a place. We have kennels filled with hungry hounds, a complete butcher's shop, even a row of cages in the cellars. The architect wondered about those and I said they were for the prey I captured, so I could keep the meat fresh.

"So now I have the resources to assure McCallum will be alive for a month at least, though not particularly recognizable after the first few days. My men will know how to work on him, though my orders will be that they may not do so without me present. I will be there tomorrow when my horse doctor castrates him." Milbridge said with a gleam, then raised the belt from where he sat and lashed out again. Duncan turned his head, taking the end of the belt on his jaw. Blood trickled down his chin.

He had been in battle before, had been tortured before. He had to focus, had to keep calculating the odds, keep considering scenarios, no matter how hapless his circumstances. They were satisfied to toy with him for now, and though Nettles and Hastings were the most dangerous men present, they had to defer to Milbridge. The earl was going to move him to his hunting lodge, which meant he might at least be seen by his friends. Milbridge's men were city toughs, not soldiers, shallow men who would not think ahead, and who would not be familiar with the tribal or ranger ways of fighting. No matter the odds, he knew his only chance of escape would be while he was being transported, before he reached the cages in Milbridge's cellar.

As Milbridge paused in his amusement to take some snuff, Hastings retrieved the dagger Lewis had tossed onto the table and began rolling up Duncan's other sleeve.

"Not his hands, Major," Milbridge said. "Not yet. The Highlander needs to be able to write for a few more days."

Defiance sparked in Duncan's eyes. "Excellent," he shot back. "I can record any number of tales of the Highland spirits protecting those who wear the plaid. Not to mention the Mohawk spirits. But then you have personal experience with those protectors. I seem to recall you losing your water when they danced around you years ago. And there were crows that pecked at the flesh of your feet. Remember the crows, my lord?"

Milbridge flushed, sputtered, and raised the belt again, then lowered it as he saw the totem pouch that had been exposed at Duncan's breast. He could have snatched it away and even extended a hand as if to do so, but then he lowered it. The tribal spirits still frightened him. "I killed that savage!" he hissed.

"That only made him angrier," Duncan said, forcing a grin to his face. "His ghost follows you. Surely you have noticed?"

The words brought a laugh from Nettles, which grew louder when Milbridge nervously glanced over his shoulders toward the shadows. He snapped at his men to form a line across the darkened hallway. Years earlier, Ramsey had mounted a private campaign on the frontier to find and kill the revered Iroquois prophet who had raised Sarah after she had been captured by the tribe. That man had been the father she had loved, the father who had woven an independent spirit around her deep intelligence, helping to create the fiery, wise woman Duncan loved and Milbridge now loathed. Afterward, Sarah had forced Milbridge to deed to her the vast frontier tract that had become Edentown, oasis for orphans and outcasts.

Milbridge broke his fearful gaze from the Mohawk pouch and lashed Duncan again. Nettles and Hastings could see that Duncan was letting the headboard break the blows, but they had grown strangely subdued. They were seeing a new side of Milbridge, which seemed to confuse them. Hastings made an inquiring gesture with his dagger.

"Not his hands," Milbridge said again. "Find something less useful for now."

Hastings gave one of his thin smiles and touched the steel point against Duncan's neck so lightly that Duncan did not feel the cut, only the blood that trickled down his throat.

"He doesn't need all his fingers to write," Nettles suggested.

Milbridge chuckled, then steepled his fingers as he studied Duncan. "You must join me at my lodge, Lieutenant. I could use someone of your imagination. Come with us tonight and I will provide amusement of a softer kind."

Nettles glanced at Hastings, who nodded. The lieutenant grinned. "There's a game we played in the war," Nettles recalled. "Who can slice off the most pieces without opening a major blood vessel. It's all about making very precise, small cuts." He reached out with both hands, suddenly grabbing Duncan's earlobe with one and slicing down with the other. Ensign Lewis gave a small, sobbing moan.

Nettles laid a quarter-inch piece of flesh on the wide chair arm above Duncan's bound hand. He had taken off the bottom of his earlobe. "You are ours now," Nettles stated, as if the shortened ear marked Duncan as belonging to them. He pushed the little lump of flesh with the end of his dagger and looked up at Hastings. "One," he announced to the major. Duncan stared at it, remembering that there was a Bedlam keeper with a mutilated ear who was owned by the War Council.

"What was your record?" Hastings airily asked. "There was a French soldier, I recall."

Nettles's eyes flashed. "Four hundred thirty-four, until that damned Indian nicked an artery." He cast a hungry smile at Duncan. "We had some savages in our company who would fry up the pieces in bacon fat and consume them. Eating the flesh of your enemies gives you their strength, they would say."

Milbridge gave a wheezing laugh. "If you're not careful, Major," he said to Hastings, "I may steal this artist from you permanently." He turned to Nettles with a businesslike air. "The horse doctor will geld him tomorrow. Usually the pain subsides enough for the subject to speak in a day or two. Then a day or two for my letters, and you can begin in earnest."

The earl stepped closer to Nettles. "What I require, Lieutenant, is that in a month's time this Highlander scum wears the expression of a pig on a spit while still having a beating heart. Can you manage that?"

Nettles offered a brisk salute. "With pleasure, sir. An iron spit through his shoulders would do the trick. Then we can hang him from the rafters as if he were in a butcher's shop."

Milbridge gave a satisfied sigh. "Maybe you can prepare a plan, a chart perhaps," he said. "Setting forth which pieces will come off on which day. Then I can more easily make adjustments to my schedule. Yes, certainly you must do so. Oh, the anticipation! What pleasure it will bring when I read it years from now. And it will help me fantasize about what I would do if I ever had that traitorous Wilkes, or even Franklin, in my lodge."

"I will write no letters," Duncan declared.

"Good for you," Milbridge replied with a satisfied smile. "Your defiance will augment the pleasure. But in the end you will do so. You will beg to do so, and to keep writing, for as long as you are writing you may keep most of your fingers. First you will write to urgently summon my daughter to New York town."

"I will write nothing to Sarah," Duncan vowed. New York town, he knew, was a domain where Milbridge's gold had bought him much influence.

Milbridge shrugged. "I can always send men to assassinate her in her home."

Duncan's fear finally welled up. "She's your daughter."

"That bitch stopped being my daughter the day she went off with those savages. If she chooses reconciliation, I will speak with her as a statesman, negotiate treaty terms, as it were. I will find her a suitable match, provide a suitable estate in the north as her dowry. Yorkshire perhaps, or distant Cumberland."

"She has a match," Duncan hissed.

Milbridge raised his eyebrows. "No. Her Highland servant will soon be no more."

"She will never leave Edentown behind."

Milbridge shrugged. "If she resists, so much the better. When the witch is gone I will inherit, for the law still sees her as my daughter and she will have no issue. It will all be mine again, Edentown and all its dependencies," Milbridge gloated, and fixed Duncan with an amused gaze as the words sank in. Milbridge would kill Sarah so he could take over Edentown. It gave a terrible credibility to his threats. Duncan's resolved faltered. He gazed in desolation at the floor.

Milbridge turned to Nettles. "Now, Lieutenant, if you want to begin your—"

"The Duke of Portland!" Lewis suddenly shouted.

Milbridge seemed to cringe at the name. "What is your meaning, boy?" he asked Lewis, who was rendered speechless by the earl's gaze. "What of the duke?"

Lewis collected himself. "He was admiring your green and gold carriage, sir, and your handsome team. He said they were as grand as the Lord Mayor's. He wants to speak with you about them, invite you to his club to discuss whether you would sell them. He asked if the coach was from the Longacre works or from Dublin. He said he would try to come back after dining tonight to see if you were here at the palace."

Milbridge seemed to have forgotten Duncan. "The duke was coming to see me?" he asked with childlike excitement.

Lewis spoke in a straightforward, earnest fashion, punctuating his words with a short bow. "I can't say when exactly, my lord, but yes, those were his words."

Milbridge's passion for cruelty was eclipsed only by his appetite for political favor. Lewis had mentioned one of the few men in London who outranked him in the social strata. The earl looked back in chagrin at Duncan, collected his thoughts, and turned to Nettles. "They have my wagon at the back door. No need for chains, they will only attract attention. Just keep your dagger point on him until he is in the cage." He shouted orders to his men, half of whom darted down the corridor, then studied Lewis for a long moment. "You too. You show promise. I saw you draw first blood."

Lewis glanced at Duncan, then quickly looked away. Had he known that the name of the duke would be one of the few that would distract Milbridge? Was it possible the ensign had lied about the duke to save Duncan, at least for a few more minutes?

Duncan did not resist as they unstrapped him and shoved him down the passage, escorted by Nettles and four of Milbridge's bullies. They made their way up a worn, cupped set of stone stairs and out into the cool summer night. He froze as he saw the wagon. Two men were struggling to upright a tall, narrow cage of iron bars, perhaps seven feet high and two feet to a side. They set it against the low sidewall of the wagon, opposite a bench where guards no doubt would sit.

Nettles began to push Duncan toward two other men who seemed ready to manhandle their prisoner up onto the wagon, then paused as the wagon driver raised a hand. A group of link boys was passing by, singing a song, lanterns and torches held high.

"Damned brats have been at it all night," the driver groused. "I'd have called the watch except many of them be Methodists too."

Duncan didn't understand until he made out the words of the song. The boys were singing a hymn. *Oh for a thousand tongues to sing.* The hymn was the one Sinner John had sung on their first failed visit to meet Franklin.

The small choir passed and he was shoved up onto the wagon and herded toward the cage.

The Mohawks called it trading the fear. In battle you had to make certain fear belonged only to your enemy. *In battle fear is the spirit killer.* You had to push it away or you would die. Trade your fear for stealth, trade your fear for hatred of your enemy. The talk about castration and mutilation was about someone else. Here within his reach was the man who had killed Robbie, the man who killed Ezra's wife and unborn child and laughed about it. He had to keep Nettles close. Milbridge had given him a gift by making it clear no one was to kill Duncan, not yet.

He stayed silent as they opened the side of the cage that served as its door and shoved him inside. The driver handed Nettles a key on a lanyard which Nettles used to lock the door. He slipped the lanyard around his neck, then took out his dagger and, laughing, made a sawing motion toward his groin.

"The pin, boy," the driver said to Lewis, pointing to a heavy iron pin that had to be slid through a coupling bolted to the floor in order to stabilize the heavy cage. Lewis pushed the pin through the coupling, then sat beside the two guards who had already settled onto the bench. The remaining men, armed with pistols and short swords, mounted horses that had been tied to the wagon wheels.

I am not an animal in a cage, Duncan told himself. I am a warrior who will make these men sorry they ever met Milbridge. He felt an unexpected spark of energy from his totem, the magical water creature, then knew he had imagined it because they were nowhere near the sea.

The wagon lurched forward, moving along the shadows behind the palace. Guards saluted as they saw Lieutenant Nettles standing in the wagon, still in his uniform. The streets were quiet but not devoid of life. From somewhere behind him a steeple clock struck the hour. As he counted eleven peals, the roving link boy choir appeared from an alley and halted in front of the wagon team, swinging their lamps and torches high as they sang out *Soldiers of Christ arise and put your armor on.* Despite the driver's seething curses, the boys were insistent on finishing their hymn, and as they continued Duncan recognized it as one of the songs he had heard coming from the Neptune's stable.

"Damn the Wesley brothers for the troublemakers that they are!" the driver spat as he worked to control the horses, skittish from the moving lanterns.

Suddenly the boys spun about and began marching down the narrow street, still singing. The driver had no choice but to follow slowly behind, and as the passage reached the broader Bridge Street and the wagon began to turn left, the boys spread and wheeled as though they had rehearsed the movement, momentarily blocking the wagon. The driver stood and lashed his whip over the boys' heads. Their tight formation began to break and by the time the wagon rolled onto the stone flags of Bridge Street they had fallen back, clearing just enough of the road for the party to pass.

As their procession veered onto the street, the last horse of their escort gave a sharp cry and reared, knocking its rider onto the cobblestones. The man rose in obvious pain, then grabbed the reins to steady the horse. "Stepped on something," he declared. "God's blood! Some fool dropped tacks all over the road!" The rider on the lead horse ordered the man to find his way back as best he could, then gestured for the party to continue. He looked back in angry suspicion at the boys, who struck up a new song.

Bridge Street. Milbridge had said his lodge was near the king's lodge, which meant they had to cross the Thames. Over the heads of the boys Duncan made out the parallel lines of lanterns along Westminster Bridge.

"Tell me," he said to Nettles, "the night at the Lick, was Ezra still saying his prayers when you killed him?"

Nettles grinned. "Some African gibberish, with his head lifted toward the clouds. Between that and the rain he was deaf to our approach. The major had picked up one of those leg bones from a buffalo or such."

"Which he used to knock Ezra senseless."

"I still had to get in that damn pit with him. What a slop hole. First the major had me pound that letter down his throat. He actually came to and struggled while I was doing so, but by then he had no real strength left."

"I didn't understand how you found his wife."

"She found us. A feisty bitch, that one. She must have seen us and run out from the edge of the forest, grabbing her own bone for a club. She actually laid the major out in the mud, but she wasn't watching me. It was the simplest thing to reach with my dagger from behind her." Nettles gave a sinister grin over his shoulder. "Tender flesh that, like butter under my blade. She called out Ezra's name and tried to crawl to the pit as she bled out. I couldn't have another body in the mud, too many questions, so I had to carry her back to the trees."

By the time the wagon rolled onto the stone flags of Westminster Bridge the link boys had fallen away completely, clearing the path. As Nettles turned his back to Duncan, steadying himself with one raised hand gripping a bar of the heavy cage, Duncan reached into his pocket and began inconspicuously loosening the knot in the cord that held the Roman dolphin charm that Xander had given him. He touched the ancient fish, then touched his own totem pouch and the bone of the *incognitum*.

"A fine night, McCallum," Nettles chided. "I'll have a woman or two and a bottle of gin at the end of this road. You'll have your new cage at the earl's lodge." He made a gesture toward the starlit sky. "Enjoy it, Highlander. Probably the last time you'll see it."

The guards on the bench laughed. One of them began sharpening what looked like a skinning knife. As the second guard produced a jar of ale from under the bench, Duncan caught Lewis's eye, then nodded downward to the pin that secured the cage. The ensign cocked his head, then slowly nodded.

"What are those drunken fools doing?" the lead outrider barked and spurred his horse forward to investigate a commotion farther down the bridge. Moments later he wheeled his mount and sped back behind the wagon as he fumbled for the pistol in his belt.

The Westminster Bridge had been built for one lane of traffic in each direction, but now two large cargo wagons, each hitched to a team of heavy draft horses, were accelerating toward them, side by side.

"Not the time or place to be racing, damn them!" the driver spat. The man who had drawn his pistol shot into the air to discourage the oncoming teams, to no avail, and the driver swerved their wagon up against the side of the bridge, scraping the low railing, in an attempt to make way for the oncoming wagons. "Blessed Jesus!" the driver gasped as the oncoming teams passed under a light.

A man was standing on the team that raced directly toward them, a foot planted on the back of each massive gray horse. No, Duncan saw, not a man. A ghost warrior, an Indian whose chest and face were painted white, and who swung an Iroquois war ax over his head. As the racing wagons passed another set of lights, Duncan saw that they were being driven by Sinner John and Darby.

Nettles's callous shell shattered at the sight of the phantom. "Dear God, that demon found us again!" he shrieked. "Shoot the thing!" The lieutenant seemed paralyzed at the sight of the warrior he had last seen on the Atlantic, flying out of the night sky to attack Hastings. Three pistols fired in quick, frantic succession, none of them striking Ishmael, now crouched for his attack, still balanced on the horses, who themselves had a ghostlike appearance. Their broad nostrils were flaring and a rumbling sound like a wild battle cry came from the massive animals, adding to the eerie effect.

"Banshees!" one of the guards shrieked and leapt off the back of the wagon, fleeing back toward Whitehall.

Most of the guards kept their wits and were calmly reloading their guns. Nettles now raised his own pistol, meaning Ishmael faced an onslaught of bullets at close range. The lieutenant, still bracing himself on the cage, seemed not to notice as Duncan wrapped and tied the cord around Nettles's arm, binding it to the cage. He carefully pried a finger around Nettles's lanyard. "Now!" he shouted to Lewis, then jerked the lanyard off Nettles's neck as the lieutenant aimed his pistol.

Duncan had fleeting images of pistols firing wildly, of Ishmael dodging a sword held by one of the riders, of the war ax slamming into a man's head, of Lewis popping out the anchor pin, and of Sinner John standing with a club in one hand and his reins in the other. Duncan wrapped the lanyard with the key around his wrist and then, with a fleeting touch of his totem, thrust his arm around Nettles's neck and threw his weight against the side of the cage. Nettles struggled in stunned surprise. Then, with a mighty heave to lift Nettles's full weight toward the top of the cage, and another shove against the side, the cage tipped. The shift in weight tumbled it out of the wagon and over the narrow bridge rail. Nettles's startled cry was choked off as they sank into the Thames.

Duncan knew he had but seconds in the black water. He ignored Nettles's flailing against the cage, confident that he would not free himself from the tight knot. He took the heavy key in his fingers and with his other hand felt for the lock.

A flash of pain shot up from his right side and to his surprise he understood that Nettles still held his dagger and was tearing into his flesh.

The strong current tumbled the cage as it sank. Nettles's thrusts grew weaker, and too late did he turn the dagger to the cord that bound him to the heavy iron. Duncan fumbled in frantic desperation, then suddenly realized he was searching the wrong side of the door. His lungs searing, he found the lock as with a shudder the cage hit the muddy bottom. In an instant he had the door open. He glanced down to see that Nettles had been pinned underneath the cage, his limp hand drifting toward Duncan. Duncan grabbed the dagger from it, then kicked toward the surface.

Strong young arms reached out as with his last ounce of strength he flung his upper body onto the landing stairs below the bridge. "The Roman fish saved him!" a boy cried out. "Don't lose him now!" As he began to slip back into the water, three pairs of arms dragged him onto the second stair, then pulled his legs out of the river.

"Mr. Duncan has avenged Robbie!" someone shouted, and with great effort Duncan pushed himself onto an elbow to look into Xander's astonished face. He had a hard time focusing on the boy. The pain in his side was ripping him apart. "Blessed Jesus, his life blood pours out!" he heard another boy cry. His world blurred and he faded into unconsciousness.

Chapter 20

F OR THE CHILL, HIGHLANDER," A scratchy voice muttered, and a strong arm pulled him up against something hard. Duncan shook his head, then groggily accepted the cup of tea from Sinner John. He had a vague memory of being lifted into a wagon by a horde of boys who had climbed in beside him. Now he lay shivering in the stable behind the Neptune, with blankets covering his legs. Nettles's dagger lay beside him.

"Xander says ye avenged wee Robbie," Sinner John said.

"The Horse Guards lost a barn and a lieutenant," Duncan replied, raising a sad grin on the stern face. "His killer is buried in Thames mud. He'll do no murder again."

Sinner John touched the wooden cross that hung around his neck. "The Lord works as the Lord wills," he intoned, then added in a whisper, "and may the bastard feel the fires of hell for all eternity."

Duncan tried to push up, then groaned at the stab of pain in his right side. "I can't stay here," he said.

"And you can't go farther without your wound being treated," said a voice from the shadows. Patrick Woolford stepped into the light of the lantern that hung on a nearby post. "They won't recover their senses until morning," he said. "And as far as they know you are dead. Again."

"But when they do recover their senses this will be the first place they look to confirm I am truly gone. Milbridge will want a body. And we can't be sure they didn't spy me climbing out of the river."

"I was watching from the bank," Patrick said. "I ran up the bridge after the melee, as if I had been passing by. Two men with broken arms, two with broken heads. And most of them half convinced they had been attacked by ghosts. No one saw you climb out of the water. They were too shaken." He shook his head. "Very few who fall into the Thames survive the strong current. And a man in an iron cage has no chance at all. His men will insist you are dead, else they will be earning the wrath of the earl."

You will die, again and again.

"I put everyone in danger," Duncan said, and once again his effort to rise was overwhelmed by the shredding pain in his side.

"We have a few hours to find you a hole to hide in. First we have to clean you up." As Woolford spoke a soft laugh came from just outside the barn.

"I need more light!" came a feminine voice. A second link boy appeared with a lantern, illuminating Ishmael standing in a washtub, shirtless, having his white paint scrubbed off by Lizzie the chambermaid. Ishmael met Duncan's gaze and rolled his eyes, then pointed to his ear. As Darby bent over him, wiping blood that was dripping onto his shoulder, Duncan put his hand to his own ear and it came away bloody. He had almost forgotten that Nettles had sliced off a piece of the lobe.

"Nicked yer lug, eh?" the bosun remarked. "No matter, just the mark of a warrior."

"I must admit I was startled when I saw those teams racing toward us," Duncan said as Ishmael stepped out of the tub and began drying himself, resisting Lizzie's efforts to help. "How could you—where did the wagons come from? And those massive horses?" His voice faltered as Patrick lifted his shirt, sending a white-hot splinter of pain up his side.

"The same teamsters who helped move the bones," Ishmael explained. "Except Sinner John and Darby wouldn't let them take the risk of driving. By God, Duncan, I thought we'd seen the last of you when that cage fell off. How is possible you could survive such an accident?"

"It was no accident. It was my one chance to escape and eliminate Nettles."

Ishmael's eyes widened in astonishment. "You meant to throw yourself into the river? But we were moments from releasing you!"

"They were reloading their pistols. All you had was a war club. You were riding into close range. They couldn't miss."

"At least four of the devils felt the blow of my club. I so wanted to use the spike end of the club, but Patrick warned me off fatal blows. When the rest saw you and Nettles had vanished as if into thin air, they were stunned. All the fight drained out of them. "Duncan—" Ishmael's emotions overwhelmed him for a moment. "I was certain I would never see you again in this world," he said, and clamped his hand around Duncan's shoulder.

"It was the only chance I would have to kill Nettles. If you had closed with him, he would have used his dagger on you. He had to die. He admitted to killing Ezra's wife and child, and to helping Hastings kill Ezra. He boasted of killing Robbie."

"So obviously," Woolford sighed, "you had to push yourself into the Thames in an iron box."

"I was certain it would be the end of Nettles. I thought I had a fair chance of surviving since the key was in my hand when we hit the water, and of course—" Duncan didn't finish his sentence, just touched his totem pouch, which they both knew contained the spirit of an otter, invincible in the water. Woolford seemed about to argue, but after a moment he just shook his head and touched a lump protruding from his own shirt. The deputy superintendent wore a totem pouch himself, at the insistence of his Mohawk wife.

Clenching his jaw, Duncan instructed Woolford to hold up his shirt as he blindly probed his wound, but the effort ended in an anguished gasp. "Hold him down," came a worried voice, "and bring another lantern or two."

Duncan opened his eyes to see William Hewson kneeling at his side, cutting away Duncan's shirt as Woolford explained how he had received his wound. Darby moved behind Duncan and clamped his shoulders with his powerful hands.

Hewson gave a despairing groan. "You let yourself be stabbed in the filth of the Thames?" he said to Duncan. "God knows what contamination we will see!" The doctor leaned closer. "That settles it," he said to Woolford. "He must come to my operating theater, and once there I will need some strong arms to hold him down."

"No!" Duncan protested. "It is too dangerous for you!"

"Too dangerous for you not to do so," Hewson retorted. "I must bathe the wound in sulfur water. Your muscle wall needs internal sutures before I can attempt the twenty or thirty external ones. I am afraid you will need some of that famed Highland fortitude, my friend."

"That, good doctor, comes in the form of a smoky amber liquid. And I pray you have enough for all of us," Woolford said.

As they lifted Duncan, the pain drove him beyond consciousness again.

He had a dull recollection of worried voices all around him, of calls for hot water, rags, vials of laudanum, whale oil lamps, mirrors, and a longer needle. Someone growled, "Damned well hold the lens steady!" He was lifted twice to gulp down whisky, but the coughing that followed brought more agony and afterward only laudanum was used.

When Duncan finally awoke Benjamin Franklin was sitting beside him, staring at Duncan while leaning both hands on his blackthorn cane. "Are you still with us, lad?" the inventor asked.

Duncan could only manage a weak nod.

"Excellent," Franklin said, then added in his matter-of-fact way, "William says if you don't die in the next twenty-four hours you will be fine."

"Dr. Franklin," Duncan said in a hoarse voice, and coughed again. Franklin raised a cup of water to his lips. "In twenty-three hours," he started, then drank again.

"Yes?" Franklin asked, leaning closer.

"In twenty-three hours please send over half a dozen Leyden jars."

Franklin gave a low laugh, then wiped at his eyes and patted Duncan's shoulder with paternal affection.

"You have to go," Duncan said. "They may still be following you."

"Nonsense. I told your friend Woolford—a capital fellow, by the way—that all that fuss must have been about your feud with Ramsey, with the Earl of Milbridge. If he thinks you are dead, then of course all the blackguards will be called off."

"They still want to stop your meeting with the king."

Franklin chuckled again. "But they don't know what I know, Duncan. We are nearly in!"

"In?"

"Nevil has asked the king for a private meeting to review His Majesty's transit observations. The king is well aware that he stumbles in explaining them and Nevil says they shall make notes together for use when he is in the banquet halls of his hunting trip, where his hosts will surely ask about June third. It is the perfect angle of attack, don't you see? The king is too embarrassed to reveal his shortcomings to anyone but Nevil, so Nevil is confident the king will accept. We propose to meet at sunset, four days before his royal ball, because everyone knows he cancels all appointments for the three days before one of his grand balls. He will be in high spirits."

"There's much to be done, then."

"Not for you. For you it is rest and recovery. Ishmael and that man Darby say they have a secret place to take you."

"If we were in Mohawk country, we would have you in a lodge, Duncan," came a familiar voice. Patrick Woolford stepped off the stairway that led up to Hewson's kitchen, holding a steaming cup. "With cedar smoke and poultices of moss and spiderwebs."

"And the old women would be singing to the gods," Ishmael said, appearing behind Woolford.

"Sounds like paradise," Franklin chuckled, then moved aside for Woolford to help Duncan with his tea. "Conawago always says the Iroquois focus on curing the spirit," Duncan recalled, "because once the spirit is cured the rest will follow." He looked up with an expectant glance at Ishmael.

"I still have to go to Bedlam every day," the young Nipmuc said.

"Don't worry about me," Duncan said, putting a hand to his head. He was feeling dizzy. It was the effects of the laudanum. "We will make the sailing of the *Galileo*," he added, not because he had any confidence he could, but because Ishmael needed to hear the words.

"And don't forget the ancient one," Franklin said. "He is still here, lying nearby."

"He?" Duncan asked.

"The ancient one," the inventor explained, sounding like one of the tribes now. "Ishmael told me. The *incognitum* watches over you."

They had found the closest thing to a tribal healing lodge in London. The walls of the corner room at the Faulkner manor held drawings of Iroquois spirit masks, in the best approximations Woolford and Ishmael were capable of. A small ceramic bowl held smoldering cones of pine incense. On the stool beside the bed were draped the white wampum beads that Ishmael had held after settling Duncan into the bed, telling the tribal spirits that Duncan must recover to help save the only living Nipmuc elder.

On the third day his new physician arrived, carrying a piece of strudel wrapped in linen. Heinz Huber clucked his tongue as he lifted the dressing over Duncan's wound, praised the precise sutures, and began asking blunt, insistent questions about Duncan's bodily functions, then asked to see his chamber pot.

Duncan managed to push himself up into a sitting position with only a dull ache from his side. "Henbane," he said as Huber finished his examination.

"I found a Flemish broker in Billingsgate who had a new shipment," the German doctor reported. "I doubled my inventory."

Duncan nodded at the news, then looked out the window over the wet slate roofs, weighing one last time an idea that had been taking shape during his bedbound days. "You said something about Vikings using henbane."

"They made a salve of it, yes," Huber confirmed. "Then rubbed it on their skin before battle. A small amount would have made them ferocious but a larger dose would have immobilized them with hallucinations."

"Maybe you can use witch hazel as a base," Duncan said.

"*Bitte?*"

"I want some of that henbane salve, just one jar."

Huber's face showed alarm. "From what I hear about your adventure in the Thames you don't need any drug to become battle crazed. And it will not offset your weakness for long, and probably will make it that much worse."

The first grin in days broke on Duncan's face. "Not for me, Heinz. One jar, just one large dose for one man. And all the rest should be ground into a fine powder for tea."

Huber stared impassively at Duncan. "You won't tell me more, I know," he said with a sigh, then lifted his package. "Greta says I must witness you eat her gift. It will be a sign of your recovery, so she can stop praying for you every hour. The housework is suffering," he added. As if on cue, Noah appeared with a small pitcher. "I requested some warm milk to help it go down."

"I will eat some of Greta's wonderful strudel only if the two of you share it," Duncan declared. They offered no objection. Feeling better than he had in days, Duncan listened as they ate and his friends offered reports on routines at Bedlam. As they finished, Noah produced a note written in Woolford's familiar handwriting. *Hastings is making urgent preparations for Boston*, it said. *He promises War Council that the Franklin threat will be eliminated before he sails.*

Duncan woke in the small of the night, feeling stronger than he had since being captured by the Horse Guards. He paced slowly along the wall of the bedchamber, once more trying to make sense of Woolford's note. Hastings had to believe Duncan dead. But why was he so confident he could prevent Franklin from meeting with the king? And what urgent business could Hastings have in Boston?

He lingered over the belongings of Conawago that hung on the wall opposite the bed, finding some solace in their presence. His old friend always traveled with few clothes, although hanging on the last peg was his favorite velvet waistcoat, which had been in fashion decades earlier when Conawago had last visited a royal court. Clothing, however, had never been particularly significant to the Nipmuc elder. What he had packed in the small trunk loaned to him by William Johnson had been the treasures of his long life, which had started in the prior century, in the year of the Great Comet, 1680. On one peg hung strands of Nipmuc beads, given him when he had left his family as a boy to be educated by the Jesuits. He had had several more but had been gradually leaving them in places sacred to his tribe.

On another peg hung a leather lanyard with a whale charm, a gift from Ishmael brought back from a visit to Nantucket. There was the small wooden spoon which the boy Conawago had impishly purloined from his mother's hearth as a memento when leaving with his new teachers. The young Conawago had vowed to himself to keep it until he could return it to her. Next was a small bundle of heather with a piece of the McCallum plaid sewn around it, a gift from Duncan years earlier. Then there was a small cornhusk doll with a quillwork dress given to Conawago decades earlier by a woman he would never speak of. Beside it was a bronze charm in the shape of a book that was inscribed with *Holy Bible* on one side and *Plato* on the other because, as Conawago was fond of saying, the Jesuits always hedged their bets.

Finally, hanging on a tattered ribbon, were two gold fleur-de-lis lockets, which Conawago had brought from the court of King Louis to give to his mother and aunt. Not for the first time Duncan felt the heartache of his friend's futile decades-long search for his family that Conawago had started as a young man and ended as an aged one. On his deathbed a few years earlier, one of his Jesuit teachers had railed against Conawago for wasting his life in his search, declaring that the Jesuits and God had given him so much that could have been used to bridge the gap between the tribes and the Europeans, but that he had squandered it. Duncan looked back at the little bronze book. Conawago said his dreams compelled his voyage, but now Duncan wondered if that guilt had also driven Conawago to his desperate attempt to speak with King George.

Duncan sat on the bed, holding what he always considered the most poignant of Conawago's treasures, the little wooden spoon. He had been a fool to be distracted by Franklin's political adventures. Nothing mattered more than getting Conawago back to America.

He ate the last morsel of the strudel, then surrendered to an urge for a cup of milk. It was past midnight and the house was silent and dim, lit only by the beeswax candle lamps at the stair landings. He stole down the servants' stairs, then onto the grand stairway, pausing by the painting that had caught his attention on his first visit. A sinewy, almost gaunt man gazed out at him over a brass plate that declared ALPHEUS FAULKNER. The man held a small enameled globe in one hand and dangled a bracelet of long white beads in the other. Duncan had taken the beads to be elongated pearls but now he was not so certain. He retrieved the landing lamp and studied the bracelet. They might have been pearls, but now they seemed more like wampum beads.

A whale oil lamp burned in the kitchen. Duncan turned up the wick, poured a cup from the ceramic jar used for milk, then sat at the big table. For Duncan, kitchens were usually the most comfortable room of a house, and that of the

Faulkner House was no exception. The scents of yeast, wood smoke, apples, and maple syrup combined to transport him to the kitchen in Edentown, where he and Sarah often sat far into the night, sharing ideas for helping the settlement, planning sowing and harvest, reviewing the accounts, or just sitting silently in the glow of the hearth.

Maple syrup. He lifted his nose, confirming the scent. He was not aware that households in London used maple syrup, originally a product of the woodland tribes and still an important trading commodity of the Iroquois. He rose and paced along the shelves, discovering a small cask sitting upright on a back shelf. Its tap was leaking. Duncan extended a finger and tested the little brown puddle under the tap. It was a high grade of syrup, an expensive grade. Madeline Faulkner must have brought the cask with her from America as a novelty for her household, he decided, then poured another cup of milk with a dollop of syrup mixed into it. As he drank he looked out the side door of the kitchen and saw that it opened across from the library, the only other room of the mansion where he did not feel out of place.

The collection of books was impressively large but most were laden with dust, long unused. One of the expansive shelves held nothing but religious tracts, many of them published decades earlier. The dust was disturbed at only two shelves, one containing richly bound volumes of novels. He ran his finger along the spines. *The Vicar of Wakefield*, *Tom Jones*, *Robinson Crusoe*, *Pamela*, *Moll Flanders*, *Memoirs of a Woman of Pleasure*, and a score of other popular works filled the shelf. The second shelf was an impressive collection of works on natural philosophy and mathematics, including Gilbert's *Magnetism*, Napier's *Logarithms*, Kepler's *Celestial Mechanics*, Bacon's *Experimentation*, Hooke's *Micrographia*, Newton's *Opticks*, and Linneas's *Systema Naturae*. There was even Franklin's *Experiments and Observations on Electricity*.

He paused, realizing the room presented something of a mystery. The well-worn popular novels were explained by the frivolous Madeline Faulkner, but not the heavily used much denser technical works. He paced along the shelves, seeing now a small step stool below the stacks of religious works. Without knowing why, he stood on it. Within his reach there was only one volume not laden with dust, on the high top shelf. He retrieved it and with a leap of his heart read the single word embossed on the spine. *Kahnyenkehaka.* It meant Mohawk, in the tongue of the tribe. He extracted a slip of faded, tattered paper that extended from the inside cover, written in a firm hand. *Iken ne Yehouah egh ne s'hakonoronghkwa n'ongwe*, it began. With a leap of his heart he recognized it, and the words of the full verse rose unbidden in his mind. *For God so loved the world that he gave his only begotten son.* It was from the book of John.

Duncan leafed through the book. He had heard of translations of the Bible into the Mohawk tongue but had seen one only once before, during the last war, when he had helped negotiate a truce with the Christian Mohawks who fought for the French in Quebec. He recalled the portrait of the stern man on the stairway. The bracelet in the subject's hand must have indeed been wampum. On the frontispiece of the book was a name inscribed in the same hand as the biblical verse. Alpheus Faulkner. It was the name from the portrait, the man who had founded the Disciples of the Forest so many years ago.

He continued to explore the library, finding another bolt of silk cloth on a chair, with a box of pins and snips of ribbon. Madeline had been using the chamber as a fitting room. The desk was still covered with papers of many sizes, and he brought the lamp closer to confirm that there were more drawings of machines, though not the same ones he had seen before. These were of flywheels and gears, with notes about weights and dimensions and the numbers of teeth in the gears. The managers sent by Madeline's father had been busy.

A creak in the floor upstairs caused him to freeze. With a pang of guilt he darted out of the library, feeling like an intruder. A peal of laughter from the foyer brought him to an abrupt halt in the hallway.

"No, my lord, you may not come in at this hour, you naughty boy," came Madeline's playful voice. "Thank you for the conveyance. Now go home to your wife."

He watched from the shadows as Madeline locked the door, then leaned against it and closed her eyes, as if collecting herself. He did not move, thinking he was well hidden in the shadows, but to his surprise she raised her head and stared directly at him.

"Why, Mr. McCallum, whatever are you doing?" Madeline asked, confusion and suspicion both in her gaze. "You really must stay in bed if you are to recover."

"I was thirsty for milk," he said as she draped her cloak over a bench.

"The perfect thing!" she exclaimed, as if he were making a suggestion. "I had more port this evening than was proper," she added with a giggle. Putting her arm through his, she led him back into the kitchen, where she quickly produced two crystal goblets and ladled each full of milk, then complimented Duncan on his healthy appearance before rambling on about her evening. It had been a private party of only forty, a "rehearsal" as she described it, for the king's royal ball. There had been too much punch, too much port, and too much horseplay between dances. "No less than three members of Parliament tried to pull the ribbons from my hair!" she reported. "One even tried to snatch my choker, the rogue," she said, and touched the gold brocade ribbon that adorned her neck. Not for the first time she looked Duncan in the eye as if about to share something, but then quickly looked away, as if he frightened her somehow. There was an air about her that he found disingenuous, but he could not name it, and still could not name the reason Sarah saw fit to befriend this shallow socialite.

Madeline had finished her glass and was wiping the thin white line from her lip when she paused, looking at the open side door, which revealed a light coming from the library. Duncan had left the lamp on the desk. "Shame on you, Duncan McCallum," she exclaimed in a mocking tone. "Stealing about among a lady's private books!"

Without waiting for a reply Madeline lifted her skirts and hurried out of the kitchen. By the time Duncan caught up with her she was pacing along the rows of books. She had pushed the stool away from the shelves and draped the second bolt of silk over the drawings on the desk.

"A library always feels like home somehow," he offered, not knowing how to explain himself. "Seeing authors from my childhood is like greeting old friends."

"So many heavy volumes," she said in her carefree tone. "So many heavy thoughts. How *do* the scholars endure it?"

Duncan motioned to the desk. "Your father's men have been busy."

Madeline made a fluttering motion with her hand. "They really need to stop intruding so often," she said and shrugged. "But I promised everything would remain confidential. As if anyone could understand them. Always talking of capital and returns and doubling the value of a groat. So mundane, so devastatingly boring. Sometimes I think my father sends them just to punish me. However shall I prepare for the royal ball with so many distractions?"

"I am a simple Highlander," Duncan said. "Such intricacies of commerce are beyond me."

Madeline flashed a tentative glance at him as if thinking of disagreeing, but then she walked to the shelf of novels and extracted one. "This one always interests the gentlemen," she said. "I understand at gentlemen's clubs they sometimes hire a lady to read it aloud to them, though I doubt a genuine lady would ever do so." She handed him Cleland's *Memories of a Woman of Pleasure.*

"Fanny Hill," Duncan observed in surprise, using the popular name for the novel.

"It will make you blush, sir," Madeline said with an impish grin. "And give you something quite engaging to discuss with your Sarah," she added, then laughed, for she had already made Duncan blush.

She lifted the lamp and herded him out of the room, stifling a yawn. He accompanied her up the stairs and returned to his room, but a quarter hour later stole back down to the library, borrowing the lamp from the landing. Madeline had been eager to have him out of the library, though he could not understand why. He lifted the cloth from the desk and studied the drawings she had covered. They were of a complex machine with many spindles and wheels. It made no sense that Madeline would be doing dress fittings in the chamber where her father's men made such drawings, especially with an abundance of vacant rooms on the floor above. He turned to a chair with milliner's tools, lifting a scrap that covered what looked like a sewing basket. To his surprise, however, there was nothing inside but cotton balls. He carried one to the lamp. No, it wasn't cotton. It was silk. He held it closer to the light, then abruptly dropped it. It had moved. He retrieved it, pulled a chair to the lamp, and carefully inspected it, probing the intricate threads.

Inside was a thin larvae that squirmed at his touch. He had never seen one, but he had read about the sericulture experiments being conducted in England and Holland in the hope of establishing a new industry. He was looking at a silkworm cocoon. Madeline had a basket of silkworm cocoons. No, he decided, they had to belong to the men making the drawings, preparing for their own secret experiments. He returned the cocoon to the basket and wandered, deep in thought, back up the stairs. He paused again at the portrait of Alpheus Faulkner, noting the dates at the bottom of the nameplate. *1660–1722.* He ascended another step and paused again, noticing for the first time a subtle difference in the shading of the wall's wood paneling. There was a lighter square around the portrait. A larger painting had been there, probably for many years, but had been replaced by the portrait of the austere, evangelical-looking man with the wampum in his hand.

The wound in Duncan's side began to throb. He grimaced as he adjusted the dressing, then slowly climbed up the stairs and returned the lamp to the landing table.

In the morning the door to the library was locked.

Sarah—I awoke from a dream with my heart hammering and realized something was in the darkness with me. Its breathing was unlike any I have known, slower, deeper, and more powerful than that of a bear or even a great ox. The sound came from the blackness on the far side of the chamber and I was too weak or perhaps too frightened to approach it. Eventually I realized I had nothing to fear, that whatever it was, it was just watching me. Then with a terrible thrill I knew it was the incognitum. *The great beast was with me. I mustered my strength and sat up on the side of the bed. "I'm sorry," I said to it. Then in a thunderous voice that seemed to come down a long tunnel it replied "I'm sorry." In my struggle to understand I was suddenly awake, in a cold sweat. It had been a dream within a dream, but one that the tribes would say had been sent to me by the gods. Since awakening I have sensed a strange, calming presence just behind my shoulder. I am not sure the* incognitum *is entirely dead.*

Duncan pulled his cloak high up around his shoulders as he knocked on the door of the brick house. Darby, who had inspected his disguise and pulled a hank of Duncan's hair over his maimed ear, had assured him that there were no watchers nearby, but still Duncan glanced nervously down the street. It was his first foray away from the Faulkner mansion since his tumble into the Thames, and though his body had largely recovered, he was not so confident about his mind. For days his sleep had been disturbed by nightmarish visions of Conawago lying in a pool of blood, Conawago curled in a fetal position and weeping, once even of Conawago being stabbed by laughing inmates of the Immortals cell as they staged the Ides of March. Even more vivid were the dreams of being in Milbridge's lodge, spitted through the shoulders, as Hastings cut away pieces of his flesh, to the hysterical cackles of the earl.

He had forced himself to go out to the Faulkner courtyard, sometimes just sitting in the sun, but more often helping Noah with the horses. The groom brought messages from Ishmael, and the day before the young Nipmuc had met Duncan in the stable to update him on Conawago's condition. Ishmael had wisely chosen to stay away from Craven Street and confirmed that no Horse Guards watchers had been spotted at the Neptune, meaning that at least for now they must be assuming that Duncan had died with Nettles. As for the dead lieutenant, Woolford had reported that no one had spoken of him dying or even as missing, but in a quiet meeting in the park across from the Horse Guards Palace Lewis had reported to Woolford and Ishmael that Hastings had cleared out Nettles's quarters and taken his name off the duty rosters. His fellow soldiers whispered that Nettles must be on one more of his clandestine missions. Lewis confided that Hastings was making preparations to leave soon on new and urgent business in Boston, news that still confused Duncan. Had Hastings decided that Franklin's opportunity to meet with the king was past and therefore the inventor was no longer a threat to the War Council's plans? Or did it mean Milbridge and the Council had launched a new plan against the inventor for which Hastings's presence was not needed? Why Boston?

When the door opened Duncan had a false name ready, but the maid had been the one who had served Duncan and Hewson breakfast on his first visit. She greeted him warmly, then led him down the cellar stairs. To his surprise half a dozen young men were gathered around Hewson's work table where, with a human skull in one hand and a writing lead in the other, the doctor was pointing out where the glands under the jaw were located. Duncan had arrived early, and the doctor was still conducting one of his private classes. He settled onto a stool in the shadows to listen, and was joined a few minutes later by Olivia Dumont, also early for their meeting. She listened with rapt attention and reacted with energetic curiosity, pushing through to the table, when Hewson produced a glass jar of alcohol that contained a human jawbone with the glands still attached.

Finally Hewson escorted his students out and returned with a tray of tea. He would entertain no discussion until he had examined Duncan's wound, pronouncing it nearly healed.

"The king sees no one for three days before his royal ball," Olivia reported. "His royal ball retreat, he calls it."

"So Dr. Franklin informed me," Duncan said.

"What he could not have told you is that the Astronomer Royal has confirmed the meeting! Just Benjamin and George and Nevil!" she exclaimed, then told them that Franklin was preparing a short speech and had ordered a new waistcoat for the occasion. Captain Rhys had taken over arrangements for moving the *incognitum*, which still lay hidden a few feet from where they sat, and had his motley company of smugglers and seamen ready to conduct the move and stand guard once the bones had been hidden at the construction yard. Through his London network and discreet distribution of coin, the captain had obtained agreement from one of the contractors that the crates could be buried in loads of sand to be delivered to the site.

"Of course Dr. Franklin is quite insistent about being conversant with the Royal Society's views on the transit," the Frenchwoman added. "Such a noble intellect, and so nobly sensitive about offending others. He was much gratified about tonight."

Duncan looked at her with new worry. "Tonight?"

"He is invited to dinner with leading members of the Society. He says it is a great honor. He had me help him select his attire, for he must not appear to the esteemed gentlemen to be some bumbling colonial. Naturally he'll say nothing about the Philadelphia calculations or the ancient creature—that news is for the king's ears alone."

"Where?" Duncan pressed with sudden alarm. "Where is he dining?"

"Why, Boodles, the club on Pall Mall. They say it overflows with dukes and earls. He said he feels like a young debutante, making an appearance at such a revered place."

"Olivia! It's Hastings's club! Probably Milbridge's as well!"

"Surely he is safe at Boodles," Olivia protested. "It is a gentleman's sanctuary. No violence would ever be committed there."

"Don't you understand? They don't need to pierce our secrets about the king's meeting. They just need to remove Franklin for a few days."

Olivia knitted her brow. "*Pourquoi*—" she began.

"The king promised a decision on the troop deployment to America before the end of the social season," Duncan reminded her. "Before he leaves to go hunting for two months. If he is undecided he will defer to his advisers on the War Council, which means that if Franklin does not meet and dissuade him soon, the troops will be dispatched. The colonies will become military encampments and the new militias will start using their arsenals to protest!"

"Surely, Duncan," Hewson protested, "no one would act against him at the club. Why, it practically sits in the shadow of St. James's Palace."

"The lair of earls and dukes? The aristocracy loathes Franklin. He will not have one friend there. They will consider it great amusement to watch him be humbled."

"But the club has rules," Hewson ventured.

Duncan replied with a skeptical gaze. "And to their minds rules are only for the lower order of men. Who is their biggest benefactor? Who invited him?"

"A messenger brought the invitation to Henry Quinn," Olivia said. "Very elegant it was, in a parchment envelope. Henry was most impressed, showed it to everyone in the house, exclaiming about what a great honor it is. It was made in the name of the Royal Society. And Duncan," she added, "I sent a link boy to check with the steward, asking when we might send a coach to retrieve Dr. Franklin tonight. The reply was that his hosts will arrange his safe return. To assure us, he told the link boy that the dining chamber had been reserved by the proprietors of Benjamin's very own home colony."

Hewson muttered a surprisingly unrefined curse. Duncan stared in disbelief.

"The biggest benefactor of Boodles," Hewson whispered, "is the Penn family."

"And the Penns loathe Franklin," Duncan said. "He sought to have their charter revoked." He stood, ignoring the pain that lanced his side, and grabbed his cloak and hat. "When is the supper?"

"Early," Olivia said. "Eight thirty."

"There's still time," Duncan said as he wrapped the cloak over his shoulders.

"You mustn't go to Craven Street!" Olivia warned. "You promised, at risk of your very life! The watchers are still there, Duncan. And we are taking precautions. Henry has a most clever plan to mislead them. Mrs. Stevenson will go outside to summon a hackney and Henry, wearing a cloak, a low hat, and spectacles, will rush out while she calls from the front door, 'Enjoy your evening, Benjamin,' while the real Benjamin darts out the rear door."

Duncan gazed in disbelief. Could the household still be so naive after all that had happened? "Then I shall go to Boodles," he declared and darted up to the street before they could stop him.

As he walked toward the Mall, he began to regret his decision. He had no plan, no possibility of entering the club itself. Turning into an alley, he waited, and his hope was realized when the wiry bosun appeared. He summoned Darby with a loud whisper and quickly explained that he was trying to divert Franklin from Boodles. Despite the skepticism that rose on the bosun's face, he did not resist, only reaching out to pull Duncan's tricorn lower over his face.

The sun had set by the time they reached the club, minutes before the appointed hour. Elegant coaches were parked along the side of the wide avenue and more were arriving. The liveried porters who met their passengers were big, strapping men who seemed more like bodyguards than servants. Duncan would have considered jumping into Franklin's coach when it arrived except that the darkness made it impossible to identify the arriving guests until they stepped under the bright lamps of the club's portico.

To his relief he spied Franklin walking at a jaunty pace along the tree-lined avenue with a link boy in escort. As Duncan turned to intercept the inventor, Darby grabbed his arm and nodded to the portico. "The big one in the livery that don't fit, he's one of the watchers from Craven Street! And that third coach past the entrance, it's got a footman wearing them tall boots!"

Duncan blended into the shadow of a big plane tree as he studied the men. Hastings's shadow men were lying in wait for Franklin, but when he turned back he was too late. Two of the men dressed as porters had intercepted Franklin and led him inside the club. Another tossed a coin to the link boy and blocked his path. The boy backed away.

Duncan quickly scanned the street. A hundred feet beyond the parked coaches was a group of perhaps a dozen link boys with lanterns and torches, waiting for customers among the wealthy who frequented Pall Mall. Opposite them were four lamplighters, chatting as they took a break in their work, beside two handcarts holding casks of the whale oil used to refill the lamps. The coachmen for the waiting vehicles were sitting in benches along the side of Boodles, smoking pipes and conversing amiably.

"They won't keep him there," Duncan said. He leaned close to Darby. "Get a hackney cab and wait a couple hundred feet down the street on the opposite side.

And make sure the horse is wearing blinders. Go!" he added when Darby cocked a questioning eye at him.

He was back at war, when there was never time to fully plan, and never time to second guess. Hesitation was death, the rangers taught. Assess your options, however limited, then act. Confuse the enemy, then strike. He touched his coin purse and hurried to the link boys.

"Tell me, men," he started, "did any of you know Robbie, who died recently?"

"Ye mean murdered by the damned horse soldiers," a tall boy growled.

"Who also tried to kill me," Duncan declared. The announcement brought them close, and he began speaking. They listened with rapt attention, and went round-eyed when he handed each a shilling. Several tried to refuse the coin, saying they would gladly help for Robbie's sake, but Duncan insisted, saying Robbie would want them to have it.

All but one of the boys stacked their lanterns and torches along a stone water trough. Five of them moved down the row of coaches, pretending to admire the horses and their fancy harnesses as they stealthily lifted out the pins that held the harness whippletrees to the coaches, the only connection between the teams and their conveyances.

Four more boys began teasing the lamplighters about who had the more important job, those of the fixed lights or those of the moveable lights, a scene Duncan had witnessed elsewhere on the streets. This time, however, as three boys inched closer from one side, the fourth rushed in from behind and seized one of the curved lighting staffs used to reach the wicks of the high lamps. As the boys sped away with a victorious whoop, the lamplighters gave chase. Duncan darted from the shadows, grabbed the nearest oil cart, and rolled it back into the darkness.

Everything hinged on his assumptions that Franklin was being kidnapped and that his captors would not linger at the elegant club. He accepted the odds, opened the tap of the cask, and slowly proceeded along the outside of the parked coaches. The oil poured out in a narrow line beside half a dozen coaches, channeled by the cobblestones. He confirmed that the link boy who had kept his torch stood ready and that Darby was standing by with a cab, then hurried forward as the club doors opened. A sputtering Franklin was dragged outside by two of the big men toward the waiting Horse Guards coach. They shoved him inside, then one of them ordered the others to withdraw, creating a frenzy of movement as their livery coats were cast off and draped over the railing along the club entry.

Duncan thrust the leaking cask under the Horse Guards coach, signaled the link boy, and opened the street-side door of the coach. The boy sprinted toward the coach with his torch as Duncan grabbed Franklin by his lapels and heaved him out, to the surprised gasp of the solitary guard inside, who had been watching his fellow soldiers.

He was pulling Franklin toward the waiting cab when the cask exploded, and he turned long enough to see flames engulf the coach and spurt up the line of oil Duncan had left on the cobbles. It would not last long, but the sudden line of flame was enough to send the teams into frantic retreat. They leapt forward, dropping their unpinned carriage bars and leaving the coaches behind. In the pandemonium that followed, coachmen, soldiers, and club porters raised angry shouts, curses, and calls for fire buckets. Some men darted after the runaway teams, others to the water trough.

Duncan had not noticed the soldier who seized his shoulder as he climbed into the cab but Franklin, already inside, did. The colonial agent raised the hard knob of his shillelagh. It slammed into the man's head with a satisfying thud.

Franklin cried out in glee as their pursuer collapsed. Darby, sitting beside the driver, shouted for him to give his horse rein, and Duncan, with one hand on the cab and one foot on the step, was nearly thrown off as the horse broke into an abrupt trot.

Franklin could barely control his laughter. "Capital, McCallum! Charge of the Highlanders! We showed the arrogant fools! How dare they try to kidnap a representative of government! Why, did you hear my Irish stick connect with that brute? He'll wake up regretting he tangled with us, I tell you!"

Darby and Duncan had quickly agreed on a circuitous route to Hungerford Market, where Darby could walk with Franklin the short distance back to Craven Street. Now Duncan saw the folly of the plan. Hastings's men would be furious and they still had the Craven Street house surrounded.

"You can't go back to Mrs. Stevenson's," Duncan warned.

"Nonsense! The cads would never dare harm me in my residence!"

"They don't seek to harm you, doctor. They seek to detain you. You have one possibility to see the king. If you miss that date, he leaves for the hunting season and the troops leave for America."

As Franklin wrinkled his brow at Duncan's words, Darby spat a curse. "Riders!"

Duncan leaned out the window to see four men on horses weaving around traffic toward them. "Faster!" Darby shouted to the driver. Seeing that outrunning the cavalrymen was futile, he directed the cabbie onto St. James's Street, which was jammed as usual. As they reached a tangle of hackneys, Duncan pulled Franklin out as Darby tossed a coin to the driver.

They wove around the hackneys to the end of the congestion and leapt into a cab that was pulling away. Several others were escaping the knot of coaches and cabs and Duncan was sure that they had not been spotted by the Horse Guards riders. Their pursuers would have to divide, following different cabs, which were already moving in several directions. He cautioned his companions not to risk showing themselves out the windows and directed the cabbie toward Covent Garden, where he knew the nightlife would mean more confusion to any followers.

Duncan's racing heart had begun to slow when, as they approached the Garden, the cabbie called down, "If it be a man on a tall black horse who worries ye, friends, he's but half a block back."

They waited until they were among a dozen other cabs, then ran to the far side of the congestion around the coffee shops, taverns, and bawdy houses before climbing into one more hackney. "Whichever route is clear," Duncan replied when their cabbie asked their destination, "just make haste!" He paid no attention to their direction, instead just casting nervous glances out the window, until the big dome loomed ahead of them. Ludgate Hill was crowded as people flocked into a service in the cathedral, apparently after concluding some sort of memorial procession. "Just in time for the Holy Cross Festival," the cabbie explained, nodding toward a line of worshipers who were arriving in a procession carrying four-foot-long wooden crosses, blocking their passage.

"Lose yourselves!" Darby barked as he leapt out. "I'll slow 'im down." He picked up a cross from the stack left by the procession, then grabbed a smoking censer that was awaiting a cleric and began swinging it like a medieval morning star. "Go!" he snapped as they stared in confusion at him.

"Dear God!" Franklin cried. "The Horse Guards are hunting us!"

Duncan did not bother to point out that if caught it would mean an inconvenience for Franklin. For Duncan it would mean death.

Chapter 21

A RANGER WAS TAUGHT TO TAKE advantage of the terrain he knew. Duncan led a frightened Franklin through the crowd and into the west portico of the cathedral, then slowed. A choir was singing. Half the pews were occupied. Clergymen in red vestments were preparing to conduct a service. From outside they heard Darby's loud shout of "Blasphemer! I heard him curse the archbishop!" then his words were drowned out by angry cries from the flock. Duncan almost felt sorry for the soldier.

"In here!" Duncan instructed, pulling Franklin into the shadowed staircase. The famed wizard of electricity said nothing until they reached the Whispering Gallery, when he halted, chest heaving, and clutched his leg.

"They know we are on Ludgate Hill," Duncan explained. "And the streets around the cathedral are thick with parish watchmen. They will be alerting the watch. More of the Guards will come. We cannot outrun them. So we outfox them. We will wait them out."

"My dear lad, we are hardly inconspicuous here," Franklin observed. "And my gout protests at every step."

"Not here. Higher, and higher still. I know a place. We can go slowly. It will be an hour before they gather enough men to search the cathedral, and Darby will be distracting them. A few steps at a time."

Franklin remained stoically silent, valiantly climbing despite his obvious pain, although often pausing to lean on his walking stick. Duncan gave him a steadying arm for the last few steps, to the Stone Gallery, but he sagged when Duncan indicated the narrow stairway up to the Golden Gallery. "Surely this suffices," Franklin said. "I am just too winded, my friend."

Duncan eyed a stack of buckets, brooms, and mops left by a cleaning crew inside the stairway. "Wait here," he instructed, then began carrying the equipment up the stairs. A quarter hour later he finally led Franklin up to the small, high gallery. Franklin marveled at the view of the sleeping city. "Astonishing. All these years and I never knew about this perch."

"Let's pray the Horse Guards are just as ignorant of it," Duncan said as he removed his cloak "Enjoy it. I need a few minutes." He carried the cleaning equipment back down the stairs, creating obstacles of buckets and mops leaning across the darkened steps.

"So this is the plan?" Franklin asked. "I fear that unless we can grow wings we are trapped."

"This is not all," Duncan said in a tentative voice. He knew he had already pushed the Philadelphia inventor to the limits of his endurance, but he led him around the walkway to the narrow ladder he had discovered when searching for Ishmael. "It leads up to a ledge for the workmen who service the gilded fixtures on top, and is on a sliding track, so that we can pull it up into the shadows once we reach the top. Ample room there for four or five, let alone two."

"Duncan, no. I simply cannot. This must suffice."

"If they find you, Doctor, they will detain you for a few days. If they find me I am dead."

"But my foot, dear lad. The gout unnerves me."

"Just a dozen feet. I will carry your stick, and at the top I can pull the ladder up out of sight. Here they have a chance of discovering us. Up there, no chance at all." Duncan touched a nearly forgotten lump in a pocket. "I have some coca leaves you can chew at the top, to ease the discomfort."

Franklin studied the ladder with a worried expression. "Can I close my eyes as I climb?"

"If you can feel for the rungs to the top, yes." Duncan looked down at the broad courtyard below. They had used up much of their hour.

He acknowledged Franklin's fortitude when, after several excruciating minutes, and a passing panic when Franklin cried out that he could not endure another moment, they reached the top. Duncan pulled up the ladder and they settled onto the ledge, out of sight from all but the birds. Duncan draped his cloak over Franklin's legs and handed him the coca leaves that Huber had supplied on his first apothecary visit.

"Quite the adventure," Franklin said, though his enthusiasm was obviously forced.

"We'll have to keep you hidden somewhere until the day of your meeting," Duncan said, "and pray they don't learn where the *incognitum* is."

"Of course they don't know. No one outside the Craven Street house knows."

"Excepting me and Patrick and Ishmael," Duncan corrected. "And everyone else who sat around the table at the Neptune to make the plans. And half a dozen smugglers. Not to mention several crew members of the *Galileo*."

Franklin made a little rumbling noise in his throat but decided to change the subject. "Was that an owl?" he asked as a winged creature flew close to examine them. Duncan said nothing.

"What a perch for November fifth!" Franklin proclaimed.

Duncan thought Franklin was referring to some new astronomical event, but then the inventor started pointing at dark patches in the landscape. "Hyde Park, Tothill Fields, the Artillery Ground, Lincoln Inn Fields," he said, naming the deep shadows. "All have displays, if I'm not mistaken."

"Displays?"

"Fireworks! Remember, remember the fifth of November, as the poem goes. You would not credit how we viewed the royal display last year. A front-row box not a hundred feet from the king! I was going to retain him in any event, but when Henry offered up some distant relative's box, our discussions were quickly concluded, I assure you."

The words tugged at Duncan's memory. "It's why Polly suggested such a gift for you this year," he said, recalling the day she had received her pearls.

"Sweet lass, but she will never match what Henry did for us last year," Franklin said, and began a lighthearted whisper of the poem, a favorite of English schoolboys. "Remember, remember the fifth of November, the gunpowder treason and plot."

Franklin had nearly finished the poem when the words faded away, and Duncan realized he was studying clouds gathering in the west.

"Has the cathedral installed your lightning arrestors, perchance?" Duncan asked.

"The fools are just working on doing so now. A committee was formed by St. Paul's to discuss it. Lightning nearly destroyed St. Bride's Church several years ago. Every steeple and tower in the city should have a lightning conductor. The clerics are always our biggest obstacles, despite their churches having the highest aspects. Why, in Boston they preached that my lightning rods were causing earthquakes, if you can credit it. I am presuming upon God, the imbeciles say, for the secrets of lightning are for the Great Jehovah alone." His words seemed to bring a painful memory to Franklin, and he fell into a brooding silence.

"San Nazaro," the inventor said minutes later. "The poor lost souls."

"Sir?"

"San Nazaro haunts me, Duncan, every day it haunts me. The church of San Nazaro in Brescia, near Venice, stored gunpowder in its vaults for the Venetian army. Just weeks ago, lightning struck the steeple and touched off the powder. They say three thousand were killed in the explosion. My God, three thousand souls."

Duncan heard something in Franklin's voice he had never heard before. "Surely you don't feel guilt over those deaths."

Franklin took a long time to answer. "I came to London for selfish reasons. The glory of political office. Preserving my appointment as deputy postmaster for the colonies. Adding coin to my pocket for serving colonial governments." He glanced at Duncan before making a new confession. "My highest aspiration was to obtain a charter for a new Ohio land company, of which I would be a founding member, with all the wealth that implies. It probably makes me no better than the starch-collared louts I am always complaining of." He paused to watch a small cloud scuttle across the moon.

"What if it had been different?" he continued, his voice strangely hoarse. "What if I had been more of a responsible Christian? There will be a terrible reckoning for me at the pearly gates. I knew with certainty that my copper arrestors would stop such disasters and save lives. I could have traveled as an ambassador for human life, to convince town fathers of the importance of installing my rods. There would be far fewer widows and orphans in Brescia today if I had done so. I could have saved them." He spoke with anguish now. "Three thousand souls, Duncan."

Duncan recalled the sadness that sometimes settled on the inventor's countenance during his long spells of staring into his hearth. "What was needed, doctor," he said, "was less stupidity in Venice about where to store gunpowder. They created a bomb under the high steeple, waiting for a spark. There has never been a successful ambassador against human stupidity."

Now Duncan was watching the clouds as well, with growing unease. "So St. Paul's is the highest point in London and it is not protected?"

"I honestly don't know how far they've gone with the project, lad, though I see no evidence of it where we sit, which is the logical location for the arrestor rods. If not, and a storm rises, just watch the hair on your forearm."

"My hair?"

"When it rises straight up you will have just enough time for a quick prayer to St. Peter to say you are on the way to meet him." Franklin's laugh was weak, and he looked away from the horizon.

"Insurance syndicates," Duncan said after a few minutes.

"Sir?"

"You should go to insurance syndicates. Many are based here in London. They are keenly interested in protecting against losses, and I hear they are expanding beyond maritime contracts to warehouses and other buildings. Tell them about your lightning arrestors. Write a pamphlet for them. Appeal to their economic interest, show them the small cost of arrestors versus the catastrophic loss of a building. Once they understand that the rods will mean fewer losses, they will become your ambassadors, spreading the word through their networks and making them conditions in their contracts."

Franklin brightened. "My God, McCallum! It's the very thing! Yes, I shall make inquiries on Fleet Street."

They spoke of little things, of Mrs. Stevenson's household and the likelihood that Hewson and Polly would soon be betrothed, then of Philadelphia and Deborah's recent shipment of dried venison, cranberries, and Franklin's precious Newtown Pippin apples. Franklin asked about the furnishings in his Philadelphia household and whether he should buy china for his wife as individual pieces or in sets. The inventor then inquired about the details of the Preston House fire, and was pressing Duncan on the performance of the fire company when he was cut off by a shout from the plaza below. A dozen mounted soldiers had appeared, quickly dismounting, and began ordering the score of people who lingered there into a line. An officer paced along the line, slapping a riding whip in his palm as he inspected each face as a soldier held a lantern to it.

"You said there were supplies there, for manufacturing," Franklin said in a tight voice.

Duncan took a moment to understand. "At Preston House? For the Covenant, yes, including some tin that you helped smuggle. But we had taken everything out already. They were saved."

"And how long afterward was Pierre Dumont murdered?"

"That very night," Duncan said.

As he spoke Franklin kept an eye on the soldiers, who were now pounding on doors of the houses surrounding the plaza. "There are some on the Privy and War Councils who think the non-importation pacts are tantamount to acts of treason. I have sent warnings."

"Warnings of what?"

"Doubtless you understand by now, Duncan. There are those in London who believe it is better to act quietly against treason. We must nip subversion in the bud, they say."

"You mean subversion as in secret meetings about an ancient beast," Duncan said. When Franklin offered no answer, he continued, "How many officers of the king are working in the shadows this way?"

"Who knows? There's been a Black Chamber in the post office for years, reading London mail. I never suspected the Horse Guards until you came with your news," Franklin said. "I have told them we have to be more careful."

Duncan fastened the top buttons of his waistcoat against the cool breeze as he chewed on the words. "America is in need of machines for production of its own goods," he suggested.

"Desperately so. The endless resources of the continent are going untapped because of the greed of men in England. It is economic servitude. They are holding the continent in bondage by their damnable rules restricting commerce. If the colonies could make the goods it needs, had its own industries, Whitehall would have to stop treating us like their serfs."

Duncan was feeling the fatigue of his strenuous day. His wound was aching. He watched the small uniformed figures below as they pulled people from their homes to question them. Gradually Franklin's words filtered through the fog of his exhaustion. Franklin had said *we* in talking about the non-importation efforts. "You're not just planning strategies for the Covenant, you're providing them with supplies and English secrets," he stated.

Franklin looked up at the moon as if to ignore him.

"The drawings of the machines." Duncan paused, revisiting in his mind the scenes with the drawings at Craven Street. "And Olivia, who took such interest in your drawing of a machine. Olivia Dumont is involved in the secrets of the Non-importation Pact."

Franklin offered no denial. Here, hovering above the world, here where Duncan had invoked the white beads of the Iroquois, here was where truths were told.

"It's why you so readily offered her lodging at Craven Street. You were already acquainted, already coconspirators in the Covenant."

Franklin kept staring upward. "Look at the shifts in color as the cloud slips by the moon," he observed. "How many shades of silver can there be?"

"And the Faulkner House!" Duncan pressed. "Is that why there are drawings of other machines at the Faulkner library?" His mind raced. "Is Olivia making drawings there? You would put Pierre's sister at risk?" he demanded.

A small laugh escaped Franklin's lips. "I doubt she has had time to make drawings there, but you have it wrong, my friend. I helped devise the Mississippi plan, yes, and I asked Ezra to help in the Shawnee country, but mostly I take orders from the Covenant leaders, not the other way around. Those agents operate in a tight group. Olivia was involved with the Covenant only recently, just before she arrived in London. I didn't know until she offered to take the drawings of the machine back to the colonies. She proposes to sew them inside a petticoat.

"The Covenant sends special requests to me from time to time through Charles Thomson, Mulligan in New York, or John Hancock, knowing that my reputation can get me inside establishments that most would be prevented from seeing. They ask only infrequently, because they say they do not want to put me at risk. The other day after the textile mill, after her alarm over your capture had subsided and after Henry left for the day, dear Olivia sat at his desk and made ten pages of notes and drawings of looms and shuttles.

"The requests from the leaders of the Covenant have been coming in the same neat hand and in code, all from Boston or New York and all cleverly glued between two sheets of paper on which fictitious correspondence from merchants is written or else written in invisible ink between lines, the kind that must be held over a flame to read. The leader even has a code name, perfectly suited to the role."

"Hephaestus," Duncan said.

"Exactly," Franklin confirmed. "The Greek god of the forge, the god of industry. The inquiries from Hephaestus are bold, I must say. Asking about the new steam apparatus in the mines, the new flying shuttle looms, the blowing cylinders being used for steel production, and even the mix of alloys used in making sword blade steel. There are those on the Privy Council who are as interested in eliminating Hephaestus and the Covenant as Milbridge has been in eliminating you."

"But why did I see similar drawings at the Faulkner House?" Duncan asked. "Madeline is so feather-headed she would compromise a secret without even knowing."

He sensed, rather than saw, Franklin shrug. "I do not know Madeline. And as I said, I am a mere private in that particular army, though I do know that Olivia is planning passage to Boston after the royal ball. I told her she should go to Paris to meet with Buffon as her brother had planned, but now she says that will have to be delayed because her business in Boston is more urgent. I deemed it indiscreet to press her, though I do know she asked Judith for lemon juice."

"Lemon juice?"

"It is one of the substances used for invisible writing, and more ladylike than the urine others use."

Duncan tried to make sense of the confusing information as he drifted off to sleep. He was aware of nothing until Franklin jammed his elbow against him. The sound of voices brought him instantly awake. Men were speaking on the outside walkway of the Stone Gallery at the base of the cathedral dome. The words were muffled by the wind, but not their angry tone.

"If I were a religious man," Franklin whispered, and his voice faded away.

Moments later he heard a cry of pain, and what might have been a clatter of buckets on the stairs to the Golden Gallery, then the approach of ascending footsteps. Duncan's heart leapt into his throat as two voices erupted from the walkway directly below them.

"Like I said," came one gruff voice, "ain't no one up here and I cracked my knee on the damned stair for nothing. That old cow Franklin would never be able to climb up here. They're gone. Probably grabbed a wherry and are laughing over their ale in some Billingsgate pub this very moment. Waste of time, and us having to be on parade at dawn."

"So now we go down and salute the major and report no enemy in sight, sir," came a weary reply. "God in his heaven, how many damned steps did we climb?"

Duncan and Franklin did not speak until long after the soldiers had retreated.

"Five hundred twenty-eight," Franklin whispered.

"Sir?" Duncan asked.

"Five hundred twenty-eight steps from the cathedral floor."

"How could you know that?"

"It's a curse. I compulsively observe. Some people rejoice at the song of a wren. I wonder how many feathers are on its breast."

"We need to stay until the crowds come tomorrow," Duncan said after a few minutes. "Hastings may have posted watchers."

Franklin sighed. "I feared you would say that." He shrugged. "So the Horse Guards strike a blow against our freedom," he said absently. "For the night, at least."

"I am learning that freedom is a complicated notion," Duncan said in a contemplative tone. "I think there may be levels of freedom just as Dante suggested there were levels of hell." Franklin turned with a questioning expression. "Ezra had a friend in the Shawnee lands," Duncan continued, "a Pennsylvania man named Boone, who I now think is something of a connoisseur of freedom. He said those of the wilds had a different understanding of freedom than those of the settled lands, that maybe it was that difference that got Ezra killed. I couldn't understand until I came to London. Here everyone is so bound up with obeying rules that they are blind to how far their freedom is compromised. If the ones sent down the Ohio to kill him had ever tasted the freedom Ezra knew, maybe they would not have enslaved themselves to men like Milbridge, and maybe he never would have been killed.

"In the wilds a man is born to liberty and his freedom can only be curtailed if he agrees. In London men only have the liberty the king gives them. Not many seem to understand that difference here. Not yet. Conawago says that the American land itself breeds freedom."

"The world needs more such wise men," Franklin said, and dropped into a brooding silence.

After several minutes Duncan motioned to the sky. "The clouds are passing us. We should sleep."

"Sleep," Franklin agreed, and took out his watch to read it in the moonlight. "My good luck piece has worked again," he said, holding the watch for Duncan's gaze.

"Again?"

"I was wearing this watch the night my son and I flew the kite in the storm. Only later did I learn that men had been killed attempting similar experiments in Europe. My son, who was just a boy then, decided my silver watch kept us alive, for he was touching the chain when the lightning struck. Later I had a lightning bolt engraved with my initials on the back." Franklin pocketed the watch and spread the cloak so it covered Duncan's legs as well. "Sleep," he repeated.

But Duncan could not regain his slumber, and knew from Franklin's uneven breathing that the inventor too was unable to relax. The clocks of London had struck another hour before Duncan spoke. "There are one hundred ninety thousand and eighty barley corns in a mile," he suddenly stated.

Franklin stirred and raised his head. "Pardon?"

"In a mile are three hundred perches, one thousand sixty-six paces, fourteen hundred eight ells, seventeen hundred sixty yards, five thousand two hundred eighty feet, sixty-three thousand three hundred sixty inches, and one hundred ninety thousand eighty barley corns. Conawago said it was a miracle that the author could count out all those barley corns because surely crows would have descended to eat them as he laid them."

"You are beyond me," Franklin confessed.

"Years ago, he and I were caught in a terrible blizzard in the northern Susquehanna country. We found shelter in an abandoned cabin that still had its roof and a workable hearth. We desperately needed fire but our tinder had gotten wet, so I was much pleased when I discovered an old pamphlet stuffed between two logs and was about to rip out some pages when Conawago stopped me. He said he was familiar with the work and we must not be so disrespectful of Mr. Saunders, the author who created it. He hated damaging the printed word. So I got out my knife and peeled away shavings from the log walls.

"Only after the fire had thawed our bones did we turn back to the pamphlet. We were trapped in that cabin for four days and took turns reading it aloud. One of my favorite entries was the detail about the makeup of a mile. We memorized most of the pages. Conawago kept saying he would like to meet this genius Richard Saunders someday."

Franklin's belly rose and fell several times before Duncan realized he was laughing. "*Poor Richards Almanack,*" Franklin said, holding his stomach.

"1733," Duncan said. "Being the first after the leap year," he recited, "and by the account of the Eastern Greek Church the year 7241."

"The very first edition," Franklin said. "We didn't know how the public would receive it."

"It was not until years later that the public learned that Richard Saunders was you."

"I wasn't going to give my own name and have farmers bringing legal action against me because my weather predictions were wrong."

"'Death is a fisherman, the world we see his fishpond is, and we the fishes be.' That was the opening for the month of May," Duncan continued. "It was the one complaint Conawago had. He said that such a dark passage should be for a winter month, not for the spring."

They watched as a cab discharged a solitary figure in the courtyard. The man faced the cathedral, then fell to his knees and lifted his hands in prayer.

"I think it was on the third day that we began challenging each other to recite a given month's page from memory. On the ninth of February you predicted snow. And high winds for the fifteenth." Franklin chuckled again. "We did catch you out that month. There was a printer's error so that there was no twenty-seventh. The dates went twenty-six, twenty-eight, twenty-nine. But February of 1733 had no twenty-ninth day."

"I was mortified," Franklin confessed. "But I couldn't bear the cost of printing a new edition. I recall a farmer in Connecticut wrote to request a refund."

"Conawago was deeply impressed. He had never studied an almanac before. I recall him saying it was the perfect way to lure the common man to greater appreciation of the world. Sharing of common knowledge is the linchpin of civilization, he likes to say, though I am certain the first time he said it was there in that decrepit cabin as the ice wind howled outside. I genuinely believe it had a lot to do with his entering the newspaper business."

Franklin's head swiveled toward Duncan. "But he is an Indian," he said, then paused and attempted a more gracious phrasing. "I understand he is a tribal elder. I never heard of such a man in the gazette business. Why, it takes such perseverance, such acute powers of observation and articulation."

"You should spend more time with tribal elders," Duncan said, trying not to take offense.

"You never told me, Duncan. Perfectly amazing!"

"He publishes the only paper west of the Catskills. He has a fine old German press." They kept watching the forlorn man below. He was advancing in slow, single steps, and after each one dropped to his knees for a prayer. "Its masthead reads *The Beacon of the Wilderness.*"

"Why, that's extraordinary!"

"*He* is extraordinary. We often travel in the wilderness together. Sometimes he finds ancient petroglyphs, and then has to stop and burn fragrant tobacco to honor them. He is like the *incognitum* in a way, aged and provoking of deep questions. He likes to camp on high ridges despite the greater winds because it gives a better view of the universe at night." Duncan felt another pang as he realized he might never again pass such nights with Conawago. "He knows the name of thirty or forty constellations, in English, Latin, and at least two tribal tongues. Sometimes we lie on the rocks and make up our own constellations. On rare nights when he is thus relaxed I can get him to speak of entering the French court, before the turn of this century. King Louis begged him to stay but he told the king a bark lodge by the Hudson awaited him, and his mother's delicious corn and bean soup. Except when he returned to the lodge, his mother and all his family had disappeared. He never saw them again. Some say they died of smallpox, others that they disappeared into the west like thousands of other tribal refugees."

"I really must meet this fellow. What tales we can exchange!"

"You may recall, Doctor, that he is a prisoner of Bedlam."

The words deflated Franklin. "Just so," he muttered. "Patients," he added. "They prefer to call them patients."

"I take it you have never visited," Duncan said.

Franklin had no reply. A man in a priest's robe emerged from the cathedral and spoke with the praying man, who rose and collapsed into the priest's arms, sobbing. Duncan and Franklin spoke no more for long minutes. An air of tragedy hung over them.

Duncan tried a new subject. "I don't understand about those steam machines for mines. In my experience mines are warm enough inside. What use would steam be?"

"Steam does the work, my boy! The machine is on the surface. It pushes a great piston and thereby powers a pump to pull water out of the depths. So many mines are in danger of flooding, and now these machines draw the water out. Such machines could break our economic servitude, don't you see! God blessed us with such vast resources in America, and so many clever mechanics. The Covenant just needs to provide the keys to unlock that productive power."

Franklin cocked his head, listening. From far below came the sound of a choir practicing for an early service. The clouds in the east were gilded by the still unseen sun. "I think they hope for breakthroughs in Boston."

"Boston." Duncan repeated the word with a chill.

"Yes, yes. They sent word to conduct our work at a more rapid pace and send everything we can to Boston for the meeting Hephaestus has called there." Franklin paused. "Prithee, forget that. I should not have spoken of it. All this secrecy. Speak only to this person, not that person. Invisible inks. McGowan or McCallum. It makes the head spin."

Duncan looked out over the city, stirring to life. "All I do is secret, sir."

Franklin considered his words and gave a sigh of relief. "Of course. You of all people can be trusted. Here we are on this sacred ground. Perhaps that makes you my priest so I can confess all my dark activities." He nodded as if to himself. "At least you can share in my amusements. A new list came across with Olivia, bless her. Parts of the new loom are desired, the new recipes for pewter being applied in Manchester, more tools for coopers, and a hunter-green dress with fawn-colored lace trim. I said surely Hephaestus means a pattern for such dresses. Olivia was very tired, and had had too much port, I suspect. No, no she says, it is for Hephaestus to wear!"

"I'm not sure I follow."

"I was stunned at first, then had to laugh. Don't you see? Hephaestus is a woman, Duncan! It's wonderful! Confusion to our enemies, eh?"

Duncan stood, alarm in his voice. "The king's advisers considered the Covenant to be treason. Traitors, the War Council has decided, are best dealt with in private so they would not become martyrs." He pushed down the sliding ladder and retrieved his cloak.

"I'm not sure I follow, Duncan," Franklin said.

"How do you send letters to those of the Pact?"

"We adhere to the highest standards of secrecy. They don't go the leaders of the Pact directly. I send them care of Hancock in Boston, Mulligan in New York, or Thomson in Philadelphia. But never directly. My messages are left at a stable in Mayfair, on Chesterfield Street. Polly usually delivers them, though she was absent the last time and Henry did me the favor of running one over. There has been a flurry of information coming across. The Boston meeting is to be hosted by a cooper named Runyon. There is a miller from Lowell very keen to hear about water-powered looms."

Duncan stared at Franklin, dumbfounded, as his words sank in. "You have to send word, this very day!"

"Word of what, pray tell?"

"Hastings is going to Boston! Hastings believes his work against the *incognitum* is nearly complete and now he turns to Massachusetts. The War Council is sending their assassin to Boston. They mean to eliminate the leaders of the Covenant!"

Heinz and Greta Huber reacted with warm enthusiasm to Duncan's request that they keep the renowned Dr. Franklin in their house for a few days. The Philadelphia inventor had been cool to Duncan's suggestion, made as they climbed down the tower steps, but his reluctance began to fade when he saw the remarkable collection of biological oddities in Heinz's shop and disappeared entirely when Greta opened the door to the back of the house and the scent of fresh pastries wafted out.

Over a hearty breakfast Franklin cheerfully answered the Hubers' eager questions about electricity and lightning. By the time Duncan departed, Franklin had called for paper and was diagramming how they might set up one of his lightning alarms in their bedroom.

As Duncan hoped, the ever-reliable Darby intercepted him soon after he left the apothecary shop. The bosun laughed as he explained how he had paid two men in dark cloaks to lead some of the guardsmen on a chase across the river, where they could easily lose their pursuers in the labyrinth of alleys. Darby had then untied and scattered the horses of several of the Guard who had dismounted to search an alley after a willing—and fleet-footed—link boy had briefly emerged to call out to his friends that they should come meet the famous Mr. Franklin.

As they approached the Faulkner House, Darby announced that the *Galileo* would be ready to sail on in five days, which meant the date of their raid on Bedlam was finally set. The ship would be anchored in the Lower Pool and a dinghy would be waiting at the agreed landing stairs before dawn. Captain Rhys, who had been in meetings with the ship owners, said they must sail with the tide, which meant soon after sunrise.

"Then we move to ever greater danger, my friend," Duncan warned. He felt a surge of emotion as he met Darby's eye. "No matter what happens, Darby, I want you to know how grateful I am for all you have done. I would gladly stand beside you in battle."

"That will come soon enough, Highlander. And this time next week you'll be standing beside me with salt spray on your face."

Duncan wished he could share the man's confidence. "I look forward to the sweet smell of the Atlantic again," he replied. Darby disappeared down an alley.

Finding the stable empty, he entered the Faulkner House through the kitchen door. "Noah?" he asked the two maids who sat at the big table drinking tea. The nearest one pointed toward the side door. He found the library door ajar, and through the crack watched as Noah slid the basket of cocoons into what appeared to be a specially designed chest, then covered it with a folded piece of silk. Watching the freedman work with such careful, earnest conviction only made Duncan wonder how he could have taken so long to see the truth. Franklin sent secret messages to a stable on Chesterfield Street.

Duncan rapped on the door and waited a few seconds, giving Noah a chance to hide his work. The groom was inspecting the hearth as Duncan entered. He turned with a smile. "I was worried about you when you did not return last night."

"Dr. Franklin and I were playing cat and mouse with the Horse Guards."

"You should rest," Noah suggested. "Your wound is still healing." He took a step toward the door as if to encourage Duncan to leave.

"They are in terrible danger, Noah."

"You mean Mr. Franklin and his friends."

"I mean all of you who are engaged in secret support of the Non-importation Pact, of the Covenant."

Noah took too long for his answer to sound genuine. "I think I have read something about that pact in the gazettes."

"You have done more than that. You have obtained silk cocoons, and the moths that will emerge will make thousands of silk worms. You have made drawings of textile and steam machines. You handle secret messages from Franklin to America, to the Covenant."

Noah took a deep breath and grew distant. "I am just a groom, Duncan."

"I have the greatest respect for you, Noah. You are much more than a groom. But you don't appreciate the danger you face. Not all the beasts and savages are on the other side of the Atlantic."

Noah offered no answer. Duncan realized he was gazing over his shoulder. He turned to see Madeline Faulkner, only two steps behind him. How had she entered so quietly?

"Noah, the blue carriage needs the team harnessed," she said, then offered an icy nod to Duncan as she stepped past him to stand between the two men. She straightened her dress and touched the matching green ribbon fastened around her neck, one of the chokers she always wore. He took it as a gesture of arrogance, as if she were reminding him of her high station.

Duncan pushed down his spleen. He had no time for the interference of the socialite. "Prithee, Madeline," he said. "I have business with Noah."

"And prithee, Mr. McCallum," she said with unexpected tartness. "Noah works in my household, not yours."

Strangely, Noah momentarily put one of his big hands on Madeline's shoulders as if to calm her, then stepped around her. "There is no need for this bile. We can speak freely, Duncan," he said. "There are already many secrets among the three of us."

"We can go out to the stable," Duncan said, and with an uneasy glance at Madeline, added, "I can help with the blue carriage."

Noah ignored his suggestion. "You were speaking of the American Non-importation Pact and something called the Covenant," the freedman said with a meaningful look at the mistress of his house.

Duncan cast another peevish glance at Madeline, who for the first time since he had known her had anger in her eyes. "Duncan," she insisted, "you need to go to your room. You need rest."

"Your groom is involved with the Covenant," Duncan snapped. "I am trying to protect him!"

"Don't be ridiculous."

"You don't understand these things!" Duncan growled, not understanding the amusement that rose on her face. "He needs to listen to me!"

"I *am* listening," Noah insisted.

"The War Council is dispatching Major Hastings to Boston. The secret messages to the Covenant have been compromised somehow. Hastings is the secret assassin of Whitehall. He is going there to eliminate the leaders of the Covenant."

Madeline gasped and her hand shot to her mouth. She suddenly seemed to have trouble breathing. Before either Duncan or Noah could react, she slumped to the floor in a dead faint.

Noah scooped her up and laid her on the divan. Duncan grabbed her wrist to check her pulse. "The damned choker!" he called out. "She has to breathe! Take that tight ribbon off her neck!"

Noah did not move. "I don't think she would want—"

Before he could finish Duncan reached up and snapped the ever-present ribbon off her neck, then stared in mute amazement. Underneath was a narrow six-strand necklace of thin purple and white wampum beads.

It was impossible. His mind raced over the anomalies and mysteries of Madeline and her household and Sarah's strange relationship with her. In that instant, with those simple beads, all was resolved.

Chapter 22

DUNCAN LOOKED FROM THE STILL unconscious woman to Noah. "You knew." He studied the narrow necklace. The beads were in a familiar pattern of two purple then one white, followed by another purple pair.

"I pledged my secrecy long ago."

Duncan acknowledged Noah's point with a weary nod. "Can you get a cool towel for her forehead?"

As Noah stepped out of the library, Madeline stirred. Her eyes slowly opened. "*Kahnyenkehaka*," he declared, using the Mohawk's name for their tribe.

Madeline hesitated, as if not understanding. "Sir?"

In answer Duncan raised the broken ribbon that had been around her neck. "*Sennihstyakitha*," he said. Your necklace.

Her hand shot to her throat, touching the beads. Her eyes flared. "You had no right!"

"I feared for your breathing, Madeline. I meant only to help you." She laid her hand over the beads for a moment, as if she could hide them. "The pattern is of the Mohawk," he said. "When in Philadelphia Sarah liked to visit her robin, they said in Deborah Franklin's household. They thought she liked to hear the birdsong from some special grove. The maid said she even had a name for the robin. Siko was the word the maid recalled. I'm going to hear my Siko, she would tell the maid. I think she meant *tsihskoko*," he said, using the Mohawk name for robin. "You are *Tsihskoko*."

Madeline gradually softened, and all pretense fell away. *"Aktsi'a,* I call her."

"Older sister?" Duncan asked, realizing he had not found all the pieces to the puzzle.

"We were taken in the same spring raid all those years ago and raised in the same lodge. Sarah is two years older, and always looked after me, even though she was but a young girl herself when captured. We vowed we would always stay together."

"But you chose London."

"My father is of the same disposition as Sarah's natural father. He loathes the tribes, is shamed by our ancestors who helped them. He had me scrubbed and brushed for hours when I was returned, until my skin bled. I was alone, without Sarah, without my Mohawk parents, without my clan or tribe. I cried for days. But eventually I realized that life was much easier if I simply pulled on another's skin when I had to deal with my father and his world. It was just a game at first. When my father left me I would run to climb the trees or go sit with the foals by the forest. Acting like the proper young lady, the desirable maiden of society, opened doors for me. Sarah chose to slam those doors, to defy her father. I learned not to defy my father but to use him, and to embarrass him just enough with occasional crude conduct to make him happy for us to live apart."

Madeline took the broken ribbon from Duncan and gazed at it. "My great-uncle was an early missionary, then when he was older he formed the charity to help the tribes. My father allowed me to renew that work in my modest way, because I convinced him it gave me reason to meet with lords and ladies and so I might find a husband among the high ranks. But I did it because it gave me an excuse to travel to America every few months. Four years ago, Sarah found me in New York town and invited me to live with her in Edentown. I was so excited, and told her it would allow me to realize my dream of starting a tribal school, but we stayed up all night talking and we finally decided I could do more to help the tribes by continuing to strut on this stage. Soliciting funds for tribal orphans and missionaries is within the province of a proper English maiden."

"Your uncle Alpheus would be proud of you."

Madeline pushed herself into a sitting position. "You know about Uncle Alpheus?"

"I have seen his book, and his portrait. It would have been a great honor for the tribes to give him a strand of white beads."

"He was the black sheep of the family," Madeline said with a melancholy smile. "I think I would have liked him very much. I had heard about him in my village long before I knew he was my great uncle. He died protecting Mohawk children from some Huron raiders."

Duncan gestured to the drawings on the desk. "You would never be satisfied to merely sit in some meetings soliciting English patrons. I had begun to believe those were Noah's work but now I believe they are yours. The robin sends songs to the colonies. No one would closely scrutinize the travel or baggage of Lord Faulkner's daughter."

Madeline studied Duncan in silence. "Sarah says you will soon be married," she said. "She says you are a great friend not just of Conawago and Ishmael, but of the *Haudenosaunee*," she said, meaning the Iroquois tribes, "and also of Patrick and Hannah."

Duncan hesitated as he saw her meaningful gaze, and he realized she was offering another piece of the puzzle. "Patrick's wife," he said, "she was the link, the one who sent Conawago to you."

"She was the third sister. *Hahnawa* lived in the same lodge as Sarah and me. The three of us were inseparable when we were young."

"Hannah. *Hahnawa*," Duncan repeated. "Turtle."

"We usually called her Dancing Turtle, for she was always jumping and skipping."

Duncan returned her smile. Among the Iroquois the women were often unseen and only subtly present in tribal councils, but they were also often the most influential participants. "The Disciples of the Forest are part of your London disguise," he ventured. "You really belong to the Covenant."

"There are many in the colonies like you, Duncan, who understand and respect the tribes. That is their great hope for survival. If their fate is to be determined by the bewigged men of Whitehall, they are doomed. The men who have the king's ear would prefer that the tribes be annihilated. The tribal elders greatly fear war between the colonies and Britain, because no matter which side they take, the other will have the power, and incentive, to destroy the tribes. And sometimes," she added, "there are more direct roles for the tribes in supporting the non-importation efforts, as Ezra and the Shawnee were doing. To avoid war there needs to be more of a balance of power between America and England."

"So the colonies need to strengthen, to become as self-sufficient as possible," Duncan observed. "That's why you copy plans of English machines to secretly send to America. You do it for the tribes. The Covenant. I should have known. It was the term used by the tribes and the early British colonists for the alliance that gave them peace for decades."

Madeline nodded and touched her beads as she spoke, as if they gave her strength. "I listen with dumb adoration as the self-important owners of factories and mills boast of their new inventions. They are not shy about speaking of such things in private. They think it will impress me, and I swoon appropriately and have them convinced it just goes in one ear and out the other." Madeline paused, seeming to collect herself, then leaned forward with a more urgent air. "But Duncan, what you said about Major Hastings being sent. We must find a fast ship and send word this very day! God help it is not too late."

At last Duncan recalled what had caused Madeline to faint. "Dr. Franklin is planning to write to Sam Adams, though it will probably take hours to compose a note and apply his secret ink."

Madeline hesitated a moment. "The good doctor never uses the ink, for we discovered he was too awkward in its application, smearing and spilling it. That is done here, in this very chamber, by Noah and me. And a single letter just to Adams won't suffice!"

"You mean a letter for Mulligan in New York. And also one for Hephaestus, the leader of the Covenant," Duncan suggested. He lowered his voice. "Franklin told me, Madeline. Hephaestus is a woman. He is a bit too loose with confidences sometimes."

He could not entirely understand the petulant look she gave him.

"Your friends in the harbor must find the swiftest conveyance!" Madeline rose and hurried to the desk, where she pulled paper from a drawer. "It must be three private letters, not by post but by private courier. One to Boston, one to New York, and one to Edentown."

Something icy crept into Duncan's belly. "Edentown?"

"Duncan, are you really so blind? You never tried to understand. Her venture with the buttons was just a way to get you and the settlement more involved in her work. It happened while you were away on business for the Sons last year. Sarah said she felt it her duty to help at a higher level, as you did, and Mr. Adams and Mr. Thomson said she was the perfect choice, and that her plan for the Covenant was the perfect way to shield their non-importation work. No one would ever suspect three women and their harmless charity, or that some of the blankets we send have plans and drawings sewn inside them. And she wrote that while you are gone to send them to her in Boston because she would be going to Boston for important meetings with artisans who support the Sons, and with those who might provide funds for new manufacturing shops. She said she didn't want you to know, because you would just worry unnecessarily."

Duncan struggled to grasp her meaning. "I don't understand. Perfect choice for what?"

"The coordinator for bringing in English secrets! The Greek god Hephaestus! Samuel Adams suggested the name of the Greek god to help obscure her identity, and she agreed, saying that Conawago, scholar of Greek literature, would love it. I told you, the Covenant was born on the frontier. The secret head of the Covenant is Sarah! Sarah Ramsey is the Hephaestus whom Major Hastings seeks to kill!"

It took him a frustrating two hours to locate the captain of the *Galileo*, but Duncan finally found Rhys pacing impatiently along the dry dock where workmen were finishing the installation of new copper sheets below the bark's waterline.

"The lubbers should have had this finished ten days ago!" Rhys snapped. "Stop for an ale, stop for a bite, stop to order more nails, stop to look at one more shiny thing dragged out of Thames mud, then stop for another ale. By God, if I had them on board I would teach them proper discipline! And the owners were no better. It will be good to leave them behind." He spoke toward the workers down in the dock but cast a quick glance at Duncan. "You seem to fare better with your blood inside rather than outside."

"Darby says five days now. Is that truly possible with the *Galileo* not yet in the water?" His heart had been racing ever since his conversation with Madeline, and he fought the temptation to jump on the next ship to Boston. Hastings meant to kill Sarah. He kept hearing her words, spoken as the Preston House burned. *A warrior needs to be blooded.* She might be expecting battle, but she would never see Hastings's attack until it was too late. All that protected her now was the final secret. Hastings did not know her name, or face.

"I told the superintendent here that she floats in the morning or by God he'll know a Cardiff flogging." He saw the question in Duncan's eyes. "A beating with a dead cod, lad," he explained. "Five days, that's what I tell the yard and the crew. We shall hold true, if it means working through the nights, so long as I conclude my business with the owners. It may mean we raise the new topgallant mast while underway, but Darby can manage it."

Duncan extracted the urgent messages he and Madeline had drafted, with Noah's help. Their letters would all go to Boston, and Hancock would see they reached the right hands, for he could not risk sending a letter to Edentown that missed Sarah because she had already left for Boston. Noah had insisted on adding a short note to his brother, who did special work for the Sons and was familiar with comings and goings on the Boston waterfront. "These must be in Boston as soon as wind and tide allow," he said to Rhys. "They can't wait for the *Galileo* and can't be trusted to the post. Who has the fastest ship on the New England run?"

Rhys took off his hat and scratched absently at his thick black hair, then gestured Duncan down the walkway, out of earshot of any workers. "I know a sleek schooner out of Salem that's leaving at midnight. She has declared a cargo of woolens, though she be mostly loading whisky for Boston, to be offloaded under the moon, if ye get my drift. Her skipper is a friend of mine from the old days. He owes me a favor."

"A smuggler would be perfect." Duncan handed Rhys the sealed letters. "And your man can say Duncan McCallum told John to pay him a full guinea for the delivery."

Rhys eyed the addressee and raised an eyebrow. "John Hancock? Shouldn't be hard to find the merchant prince. I'll hire a wherry over to the schooner this very hour." He began to turn, then paused. "Unless I hear otherwise, Duncan, the *Galileo* will be waiting in the Lower Pool on the appointed night, provisioned and ready to sail. I will burn two red lanterns on the port side."

The captain lingered a moment more, studying the addressee of the letter Noah had added. He wrinkled his brow. "Where would such a man be found? Is that the right spelling?"

"He works with Mr. Hancock in his shipping business and is often on the docks. You met Noah, Miss Faulkner's groom. This man is his half brother. The spelling is correct, yes. Crispus Attucks."

The hackney driver had to wake Duncan as they reached Faulkner House. His last sleep had been the fitful naps on top of St. Paul's, and now the climb up to his room proved exhausting. Madeline had gone to find Olivia and he was grateful for the quiet as he finally collapsed onto his bed.

He had slept less than an hour when someone began shaking his shoulder. "Duncan! There's a woman at the kitchen door," Noah announced.

Duncan rolled over, away from the groom.

"She is most insistent! I can make out your name and that of Dr. Franklin, but I'm not sure about the rest. I have no German."

Greta Huber was nearly inconsolable. Although Duncan knew she had a good command of English, apparently her native tongue prevailed in her distress. They sat in the kitchen, encouraging her to drink tea. Noah finally offered her a small glass of brandy. She quieted, staring at the glass, then drained it in one gulp. She gasped, clenched her fists on the table, and when she looked up her eyes had cleared.

"Duncan, it is all my fault!" she groaned, finding her English. "He is gone. The great man vanished!"

It took another few minutes and another glass of brandy before Duncan was able to piece the story together. Franklin had slept for several hours after his breakfast with the Hubers, but when he woke he was very restless, and despite Duncan's warnings had insisted on making a quick visit to his home to fetch clothing. Heinz and Greta had argued with him, and it was finally agreed that he would not go home but to a safe house close to home, whose owner could retrieve what Franklin needed.

"Dr. Hewson's," Duncan suggested.

"*Ja, ja*, Hewson," Greta confirmed. Heinz had customers in his shop, so it was agreed that Greta would accompany Franklin. She had accepted Franklin's suggestion that they climb out of their cab a block away from their destination, to "gauge the territory" in Franklin's words. All seemed fine until they were fifty feet from Hewson's door, when suddenly there was a loud whistle and four large men ran at Franklin, knocking Greta to the ground. They threw him into a coach and sped away. On her tearful return, Heinz had insisted Duncan should have the news and Greta had resisted her husband's offer to go, saying it was her duty to carry the message.

Noah had a strangely calming effect on the German woman, holding her hand and explaining in his slow, deep voice that she had done no wrong and that surely no one would harm the famous inventor, only confine him for a few days. By the time she had collected herself sufficiently to depart, she had warmed to Noah enough to extend an invitation to him for tea.

A quarter hour after Greta's departure Ishmael arrived, gasping for breath. "He's taken, Duncan!" he announced. "Franklin is taken!"

Duncan and Noah exchanged a confused glance. "How could you know that?"

"The Natural Philosophers!" Ishmael said. "Archimedes! Copernicus! Newton!"

"Ishmael, have a seat," Noah suggested. "Collect yourself. You are making no sense."

"Hastings and his men stole him away and brought him there this afternoon! Taggart the keeper was troubled by it and took me upstairs. I saw him! Benjamin Franklin is imprisoned in the Natural Philosophers chamber at Bedlam!"

Noah insisted on accompanying them to Bethlem Hospital, but without explanation separated from Duncan and Ishmael as they approached the entrance, hurrying along the front of the building as if bound for a different entry. With an hour left in the visiting period. Ishmael led Duncan at a fast pace to a chamber on the top floor not far from the Immortals. Images of Franklin's likely plight as an inmate gnawed at Duncan. The inmates were capable of violence when their doors were closed, and in some chambers the long-term patients resented the arrival of a new member of their personal asylum. Even if there was no harm done to Franklin's person, Duncan feared for what he might do under the influence of Bedlam's drugs. The inventor in his normal state did not always conform to social expectations. Would he climb into the tub with Archimedes and squabble over the toy boat? Would he decide to take one of his air baths?

They slowed as they reached the cell, encountering a surprisingly large crowd of onlookers, who were eagerly tossing coins and pieces of fruit through the bars. With a wrench of his heart Duncan saw Franklin sitting in a wooden armchair near the rear wall. The keepers had thrust a willow branch into a wall sconce above him and fastened a string to it. A key was tied into the string and the other end of the string was tied to Franklin's wrist. The tension of the willow was enough to gently lift his wrist, the weight of which then dropped it back into his lap after a second or two, giving the impression that he was flying his famous kite. As if the props weren't sufficient, a pasteboard placard over his neck, like those worn by Archimedes, Copernicus, and Newton, proclaimed FRANKLIN in bold letters. The wizard of lightning had been hidden in plain sight.

Franklin gazed absently at the side wall as his left hand methodically rose and fell. Every few seconds he reached into the air with his right hand as if trying to touch something invisible to the rest of them. The kindhearted inventor had been heavily dosed, probably with a strong mixture of laudanum to sedate him and henbane to trigger hallucinations. Duncan clenched his fists, trying to control the fury that seized him. Ishmael sensed his reaction.

"Do nothing," he warned. "At least we know where he is. Tip our hand and he will be locked away far from view."

"Dr. Granger," came a whisper from beside him. Duncan turned to see Noah, wearing one of the tunics for the lower staff and holding a stack of towels as part of his disguise. "He was brought here by soldiers under orders from the Earl of Milbridge, they said. He underwent treatment by Dr. Granger, who announced that he was suffering from a pathological delusion that he was the electrical inventor from Philadelphia. Everyone on the staff is laughing about how similar he looks to the famed inventor, though most say this man is fatter than the real one."

Granger. The name was like a bitter pill on Duncan's tongue. The instructions of Granger, royal physician and allied with Milbridge and the War Council, would never be questioned by the keepers.

Duncan felt a pressure on his arm and discovered that Noah had clamped one of his big hands around his bicep. Ishmael stepped in front of him, partially blocking his view. He realized he had slightly bent, as preparing to launch himself in battle. If Milbridge had been in his reach at that moment Duncan would have beaten him to within an inch of his life, no matter the cost.

"He's not going anywhere," Noah said.

Duncan gazed forlornly at Franklin, who was clearly no longer connected to reality. The inventor took no notice of the obese man in the empty bathtub who cried "Eureka!" every few moments or the pretend Copernicus gazing through a pasteboard tube and randomly shouting out the names of planets. Franklin mindlessly let his hand rise and fall with the tension on the make-believe kite string.

"Watch out for the lightning, Ben!" an onlooker hooted.

"A penny saved is a penny earned," cackled another, raising laughter. Duncan wanted to pummel the man.

"It's only a few days," Ishmael said. "We will retrieve him the night we remove my uncle."

Duncan choked down his rage. "A few days in there can crush a man's soul," he replied. He said nothing more and allowed his friends to shepherd him to Conawago's cell. Ishmael reported that he had instructed Taggart to stop serving his uncle the doctors' brew. The keeper had refused, saying it would be the end of him if the doctors discovered it, but he did take over the distribution of the tea and was making sure Conawago received only half the usual amount.

Duncan pushed through the crowd at the Immortals' cell, in his dark mood ready to swing at anyone who protested. His heart sank as he saw the effects of the reduced dosage. The old man sat on a low stool along the back wall. His eyes were no longer unfocused. He was staring at his hands and weeping.

A new crier was on the box. "The esteemed Aristotle will not be performing today," he announced, pausing to adjust his mophead wig. "He has been seized by the melancholy of antiquity. He cannot locate his beloved Parthenon!"

They watched for several minutes, then Noah pulled Duncan toward the side stairs. They opened the stairwell door to the sound of a fearful moan.

Ishmael had the keeper Taggart backed into a corner and had pulled out the crumpled deerskin pouch Conawago had left at Faulkner House. Taggart was staring at it with a wide-eyed, terrified expression. Ishmael acknowledged Duncan and Noah with a quick nod but did not turn from the keeper. "I was explaining to Mr. Taggart that these are the private parts of the last man who lied to me," Ishmael explained. He emphasized his threat by drawing his belt knife.

"I didn't lie, sir!" Taggart cried. "Prithee, sir, I swear it! I would never lie to one of the tribes."

"You didn't tell me everything. Were you there when Mr. Franklin was brought into the hospital?"

"Yes sir, yes. Dr. Granger likes a tea with brandy when he works. 'Tis his habit. I always bring it to him when he is in his examination room. He was with that man they put the Franklin placard on."

"You put on the placard?"

"I have to write whatever I'm told. The other man said to do so, and he and the doctor laughed about it. The doctor said it was a splendid idea, that the earl would be most amused."

"The other man?" Ishmael asked as Noah shed his borrowed tunic, laying it on the stairwell.

"The officer in the brocaded uniform. Hastings, the doctor called him, like the battlefield of the Normans. 'Major Hastings,' says he, 'you are a treasure. What an inspired idea the earl had, to send this one here, and what prowess it took to so secretly bring him here. The alternative might have been embarrassing for the king at this particular moment.'" Taggart looked away, staring at his feet now. "'No need to spill blood unnecessarily,' the doctor said."

"What else?" Duncan demanded.

"Then that major said the poor old lout would probably enjoy a week of hallucinations. Flying kites with unclad maids and such." Taggart glanced up. "His words, sir."

"Then?" Duncan pressed.

"Then an orderly came for the major and said they had to leave. His baggage was aboard, the orderly reported, and the Boston ship would not wait much longer as the tide was shifting."

"He sailed today?"

"A few hours ago would be my guess."

Ishmael looked away and Taggart inched toward the gallery door.

"One more thing, Taggart," Duncan said. "You are giving only a half dose of the Granger tea to Aristotle?"

"Aye, sir, as the young gentleman requested."

"The same for Franklin," Duncan instructed. He saw the expectant expression on the keeper's face and handed him a coin.

"At your service, sir," Taggart said, and with an anxious glance at Ishmael backed away.

As they reached the bottom of the stairs a forlorn cry echoed from above.

"I'd sooner be a slave again than to live like that," Noah whispered.

"Milbridge should be put down like the mad animal he is," Ishmael hissed.

"Years ago we had him tied to a tree," Duncan recalled, "in the Mohawk forest. It would have been so easy to slide a blade into him. The Mohawks wanted to but I convinced them otherwise, because he was Sarah's father. Crows flew down to peck at his flesh and I scared them away. Now, looking back on the misery he has caused, I feel responsible for it all."

"A turtle with two heads!" Hewson exclaimed. "The wonder of it! And is that the foot of the mythical ostrich?"

They did not dare let the Stevenson household know where Franklin was, for Mrs. Stevenson would undoubtedly raise the kind of fuss that would assure the inventor would disappear from Bethlem. The next morning, however, they did arrange to meet with Franklin's physician. Now, as Hewson exclaimed over Huber's collection, Duncan had to pull him away. Over tea in the back dining chamber, he asked both Huber and Hewson to indulge him, and soon his friends were uneasy conspirators walking at his side as they passed through the arch leading to Bethlem Hospital.

Hewson stifled a cry with his fist against his mouth when he saw Franklin. The inventor seemed little changed from the day before, his arm still going up and down every few seconds.

"*Mein Gott!*" Huber cried as he saw his former houseguest.

Franklin glanced up without recognition when Hewson shook the barred door and called his name to no avail. Duncan pulled him back to a window on the other side of the gallery.

"This is unforgivable!" Hewson snapped.

"As is the imprisonment of my friend Conawago," Duncan said.

The words quieted Hewson, who had been reluctant to help Duncan at the hospital. The anatomist gazed through the barred doors in silence, then finally turned to Duncan. "But you have a plan," Hewson stated, as if finally agreeing. "Some hope for their release."

"Our chances would be better with your assistance," Duncan said. "Both of you," he added as Huber stepped to his side. "Our troop has sailors, Indians, link boys, smugglers, and a Highlander. The only thing missing is doctors."

"You're going to tell Milbridge where the *incognitum* is?" Woolford asked. "Duncan, you must take more time to rest. You are not thinking clearly." They were sitting in the library of Faulkner House with Noah, Hewson, Ishmael, and Madeline.

"We are going to tell him on that final day, the last possible day for contact with the king. Later in the day he will get a note purporting to have been stolen by the Guards from one of our runners." Lewis had offered no protest when Duncan and Ishmael had approached him in an alley near Carven Street, and in fact seemed eager to help confound the earl again. "The note will confirm that all is in place to transport the *incognitum* to the Royal Observatory after sunset under wagonloads of sand."

"Will they truly believe such a note?" Woolford wondered.

"They will, because it will be in Franklin's secret alphabet. And seizing control of the bones will be the crowning victory for Milbridge, one he will not want to share. He lusts for those bones. He will have to have those bones because they will give him even more leverage with the king."

Woolford tried to see through Duncan's grin. "But?"

"First, the bones will not be there. Franklin will not make his meeting with the king if he is in Bedlam, so no need to move them. But Milbridge will be ravenous, and will have to be certain no one discovers the bones before he reaches them. So, more importantly, the note will assure that the earl will be racing along the King's Road in the early evening after receiving the message." Duncan chose his words carefully. "It is the kind of battlefield intelligence a commander dreams of. It means you can intercept him."

"Me?" Woolford protested. "Duncan, you do know he is acquainted with me?"

"It is an expedition for a ranger to lead. You can use men of the *Galileo* and some of the smugglers. He will never see you. You will command from the shadows. By the time you are with him he will be unconscious. Dr. Hewson"—Duncan turned to William Hewson—"will calculate the dose of laudanum needed for a man of, what? Sixteen stone?"

"More like eighteen or nineteen," Hewson corrected. After witnessing what Milbridge and Granger had done to Franklin, he had become an enthusiastic member of their conspiracy.

Duncan unrolled his chart and laid it over the desk, then indicated the King's Road. "Here," he said, pointing to a sharp bend in the road between two guard posts, "is a blind spot. I was thinking of a wayward herd of cows blocking the road. The green coach will have to stop. Half of your men will stop the coach, the other half rush in to administer the dose. It will be done in less than a minute."

"He travels with two footmen and a driver," Woolford reminded Duncan as Ishmael placed a walnut shell at the bend in the road. "They usually have pistols."

"Who no doubt were part of the plan to carry me in a cage to be mutilated by Milbridge. You will have the element of surprise. You need not be gentle with them. Tell your men they can keep whatever booty they may find, including any of those weapons. Let his men think it is a robbery."

Woolford frowned, studying the map. "A fallen tree limb might be better. Cows are such unpredictable creatures."

"And loosen the team to add to the confusion," Ishmael suggested. "Scatter his precious Friesians out into the wheat fields."

"The tactics are for you to decide, Patrick," Duncan said. "Just get him to Noah at the Bedlam laundry house, no later than nine in the evening."

"Laundry house?" Woolford asked.

Duncan grinned again and gestured to Noah. "Take those details up with the captain of that particular company," he said, raising a mischievous smile on the groom's face. Duncan turned to Ishmael. "Next?"

Ishmael consulted the list in his hand. "The carriages will be waiting by Moorgate at midnight. Greta says she will keep them there no matter what the clamor."

Woolford rolled his eyes. "The clamor?"

"The link boys will release the sheep at the appointed hour, then light a bonfire in the center of the grounds with a barrel of ale beside it."

"For the sheep?"

"For the neighbors. The gate will be opened. The link boys will have spread the word that there is to be a celebration under the moon. For St. Michael's day."

"St. Michael's day is not until the end of September," Woolford pointed out.

"St. Michael is the protector of Scottish warriors," Duncan replied with a grin, "and any day Scots offer free ale, that will be St. Michael's day." He had hoped that they would find a more subtle way to deal with Bedlam but now, sitting with his friends as they planned their campaign, he knew it was always going to end like this. He had argued with Ishmael, because of the many dangers, but in the end had no other solution. "It's what the gods need," Ishmael had said with finality. "It's how we get back our honor."

The dangerous gleam Duncan had seen on Woolford's face before ranger missions in the war began to shine again on his friend's countenance. He sipped tea as Duncan explained the planned sequence, altered slightly now to include Franklin, then began making notes of supplies, starting with hooded cloaks, clubs, ropes, and ale.

The deputy superintendent looked up when he finished writing. "If any of us are caught there will be no mercy. Some tribes will slowly roast their captives over fires. The earl and his friends will think of something much more painful."

"Which is why, Patrick," Madeline said, "we shall have disguises. No one must be recognized at Bedlam."

"But there is no time for all of us to find—"

Madeline held up a hand to interrupt him. "Allow me to address that particular challenge," she said with an impish smile. "Do you not know I am a wizard of wardrobes?" She lifted a quill from the desk and stuck it upright in her hair.

Chapter 23

THE SKY WAS CLEAR AND the moonlight brighter than Duncan would have preferred for his raid on the castle keep of lunatics. The two coaches emptied by the northeast corner of Bedlam's high wall, met by Sinner John and more than a dozen eager link boys. His party had eagerly accepted the apparel Madeline had distributed at the Neptune's stable. Some wore leggings, others old waistcoats painted with tribal signs. All had put on headbands of sorts, most with feathers, and some of the sailors had even braided feathers into their hair. Those wearing sleeveless waistcoats over bared torsos had mimicked the ghost warrior by sprinkling flour on their arms. Darby, who had already thrown a rope with a grapnel over the wall and climbed to the top, sat and watched with amusement as a figure wearing a cloak and an oversize tricorn hat applied paint to the faces of a line of the volunteers. All of the patterns were configurations of lightning bolts.

As the last man was painted, Duncan approached the cloaked figure, who wore Iroquois leggings and moccasins, and lifted away the hat. He contained his surprise and just shook his head. "No. It is too dangerous. You have too much to lose." It was Madeline Faulkner, wearing a belted green linen shirt over her leggings. Several exotic feathers, no doubt stripped from some high-fashion hairpiece, extended from her headband. Her wampum necklace was uncovered.

"Duncan, did you think you were going to lead a Mohawk raid without me?" she asked, and flung her cloak into the nearest coach. "I am more Mohawk than anyone here," she added. Without waiting for a reply, she flipped her braided hair over her shoulder, grabbed the rope, and adeptly scaled the wall.

He watched with a mixture of admiration and fear. If she were caught, her life in London would be over, and her father's wrath, like that of Milbridge for his own daughter, would know no bounds.

"Ishmael?" Duncan asked. The young Nipmuc had left two hours earlier than the rest, to help Noah, but had promised to join them at the wall. He turned to Sinner John, whose only concession to disguise had been to drape a black handkerchief over his black britches, a pious loincloth, and to paint two black crosses on his cheeks.

"No sign of him," Sinner John said, and began helping the link boys up over the wall.

Duncan waited until all the others had climbed the wall, then surveyed the shadows with increasing worry and grabbed the rope. They could not afford to wait.

The night patrols around the grounds were usually conducted by two pairs of guards, working different sections of the broad gardens and field in front of the hospital building. Duncan watched as the link boys darted along the wall toward the sheep pens on the other side, then motioned his company along the adjoining wall, shielded by the shrubbery that grew there. His heart was leaden by the time they reached the building.

Madeline noticed his hesitation. "What is it?" she asked.

"Ishmael. His tame keeper agreed to keep the last window on the top floor open," Duncan explained, gesturing to the window high overhead, "because Ishmael, who has a careless disregard for heights, was going to scale the ivy vines and mortar joints to it, then run down the stairs to unbolt the side door for us. He was with Noah and Woolford but should have been here by now. Something is already amiss and we've barely begun," he said with new foreboding. He studied the shadows along the building, praying for sight of Ishmael, then turned back as several of the men began to softly laugh. With the agility of a Mohawk warrior, Madeline Faulkner was climbing the building.

He watched breathlessly as she advanced up the heavy vines. When, twenty-five feet in the air, she reached the final few feet, which were devoid of vines, she paused only a moment to study the mortar cracks, then began climbing again. In less than a minute she was in the window. A minute later the door on the side of the building swung open. Madeline stood beside a grinning Ishmael, who motioned the company up the stairs, brandishing a big key.

"The keepers have been taking a long tea break, enjoying the special brew prepared by Dr. Huber and served out by Noah and his friends. Their thirst seems encouraged by the trays of pastries baked by Greta," Ishmael reported. "And Patrick arrived with his overstuffed cargo, unconscious but unharmed."

"Late, I take it," Duncan observed.

"Not late. But we had some special preparations for our guest that required extra time," Ishmael said enigmatically. "And who should we meet but the mysterious Dr. Granger," he added. "He proved to have a great fondness for German pastries and enjoyed a double serving of the special tea served out by Taggart, complementing its flavor." The Nipmuc turned and without further explanation darted up the stairs.

They confirmed that the top gallery was empty, with dim lamps burning on hangers every fifty feet along the corridor. Ishmael ran to the door of the chamber of the Savages and with his forged key unlocked the door. As the patients inside, all wearing their own makeshift tribal clothing, stirred and began drifting out into the hallway, Duncan dispatched half a dozen of his own company to create chaos at the far end. Ishmael kept opening more cells as Duncan and Madeline ran to the main stairwell. Duncan froze as he saw several keepers in brown tunics on the stairs below.

"No, Duncan," Madeline whispered, seeing his fists clench as if for readying for a fight. "It's working. Stay true to our plan. We must walk unflinching through the enemy camp." She pulled him down the stairs.

To his immense relief Duncan now saw that Huber's brew was having the desired effect. Some of the keepers were simply sitting on the stairs, smiling dumbly into the air. Others were engaged in animated, if disjointed conversations.

"I swear it, Jimmy," said the first keeper they passed to his companion, sitting dreamily on the step below, "there's a great bear sitting in the water closet. And he's reading a newspaper."

"Mind yer feet, ye oaf," his friend said. "Yer going to squish the pretty frogs!"

Madeline squeezed Duncan's arm. "Granger!" she whispered in warning, nodding toward a distinguished-looking older man. The nefarious Dr. Granger was walking arm in arm with a large man in a pink dress, zealously speaking about a unicorn he had spied on the second floor.

Soft laughter came from a keeper sitting close to them. Taggart had been surprisingly easy to recruit for their final plan, and had actually given back half the extra coins Ishmael had offered. He had refrained from drinking the tea he had served and was now obviously enjoying the consequences. "Two cups of the brew for him," Taggart said, indicating a man stumbling down the gallery, frantically looking over his shoulder. Duncan recognized the cruel overkeeper with the maimed ear. "I told him if he had ever killed anyone, their ghosts will be chasing him this night."

"Make way for the Indian princess!" called another as he greeted Madeline with a deep bow. She reached the entrance doors a few paces before Duncan and released the bolts. They each pushed one of the heavy doors open. At the sight of the bonfire the link boys had lit in the center of the courtyard, the disoriented keepers began drifting outside, moving like moths to the flame. As Duncan watched, two of the outside guards dashed past the fire, chasing several sheep. On the far side of the yard the wide entrance gate was open, and bystanders from outside were wandering in under the arch, attracted by both the unexpected sounds of celebration rising from the link boys and the sight of the cask of ale on a rack erected near the fire.

A refined-looking gentleman in a patient's gown touched Duncan's arm. "Pardon me, sir. Have you seen Cromwell?"

Chaos was descending upon Bethlem Hospital. The handful of keepers who had not taken a tea break were desperately trying to subdue their hallucinating colleagues, a task made more difficult by the fact that several had traded their brown tunics for the more fanciful garb worn by some of the patients.

Duncan turned back inside as Noah appeared from the rear of the building with three other broad-shouldered men, carrying one of the large wicker trays with long handles that were used as laundry pallets. From under a pile of towels and linens on the pallet a foot extended, wearing a silver-buckled shoe. Duncan pushed ahead of them, clearing a path as they carried their heavy load up the stairs. Darby arrived with three of his crew to relieve them at the first landing. When they finally reached the still-locked cell of the House of Lords, the upper gallery was nearly empty. Only a few of the patients in the chamber awakened as Duncan unlocked the door and hung a lantern on the wall. They watched in silent fascination as the obese man was deposited on a cot at the rear of the chamber. Duncan cautioned his companions not to touch the henbane salve that Huber had rubbed onto the man's back, then asked Noah to bring the lamp closer.

"On his head," Duncan asked, "is that a bruise? Was he dropped?"

Noah grinned, then stepped aside as Ishmael approached. "Noah has a friend who is well known for his ink work," the Nipmuc explained. "It was a hurried affair. As he worked, I repeatedly told the gentleman that if he ever lifted a hand to harm Sarah or her friends, the gods of the Iroquois would haunt him forever. The crows would be watching him, I said. I am not sure if he understood in his daze but he has this reminder. His new pet will never let him forget. He started weeping, so I think part of him heard me."

Duncan held the lamp closer. Along the front of Milbridge's bald scalp was a fresh tattoo of two crows, Mohawk messengers to the gods. Milbridge would be wearing wigs and nightcaps the rest of his life.

"Time for a change in wardrobe," Madeline said, and helped Noah pull away Milbridge's elegant waistcoat, handing it to Duncan. One of the patients readily agreed to trade his soiled tunic for the coat, but Duncan decided first to rub it in the dirt on the floor. He paused over a bauble pinned inside the coat, over the chest where it would have been readily visible to Milbridge but no one else, as if for the earl to glance at in private amusement. Duncan pulled it away before handing the coat to the eager patient. It was one of Milbridge's golden tokens. He had seen it before, for it was an identical version of the pin Nettles had been wearing. POMPA FULGUR VINCERET, it said, over a bursting star superimposed over a lightning bolt. Duncan paused for a moment, once more trying to understand the message, "Fireworks Conquer Lightning," then Ishmael pulled him away.

As they propped Milbridge against the wall, Madeline set a pasteboard crown on his head with two long ears, then draped a placard around his neck that declared in two rows of bold letters: EARL MILBRIDGE, ROYAL DONKEY. As she did so the earl began to stir. Milbridge did not resist, but raised a hand as if to fend something else away. "The crows! Not the crows!" he desperately moaned, batting at the air.

They left the pompous lord in his new court, straightening the pasteboard signs that hung on several other inmates, declaring Lord Grafton, Lord Hillsborough, and three other luminaries of Parliament. If Milbridge drank the usual tea of the patients in the special wards, it could be days before the truth of his identity was discovered.

Hewson and Huber joined them as they reached the inventor's cell. "William? Is it you, William?" Franklin asked in a fearful voice as he studied Hewson, the first to enter the chamber. "The horror!" he cried, then seemed incapable of further speech. He rose with great difficulty, then fell back onto his cot with a groan. Darby and his men, standing by with the laundry pallet, gently eased Franklin onto its platform, then lifted it and headed for the stairs with Hewson at his side.

A patient pushed past Duncan as he watched Franklin disappear down the staircase. "Jimmy, come see!" the man called as he reached the window, where the flames of the bonfire could be seen. "It's Guy Fawkes Night!"

Duncan hesitated, extracting the golden pin he had taken from Milbridge. There had been one last enigma he had failed to pierce, the cause of all their misery. Now the answer struck him like a lightning bolt.

Ishmael waited for Duncan at the Chamber of the Immortals. His hand trembled as he unlocked the door. Conawago sat in the back corner again, sitting on his cot and rocking back and forth. He seemed to take no notice when Ishmael and Duncan gently lifted him, other than uttering a low "Oh, bath already?" They threw his arms across their shoulders and pulled him out into the gallery, leaving the door open for the inmates to wander out.

As they reached the cool night air, the old Nipmuc began making low humming sounds. Before reaching the coach, his weight still supported by Duncan and Ishmael with Madeline and Noah clearing a path through the now crowded courtyard, he began what sounded like another of his recitations in Greek. Ishmael, spectator to such performances for weeks, recognized it. "An account of the fall of Troy," he explained. Conawago seemed to have almost no physical strength left; they had to lift him bodily into the coach. His mind drifted and he gave no sign of recognition of where he was or whom he was with. As he settled into the seat, he began a bawdy song of French trappers that Duncan hadn't heard him sing for years.

Darby arrived with the crewmen of the *Galileo*, confirming that Franklin and the doctor, with Noah as a guard, had boarded the coach for Craven Street. With a victorious gleam in his eyes, Ishmael climbed in beside his uncle and offered a hand to Duncan. Duncan hesitated.

"I can't," he said, his heart sinking. "Get him on board. Tell the captain to wait as long as he can, but the *Galileo* must be gone with the tide whether I am on board or not." He gestured Darby to take the seat meant for him.

The bosun hesitated. "Ye need to be with us, Highlander."

Duncan held up the golden pin. "Remember, remember the fifth of November," he said, then motioned Darby up and pushed the door shut.

He set off through the streets in the loping gait of the forest runner, ignoring the calls of watchmen. He had four hours to save Franklin, again, and if he missed the *Galileo* he might not be able to save Sarah. By the time he reached Craven Street, after a stop at the Neptune to enlist Mrs. Laws's assistance, an informal celebration was already in progress. Hewson, Polly, Olivia Dumont, Henry Quinn, and the Stevenson household staff were welcoming Franklin "back among the living" as Hewson declared in the toast that was underway when Duncan and the innkeeper appeared at the top of the stairs.

Mrs. Stevenson warmly greeted Clementine Laws as an acquaintance from the market. Franklin, looking much revived, spread his arms and gave Duncan an uncharacteristic embrace. "How can I ever repay you, McCallum?" he asked.

"By continuing to be the voice of conscience in Whitehall," Duncan replied with a smile.

"They have not heard the last of me, I assure you! And we shall have such a feast tonight!" Franklin declared, and turned to Mrs. Stevenson. "Roast beef, Meg, and the new case of claret! Duncan will be our guest of honor!"

"I would like that of all things," Duncan said, "but I fear this is farewell. I am away at dawn."

Franklin sighed in disappointment. "With Conawago I pray," he said, and hesitated. "Is he—did he—" Franklin was not sure how to complete his question.

"He is away from Bedlam," Duncan said, "and sails to America with the tide." He desperately wished he could say more, but his old friend had given little hope that his crushed spirit could be mended.

"I should have—" Franklin paused and started over. "I should have taken your friend's plight more seriously. I didn't quite grasp how dire things were at that particular institution. They dosed me out of my wits. Before I stopped drinking that dreadful tea I saw things! The *incognitum* was chasing me! The citizens of Venice were coming for me with a noose," he groaned. For a moment, Franklin drifted into one of the absent stares Duncan had so often seen at Bedlam, then just as quickly he was back, gazing sheepishly at Duncan. "I saw things," he whispered.

Duncan nodded. "It will take some days for the medicine to fully dissipate," he said, then added, "I'm afraid your date with the king has gone by." Despite their victory that night, he still felt a sense of failure. The purpose of their costly effort to retrieve the *incognitum* had been frustrated. The colonies would be invaded.

"The date is past, but the ladies have a clever plan! I am going to write a letter to the king announcing that I have been preserving the bones and the American transit calculations for him alone, then recounting all that the Earl of Milbridge and the clandestine soldiers did to prevent the king from receiving them."

"It will never get to him."

"That's what is so brilliant!" Franklin, showing fatigue again, stepped to the mantel, touched the solitary Leyden jar, and with a satisfied moan let the electricity revive him. "The distaff connection! Olivia and Madeline had the inspiration. What better couriers!"

"Couriers?" Duncan asked.

"Olivia and Madeline have all the talent and, one might say, all the other assets to be the most desirable maidens at the royal ball. The king will most certainly dance with one or even both."

Olivia took up the explanation. "We shall each have a copy of the letter in our bodice, Duncan, and tell the royal George that it is for his eyes only, that we know not the contents but agreed to deliver it to the king because we adore him so, and that we know he wants to be a man of the real truth, not the truth arranged by his advisers. And there will be another copy that we will give to Queen Charlotte, who plays the mother hen to all the eligible maidens in attendance. The queen will insist he read it, we are certain."

"But still, just a letter," Duncan said.

"Not just a letter," Franklin corrected. "A coup de grace. A decisive stroke! Truly inspired!" He raised his glasses to the ladies, then saw the confusion in Duncan's gaze. "A copy shall also find its way to the prime minister, who has the final meeting with the king just before he leaves for his hunting tour. The balance of power is precarious. A handful of votes one way or the other determines most outcomes. If the king were to lose votes in the scandal these revelations would inevitably cause if publicized, the army's plans will never stand up in Parliament, and he will have to back away from half a dozen other initiatives. The Whig prime minister and the king will reach the obvious accommodation. The army will have to abandon its plans."

"But the *incognitum*?" Duncan asked. "And the transit observations?"

"I am proposing that the king publish the transit observations himself, announcing them as a gift to the people of England from America. No intrigue, none of the Royal Society's favoritism. They will be available to everyone, as if they were published in my almanac." Franklin smiled at Duncan. "I seem to recall an old tribesman saying that the function of civilized society is to advance the common knowledge."

A smile slowly grew on Duncan's wary face. "And the *incognitum*?"

"I will explain to the king that I shall send an itemized list of the relics to the Royal Palace and the Royal Society at the same time, stating publicly that I will formally present them to the king when he returns from his hunting season."

"The real leverage point isn't the bones," Duncan suggested. "It is what our enemies did because of the bones."

"Exactly!" Franklin exclaimed. "A circular kind of justice! A solution worthy of a great chess master," he added, then took the hands of Olivia and Madeline in each of his own. "Chess mistresses!" he corrected with a hearty laugh.

As Duncan digested the plan, his approving smile grew. He caught Mrs. Stevenson's eye as she carried a tray toward the stairs. "Allow me, ma'am," he said, then nodded to Mrs. Laws as he descended the stairs. Once in the kitchen he asked Mrs. Stevenson for her forbearance in allowing some other visitors invited by Mrs. Laws to use the servants' rear stairs.

Minutes later, as he helped arrange new refreshments brought from the kitchen, he asked who would write the momentous letter to the king. "Such a challenge," he observed, "but such a glorious accomplishment when it is completed. Who is up to the task?" he wondered out loud.

Franklin threw a cheerful nod toward his secretary, who was pouring more claret into Olivia's glass. "We will compose it together. Henry is always an excellent collaborator."

"Oh," Duncan said, feigning surprise. "Such a task. No doubt candles will burn far into the night. Four identical letters. With a copy for the desk here. Not to mention the copy for the War Council."

Franklin cocked his head at Duncan. "No, no," he said with a tentative chuckle. "Secrecy is all."

"Remember, remember the fifth of November," Duncan abruptly said, taking in the entire company with a sweeping gaze.

"Duncan?" Hewson asked. "You're very tired. Perhaps you should sit. Have some tea."

"Very tired indeed," Duncan agreed. "Tired and still recovering from my wound. So much so I almost forgot the greatest mystery about the death of our friend Ezra," he said. "When I extracted the letter that Lieutenant Nettles had pounded into his throat, his cousin said dark magic was at work, because he had seen the letter for Dr. Franklin torn up and dropped into the Ohio. Except it wasn't magic. There were two letters, the original and the copy brought to America by Hastings and Nettles, made here in this room."

"Nonsense," Quinn insisted. "We are most careful about who has access to our desk. I close it up every night."

"We would never touch Benjamin's desk," Mrs. Stevenson said, sharpness in her voice now.

Quinn turned to Franklin. "I told you about those men who repaired the windows last spring, sir. They tended to ask too many questions about you. I was never too comfortable with them."

Franklin brightened. "There, you see, Duncan. Unfortunate, but no concern at present."

"I recall you speaking about the wonderful front-row box you had for the royal fireworks on Guy Fawkes Day," Duncan said to the inventor.

It was Polly who responded. "Oh yes, we all went, it was the most spectacular display. We called it a double celebration because of Henry's arrival."

Duncan found no joy in the response he had been waiting for. "So November the fifth was the date your service began, Henry?" he asked the secretary.

"Who can recall such things?" Quinn replied. "The months fly by so quickly it all seems a blur."

"Oh no, of course it was, because Benjamin loves fireworks so," Polly exclaimed. "Don't you recall, when we were interviewing you, Henry, you mentioned that your cousin, some duke or earl or such, had a box he could not use and if we could but conclude arrangements in time we all might celebrate together . . ." The last few words trailed off and she looked at Duncan with new concern.

"Remember, remember the fifth of November," Duncan said again, and held up the pin he had taken from Milbridge. "A private victory token of the earl's. 'Fireworks Conquer Lightning,' it says. It never really made sense to me until tonight. The timing is everything. In order for Hastings to arrive on the Ohio in time to intercept us, the War Council would have had to begin receiving the secrets discussed in this house last autumn. Say early November. Secrets about the Covenant and the mission for the *incognitum*." Duncan turned to Franklin. "You wrote to Charles Thomson and your wife about the *incognitum* in November. I saw the letter. Your wife gave it to me, to inspire me on my mission. I suspect your letter to Ezra about his mission for the Covenant was sent at the same time."

The joy of their celebration left Franklin's face. "I don't know, Duncan. I suppose. Yes, two or three days after the fireworks, I recall. But we would never have kept copies, not like other correspondence. Though of course Henry often helps me with final composition."

"No, no," Quinn insisted. "I am sure I would have recalled if I had been present. I may have been at the fireworks but I didn't start until much later in the month." He turned in surprise at the sound of the desk cabinet being opened. Polly was running her fingers along the thick pasteboard folders that contained copies of correspondence, arranged by month.

"Here we are," she declared, extracting a folder. "Correspondence for November 1768."

Quinn stepped to the desk, reaching for the folder, but Polly ignored him, stepping to the window seat. Seconds later she pulled out a sheet of paper. "The very first one in Henry's writing. A letter to Lord Hillsborough, dated November sixth."

Franklin broke the silence. "It doesn't signify, Duncan," he said.

"Who recommended Henry to you?" Duncan quietly asked as Quinn, with some irritation, took the folder from Polly.

"The Royal Society. Impeccable recommendations."

"The Royal Society that helped to kidnap you at Boodles. How many of its members also serve on the War Council? Three, four? A half dozen?"

Franklin had no reply.

Duncan spoke in a slow, contemplative voice as he sipped his wine. "I recall being struck by the paintings of the great masters when I was young," he related. "My Dutch schoolteacher pointed out that it is the little things, the subtle tint of a cloud, the hint of fire in a horse's eye, the tiny point of color on an autumn leaf that make the masters' paintings so complete. The magic is all about many inconspicuous pieces joining to create the whole. Any one of them would not signify on their own," he added with a meaningful gaze at Franklin.

His listeners gazed in mute confusion. "Duncan, you're obviously tired," Mrs. Stevenson said. "Do have some tea."

"There's information in Whitehall about you, sir," Duncan continued. "Hidden things, some of those subtle things that no one else should rightly know, that on their own may not seem important, even."

"Some ham, perhaps?" Mrs. Stevenson said, extending a small platter toward Duncan.

He declined with a smile, glancing at Mrs. Laws as she slipped into the back hallway that led to the water closet and the rear stairs. "Newton Pippins," he said. "You told me, sir, it was one of your greatest secrets, that no one out of this house knows about your secret shipments of Newtown Pippins, because the supply in Pennsylvania was so limited. But the War Council knows. I have a witness who heard the War Council discuss them."

Franklin was growing impatient. "Impossible! And prithee, Duncan, why would such an esteemed body fuss over my apples? Why are we speaking of such trivial things?"

"The truth often dwells in the subtle pieces, as I said." Duncan reached into his pocket and extracted the slips of paper Woolford had given him and handed them to Franklin. "The printer's mark of crossed swords means it's from the press the War Council uses for internal documents."

Franklin sagged as he read the couplets.

"You are right, Doctor," Duncan said. "Who would fuss over such things? The apples aren't important except they prove that information has been leaking out of this household to the War Council. These are just mocking ditties written by the one who supplies information to them. I assure you they have had much more information from this household, for many months. Fatal information, you might say. Like the details of the expedition to the Lick, the mission of Ezra, the name of Mademoiselle Dumont, and the existence of the Covenant. It was your letter that suffocated Ezra, but not the original. It was a copy provided to the Horse Guards, probably the same day you signed that original. I would have realized that eventually since the copy would not have your original signature, but the Shawnee burnt the letter, so their gods could see it. If we had not been so careful in hiding the *incognitum* they would have captured it long ago. As it is, they were given a letter to the prime minister in which you spoke of spies, and that resulted in a raid on your friend Joseph Priestly's house. And the pending presence of the leader of the Covenant in Boston was revealed to them in a secret letter you sent to Faulkner House, though not with the usual trusted courier," Duncan said, with a glance to Polly. "Not to mention the notes you keep about the details of the enigmatic Hephaestus."

Mrs. Stevenson pushed forward, her face flushing with anger. "Mr. McCallum! Do you suggest we would spy on our Benjamin? You go too far!"

"Of course not, dear madame. Not your family. Not your servants. There is another." He turned his gaze toward the stairway, toward which Henry Quinn was inching, and nodded at the secretary. "Someone who knows about apples and cranberries and everything that is written down in this chamber."

"You make light of my honor, sir?" Quinn snapped. "I should call you out!"

"If I had but the time," Duncan replied in a frigid voice. "And you left your honor behind when you joined with Major Hastings and his assassins."

"Henry?" Franklin asked. "Tell Duncan it is not so!"

"That blood is on your hands," Duncan continued. "Ezra, his wife and child, Pierre Dumont, even poor Robbie. Not to mention the new danger in Boston because of the secrets you stole."

Hewson moved to block Quinn's path to the stairs. The secretary hesitated, as if wondering whether to continue the game, then flung the folder in his hand at Duncan, sending sheets of paper fluttering through the air, and leapt toward the shadowed rear hall. He had nearly disappeared when a pewter knob materialized out of the shadows and slammed into his skull. He collapsed onto the floor, unconscious.

Mrs. Laws appeared from the darkness, balanced on her solitary foot. "Thank you for that pleasure, Duncan lad," she said with a satisfied smile, and with the help of Hewson hopped to a nearby chair to reattach her wooden leg. She looked up as if just noticing her silent onlookers. "Mr. McCallum asked if I would be prepared to repel boarders in the back hallway." She affectionately tapped her false appendage. "Ain't used her since the Barbary Coast, but she still works just fine."

Franklin had collapsed into a chair. He stared in stunned silence as Clementine Laws manipulated her limb into place. "Henry?" he gasped. "My Henry?"

As Mrs. Laws arranged her skirts, three men appeared in the shadows and bound Quinn's hands and feet. Sinner John and two others propped the unconscious man up and tied a gag around his mouth. One of the others was a thick-bodied, nautical-looking man; the other, thin and dressed in dark clothing, stayed in the shadows, keeping his back to the parlor. "We will deal with him, never you mind," Mrs. Laws declared, recognizing her onlookers' question.

"Surely you're not—" Mrs. Stevenson began. Not wanting to voice her real question, she just said, "He's an educated lad."

"Not going to harm the one who provided the means for so much suffering?" Mrs. Laws asked with a rather sinister smile. "This traitor and abettor of assassins is going straight to the Thames," she announced and paused for dramatic effect, causing Mrs. Stevenson to swell up with an apparent protest. "Where he will continue his education. He will be put on board a whaler sailing in the morning for the South Seas, which means he'll have a couple of years to meditate on his sins."

Mrs. Stevenson sighed and nodded her approval.

"Better than he deserves," Hewson declared as he gazed into the shadows where Quinn had disappeared.

"Better than he deserves," Duncan agreed. "But there's been enough killing. And we need to go—" He paused as the second man helping Sinner John stepped into the light of the parlor. "Ensign Lewis!" he said in surprise, and suppressed an urge to run to the window in search of Horse Guards.

The youth turned a bruised, worried face to Duncan. "Just Lewis, sir. I'm done with the army."

"They deal harshly with deserters," Duncan warned as the words sank in.

"I'm done," Lewis repeated, "whatever the cost. I have much to atone for." As he spoke, he drew a long belt knife and fixed Duncan with a sober, determined expression. Polly Stevenson stepped behind Hewson. Mrs. Laws raised a restraining hand as Hewson warily advanced toward Lewis.

"They tried to turn me into a demon. But my mother raised no demon, just a boy who was too easily led astray," Lewis told Duncan. "You said you were of the western Highlands and the Hebrides. Like my own people, until a few years ago."

"Aye," Duncan said uncertainly, then tensed as Lewis advanced with the knife outstretched.

"My mother told me how small clans and broken men could make blood oaths to stronger clans," Lewis said, his voice growing more confident.

Duncan lifted an arm in defense as the knife swung out. But Lewis reversed it and knelt before him, extending the hilt to Duncan in both hands. "I swear myself to you, Clan McCallum. I don't know all the proper words but I will try. I swear my lifeblood in allegiance to Clan McCallum, to protect you and do your will, and if ever I were to betray that oath then may this cold steel pierce my heart."

Duncan stared, stunned. Olivia Dumont softly clapped her hands.

"Bravo!" Franklin said in a loud whisper.

"Good lad, that's the way of it," Mrs. Laws declared, and Duncan realized she had helped Lewis muster his courage.

Franklin made a rolling gesture toward Duncan, as if telling him to proceed. But Duncan himself did not know the words. He had been a boy when he had last seen such a ritual, at a clan gathering.

"I accept your allegiance and your oath, and may the good St. Michael protect us both," Duncan said, clasping his hands around Lewis's, which still held the blade. "I fear I have little to offer you, Lewis."

"No sir, you have the best of all to offer. America!" Lewis grinned. "I have passage on the *Galileo*," he said, with a meaningful glance at Mrs. Laws that Duncan did not understand.

"Which means we must go," Duncan said. "The *Galileo* leaves on the tide."

"Thaddeus Rhys will nae be sailing without us," Mrs. Laws declared.

Duncan hesitated, trying to recall if he had ever heard the captain's Christian name. "Us?"

"Thaddeus had money from his old smuggling days tucked away. I had money set aside. The inn has been prosperous. We pooled our resources, ye might say."

"Might say what exactly?" Duncan asked.

"We are the new owners of the *Galileo*! And Sinner John will mind the Neptune while Thaddeus and I take our maiden voyage to Boston."

Duncan was not sure why, but he laughed. The laughter spread through the chamber, then faded as a commotion rose at the front door. Mrs. Stevenson darted to the head of the stairs, then froze and looked back at Duncan, who now heard loud whispers in the Nipmuc tongue. In an instant he was beside her, and stared down as Conawago, braced on each side by Ishmael and Darby, slowly ascended to Franklin's parlor. Conawago began to laugh and cry at the same time as he saw Duncan. When he reached the top of the stairs, he threw his arms around Duncan and gave a long sob.

"We were in the carriage approaching the river," Ishmael explained, "when he just looked up and said, 'I was in a long dream but now I awake.' He embraced me, then he asked for you. When I told him he insisted he had to come to meet Dr. Franklin, whom he knew to be a noble man and a kindred spirit."

When Conawago finally released Duncan, they turned to their host, now standing beside them. Benjamin Franklin was weeping too.

"There is but one noble person in this chamber, sir," the great inventor said to Conawago, "and that is you." Franklin helped the old Nipmuc to his favorite chair by the hearth and called for refreshment. Duncan stayed at the side of his old mentor, who reached out and held his hand as Franklin spoke of his own captivity in Bedlam, his adventure at the top of St. Paul's, and then of Duncan's remarkable mission to the Lick. Conawago, whose voice was hoarse and weak, offered nods and smiled in reply, punctuated by tight squeezes of Duncan's hand. Eventually his old friend just stared into the hearth with a dull smile as new toasts were offered.

More food was brought and they ate a makeshift breakfast as the first rays of the new day filtered into the room. Franklin, who had recovered enough to enjoy a thick slice of bread and marmalade, kept looking at Conawago and Duncan and repeatedly seemed about to speak, but words seemed to fail him for once.

"You can't leave," he finally said. "Conawago and I have so much to talk about. Days and days we must talk. The French court! The first George court! The tribes! The Jesuits! The stars! Do you not know what a treasure this man is?"

Duncan smiled. "I think we know that above all else."

"And you, Duncan," Franklin continued. "How valuable you are! How priceless your contributions! You do not even blink when the War Council roars! We need you!"

"Which is why I must return. You forget that my pursuit of Major Hastings is not over. He returns to America to sow more despair."

Franklin offered a reluctant nod.

"Mr. Conawago and Mr. Duncan reside at Edentown on the New York frontier," Polly Stevenson said. "Surely the deputy postmaster for the colonies can find a way to get mail there."

"We do get mail," Ishmael observed, "twice a month in warm weather. And we can add this household to the subscriber list for our newspaper."

"Perhaps I can send a note on London life for publication from time to time," Franklin suggested. His face colored with emotion, then he jerked his head toward his bedroom. "Prithee! Tarry a few more minutes." He disappeared into the chamber and returned with a folded piece of muslin, which he unwrapped to reveal a shiny piece of wire. "The finest English copper," he explained. "Duncan, next time you visit Philadelphia you must use this to bypass the bell on my lightning alarm, for my dear Deborah's sake." He hesitated, then lifted the silver watch from his pocket and unfastened the chain. "I want you to have this, Duncan, as a small remembrance of the night on top of the cathedral when time seemed to stand still."

"Surely I cannot," Duncan protested as Franklin extended the expensive watch, his good luck charm inscribed with a lightning bolt.

"Surely I can," Franklin rejoined, "and a pittance it is for what you have done for me. For all of us. The only thing that is certain in the royal court is the king's fear of scandal. Events did not go as planned, but events did conspire to reach our aspired result. I am confident no troops will be sent."

"For now," Duncan said.

"For now," Franklin agreed. "Not for a year or two at least. Which gives us time to heal the wounds, to find the compromise that will avoid rebellion."

Duncan took the watch, and the hand that Franklin extended. "My influence may be slight, Highlander," the inventor said, his voice swollen with emotion, "but if there is ever anything in my power to do for you, you have but to ask."

Mrs. Stevenson rushed forward with tears in her eyes, and before Duncan could react, threw her arms around him in a motherly embrace.

"I look forward to reading of your work on the lymphatic glands," Duncan said as Hewson offered his hand. "You will go far, William. The Royal Society will soon be issuing you medals."

"I shall sail on the first ship to Boston after the royal ball," Olivia Dumont promised as she embraced Duncan.

As Madeline Faulkner, still in the garb of the raid, approached Duncan for her farewell, Franklin seemed to take full notice of her Indian disguise. "Oh my," he said. "Most striking." He looked up at Duncan. "This is an excellent subterfuge. I shall write to Sam Adams and suggest a Mohawk disguise if ever he has a mission in Boston."

At last they helped Conawago to his feet. He was exhausted beyond words and once more seemed to have become disconnected from his surroundings. He responded with weak, silent smiles to the enthusiastic farewells his new friends extended. At last he put an arm over Duncan's shoulder for support and gestured to the stairs.

"Home," was all he said.

AUTHOR'S NOTE

THE DEBATES TRIGGERED BY THE eighteenth-century discovery of the mysterious *incognitum* in a salt lick near the Ohio River became a touchstone of the turbulent times. Scholars, clergymen, and political leaders on both sides of the Atlantic offered sharply divergent interpretations of the huge bones and their origins. Whether viewed as a reminder of holy wrath, evidence of a giant race of humans, or a provoking suggestion of a world unknown to man, this monster of the western frontier challenged conventional thinking. The bones took on a uniquely American character—a bit defiant, a bit troubling to European institutions—adding one more piece to the puzzle of the evolving American identity.

The ever-inquisitive Benjamin Franklin requested relics of the *incognitum* to be sent to him in London for study, which resulted not in identification of the fossils—he accepted that the tusk was from an elephant-like creature while insisting that the tooth was from a carnivore—but rather in the extraordinary insight that they might indicate a physical shift in the continents over time. A generation later, with the mystery still unsolved, Thomas Jefferson dispatched Lewis and Clark on separate expeditions to what had become the famous Bone Lick, which eventually resulted in remains of the *incognitum* being strewn about the East Room of the White House as the president pondered them. The saga of *incognitum* inquiries, including fanciful skeletons assembled from various bones, is a fascinating, sometimes amusing, tale of the uneven progress of science, reflected in more detail in Stanley Hedeen's informative book *Big Bone Lick* and Paul Semonin's *American Monster*. Only in the last century did paleontologists confirm that the Lick held the remains of both the woolly mammoth and the mastodon, in addition to other prehistoric creatures. Generally neglected in our history books is the fact that the first recorded identification of a fossil in America occurred in the early eighteenth century, made by slaves on a Carolina plantation who recognized the features of elephants among the remains of what was later identified as a mammoth.

Widespread excitement about the transit of Venus on June 3, 1769, was closely aligned with the *incognitum* phenomenon in both time and popular reaction. Preparations for the transit reflected how intellectual inquiry and dialogue were becoming democratized as American colonists caught "transit fever" in anticipation of the planet's movement across the face of the sun. Benjamin Franklin also had a deep interest in astronomy—years earlier, for a prior transit of Mercury, he had printed and distributed at his own expense instructions for its observation, which was ultimately frustrated by inclement weather. The Royal Society and King George III went to considerable efforts, including construction of a new Royal Observatory outside London, to ensure that the British government played the leading role in measuring the 1769 transit.

The king no doubt shared the surprise, if not outright shock, of many Royal Society members at discovering that scholars in Philadelphia had captured the best observations and were able to offer up the long-awaited calculation of the earth's distance to the sun. For the first time, the natural philosophers of the colonies took center stage in the Western quest for knowledge, a development that proved deeply galling to the detractors of Franklin and his allies. Franklin proudly published the Philadelphia results in the journal of the Royal Society, and eventually the king's official astronomer acknowledged publicly that the best observations were made not by "the schooled and salaried astronomers who watched from the magnificent observatories of Europe but by unaided amateurs in Pennsylvania."

By 1769, Franklin, easily one of the most complex and colorful of our founding fathers, had already lived in London for over a decade in his capacity as agent for several colonial legislatures. His experience there in many ways personifies the transformation of the American identity. In his official role, his emphasis gradually shifted from judiciously explaining the efforts of Parliament to the colonies to ardently advocating the views of the colonies to Parliament, a process that caused him to be increasingly shunned by the aristocracy. Throughout these years Franklin clung to the belief that if he could only reach the rational, moderate king, compromises could be reached to avoid bloodshed. In retrospect, this assumption was woefully misplaced, for more than any other aspect of British government action, it was the king's stubborn resentment that caused the revolution.

While there is no direct evidence that Franklin engaged in covert activities for the Sons of Liberty, he clearly supported the Sons' goals, and it seems likely that the patriotic inventor would have quietly offered suggestions to support American manufacturing. With respect to his opposition, however, it is well documented that the British government engaged in its own clandestine activity through such agencies as its Black Chamber. Decades after Franklin's death, records revealed that during his later tenure as a diplomat in Paris, his longtime confidential secretary was a spy for the British government, who every week deposited copies of Franklin's documents in a hollow tree for London to read.

Despite his strained relations with officials, including his own son, Franklin's insatiable appetite for knowledge of the natural world kept him in good stead with many scholars in London and drove ongoing experimentation at Craven Street. Among his ambitious projects during this period were the first chart of the Gulf Stream current, a three-wheeled clock, his widely celebrated armonica musical instrument, and his new phonetic alphabet. It was during 1769 that Franklin began using this simplified alphabet in correspondence with Polly Stevenson, his landlady's daughter, with whom Franklin developed a close, decades-long relationship. As portended in these pages, Polly did indeed marry Dr. William Hewson, who in late 1769 was awarded the coveted Copley Medal of the Royal Society for his pioneering work on the lymphatic glands. Hewson's promising career was cut short in 1774 when he accidentally cut himself while examining a cadaver and died of the resulting septic infection. After the Revolution, Polly moved to Philadelphia and was with Franklin at his deathbed in 1790.

As the acclaimed father of electricity, Franklin also remained active in research into the nature of electrical energy and the use of lightning rods. His London detractors attacked him, among many other ways, by alleging that Franklin "disobeyed" and embarrassed the king by advocating sharp-tipped rods when the king had installed blunt-tipped rods at his palace. The image of a sharp-tipped rod became one more symbol of independence in America, and another source of disapproval in London by those who insisted the king should lead the advancement of knowledge. Franklin remained a zealous advocate of his lightning rods, or "arrestors," and no doubt experienced deep frustration over the slow pace of their adoption. The inventor knew with certainty that his arrestors saved buildings and lives, but often he met with stubborn, irrational resistance. Franklin had to endure the destruction of countless buildings and the loss of many lives, the worst tragedy being the 1769 disaster at San Nazaro near Venice, in which a single lightning strike claimed three thousand lives. As reflected in Franklin's confession at the top of St. Paul's Cathedral in these pages, I have often wondered how the compassionate inventor would have felt, knowing that if his lessons had been heeded, or his advocacy more vigorous, thousands of souls could have been saved.

Bethlem Hospital provides another intriguing lens on eighteenth-century society. The hospital, dating to the thirteenth century, had by the time of this novel substantially changed from the site of gothic horror associated with its earlier existence, evolving into a large facility styled like a French palace where techniques of then-modern medicine were applied. Yet there were still many aspects of its treatment of patients that we would consider hideous today, including extensive application of blistering, emetics, and daily immersions in cold water. Doctors were known to practice a "trade in lunacy" and for many decades Bedlam was a public amusement where visitors could pay a penny to view the patients, especially the extreme cases confined to the wards on the top floor.

The year 1769 poignantly reflects the events, people, and struggles that are transforming both Britain and the American colonies during this revolutionary period. In the west a woodsman named Daniel Boone has reached the Kentucky lands, ironically opening that frontier up to a wave of the settlers he had been trying to leave behind. In Britain, Scottish engineer James Watt has obtained a patent for his new steam machine. John Wilkes, passionate advocate of liberty, has been blocked from taking his seat in the House of Commons, stirring further unrest on both sides of the Atlantic. Protests by colonists are growing louder and more widespread, fueled by the defiant Massachusetts Circular Letter, which has been penned by leaders of the Sons in reaction to the punitive Townshend duties. Legislatures speaking in support of the Letter are being dissolved by royal governors, reflecting the punitive policies of Whitehall. Non-importation pacts are becoming a primary weapon against British tyranny, driven by remarkable grassroots efforts aimed at expanding American production of common goods, often led by women. Mothers and daughters of New England, for example, are organizing classes to teach spinning and weaving, transforming thousands of hearths into venues of protest while generating vast quantities of cloth to substitute for imports. Loyalists are even complaining of pastors who preach "manufacturing" instead of the gospel from their pulpits. By many such measures, 1769 is the year in which colonists find their American voice. The year is also the last year of peaceful resistance in the colonies. The powder keg that is occupied Boston is about to explode.

ELIOT PATTISON

© Jed Ferguson

ELIOT PATTISON is the author of the Inspector
Shan series, which includes *The Skull Mantra*, winner
of an Edgar Award and finalist for the Gold Dagger. He
is also the author of the five previous titles in the Bone
Rattler series, most recently *Savage Liberty*. Pattison
resides in rural Pennsylvania with his wife, son, three
horses, and three dogs on a colonial-era farm. Find out
more at eliotpattison.com.